Frozen Sky 3:
Blindsided

Jeff Carlson

International bestselling author
of *Plague Year* and *Interrupt*

Jeff Carlson
www.jverse.com

FILM/TV

Lucy Stille
APA Agency
135 West 50th St., 17th Floor
New York, NY 10020
212-205-2139
www.apa-agency.com/

LITERARY

Laurie McLean, Partner
Fuse Literary Agency
P.O. Box 258
La Honda, CA 94020
650-922-0914
laurie@fuseliterary.com

First Edition

ISBN: 9780996982365 (ebook)
ISBN: 9780996082372 (print)

Cover design and artwork by Jasper Schreurs

Formatting by Polgarus Studio

European Space Agency maps and schematics by the most awesome and talented Jeff Sierzenga. Reproduced with permission. Copyright © 2016 Jeff Sierzenga.

Other Books by Jeff Carlson

Interrupt

The Europa Series

The Frozen Sky

Betrayed

Blindsided

Battlefront

The Plague Year Trilogy

Plague Year

Plague War

Plague Zone

Movie Scripts

Plague Year: The Screenplay

Shadow Of The Living Dead

Short Story Collection

Long Eyes

Praise for
The Frozen Sky

"I'm hooked."
—Larry Niven, *New York Times* bestselling author of *Ringworld*

"A first-rate adventure set in one of our solar system's most fascinating places."
—Allen Steele, Hugo Award-winning author of the *Coyote* series

"Pulse pounding."
—*Publishers Weekly*

"Intelligent and entirely new. Highly recommended."
—Seanan McGuire, *New York Times* bestselling author of *Feed*

Praise for the
Plague Year trilogy

"An epic of apocalyptic fiction: harrowing, heartfelt, and rock-hard realistic."
—James Rollins, *New York Times* bestselling author of *The 6th Extinction*

"Chilling and timely."
—*RT Book Reviews*

"Ingenious."
—*Publishers Weekly*

"I can't wait for the movie."
—*Sacramento News & Review*
"Compelling. His novels take readers to the precipice of disaster."
—*San Francisco Chronicle*

Praise for
Long Eyes

SIXTEEN STORIES ABOUT STRANGE WORLDS, BIOTECH, COMMANDOS AND THE GIRL NEXT DOOR.

"Striking." —*Locus Online*

"Exciting." —*SF Revu*

"Chilling and dangerous."
—*HorrorAddicts.net*

Praise for
Interrupt

"Let's be honest: Carlson is dangerous. Thumbs up."
—Scott Sigler, *New York Times* bestselling author of *Alive*

"The ideas fly as fast as jets."
—Kim Stanley Robinson, Hugo Award-winning author of *Aurora*

"This book has it all — elite military units, classified weaponry, weird science, a dash of romance and horrific global disasters. Carlson writes like a knife at your throat."
—Bob Mayer, *New York Times* bestselling author of the *Green Berets* and *Area 51* series

"Terrific pacing. Dimensional characters. Jeff Carlson delivers everything and more in a killer thriller."
—John Lescroart, *New York Times* bestselling author of *The Fall*

For the real Ashley Sierzenga,
smart, strong, talented,

and for her father,
the Real Jeff,
a great family man,
a great engineer,

Both of them adventurers
and my friends.

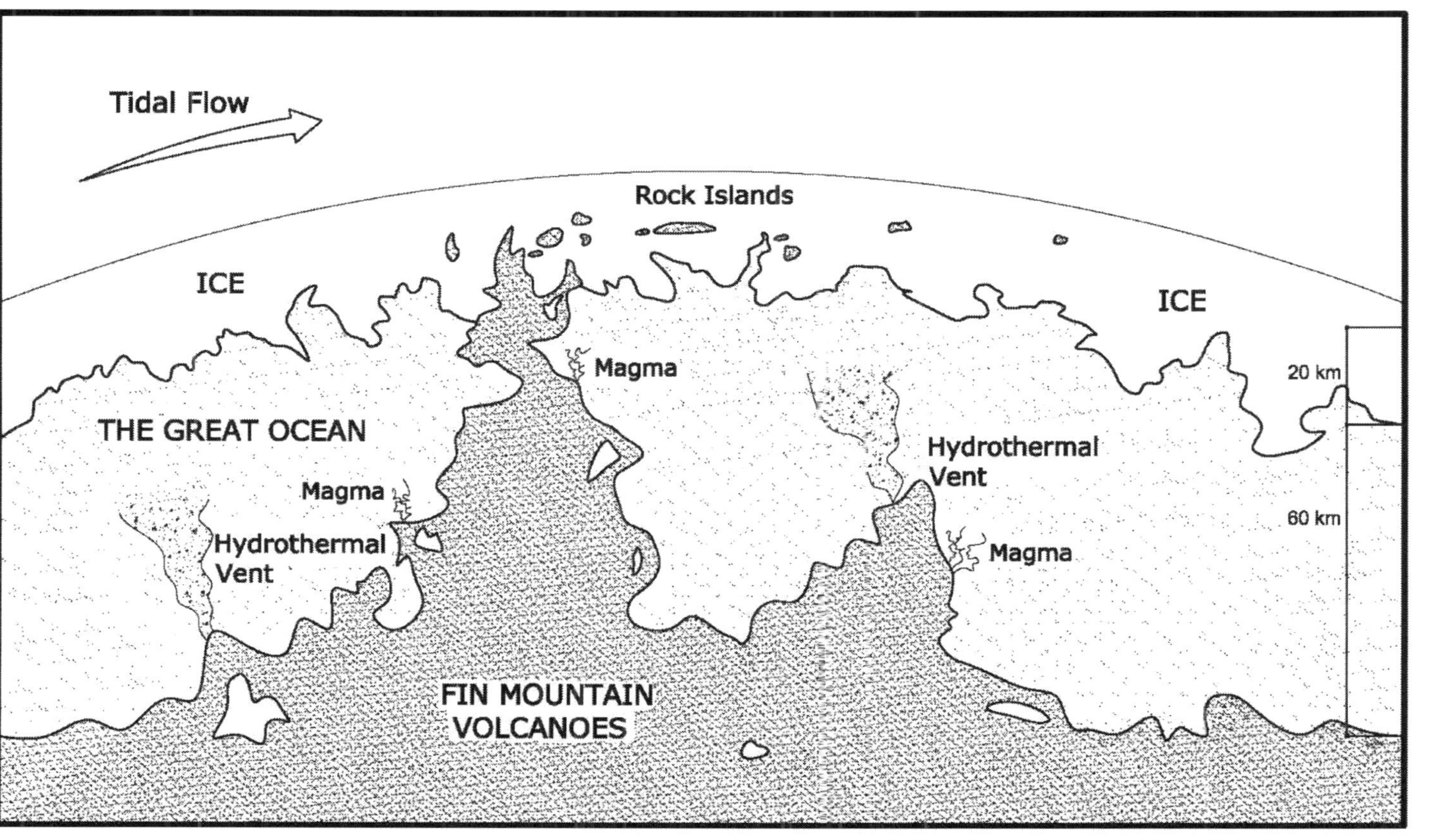

Europa's Southern Pole

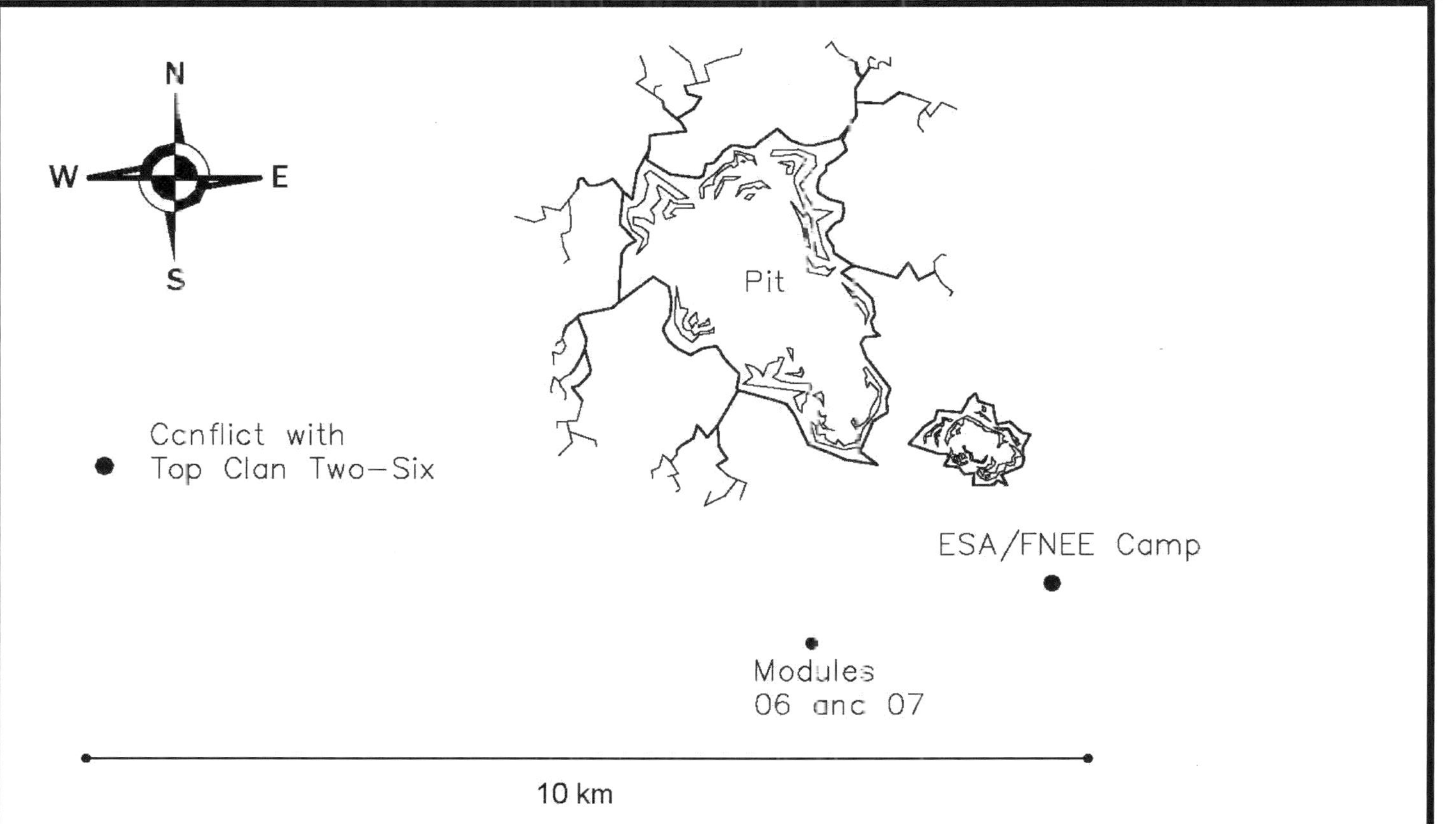

Surface of the Southern Pole

Glossary

2MS
Multibeam Model- and Sim-assisted Sonar.

AIs
Artificial intelligences ranging from Level VII super computers to human-like Level II and Level I personalities.

Altercast
Alternating frequency broadcasts used for stealth and security.

Alumalloy
A lightweight ultra-high tensile nano composite aluminum alloy.

A.N.
The Allied Nations, a world council formed November 25 2096 after the dissolution of the United Nations.

APAQS Module
All-Purpose Atmosphere-Equipped Storage unit.

AP mines
Anti-Personnel mines.

AP/CEW pods
Anti-Personnel / Counter Electronic Warfare devices typically used to protect fences, entrances or locks from unauthorized entry. AP/CEW pods often contain tasers, mace, scramblers and low-level AIs.

AMAS
Anti-Missile Anti-Satellite defensive systems.

ATMP
All-Terrain Multi-Personnel vehicle, a.k.a. "jeep."

CEW
Counter Electronic Warfare.

Con Foam
Construction foam, a number of pliable expanding materials which are typically airtight, watertight and pressure resistant when cured into solids.

Crypto
Encryption.

Data/comm
Data and communications.

Deuterium
A hydrogen isotope used as fuel in cold fusion reactors.

DGSE
Direction Générale de la Sécurité Extérieure, a.k.a. "the Directorate," French national security.

DMsP
Dense Materials Penetrating radar.

DNA
Deoxyribonucleic acid, one of the three major macromolecules found in all known terrestrial lifeforms and also found in all Europan lifeforms including "sunfish."

DSAMs
Disposable handheld surface-to-air missile launchers typically known as a

OneSAM, TwoSAM or FiveSAM depending on the number of missiles preloaded into each size.

DSSC Module
Deep Space Self-Contained habitation unit.

ELF
Extremely Low Frequency radio waves.

EMP
Electromagnetic Pulse.

ESA
European Space Agency.

ESUs
Emergency Survival Units.

EUSD
European Union Space Defense.

FNEE
Brazil's *Força Nacional de Exploração do Espaço.*

HESH
High-Explosive Squash Head projectile rounds.

HUD
Heads-Up Display.

HKs
Unmanned "hunter-killer" probes or mecha.

LRAs

Line Replacement Assemblies are standardized cybernetic or electronic components that can be quickly replaced in damaged suits and mecha.

MAID/comm

A briefcase-sized Mobile Artificial Intelligence data/communications unit.

Mem Files

Coupled with holo recordings and after-action reports, these immersive recordings of cyber-assisted, individually-tailored biological feedback result in "memory files."

MI6

Britain's Secret Intelligence Service, commonly known as "MI6" based on their designation as Military Intelligence, Section 6.

MMPSAs

Mobile Multi-Purpose Sensor Array mecha.

MP7

Modifizierte Maschinepistole 7A50, a 30mm Hechler & Koch machine pistol Assault Model 50 modified for airless environments.

NASA

U.S.A.'s National Aeronautics and Space Administration.

NATO

The North Atlantic Treaty Organization.

OBP

Optimized Blood Plasma.

Plastisteel

A combat-grade ballistic armor forged from polyproylene nickel chromium molybdemun nano composites.

PSSC

The People's Supreme Society Of China.

Q-and-E

Quarantine and Evaluate.

Rems

The Roentgen Equivalent In Man, a unit measuring the biological effects of absorbed doses of radiation named after the German scientist William Röntgen, who discovered X-rays.

ROM-4 AP Mecha (FNEE)

Remote Operated Mecha, System 4, All Purpose.

ROM-6 SD Mecha (FNEE)

Remote Operated Mecha, System 6, Self Defense.

ROM-12 GP Mecha (ESA)

Remote Operated Mecha, System 12, General Purpose.

ROM-20 LRSS Mecha (PSSC)

Remote Operated Mecha, System 20, Long Range Self-Sustained.

SETI

Search for Extra-Terrestrial Intelligence.

SCP

Sabotage and Control Program.

Sharecast

A transmission linking two or more suits, mecha, ships or satellites.

Showphone

A short-range communication device incorporating visual displays with audio transmissions.

Slavecast

Similar to SCPs, slavecasts are brute force transmissions intended to seize control of hostile suits, mecha, ships or satellites.

Spy sats

Stealth-equipped surveillance satellites.

SRHEL

Short-Range High-Energy Laser communications.

STAT Missile Launchers

Surface-To-Air Twin missile launchers.

USAF

United States Aerospace Force.

VRAP

Variable Rapid-Fire Armor-Piercing projectile rounds.

BLINDSIDED

1.

Ben said, "Watch your back!"

Vonnie swung around in her suit, lifting one arm to protect her face. In her other hand she held a sword. Curved and lined with saw teeth, its blade was a wicked crescent.

The tunnels were empty. She heard dripping water. Darkness surrounded them and her eyes felt as wide as plates.

"What do you see?" she asked.

"Movement, four contacts," Ben said.

"No. There are more," Ash hissed.

The three of them weren't supported by their allies or their mecha, which left them vulnerable on their flanks. Sims allowed them to map several hundred yards of the catacombs — a maze twisting in every direction — but the shifting ice and trickling water created dead spots in their radar. Noise affected their seismography.

Gas vents filled this region of the frozen sky. The catacombs sagged into low crawl spaces or melted apart in steaming caverns. The ice was pocked with holes.

Some of the holes moved as if giving birth. Muscular round forms dropped onto the tunnel floor.

Suddenly there were twelve sunfish on the ice.

Screeching and piping, they writhed their many arms. Most of them were savage males. Their song was ravenous. The matriarchs were hungry, too. This was a poor tribe. Four males showed red fungal infections on their waxy skin. They were scrawny and ill.

"Oh shit," Ben said.

Vonnie nodded grimly and hefted her sword in both hands. "Get ready to fight."

New sunfish always seemed to have heard of the Earth crews who'd landed on Europa. The tribes could sing to each other through several kilometers of ice, and ESA biologists thought the matriarchs sent runners to deliver warnings to each other, but the tribes who hadn't personally dealt with human beings rarely understood the power of lasers or projectile guns... not until they'd been shot.

Vonnie's blade was meant as a deterrent. Sunfish faltered at the obvious cutting edges of medieval weapons. All of the tribes revered metal.

"Don't move!" Vonnie shouted, using her helmet to broadcast her real voice as well as its equivalent in sonar. —*We hear you! Don't move!*

—*Danger! Attack!* the males shrieked.

—*There is no danger,* Vonnie cried. —*We are here for a friend. We're searching for him.*

—*Attack! Attack!*

—*Don't make us hurt you!* She kept her elbow close to Ben, covering his side.

Behind them, Ash laid a hand on Vonnie's shoulder, establishing contact even if their heads-up displays placed them within centimeters of each other.

Ash's voice was rigid with fear. "They're boxing us," she said. "Four ahead, two left, six right."

Vonnie spoke in a reassuring tone. "We can talk to them. We'll make them listen." She gave her AIs a prearranged command. "Combat menu, Samurai One."

Their scout suits took over. Two hundred and twenty kilos of armor, computers and ordnance, each suit was capable of carrying whoever was inside it like a person inside a robot. Unassisted, nobody would have been able to swing their heavy weapons... but in their suits, they were giants.

They danced with the menacing grace of ancient Japanese warriors. Their blades whirled in a high-speed pattern, every lunge or spin carefully orchestrated to blend their trio into a powerful whole.

Ben and Ash had battle staffs with axe heads on either end. Vonnie preferred her sword. She'd practiced for hours with the long scimitar, and, not coincidentally, its saw teeth resembled the stubby spikes on a sunfish's topside.

Despite their knack for exquisitely subtle nuances in speech and body language, the sunfish were literal creatures. They liked clear connections. The teeth on her blade were a message that even with her size, she needed defenses, too.

—*Food! The intruders are food!* the males shrieked.

—*We will destroy you if you attack! We are invincible and you are small! Our weapons are steel!*

—*Your name? Your name?* the matriarchs called.

Vonnie frowned at the question, and Ash whispered what she was thinking. "They should know who we are," Ash said.

The three of them were 6.8 klicks from their base, well inside the boundaries of the territory they'd claimed. Their scouts and mecha ranged as far as fifteen klicks. They'd placed markers everywhere.

"Cancel one," Vonnie said, stopping the *Samurai* program. It ended with their suits in a confident pose. Vonnie knelt at their center as Ben and Ash stood over her, weapons out. —*We are Ghost Clan Thirty!* she cried.

—*Your name? Your name?* a matriarch screamed.

—*We are Thirty!*

The sunfish hadn't declared their own identifiers, which was odd. Were they testing her or had their group intelligence been lowered by the predominance of savage males? Vonnie couldn't believe this tribe had traveled from so far away that they hadn't learned of the wealthy, dominant *Ghost Clan* who ruled Europa's southern pole.

She also didn't understand their stubborn repetition, which led her to one inescapable truth.

Walking into the ice was a death trap.

It's the same fight every time, she thought. *Detect, pursue, ambush.*

During the past months, Earth agencies had encountered fourteen tribes in addition to a few loners and rogue pairs. Each meeting had begun with violence.

The two males on Vonnie's left shifted closer.

"Here they come," Ben said.

"Wait. Check your display. They're maneuvering so they can cross their sonar with the six males on our right."

"They're going to jump."

"I'll stop them if they do."

Ben nodded, clutching his axe. Like most of the ESA crew, he mourned the sunfish they'd lost, but he had yet to bend his heart around the fact that killing some of the natives was necessary to save their race.

Vonnie had struggled with this lesson herself. The horror and fascination she felt toward the sunfish were impossible to separate. She admired so much about them.

Emulating their best traits, she'd developed an extreme sense of paranoia. Sometimes it let her predict the future. That spooky feeling heightened her composure as Ash grew louder, even frantic.

"Why don't they know who we are!?" Ash shouted.

"They do," Vonnie said. "It's a trick. There are more of them in the catacombs above us."

Ash gaped at her. "What?"

"All systems up. Link to me."

"Oh shit," Ben said as he synchronized his gear block with Vonnie's suit. Ash did the same.

They had ventured beneath the surface with a minimum of active hardware, using only radar and neutrino pulse. Spotlights were like torches in the cold. Sonar held a greater risk. Any disturbance brought predators, including the tribes. The weight and noise of their suits had probably attracted these sunfish, so Vonnie considered herself responsible for what happened next. Blood or peace?

"Burn 'em," she said.

Their spotlights switched on. The ice blazed. Unseen, their infrared and sonar exploded outward like a shockwave.

The sunfish recoiled, screaming.

—*WE ARE GHOST CLAN THIRTY!* Vonnie roared. She opened her posture with her sword in one hand and her laser on her other wrist. The laser flared, slashing into the wall.

A quarter ton of ice crumbled at their feet.

—*Magma! Quakes! Magma! Run!* a matriarch screeched. She equated Vonnie's laser with flowing lava.

Vonnie also heard distant cries. The sunfish hidden overhead had reacted to the terror of their kin by promising help. In doing so, they revealed their positions. Her sensors estimated there were twelve of them. The tribe was about to double in number. Would more warriors convince them that they could defeat three astronauts?

Ash and Ben added to Vonnie's roar, their suits mimicking hers exactly. —*We can destroy you or we can be allies! We have great strength but we need advisors and guides! We are rebuilding the empire!*

Vonnie pinned the nearest males in her spotlight. They cringed. They looked like albino shadows on the ice. Sunfish had no eyes, but they were heat sensitive. Ben thought they also possessed crude photo receptors among the thousands of pedicellaria and tube feet that lined their undersides.

—*Fire!* they shrieked. —*Crush it!*

Like a targeting array, they were providing coordinates to their kin. Overhead, the ice vibrated as the hidden sunfish scurried and dug.

Ben looked up.

"Move with me," Vonnie said as she paced toward the matriarchs. The matriarchs retreated, dragging the savage males with them.

—*Run! Run!* they cried.

"Lights off, lasers down," Vonnie said. Darkness enveloped them. —*Feel the cold!* she screamed. —*We control these fires, and our strength can be yours. Join us. Our empire includes many sunfish.*

Quivering, two of the matriarchs reversed course. They prodded their way through the males and lifted their arms to expose their tube feet. Tasting the air, listening, they studied Vonnie with the intensity of blind children sifting through a million elusive details.

She knew they could read her tension. They heard her rapid heartbeat and her shallow breaths. They couldn't smell her inside her suit, but she didn't doubt they would discern every clue in her body language as she produced adrenaline and sweat. She tried to master her nerves. At her best, she could project certainty and resolve.

The males shrieked, disrupting the exchange between Vonnie and the matriarchs.

—*Tell your tribemates above us not to attack!* she screamed. —*We can hear them. We'll kill you all. Let us help you instead.*

—*Why? Why?* the matriarchs screeched.

—*We need advisors and scouts. Join us. We have safe homes. We have limitless food.*

The matriarchs piped among themselves. Their tone was bewildered. It was hungry and yearning. They used their song to quiet the agitated males.

"I think the noise above us stopped," Ben said as Ash blurted, "I am never coming down here again."

Vonnie didn't have time to comfort Ash. The matriarchs were discussing her offer! She needed to persuade them, so, like a sunfish, she boasted of her tribe's potency once more.

—*We are Ghost Clan Thirty!* she cried.

At last, the matriarchs answered with their own name. —*We are Top Clan Two-Six!*

The combination of small amounts meant they were the dregs of their race, outcasts condemned to the desolate areas at the top of the ice. Possibly they were homeless nomads. That was why they'd ignored the ESA markers. Starving and weak, they'd assumed they were unworthy of an alliance.

But I got through to them, she thought. *We can nurse them back to health, teach them, help them. We…*

The ceiling collapsed.

Three tons of ice hit the floor where Vonnie had been standing with her friends. Shrapnel clattered off their suits. Ash staggered and Ben sank to one knee, banging his arm against Vonnie's leg.

There were sunfish in the avalanche. A spasming male fell out of the pile, squashed and bleeding.

—*We are Two-Six!* the matriarchs shrieked.

—*No! Please!* Vonnie yelled. But to their kind, begging was taunting. If there had been any chance of changing their minds, she'd wasted it by speaking to them like they were people.

The sunfish launched themselves into the air, a swarm of tough-skinned bodies. All twelve acted as one. Some of them bounced into the wall. Others shoved each other in mid-air to alter their trajectories... careening up or down... spinning off the ceiling or the floor. They converged on the astronauts as a single group.

Vonnie's radar tracked another swarm from behind. Ten sunfish jumped clear of the avalanche or poured through the gap overhead. She heard Ash shout.

The matriarchs slapped aside Vonnie's blade. They clawed on her helmet and ripped at her neck.

2.

Briefly, there had been peace. It lasted twenty-three days. Yet even in peace, their lives were hectic. The ESA and FNEE crews had been busier than ever with the sunfish, constructing more mecha, securing their borders and reaching out to neighboring tribes.

Meanwhile their genesmiths were devising medicines for the sunfish and cataloguing an excess of DNA samples. The tribes brought them living pieces of bacterial mats, fungi, several species of bugs, eels, and the desiccated corpses of two furred animals that looked like ferrets with gnawing teeth and digging claws.

Dawson had been pleasant of all things. He was chatty and jovial while Harmeet turned pensive. Dawson was exuberant about their new wealth. Harmeet seemed uneasy. Vonnie couldn't guess why, although as the ESA's lead biologist, Ben said they were finding more puzzles than answers in their research. There were too many unknowns on Europa, too many holes in its evolutionary history.

Vonnie liked Harmeet. The older woman was her friend and a steadying influence. At dinner, Vonnie had tried to draw her out with layman questions about her work. Harmeet shook her head and murmured, "I'm okay, Von. Maybe later."

Everyone was running on too little downtime. All of them were frayed except Dawson, who'd always been a loner even if he showed it by relaxing when everyone else felt overwhelmed.

"No rest for the wicked," Koebsch said, smiling at Vonnie when they met in a corridor.

"Yes, sir," she replied.

Their schedules let her pretend she wasn't caught in a triangle between herself and Ben and Koebsch. She was still sleeping with one and exchanging complex glances with the other, which wasn't fair to any of them.

She'd found a new confidant in Sergeant Tavares. It was good to commiserate with someone, although Tavares was younger and less experienced than Von. The Brazilians were grappling with the same dilemmas. Worse, their squad was military.

Fraternization between ESA Commander Peter Koebsch and his subordinates was discouraged but not *verboten*. Among the FNEE, sexual relations were a punishable offense.

Five days ago, Vonnie and Tavares had stolen a moment to talk while they rigged new data/comm units on the exterior of the FNEE hab module. Silencing their radios, they'd clonked their helmets together. With their voices carried by conduction, not radio, no one else could hear.

Tavares confessed that the FNEE squad was strained to the breaking point. They were in peak physical condition and most of them were in their twenties. None were older than thirty-five.

Their daily meds included pills to mute their libidos, but her squadmates discarded those pills as a matter of course. Honor demanded it. Unfortunately, she was the only female; the men had been snarling at each other for months; disputes were common; and during their reports to Earth, they'd concealed several injuries caused by fistfights between Captain Araújo and Lieutenant Santos, including a fractured arm when Santos threw Araújo against a supply locker.

Honor demanded it.

They would rather beat each other like apes in a high tech cage than ingest a pill to soothe themselves. They conspired against their leaders on Earth, hiding their bruises, lying about their confrontations. Somehow, in fact, the men's beatings brought them closer together.

From what Vonnie had seen, the FNEE squad possessed a remarkable *esprit de corps*. They were like brothers. Their physical frustration was evidence of their vigor.

Tavares met Vonnie's gaze and spoke frankly. "I want to help my squad. Tell me if I am crazy."

"What do you mean?"

"I can… I'm why they fight."

"That's not your fault."

"I know a solution. You know it, too." Tavares ducked her eyes. "I'm not sure I can go through with it."

"Then you shouldn't."

"I should."

Tavares wanted to sleep with most of them. She said she was genuinely attracted to Araújo and Pereira. She liked all of the others except Santos, and she sympathized with him. They were a long way from home. They'd faced many forms of death in the ice and in the sunfish.

"But I can't," Tavares said. "If I choose one, the others will kill him. Lately I've tried not to talk to anyone. We…"

Vonnie grimaced as she contemplated the young sergeant's loneliness. She wondered again why the FNEE mission planners had put seven men with one woman. It was a stupid mistake. They intended to remain on Europa for years. Wouldn't a balanced group have been better? Or eight men?

Tavares had buzzed her obsidian-black hair into a masculine cut and she kept her uniform collar buttoned to her neck, but she couldn't disguise her cheekbones or her hazel eyes.

To say their conflicts were entirely centered around her was simplistic. Like the ESA crew, the FNEE squad had been cooped inside their module for months, but her presence amplified their discontent. She was the star around whom the men circled and crashed, untouchable, unavoidable, an irritant and a treasure.

Tavares said, "If they see me talking with one man or if I sit by the same man twice for meals, they argue. Santos picks fights with them. Araújo defends everyone even when they don't want his protection."

"Each man has found his role in the group."

"They need to get outside, but there's nowhere to go. Colonel Ribeiro gives them demerits or unpleasant jobs when he can. I had to ask him to work with you today instead of sending Santos. I… I touched his arm and he stared at me. I don't think they realize how *pertubado* they've become. So much of their shouting seems normal. They need more people."

Was she asking Vonnie to arrange a social event? On occasion, ESA and FNEE personnel met face-to-face. Mostly they communicated by radio or showphone. Vonnie supposed everybody could fit into Module 01 if they squeezed in tight.

I guess that's the idea, she thought like a sick joke.

The subtext would be an insult — the expectation of promiscuity — and Vonnie and Ash and Harmeet were the only surviving females among the ESA.

They were outnumbered by their own men, who'd also developed a convoluted hierarchy in response to their circumstances. Henri and Ash had paired up. Koebsch and Ben were rivals for Von. O'Neal was deferential to the three women and especially kind to Harmeet, who permitted his attention, while Tony was gruff with them and Dawson maintained his snobbish gentlemanly air.

We're not the answer, Vonnie decided. *Mixing our crew with their soldiers would create new hassles.* "Your men should take their pills," she said. "Haven't your people on Earth seen their blood work?"

"Our medical systems aren't automated like yours. Lieutenant Carvalho analyzes our blood samples and enters his assessments manually."

"He's faking his results to show everything's okay? That's idiotic. It's selfish."

"It is what we decided to do," Tavares said. Her tone was stiff. Vonnie realized she needed to tread cautiously. Yes, the FNEE had inferior equipment, but she'd offended Tavares by implying they had poor discipline.

"None of this is your fault," she said. "You should tell Earth what's happening."

"I will not report my squad."

"Um. Let's try something else. Are more FNEE ships coming to Europa?"

"You know two more of our spacecraft arrive soon."

"I mean will they land or stay in orbit."

"This is classified. I cannot say."

"What difference would it make? We'll find out for ourselves in another week."

"If I say, you could have time to prepare."

"Prepare for what? Tavares… Claudia… I want to be friends, but I can't help if you won't let me."

"Please be my friend. I enjoy your company."

"Okay. Me, too. Maybe our commander can talk to your colonel about sharing more food or entertainment." Vonnie glanced up as if she could spot the incoming ships. She was worried. She wanted Tavares to see her concern, but Tavares brightened.

"Thank you, Von. Thank you."

Can she be that naïve? Vonnie wondered, although she didn't think the young sergeant's warmth was an act. *I used to be the same. I looked for the best in everyone. Is that why they chose her? She'll give her squad everything she has…* "We'd better get back to work."

Tavares nodded, and they leaned away from each other, separating their helmets. They returned to wiring the data/comm units.

When they were done, they hugged in their bulky suits. Tavares looked like she'd made her decision. Vonnie tried to smile. "I'll call soon," she said.

But as she strode back to Module 06, she stopped and searched the blackness. Moons glittered in the void, outshining the stars. Even the sun was a cold white dot. On the looming face of Jupiter, its clouds roiled in an endless storm.

Are the FNEE planning a double-cross? If they betray us to the PSSC, we can't stop them both.

When an automated rover first discovered bugs inside the catacombs, there had been five robot tankers above Europa. Now there were ESA, NASA and PSSC spacecraft on its surface and a FNEE ship in orbit. Seven tankers and five probes crowded nearby. So did an unknown number of spy sats.

Twenty of those satellites belonged to the ESA or NASA, who shared most of their data. Five more belonged to the FNEE, who contributed information to the ESA.

They'd identified a high-gee PSSC fighter holding position above Europa's southern pole. Less brazenly, American and Japanese hunter-killers lurked among the debris of Jupiter's nearest rings. Koebsch said there were more HKs in-system. They'd snatched a bit of Iranian code from an otherwise undetected rig, and an automated NASA probe was slowly drifting back from Neptune.

More crewed vessels would arrive during the next weeks including the two FNEE ships, a PSSC destroyer, and the EUSD cruiser *Jyväskylä*, a Marauder-class firing platform named after a Finnish city obliterated during the One Day War.

The intricate dynamics of the men and women on the ice were mirrored proportionally by the craft overhead. The character of each crew was reflected in their governments' actions.

Brazil wanted to prove they belonged among the major nations. On the net, Vonnie had seen NATO analysts who said the FNEE couldn't afford to boost two more ships, but they'd done it anyway with their slapdash bravado, rushing to beat PSSC and EUSD reinforcements to Europa.

NATO security briefings said the FNEE ships contained sixty mecha and twenty soldiers. Ten were female. They'd improved upon their gender imbalance, but the show of force was a larger error.

China had serenely moved to demonstrate its superiority. They did not warn their opponents. Nor had their astronauts communicated with the other crews on the ice. They'd simply routed their destroyer toward Europa and it advanced like an emperor toward his throne, presuming everyone and everything would clear its path. It had overtaken the FNEE ships. It would arrive before them.

Then the Americans made their own show of force. The war had crippled them, and, long before the missiles fell, their country had seen a devout push away from science and technology. Their economy had fizzled. They'd sold their debts to China and other nations, further impairing themselves by paying interest for three generations. As always, however, the best of them were plucky and brave and rebellious.

NASA had put one crew on Europa. They couldn't send more, yet, working on a shoestring budget, the American military and civilian agencies brought every available probe to Jupiter. Many were combat capable. Any device under acceleration could serve as a missile.

Much like Brazil, America wanted to prove itself again, but whereas the Brazilians regarded themselves as upstarts, the Americans were tainted by the anger of fallen kings. Wheeling and dealing, they called in every marker or made demands upon their friends.

Japan and Israel sent more probes.

Rogue nations or PSSC allies like Russia and Iran did the same, adding to the powder keg.

Vonnie liked to think the European Union had responded with the most elegant approach. They allocated a single cruiser to guard their interests but they did not provoke China by sending a full strike wing.

Meanwhile, on Earth, the diplomats and lawyers attacked each other with words. The politicians squabbled among themselves and redoubled the pressure on their crews, urging them to solidify their claims on Europa. It was a spectacular mess. Vonnie couldn't imagine what the sunfish thought of human beings. Their species shared many traits. Loyalty. Possessiveness. Competition. Mistrust. But in comparison to the scattered tribes, humankind's social groups were clumsy and ponderous. They tripped over themselves, blundering along, led by morons and thieves as well as honest souls.

Vonnie knew better than to think she didn't have her own shortcomings. When the order came to send people into the ice, she'd volunteered.

Berlin wanted every possible rationale to stand up to China in the world courts. To them, having astronauts beneath the surface was proof of ownership. Fine. Joining the sunfish was what she'd wanted.

Her crewmates were less enthusiastic, but most of them had entered the catacombs. They went in pairs or quartets because even Vonnie wasn't sure if they were safe. The treaty they'd formed had been with the combined groups of a Top Clan and a Mid Clan, and the tribe's mood was jubilant.

The matriarchs were drunk with power. The unusual conglomeration of both breeds would have been successful by itself, but wedding themselves to the ESA offered more resources than they'd known in millennia.

Backed by tools and food, the new tribe had swiftly grown. They'd expanded their territory and adopted three more Top Clans into their ranks.

As an engineer, Vonnie led the effort to reinforce the tunnels beneath the ESA/FNEE camp with epoxy, mesh and steel, building homes for the sunfish, sealing key spots and pumping heat and air into their nests.

She was called *Young Matriarch*, a traditional role for vibrant, ambitious females. Every astronaut had a sunfish name, even those who remained on the surface like Dawson.

The tribes heard everything. They had survived Europa's turmoil by judging the qualities of everything around them based on the slightest sound or shape. They were almost clairvoyant. They reached conclusions with AI speed, except that unlike computers, the sunfish were biased.

Dawson was *Old Foe* due to his spiteful relationship with Vonnie. Others who'd clashed with her also had names with unpleasant connotations. Colonel Ribeiro was *Loud Warrior* and Ash was *Biting Female*, although the tribe's concepts for 'loud' and 'biting' held respect. Even their term for 'foe' was approving. More than anything, they celebrated strength and wits and courage.

O'Neal had been bewitched by the contradictions inherent to sunfish thinking. They were the mystery he'd waited to solve since he was a boy with an IQ of 165, few friends, and the dream of escaping the poverty- and gang-ridden streets of Belfast.

His name was *Wise Scout*, a reliable male advisor. As the ESA linguist, O'Neal coordinated the development of their translation programs. On Earth, thousands of better-trained interpreters and polyglots pored through his data, but O'Neal was the man on the scene. During the past week, he had begun meeting with the sunfish in person.

Four hours ago he'd disappeared into the ice.

3.

Vonnie lowered her sword in one fist as she used her other hand to pry a twitching male from her chest. The corpse flexed two arms. Even in death, the sunfish had predatory impulses.

At her feet, thirteen more small bodies squirmed. The rest of the tribe had fled.

Their blood smoked in the subzero atmosphere. A male rolled over pitifully. His arms curled. He clacked his beak. Vonnie aimed the point of her sword, ready for one final assault, but the male sagged. He lay motionless.

Inside her suit, she was shaking.

"Christ," Ben muttered. "Oh Christ." He patted his armored glove on her armored hip. "You okay?"

"No."

"Are you hurt?"

"No, I'm fine. I..."

In the brilliant lights radiating from their gear blocks, Ben turned to study Ash. All three of them were caked in frozen gore. He said, "Ashley? It looks like they got your leg."

"I'm fine, too," Ash said.

Vonnie felt like throwing up. Adrenaline pounded in her ears and she stared at her gloves as if they belonged to someone else. They seemed to float away from her above the carnage of the sunfish. "My hands..."

Ben said, "You're in shock. Take a sedative, both of you. We all should. Then we're getting out."

"No, I want to feel… This is how we should feel." Suddenly she thought of the FNEE squad's refusal to take their meds. Maybe now she understood. She wanted to be herself even if she felt stunned and melancholy.

He said, "You're not thinking straight. Our sonar calls were like a beacon. If there are other tribes in the area, they'll come for us."

"No pills."

Their radios crackled with a new voice. "Scout Team, this is Koebsch. Report."

Ben didn't welcome the intrusion. He tilted his helmet up as if challenging the other man, who was in camp far above them to the south. "You saw the whole thing, didn't you?"

"Yes. Report." Koebsch was authoritative.

Ben was rude. He gestured impatiently and said, "We'll be all right."

"Von?" Koebsch asked. "We're here for you. Let us know if there's anything you need." In that moment, his formal tone became something else. He was consoling her, but she didn't want to be the prize in a contest between the two men. She wanted to redeem herself. She stared at the dead sunfish, wondering what else she could have done.

Ben touched her hip again. "The attack wasn't our fault," he said.

"We didn't have to come down here! We didn't even have to send mecha. O'Neal might…" Vonnie stopped when she realized Ash was bent sideways.

The young woman propped herself on her axe like a crutch. Between her ankle and thigh, the plastisteel was scored with ragged marks.

"Ash, your leg!"

"I'm fine. I might have some bruises."

"She needs attention," Koebsch said and Ben snapped, "It's under control."

"You should've noticed her injury," Koebsch said.

"Goddammit, there are bodies everywhere. We're not relaxing with a hot coffee like you are."

Vonnie crouched beside Ash. Their displays would have blared with alarms if Ash's suit was losing pressure, but Vonnie needed to see for herself that Ash was okay. "What did they hit you with?" she asked.

"I don't know."

The marks were shallow yet numerous. The sunfish had hacked at Ash's leg with something. Metal blades? Vonnie decided no. The marks were too blunt. More likely, they'd scavenged ceramics or plastic composites from some of the mecha lost in the ice.

Keeping her glove on Ash's knee, Vonnie surveyed the tunnel. The sloppy, eviscerated corpses hid any artifacts from sight, but her radar spotted four dense baseball-sized chunks in the mess. Each chunk was a rock shaped like a pyramid with jagged edges and points.

She shared her radar images with her crewmates. "Ben, grab them, please."

"How is her suit?"

"I'll patch it. Her med systems can deal with any contusions." Vonnie opened her tool kit. "Ash, you swear you're okay? Nothing sprained?"

"Affirmative."

"She's as tough as steel," Vonnie said. "We both are." She didn't want to talk more about sedatives.

Ben nodded. He strode away.

Vonnie rubbed her fingertips on Ash's leg. Then she applied strips of glue and nano mesh, filling the abrasions. The damage was barely more than cosmetic.

This was the worst they could do, she thought. The starving Top Clan had been no match for ESA armor. As soon as they'd learned what to expect, one person could beat twenty sunfish. The tribes' best strategy was to drop ice or rock on their enemies. Avoid the trap, minimize the threat.

Given time and superior numbers, sunfish could crush suits or mecha, but they would never have time again. The AIs had invented specific combat routines to deal with their swarm tactics. Vonnie had replaced the suits' welding lasers with anti-personnel Lance 515s, and, in heated sheaths on their waists, each of them carried a modified 30mm Heckler & Koch MP7 loaded with HESH rounds.

Berlin did not want more casualties. The politicians couched this decision in phrases like *'sparing no effort to defend our astronauts'* and *'ensuring our borders with our new allies.'* The reality was some tribes would listen to reason; some wouldn't; and the human presence on Europa was not only permanent, it would expand.

Vonnie couldn't save every group of sunfish. Somehow she needed to accept her failures with her good deeds. She'd accomplished so much, but she felt like a murderer.

She finished patching Ash's leg and glanced up. Ash was watching Ben as he sorted through the corpses. They were stiffening. His boots crunched on frozen webs of blood. A blotch of meat stuck to his shin. She shouldn't have been so casual in telling him to take the job.

"Thank you, Ben," she called.

"Yeah. God. I suppose it had to be done." He drove his axe through a crimson sheet of icicles. Then he shoved aside a disemboweled matriarch and leaned down to grab one of the objects on their radar.

Ben had entered the catacombs to meet the sunfish for himself. Like Vonnie, he hoped to show everyone on Earth that the tribes were useful and friendly. As her lover, he had the added motivation of protecting her.

He's a good man, she thought. *I should let him do more to take care of me. He'd like that. I just don't want him to lord it over Koebsch.*

How do I stop them from bickering with each other?

Ben returned with his axe attached to the magnetic clamps on his back. In his gloves, he cradled four rocks. Although scratched and chipped, each rock was a solid pale grainy chunk, not the porous lava common among Europa's fin mountains.

"It's granite," he said. "All four pieces are granite."

Vonnie frowned. "That can't be right."

"What's wrong?" Ash said.

"We're at least seventy kilometers above the ocean floor, maybe eighty or ninety."

"So what?"

"Ash, there's no granite here," he said. "The mountains don't have the age or the composition to produce this form of rock. The ocean floor is the only continental crust on Europa."

"Maybe that's where they got it."

"Seventy kilometers away?"

Koebsch spoke on the radio. "Ben, I want full scans of the rocks before you leave."

"Wow, I didn't think of that," Ben mocked him.

"Just do it."

"What about the bodies?" Vonnie asked. "Should we leave them for the survivors? We might gain some standing with this tribe if we do. They need the food."

"We want samples from each corpse, but that's a good idea," Koebsch said.

Muttering, Ben set the rocks on a clean patch of ice. Vonnie and Ash joined him. They formed a triangle as Ben chose an auto program from his display.

In tandem, their gear blocks swept the chunks of granite with radar and neutrino pulse.

When the scans were complete, Ben knelt. His left glove seized the largest rock, then the next and the next. Micro drills in his ring finger buzzed into each stone. The samples remained isolated in the detachable hollow drill bits, which he stored in his chest pack.

Ash said, "Couldn't geysers or storms carry different materials into the ice?"

Ben secured each rock in a sterile foam block. "It's possible. The distance makes it unlikely. Even if a natural event lifted granite from the ocean floor, how would a Top Clan find it? The ice is twenty kilometers thick. From what we've seen, the Top Clans move laterally over long distances, but if they travel more than five klicks downward they're in Mid Clan territory. Below the Mids, they don't even have rumors of what's farther down."

"Actually, that might not be the case," Vonnie said. "O'Neal was starting to think otherwise."

Ben stood up. "What are you talking about?"

"We hardly know anything about where the sunfish evolved or how far they've spread." Vonnie tipped her head forward, waving for Ben and Ash to do the same. Then she chopped her hand at her throat. She switched off her radio and cameras. So did Ben. They put their helmets together and waited for Ash.

Reluctantly, the young woman complied.

None of the astronauts were supposed to cut communications. First, maintaining contact was a safety measure. Second, Berlin demanded full transcripts.

As a British agent, Ash had additional orders. Her handlers wanted direct access to the ESA crew. Vonnie couldn't stop Ash from reporting her secrets, but she hoped she'd sway Ash to keep quiet for a while. She'd give Ash something personal to divulge instead. As an unofficial policy, Berlin overlooked the occasional blackout. They knew their people needed private encounters like Vonnie's meeting with Tavares. If Ash offered a dirty bit of gossip to MI6, they might believe that was why Vonnie had asked for radio silence.

"The things I'm about to say… You can't tell your bosses on Earth. Tell them Ben and I went off-line because we're fighting. Tell them he's mad because O'Neal has been flirting with me like Koebsch."

Ben said, "What?"

Ash might have smiled at his response. Vonnie caught one glimpse of humor in Ash's face before her expression hardened. Ash had never acknowledged that she served two masters. She didn't like it when anyone brought it up.

She was so young. She believed in black and white where Vonnie saw impure shades of gray.

All of them had been startled when they discovered O'Neal was gone, but Ash had cursed him as an idiot while Vonnie reserved judgment. He'd disobeyed their most cardinal rule. He'd gone into the ice alone. Now he was either dead or lost or exactly where he wanted to be.

Like most of the crew, Ash thought O'Neal had made some horrible mistake. Vonnie was willing to assume he knew what he was doing. He was an intelligent man. Yes, he was wonky. He spent too much time with his computers, but he had a good soul and he'd pointed them in the right direction more than once.

"Everything has been different since our treaty with the sunfish," Vonnie said. "O'Neal was learning things he didn't tell Earth. He learned things he didn't tell *us*."

"He told you?" Ben asked.

"Yes. I was…" Vonnie paused at his scowl. "For Christ's sake, Ben, he didn't tell me because he wants to get into my pants. He told me because I'm the stupid famous troublemaker who loves sunfish more than her own kind. Right?"

"Yeah." But there was jealousy in his eyes.

"During the past month, the tribe has quadrupled in size. We've had so many sunfish to interview, O'Neal's research took a quantum leap."

"Good." Ash shrugged. "What was it?"

"Some of it's complicated."

"You didn't warn Koebsch?"

"I didn't think O'Neal was going to disappear. He just talked a lot. He always talks a lot. The main thing he focused on is how difficult it is for the sunfish to lie. They don't hide anything from each other, not their emotions, not their plans. In a lot of ways, a tribe functions like a group mind."

Ash shrugged again. "Roger that," she said as Ben grunted, *Mm*, not because he was curious about the sunfish.

He was grouchy that *she* had lied.

"O'Neal said there are more layers in their songs than we realized. The more data he soaked up, the better he could translate. His work began to snowball. Suddenly he was hearing subtexts we'd missed."

"Enough," Ben said. "What's the secret?"

"They can lie by omission. All this time, we thought there were gaps in what the sunfish know about themselves. Now it looks like some topics are prohibited. Their own history is at the top of that list, but when O'Neal questioned the matriarchs directly, even if they didn't answer, he caught hints of what they meant to hide. There's an inner circle among the oldest females. They know more than they share with the other sunfish. The ignorance is deliberate."

Ash said, "Why would they do that? To stay in power?"

"That's one reason. They also want to keep their tribes away from something. O'Neal thinks it's an ancient place from the empire, maybe ruins."

"We've found ruins before. Why would that matter?"

With their helmets pressed together, Ash's face was ten centimeters from Vonnie's, which made each word more intimate. Vonnie could have been polite. Instead, she was accusing. "O'Neal didn't share what he'd learned because we know who you work for. Too many people want an excuse to kill the sunfish and go back to full-scale mining."

Ash hardened again, stung by Vonnie's scorn. "Why tell me now?" she asked.

"Because you put your life on the line for him. Because you risked yourself for me and Ben. We're supposed to be on the same side."

"Von, *you're* the one pulling strings. You let us think this was a rescue mission into an unpopulated zone. We thought O'Neal had been abducted by our own sunfish, so we couldn't bring them with us."

"I didn't—"

"We could have used them as scouts! We could have had reinforcements."

"I didn't think O'Neal knew what he was talking about. I'm sorry. Now we have to assume he's right." Vonnie took a deep breath and said, "There's another part of what he learned from the matriarchs."

Ash was also regaining control of herself. She shut her eyes and opened them again, her anger dimming slightly. "Go ahead."

"He thinks there are more sunfish than we ever guessed," Vonnie said. "A lot more."

"That would change everything," Ben said, lecturing her. "Earth thinks we're dealing with a few remnant tribes. Our entire program is based on the idea that we can take charge of their last survivors. How many does O'Neal think are out there?"

Vonnie swallowed to clear the lump from her throat. In that instant, the vast, echoing catacombs felt tighter. Her skin prickled with claustrophobia.

"Von?" he asked. "How many?"

"Hundreds of thousands," she said.

4.

"Are you kidding!? We can't keep that kind of information from Berlin." Ash spit each syllable like acid. Left unspoken was the threat that she would contact her superiors with MI6.

"Ash, wait," Vonnie said.

"No! It sounds like we're standing on top of an army. A massive army. That many sunfish could overrun us."

Ben said, "Our estimates never exceeded a few thousand survivors."

"We've been operating with limited data."

"But his new numbers are based on hearsay. Just because the matriarchs have stories about other sunfish, that doesn't mean anything."

"They don't lie, Ben."

"You just said they do."

"They deceive the stupid members of their tribes, not each other. Most of the males are barely more than animals."

"Hold on," Ash said. "I've seen them read our thoughts and we're not even the same species. I know they can read each other. How could the matriarchs keep secrets?"

"They have more than one language." Vonnie raised four of her fingers in a row. "Sound, scent, behavior, shape." She added her thumb, making five as she said, "The matriarchs also have a stylized form of communication for themselves. O'Neal said they tap and scrape their pedicellaria against each other like a combination of Morse code and Braille. It's unobtrusive. It took him days to see it."

"Wouldn't the other sunfish know the matriarchs are hiding something?"

"Yes. It's forbidden to ask. They don't have religion, but they do believe 'the Old Ones' were greater than any tribe now. Most of that knowledge is gone. Some of it exists as legends or cautionary tales. If a lesser sunfish gets too curious, the matriarchs can... O'Neal said they'll damn him. He's ostracized and shut out. They punish him."

"So the lesser sunfish learn not to ask questions, and we never realized we were missing the whole picture."

"Not until O'Neal surrounded their nests with his arrays. Look. The proof is how quickly our clan expanded. The nearest loners and tribes joined us because they were attracted by our food. But according to our models, there shouldn't have been that many sunfish in the area. We decided it was a fluke. O'Neal thinks we totally miscalculated how many of them are alive."

"We need to tell Berlin."

"Don't. Please. Give us more time."

"Time for what?"

"We're learning so much. New sunfish join our clan every day. They make us stronger. We're governing more territory. All of it could go up in smoke if Berlin panics."

"What if we're attacked?"

"We're less likely to be attacked if our clan is the dominant force in the area."

"Ash, I agree with her," Ben said.

The young woman's laugh was sharp. "You two don't know sunfish politics as well as you think. Nobody does. If the ice is heavily populated, our clan's expansion into new territory could be what sets off the other tribes. Our sunfish could turn against us. Some of the refugees we've taken in might be spies. Too many things can go wrong."

"If we bring more ships and mecha, so will the Chinese," Vonnie said. "So will Brazil. If we go on a war footing against sunfish we've never seen, that could be what sets off the other *people*. It's not the balance of power in the ice that I'm worried about."

"So we just wait?"

"Hell no. We find O'Neal and whatever he's looking for. Then I want to talk to the matriarchs. We might want a new strategy. First we need more time."

"A few days won't matter," Ben said.

Ash shifted uncomfortably. All of them had emergency lights on their displays, an urgent call from the surface. Their radio silence had lasted too long if it was really meant to conceal a lover's spat between Vonnie and Ben.

"We should answer Koebsch," Ash said.

"What are you going to tell him?"

"I'm not sure." Ash flared again. "You should've warned us what we were getting into! We thought this area was deserted!"

"I thought so, too, but we weren't in much danger with our suits, were we?" Vonnie looked at the shredded corpses. "There are three of us. Imagine what will happen if other tribes try to attack the FNEE gun platforms. We're safe. Let's give O'Neal more time."

With a rough shake of her head, Ash switched on her radio and cameras. "Scout Team online," she said as Von and Ben reactivated their own audio/visual channels.

"What are you doing?" Koebsch asked. From their vital signs, he knew they were nervous. He'd seen their heart rates rise and fall. He said, "I understand if you needed a minute to grieve for the sunfish..."

"No, sir." Ash glanced at Vonnie with a combative look. "We were talking. We, uh." Ash's first loyalty was to MI6, but that same quality — her devotion — worked against her now.

She owed Vonnie her life.

"Von and Ben were arguing about O'Neal," she said. "Von admitted she's spent time with O'Neal lately."

Koebsch's voice was cautious. "That's correct. Vonderach assisted O'Neal in placing our sensor arrays around the sunfish colony."

"She did more than that," Ben said sarcastically, playing his role as the offended boyfriend.

"Sir, I don't want to get involved," Ash said. "It's an interpersonal issue. My teammates say they'll put it behind them until we're back at camp."

"Um. Roger that." Koebsch obviously had questions, but he didn't want any of it on record. "You should get moving."

"Let's go," Ben said.

Vonnie didn't chime in. She wondered what her detractors would think when they heard this conversation. Would they believe she was now involved however casually with three men? Another blow to her reputation was a small price to pay. She was pleased Ash had gone along with the sham.

She opened the kits on her chest as she strode toward the dead sunfish. She reached the closest body and knelt, jabbing two patches of its skin with a lab pack.

Ben appeared at her side. He produced his own lab packs. They worked their way through the dead.

Ash followed, although she didn't join in. She stood guard, sweeping the tunnels with her radar as Koebsch said, "Let's get you to the surface. I have escape routes prepared."

"No, sir," Vonnie said. "We're not going anywhere until we find O'Neal."

"That's commendable, but we never planned for you to travel so far. I'd like to send in mecha. You're approaching an unstable region."

"O'Neal can't wait."

"If he's... No one wants to make a bad situation worse. I shouldn't have asked you to go."

"You made the right call."

O'Neal had vanished ten minutes before they noticed he was gone, which was inexplicable at first. Their suits carried transponders. Even if he hadn't been linked to the ESA grid, radar and seismography tracked every movement beneath camp and their radios were always live.

He could have yelled if he was in trouble. Their beacons should have pinged when he left Zone One, the nearest section of ice surrounding Submodule 07. Zone Two extended a kilometer in all directions. Both zones were crowded with retaining walls, pipes carrying oxygen and heat, MMPSAs, burrowers and larger mecha.

O'Neal had walked through each boundary without a peep. He'd gained another minute while Koebsch called him again and again. Even if his gear block was smashed, his transponder should have been live. He could have used it to signal an alarm.

He'd turned it off. Why? Was he under duress?

The playback from their sensors showed him leaving with a swarm of matriarchs. Then they'd lost him among a strand of rocks and gurgling streams. O'Neal looked like he was at the front of the group, but sunfish tended to lead from the middle. Koebsch assumed he was a prisoner. O'Neal might have foxed the ESA grid because the matriarchs threatened to hurt him if there was any sign of pursuit.

Koebsch almost sent mecha after him. The ESA/FNEE lines were peppered with GPs and doppelgängers. The FNEE also had gun platforms standing by, but the sunfish responded differently to people in suits than they did to machines. They would hear anything that followed them, and their greatest esteem was for the engineer they called *Young Matriarch.*

Koebsch had decided that if Vonnie went after O'Neal, her presence could make a difference. Equally important, she had been well-positioned to direct a rescue mission.

Vonnie and Ash had been in Module 06 running maintenance on its scout suits. Nearby in their cargo tent, wearing his own suit, Ben had been painting a quartet of mecha with lab-grown pheromones. They wanted to bring the segments of a power plant into Zone Two. Ben thought he could keep the sunfish from investigating the new hardware in their nosy, violent manner if the mecha smelled like egg-laying females.

As the two women had armored up, Ben dabbed the pheromones on himself. When they joined him, he painted them, too.

Then they'd gone into the ice.

The scent didn't protect us for long, Vonnie thought. *Ben hoped it would pacify the tribes. Did it attract them?*

Troubled, she stood over one of the dead males. His fungal infections were more advanced than any she'd seen before. The red swelling was tinged with black bumps. She took a new sample and secured her lab packs.

"Ben?" she asked.

"I'm done." He wiped his glove on his hip as if absolving himself of killing the sunfish by cleaning his hand.

She liked him for it. He tried to be tough, but he was a teddy bear. Her bear. Sorting through the grotesque corpses had shown a lot of perseverance and he'd done it twice, once for the stone tools, then to collect DNA.

"Why are you so awesome?" she asked before she remembered she was on an open channel and they were supposed to be stinging from a fight.

He beamed. "Am I?"

She grinned at the spark in his eyes. She had never been good at masking her emotions. Maybe that was why she related so well to the sunfish. She would have liked to embrace him. Instead, she punched his shoulder and feinted at Ash, wanting to include her.

Ash rolled her eyes, exasperated.

Vonnie laughed. It was good to feel connected to her lover and her friend in this dark place. "Get ready to run," she said. "I'm going to scream for the survivors. I'll invite them to eat, but I'll challenge them first. Maybe we can scare them enough that they'll submit."

Ash said, "If they hit us again, they'll use an avalanche or a flood. Watch your radar."

Koebsch said, "Listen to her, Von. We're picking up a lot of activity. We don't have full maps of the area, but we know it's corroding. There are too many rivers and lakes."

"Yeah." Vonnie's laughter had come and gone like the sun cutting through a bank of clouds, and she missed that happy feeling. "All systems up. Link to me."

Ash said, "We can't stay here and negotiate."

"If the sunfish are digging traps, pitfalls and avalanches will slow us down more than convincing them to let us pass. Maybe we can form a truce. They might know where O'Neal went."

Ash nodded. Then she grumbled, "I fuckin' hate this place."

Vonnie nearly laughed again. She bared her teeth in an audacious grin and thought, *I love it.*

5.

She was better at playacting with the sunfish than she was at pretending with people. She thought that was because she had no patience for fools or greedy shitheads whereas the sunfish were child-like in many ways.

Yes, they were vicious and foul. They ate their own feces. Their ate their dead! But they were smaller than human beings and they knew less about their own world.

They were ignorant of the universe beyond the ice. They could have been boys and girls stuck inside a huge apartment building with its windows boarded up. They knew something existed outside the building's walls. They had names for the vacuum that swept in and asphyxiated them from time to time, but they'd developed only the barest concepts of space.

Like kids, they were pure in their needs. Eat. Sleep. Fight. Explore. In combat, they were berserkers. In mating, they were as ruthless as sultans and queens, lording their prowess over each other… yet even their sexual posturing reminded Vonnie of teenagers in the closed environment of high school, believing they were capable and mighty when they had so much growing ahead of them.

That was why she showed compassion to the tribes. It was why she encouraged them. If a technologically superior race landed on Earth, humankind would need those intruders to offer the same tolerance and generosity.

She tried to speak in their terms, which always dealt with comparative strength. To help them, she conducted herself like a bully on a playground.

In the beginning she'd resisted intimidating them. Now she tried to have fun with the necessary bluster. Her amusement helped her sound like a seasoned leader dealing with inexperienced youngsters.

—*I am Young Matriarch!* she cried into the ice. —*We own your dead, but our clan is powerful and rich! We do not want this rancid meat!*

Were they listening?

—*We leave it for your feeble tribe! We'll let you eat if you submit to us!*

Something scraped in the catacombs on Ben's side. She pictured the survivors creeping toward them. Radar and seismography were inconclusive. The ice was too wet. What if the sunfish were digging overhead or sneaking through the chasms below?

"Movement," Ben said. "I have two targets in the tunnel to the east. Six targets now. Two matriarchs, four males. They're coming fast."

Vonnie stepped past him with her sword. "I can—"

"Movement!" Ash yelled. "Movement above us west and north! It's too big if—"

Ben muttered once. "Dammit."

Vonnie stared at the rushing mass on their radar. It was water. Less than a kilometer away, an immense, multi-pronged flood was surging down through the ice. It bludgeoned into the catacombs, falling and splashing and welling up again as it filled every pocket and cavern.

"The sunfish opened a lake somewhere above you!" Koebsch shouted.

"Where do we go!?" Ash yelled as Vonnie swept her infrared across the ceiling, wary of more sunfish. Ben misunderstood what she was doing and hollered, "We need to seal the roof!"

"It won't hold," Vonnie said. "We can—"

New alarms flashed on her display. Too late, she turned. Muscular tentacles swatted her chest.

She had forgotten about the sunfish in the tunnel. The two matriarchs fled as the four males attacked, scratching uselessly at Vonnie and Ash… but the sunfish didn't need to hurt them. The sunfish were delaying them.

The four males were a suicide squad.

"Go! Go!" Vonnie shouted. She moved away from the hole in the ceiling, jabbing at the male on her neck.

Ash fell. Ben grabbed her. A male slithered off of Ash's shoulder and leaped into Ben's helmet, its beak rasping on his faceplate, but Ben didn't let go of Ash. He dragged her upright. They stumbled after Vonnie, the sunfish biting and lashing.

"The flood is almost there!" Koebsch shouted.

We're too close, Vonnie thought. She'd hoped to run twenty meters into the tunnel. Five meters would have to do.

The male chewing on her helmet obscured her eyes but not her sensors. She aimed and fired, cutting above them with her Lance 515. The laser widened the hole in the ceiling. She brought down the wall, too.

"Hold onto me!" she yelled, reaching for Ben and Ash.

The sunfish were a pale, spastic nightmare. Ben's faceplate was slobbered with blood. Vonnie grabbed his arm but her hand was knocked away. Ice slammed down on them in chunks.

A block caught Ash's head. It dropped her like a hammer. She fell onto her stomach, where she was struck again, her prone figure taking hits on her legs and spine.

Vonnie didn't see what happened next because she was knocked flat. Ben's outstretched arm landed beneath her. Despite the impacts on her shoulders and hips, she felt him jerk as the ice pummeled him, too.

One of the sunfish was crushed. Its blood stained the white avalanche. Another sunfish flailed in the tiny space beneath Vonnie's chin, invading her head with noise.

Her skull buzzed with its shrieks and she couldn't lift either hand to kill it.

"Von!" Koebsch shouted.

She thought she was screaming. She thought she would die. The ice thundered onto her like enormous fists, although there were fewer blows as the weight increased, pinning her, squeezing her.

The male caught under her chin dug its beak into her collar assembly. It popped one of her locks. Vonnie couldn't move. She was intensely aware of the seam connecting her helmet to her suit. If it tore open…

The flood rammed into the shield she'd formed. Water squirted through every gap. The deluge stole most of the ice, which spun away, clunking and banging. The noise was incredible. A current took the dead sunfish. Ben's axe flipped into Vonnie's shoulder, a steel-on-steel *thunk* unlike the clattering ice.

The male chewing on her neck let go. He tumbled past her face and swam away with an elegant movement like an Earth squid. His arm tips touched her helmet as lightly as a kiss goodbye, propelling himself into the maelstrom.

Ben had been lifted sideways by the water. It was taking him! Pinned beneath her, his arm scrabbled to hold onto something — anything — and she clung to the tunnel floor with every gram of energy in her body.

"Ben!" she screamed.

She felt herself lifted, too. Her boots were drawn upward, then her shins and thighs. The cascade tugged at her legs like she was a flag

Without warning, the water receded. Her head emerged. She flopped onto her belly. Puddles remained and slush dripped around her, but the newly scoured tunnel was refreezing into smooth, solid surfaces.

Not so solid in places.

As she rose to her feet, a vein on one wall slumped apart, then a larger spot. The floor had melted and split The ceiling was a yawning mouth.

Vonnie looked for Ben and Ash. They were nearby. Ben had risen to his hands and knees. Ash didn't move.

Koebsch was in Vonnie's ear. "Her vital signs are good," he said. "You saved their lives. I think she's stunned. Ash, can you hear us?"

Somewhere far below, the world shuddered as the flood broke through another section of the catacombs. Vonnie and Ben reached for each other, anticipating the worst... but the tremor passed. Their tunnel held.

"I'm all right," Ash said. Her suit creaked as she raised herself up.

The three of them were coated in ice. Wet clumps grew from their chest packs and gear blocks. The severed arm of a sunfish was frozen to Ash's hip. Most of the corpses had vanished, although the tunnel was streaked with dark splotches of blood.

Vonnie sidestepped the crevice in the floor. Ben followed. More drips and slush pattered down as they hurried to Ash.

"I'm sorry. Let me help you. I'm sorry," Vonnie said.

"Don't be," Ash said. She hugged Vonnie. "If you hadn't weighed us down, we might've been swept away. We could've been separated or killed."

Vonnie shook her head. "We shouldn't have been here in the first place. I..."

"Stop," Ash said, surprising her. "Don't apologize. You were right to bring us after O'Neal. The problem is knowing whether or not those sunfish got what they wanted."

"They'll attack us again."

"Maybe not." Ash looked exhausted and hurt, but her eyes were clear. "I think you missed something when you talked to them. Look at the transcripts from our AIs. The way they kept asking our name... They were showing their approval of our strength. Otherwise they would've killed us."

Ben said, "You're nuts. The tribe ambushed us as soon as we met."

"That's not how I saw it." Ash tapped her finger on the lab packs on Ben's chest, reminding him of their blood and tissue samples. "Most of the sunfish we fought were savage males. The matriarchs always try to reduce the savages in their colonies, right? Arranging for them to die is a way for the females to improve their breeding pairs."

"*We* almost died in the flood."

"No." Ash shook her head. "If they wanted to kill us, they would have waited for us to go further west. Don't tell me they didn't know exactly where the water would fall. Volume and spatial relations are their thing, and that last group of sunfish came from the east. They were decoys. Their objective was to keep us near the edge of the flood or even draw us away from it."

Vonnie was still processing her own injuries and fatigue. She'd wrenched her shoulder. Her forehead was bruised. She stared at Ash, who'd never been an expert in any regard to the sunfish.

As a pilot without a ship since they'd landed on Europa, Ash's jobs were data/comm and maintenance. She excelled at those tasks, and, if anything, she'd given as little attention as possible to the native ecologies. Vonnie felt like a brand-new Ash had stepped out from behind a curtain.

She's been faking. We knew she was smart, but she's been hiding some of her education. How much of her MI6 training includes military tactics? She's treating the sunfish like an organized guerrilla force.

Testing her, Vonnie said, "I've never heard you talk about the tribes like this."

Ash didn't deny it. "I've never been down here before. Now things make more sense."

"But you've been studying our files."

"Of course."

Vonnie had to admit turn-about was fair play. She had deceived Ash and Ben when she brought them into the ice, but she should have known Ash was more than a willing pawn. The young woman had always had her own agenda.

She must have a list of standing orders from her handlers on Earth. Something they want is available here. What is it? She hates the sunfish, but she'll do her job, and MI6 is about influence and control. Does she think we can expand our power over the local tribes if we keep pushing now?

Koebsch must have been mulling over the same questions. He said, "Ash, what do you think the sunfish were after?"

"They closed off our path. Whatever O'Neal is searching for, they don't want us to find it. Maybe it's more than ruins. Maybe it's a larger colony than we've seen."

"And now we can't get there," Ben said.

Koebsch said, "I have mecha closing on your position. We also have rovers on the surface."

Ash said, "How long until the mecha arrive?"

"Thirty minutes."

"Sir, we can't wait that long."

Vonnie smiled ruefully, liking and not liking her friend's new take-charge attitude. Later, they needed to talk. Now she studied her display. Her blade carried a homing device. So did their axes. "There's my sword," she said. "I see Ben's axe, too. The flood took Ash's about a klick below us."

"Leave it." Ben walked to the gaps in the floor and tore at a crevice.

Beneath a layer of new ice was his axe. He tugged it loose as Vonnie retrieved her sword. "Here, Ash," he said, holding out the axe.

Ash accepted it. "Thank you, Ben."

Vonnie glanced surreptitiously at her again. If there were hostile tribes ahead of them…

"Come with me," Vonnie said.

The Chimney and The Cathedral

6.

Vonnie swept her sensors across the hole where the ceiling had been, listening for the matriarchs. Below the hole was a steep pile of ice. It compacted and sagged as she climbed. Halfway up, she braced herself, securing two good footholds before she bent and extended her arm.

Ash took her hand. She scrambled up.

They stood together near the top of the heap. Ben could hear them, of course, but it felt like a private moment, which was what Vonnie wanted. Words weren't enough. She needed to physically remind Ash that for now their friendship was more important than MI6.

"Here's what I think," she said. "The three of us are the perfect team. I'm engineering, you're navigation, he's planetary. If we help each other, there's no reason why we should retreat or spend time looking for a way around the flood. We'll go straight through."

"I agree," Ash said.

"Let's go *toward* the lake they opened so they can't wash us out again. There's no water left. We'll maintain a diagonal bearing westward and upward. The problem is if they drop more sections of the ice. There will be spontaneous avalanches, too. This area is a mine field."

"Like my dad's house at Christmas," Ben said.

Ash and Vonnie burst out laughing. They were under so much stress, their moods ran hot and cold. Tension made them mercurial. Minutes ago, they'd faced their deaths. Now they poked fun at each other.

"If everyone on Earth hears you say that, you're going to sound very mean," Vonnie said.

"My dad won't notice. He's usually as drunk as the Italian president."

Koebsch spoke dourly on the radio. "Stop. Remember you're on a recorded line."

"The president won't notice. He's as drunk as my dad."

Ash put her glove on her faceplate as if covering her mouth. Vonnie snickered. Standing by the pile of ice, Ben grinned at the two women. Their camaraderie was a shield. It protected them from horror and pain.

"Let's get back to work," Koebsch said. "Our rovers are above you."

Three kilometers overhead, the rovers swept the ice with neutrino pulse, DMsP radar and seismography. They had a preliminary schematic of the area in seconds.

"Looks good," Ash said. "Boost me."

Vonnie would have liked to go first, but she supposed Ash had combat training. The young woman had handled herself well, although she'd taken some damage to her leg. Was that because Ash had deliberately absorbed the brunt of the assault?

"Up you go," Vonnie said.

Ash stuck her axe to the magnets on her back, freeing both hands. Vonnie shoved on her rump. Ash scrambled into the space overhead.

"Ben, you're next," Vonnie said, maintaining her footholds on the pile of debris.

He climbed.

Above them, Ash extended the handle of her axe. Ben reached Vonnie and kept going. He seized the axe and dug his toes into the wall.

Vonnie went after him.

She ascended into a new space and stood beside her friends. The flood had torn through this hollow like a brush, smoothing the ice.

Ash led them through five hundred meters of tunnels. They squeezed past several barriers where the deluge had pulled down walls or ceilings. Ash was decisive and confident. Then they found another hole leading up.

They climbed through until Ash stiffened. Vonnie and Ben became statues like her. "Don't move," Ash whispered.

Overhead, the flood had scoured a series of cracks, fusing some, dissolving others, creating a lacework of pillars and veils. Much of it was impassible. Elsewhere, Vonnie saw open paths... but the ceiling stretched into malformed teeth and blobs as large as hab modules.

They stood beneath a hundred straining tons of ice. It looked like a madman's cathedral that had tumbled upside down with its imploding contents captured in a three-dimensional snapshot. It teetered, waiting to fall. The strain was palpable. Only a flash-frozen rime of water kept it intact.

"We'll go north," Ash said. "Hurry."

Vonnie didn't have a better suggestion. She'd wasted a precious heartbeat gaping at the cathedral, so Ash stayed in front. Ben took the rear, putting himself in the greatest danger of being caught by a collapse. "After you, m'lady," he said.

Funny and brave, she thought.

They moved softly in their heavy suits. Overhead, many pieces swayed with an ominous noise. *Krakack!*

They left the creaking mass for a new cave. The flood had overshot this cramped space. Its floor canted upward and Ash led them higher.

Then she paused, confronted with a narrow gap. Their suits wouldn't fit. She said. "I thought..."

Vonnie patched into Ash's radar. If they could excavate four meters, they'd reach a wide chimney. Below them, the chimney fell 924 meters until it was clogged by slush and ice. Leading upward, the chimney rose 103 meters before it branched into a dozen channels. Most of these smaller channels went laterally into the ice. Some had been closed by the flood.

Ash exhaled loudly, letting them hear her disappointment in herself. "Von, if we dig, will it drop the ice behind us?"

"It'll drop everything."

"I didn't know where else to go. The maze is... This was the only way through. I thought the gap was larger."

"You're doing fine. We can make it."

"How?"

"See these formations on our maps? An older layer runs through this area for at least ten square kilometers, maybe more. It probably dates back thousands of years to when it was on the surface. It's fractured and tipping east, but it still works like a foundation. We're up against a load-bearing section. As long as I don't weaken the sides of the gap, I can carve a trench for our suits. Koebsch, do you see anything I missed?"

"No. I'm routing our mecha away from your position. I don't want them to set off an avalanche. They'll have to meet you further west."

"What about the chimney?" Ben asked.

"The flood must have stripped away anything that wasn't solid," Vonnie said. "We can climb it. We'll rendezvous with the mecha higher up."

"It looks deep."

"We don't want to go down. We're going up."

"Von, it's a gas vent."

"It's dormant. There's no pressure flow."

"Not yet. If the flood melts open the base of the chimney and there are volcanic systems below us..."

Vonnie frowned.

They didn't want to find themselves caught in an eruption of superheated gases. They couldn't stay where they were. They couldn't go back through the cathedral.

"Let's send a beacon down there while I excavate," she said. "It can warn us if the chimney's opening up."

"Roger that." Ben detached a fist-sized mecha from his chest. He passed the machine to her. She placed it in the gap. On his command, it scurried forward.

Then it jumped into the wisps of air. Given the low gravity, it would endure its impact with the slush at the bottom of the chimney. How long would it transmit after it sank into the morass?

Vonnie activated her Lance 515. Their suits darkened their faceplates to compensate for her laser's ruby light.

Below them, Ben's mecha splashed down. It immediately reported heat. The flood wasn't solidifying. Bubbling threads of liquid water were prying up through the slush.

Vonnie kept her attention on her trench. She finished her initial cuts and pulled at the ice, scooping debris onto her legs as Ben said, "It's ten meters down. Fifteen. Temperatures increasing slightly. Holding at nine degrees Celsius."

Ash said, "What does that mean?"

"Good news, bad news. I can't tell how far the chimney goes. It's plugged with ice. There's rock in there, too. The mecha's radar won't penetrate more than a few hundred meters."

"I need two minutes, but I can do it in one if you want to gamble," Vonnie said.

"Don't," Koebsch said. "An avalanche behind your position could push down onto the systems underneath the chimney. It's all connected."

Ben said, "That's my point. I can't tell if the chimney leads to thermal vents or hot springs. Something's brewing down there. Water and magma would be the worst combination for us."

Vonnie realized she was sweating. She squinted through her display at the bright ruby star of her laser.

"Ninety seconds," she said.

"Here's a fun puzzle while we wait," Ben said amiably. "Allow me to prove I'm smarter than Ash."

"Doubtful."

"What if that last group of sunfish were trying to retrieve their granite tools before the flood hit?"

"A few rocks can't be that important."

"*Au contraire*, m'lady. A granite tool must be rare indeed to the Top Clans. It could be the kind of thing they've handed down for generations."

"Yeah." Vonnie had the dark thought that Ben just wanted to get his theories on record in case they were killed. Characteristically, he wanted to preserve his findings as much as his life.

"This is an Earth-like world, so we assume many of the same mechanisms," he said. "Granite is formed by the fractional crystallization of magmas within a continental crust. It's not a rapid process. The bases of the largest fin mountains may be old enough to produce A-type granite, but for the most part these mountains are temporary structures. We think they're less than a million years old. They don't have the age or the composition to form other granites. The tools we found are igneous protolith. I-type. That rock must have formed beneath the ocean floor."

"Boring!" Ash joked, and Vonnie heard the grin in Ben's voice when he said, "You're a pilot. Nobody expects you to understand real science."

"Von is a pilot, too," Ash reminded him.

"You're both halfwits."

Vonnie's trench was nearly complete. *Made it!* she thought, lifting her arm for the final cut.

Then the world shook.

7.

The floor rattled. Frigid gusts of air surged through the chimney, washing over Vonnie's helmet.

Behind them, the cathedral dropped. It fell like a comet onto the tunnels below. Dust billowed through their little cave. They toppled. The world shook again. The cave tilted and its wall cracked.

The frigid air rushing up through the chimney became hot swirls of gas. Vonnie dragged her friends into a ball, yelling, "Tuck in your arms and legs!"

If there was a volcanic eruption, one or two might survive if another deflected the blast.

One might die so the others lived.

She wanted to be with them in the end.

Then it stopped. The ice thrummed but it didn't shake. She heard dull crunching booms. Nearby, a slide was in progress.

"Vonnie! Go!" Koebsch yelled.

Her hands jittered and her mind was blank. "You want us to climb the chimney?" she asked.

What choice did they have?

On her display, temperatures were spiking. *Seventeen degrees Celsius. Nobody's hurt. Our maps are changing as we speak. Too much noise and motion.* Grasping for a smart decision, she said, "Can we retreat through whatever's behind us?"

"There's nothing left. It's a sinkhole. The ice is dragging itself down."

Ash stepped toward the trench. Vonnie grabbed her arm and said, "Let me. I'll rig some bolts and wire. We'll need them if..."

Ash rummaged through her hip packs. She gave Vonnie an extra tool kit. Vonnie attached it to her chest. She crawled into the trench. The world groaned.

They heard a bone-jarring shriek of colossal masses grinding at each other. Her claustrophobia felt like a rat in her brain. She fumbled with her rappelling gear and almost dropped the bolt gun.

She looked into the chimney. It was about six meters in diameter, its sides stained with minerals and sulfur. Some streaks were reddish. Some were yellow or black.

She took a spool of molecular wire and clipped the line onto a climbing bolt. Examining her radar, she fired. The ten-centimeter bolt would telescope to fifteen centimeters inside the ice, extending a cloud of plastic filaments like a tree's branches.

Below her, the chimney burbled. Eddies of gas rose past as she sank four more bolts, weaving a net like a pentagon. With three people on the quaking walls, she predicted at least one of them would lose their grip. Her net needed to catch a 220 kilo suit — but she was taking too long.

"Von?" Ash called nervously.

"Don't follow until I say so." She fired a sixth bolt into a hardened old patch of rock dust, anchoring the wire, which she fed through her belt.

She attached the gun and five more bolts to her arm. Then she extended claws from her boots and gloves.

She climbed out.

She gained less than a meter before the wall crumbled under her feet. A wet patch sloughed away. "Whoa!" she yelled, jamming her gloves into the ice.

Clinging there, she contorted her upper body and shot another bolt, leading herself up the wall.

Invisible bands of heat curled upward, softening the ice. Blots of moisture swatted her arms and her helmet. Somehow she climbed another meter. Then another. Her thoughts concentrated into an emotionless point. The distant rumbles couldn't touch her. The sleet pattering down and the gases swirling up were irrelevant. There was only the climb.

Her knees banged against the wall. It crunched under her gloves and feet. She found her next handhold, her next toehold, the placement of her next bolt.

She was thirty meters up when she stopped beside a fragment of basaltic lava embedded in the wall. The rock was wider than her body. One surface was carved with sunfish hieroglyphics. She couldn't stay to run her translation programs, but she deftly scanned the rock.

Above, she located other fragments. Many were deep in the ice. They were jumbled or smashed or obscured. Her experience was the many pieces had once fit into a lumpy whole like the page of a giant book.

"You see this?" she called to Ben.

"Keep moving. Ash and I will scan it from different angles as we go past. We should get enough to work with."

Vonnie was already pondering the shapes she'd seen. One was familiar. Typical of the sunfish, it was self-contradictory, a warning and a welcoming.

Four of the shape's arms bent outward and counter-clockwise. Four bent inward and clockwise. Its body was equally conflicted. Its center was lowered as if bowing while its outer muscle groups were bunched as if preparing to leap.

It was a symbol from the empire. A landmark. An invitation. Vonnie wanted to drill for samples. They needed to put a date on the carvings, but she climbed, abandoning the rocks to their destiny.

When she was forty meters up, Ash said, "I'm coming out."

Vonnie sank another bolt into the wall. "Give control of your suits to the AIs. Let them bring you up."

"What about you?"

More than one answer occurred to Vonnie. Auto programs would maximize their agility and coordination, but she'd learned to depend on her plain old human instincts before any machine. She used their AIs in combat. Otherwise she preferred her own reflexes. Unfortunately, her friends lacked her experience in the ice. In time, they might share her skills, but now she needed them to become machines. She needed them to act like scouts obeying a matriarch.

"Do what I told you," she said. "If you fuck something up, it could kill us." She began climbing again without waiting for a reply.

Ben's suit went on auto. Ash switched over, too. They scaled after Vonnie like steel spiders.

Human beings might have crowded each other. The suits distributed their weight efficiently, never less than two bolts apart, always compensating for each other.

Vonnie was slower. She tapped at nubs of ice that her radar deemed were solid. Angling to her left, she bypassed a crack that her targeting systems identified as a useable handhold. She was waiting for something. A sound.

Drips and blots fell around her like rain.

They were seventy meters up when Koebsch spoke on the radio. "Von, you need to hurry."

"I hate to say it, but he's right," Ben said. "The slush at the bottom is over twenty degrees. More gases are bubbling out. Christ, that's why the ice is thawing."

"Put your suit on auto," Koebsch said. "You can stay in the lead. Just let it climb."

"No." Vonnie had a bad hunch.

"We'll fry in here!" Ash shouted.

Vonnie maintained her steady pace. She hooked her claws into the wall. Twice she dry-fired her bolt gun in even amounts, one two, one two.

"We're almost out," she said. In ten meters they'd reach the first branches leading away from the chimney, although most of those holes were shallow pockets or dead-ends. "Are we tracking any sunfish?"

"Yes," Koebsch said.

"Oh God," Ash murmured, but Vonnie felt a preternatural sense of fate.

"Why aren't they on my display?"

"They're not using sonar and they were hidden beneath a cluster of rock," Koebsch said. "They're coming out of the northwest above you. Von, there's something strange about their radar signature. They're carrying metal and rock."

"Metal. That means they're our sunfish."

"Maybe not," Ash said. "Another tribe could have killed O'Neal and taken his suit apart."

"It looks like an intact suit with most of its equipment spread among the sunfish. Here." Koebsch patched them into his datastreams, which showed the sunfish dragging O'Neal down through zigzagging chasms.

They poured through the ice like a living flood. Among their muscular eight-armed bodies were a variety of objects; the dead frozen meat of eels; kernels of ice; stone tools; and ESA kits and gear, some unscathed, some beaten flat or torn into ragged strips.

"He's alive," Koebsch said. "His suit has power. We're hailing him. No response."

"How many in this group?" Vonnie asked.

"Thirty-two."

"Then they're not the matriarchs who left with him, and the survivors of the tribe we fought went southwest. These are new sunfish." *New sunfish again*, she thought. *It's like O'Neal said. There are more of them than we imagined.*

Ash said, "How long until our mecha arrive?"

Koebsch said, "Seven minutes. The sunfish will reach your chimney in four."

"What about our assets on the surface?"

"Our rovers can't do anything except make noise if that would help. Maybe they could cause a cave-in..."

"Let the sunfish find us," Vonnie said. "We have the dominant position. We're beneath them. They're doing our job for us if they're bringing O'Neal."

She reached the first pocket in the chimney's wall and scrambled over its rim, firing a new bolt into its floor. With the wire firmly set, she yelled for Ash and Ben. "Let's go! Full speed!"

Their suits swarmed up the ice. They joined her.

Ash leaned too close, her eyes flashing with accusation. "You *wanted* the sunfish to come. That's why you were so loud. That's why you kept clicking your gun. I thought you were scared, but you did it on purpose."

"They were coming anyway."

"This is the worst possible place to deal with a new tribe. Why did you bring them here?"

"They have O'Neal."

"You were loud before we knew that!"

"I want to learn why the other tribe caused the flood. What are they trying to hide? The hieroglyphics? Are there more ruins above us?"

"Von, start climbing again," Ben said. "We don't want to be stuck here when..."

"Too late," Ash said colorlessly. Her anger with Vonnie had taken the wind out of her. She let her chin droop. Then the slithering noises of the sunfish spilled into the chimney, and Ash's chin rose again. She was prepared for battle.

Vonnie felt awe and pride for her friend — if they were friends. Vonnie had sworn to work as a team, but she'd hijacked Ash and Ben, although the circumstances warranted it. She thought Ben understood. Why didn't Ash? If they ran, the sunfish would pursue and attack. Meeting this tribe inside the chimney increased their status.

I'll make it up to you, she thought. *I will.*

Ten meters up, four sunfish skittered through a chink in the wall. They were matriarchs, healthy and aggressive. Behind them was the bustling tribe. They screamed down at the astronauts, adding their sonar to the storm of dripping water and warm gases.

—*You are death!* they shrieked. —*Floods and quakes! Burning and slides!*

Ash raised her Lance 515.

"Don't fire," Vonnie said as she raised her weapons, too. Ben took the axe from Ash's shoulder. More sunfish scrambled into the chimney. They were savage males. They pried at the ice.

"They'll drop the wall on us!" Ash shouted.

Vonnie shook her head. "Haven't you learned anything yet? Listen to them. They're praising us."

The matriarchs barged in among the males, stopping them from tearing the ice. Through smell and touch, they seduced the males, who joined their song. —*Geysers and heat! New water! Poisons and salt! You are death! You bring death!*

"Thosc are compliments?" Ash said with contempt.

"Their word for 'death' also means opportunity," Ben said. "Upheaval destroys their homes, but it can open deposits of bugs or eels that were killed years ago. They probably find some of their best food supplies after major events."

"That has nothing to do with us. They know we didn't cause the flood," Ash said.

"Do they?" Vonnie asked. "They heard us fighting right before..." Her voice lifted in excitement. "The matriarch below the rest of them is Michelle! She's from our clan."

"The AIs recognize some of the voices in the main pack," Koebsch said. "At least three of the females are the ones who left camp with O'Neal."

"Wait," Vonnie said. "Wait."

Her thoughts were a blur. Trying to connect their disordered clues and evidence, she peered at the hard shell of minerals across the chimney.

Her radar penetrated into the tunnels, where a phantom moved among the savage males. It was too big for the meager spaces in the ice. It wandered — not aimlessly but urgently — ducking and kneeling and rising again, trying anything to find enough room. It had struggled closer while Vonnie, Ash and Ben were preoccupied by the sunfish.

Finally it pressed through the gap in the chimney's side, knocking a white spray into the drizzle. It was an armored hulk with two arms, two legs, a torso and a head.

It was O'Neal.

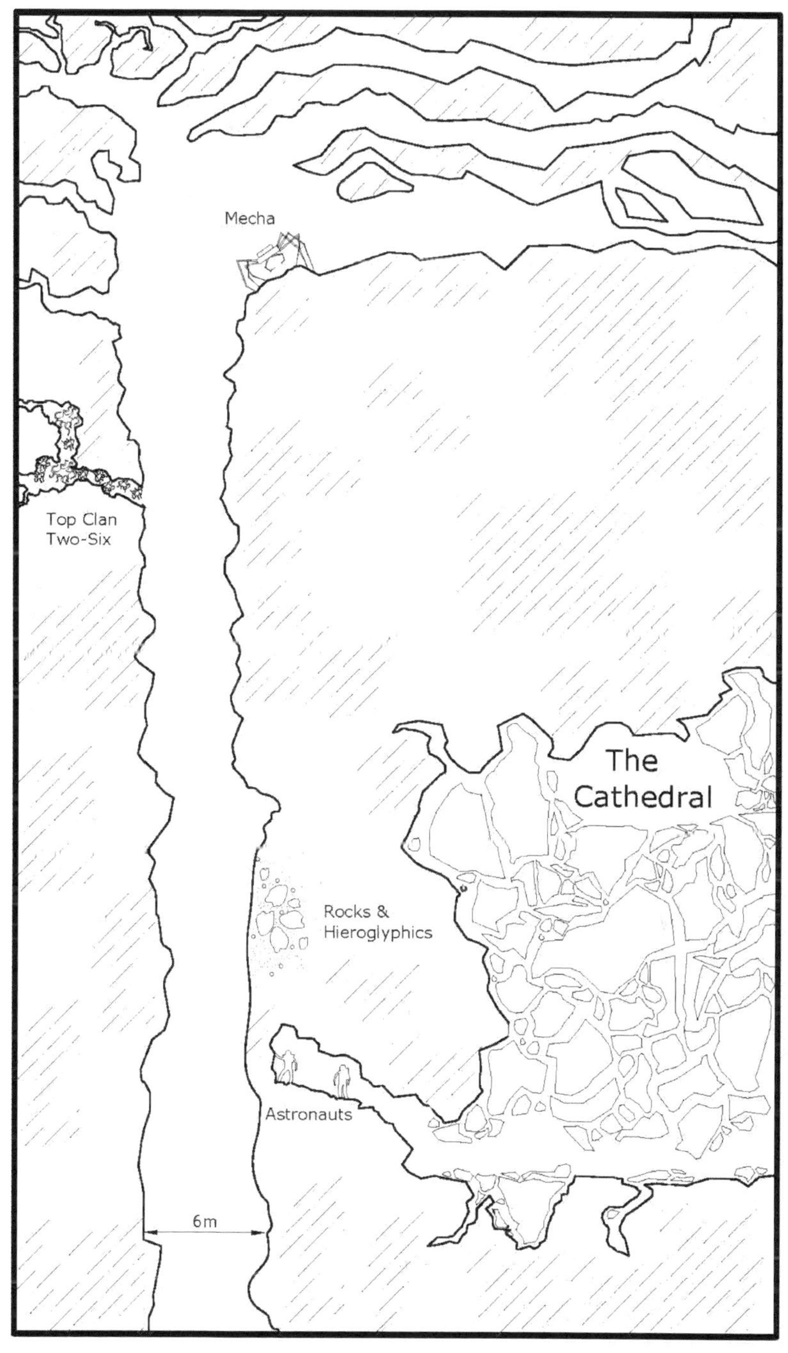

The Chimney and Top Clan Two-Six

8.

His suit provided no links with theirs, no radio, no data/comm. He lacked his sensors and spotlights. His gear block had been smashed. Even his voice box was useless. Blood-stained ice stuck to the remains of his collar assembly. His left arm hung limp, its laser gone, its elbow joint crushed.

His faceplate was pitted and his chest had been scored with the filthy impacts of stone tools or a rock slide.

He waved at them.

The wordless *hello*, the casual arc of his hand, looked like he might have been greeting them inside their hab modules.

Ash went ballistic. "What is *wrong* with you!?" she yelled. "Why are you down here?"

"Ashley—" Vonnie said.

"You almost killed us!" She was yelling at O'Neal, but she threw a bitter glance at Vonnie. "This place is falling apart! Let's go! Let's go!"

"Not yet," Vonnie said with practiced calm. It was a state of mind she'd learned from the tribes.

O'Neal had trained himself, too. The sunfish responded to emotional turmoil with fear and rage. By the same token, they admired self-possession. Given a strong example, they might emulate her composure.

Vonnie stepped in front of Ash, blocking Ash from the sunfish, hoping to present a united front.

The matriarchs buzzed. They were thrilled by the confrontation between the astronauts. Two matriarchs glommed onto O'Neal and were accompanied by four males. They snarled themselves around the legs of his suit.

—Biting Female asserts herself! they shrieked. *—Love and ambition. Hunger. Protectiveness.*

Ash flinched at 'love.' The translation was approximate. To sunfish, it meant fealty. To Ash, perhaps, it implied she was dependent on Vonnie.

She needed to show otherwise. She leaned into the warm sleet and shook her fist at O'Neal. "You stupid asshole! We should leave you here to die with your little monsters!"

—Kill him? Kill him? they cried.

"For Christ's sake, watch how you act," Vonnie said. "He can't hear you and they take everything literally."

Vonnie zoomed on O'Neal with her cameras, inspecting the scuff marks on his faceplate. His cheeks were pink, his eyes bloodshot. Sweat rolled from his curly brown hair. He looked like he was breathing through his mouth. Her AIs said his respiration was elevated but there was zero panic in him.

"We have a bigger complication than no radio," she said. "His heat exchangers aren't a hundred percent. You can see where he jury-rigged his panel circuitry to compensate. He's baking inside his suit."

"That's easy to fix if they let us," Ash said.

Vonnie thought she'd succeeded in engaging her friend's intellect, making Ash think instead of feel, but the naked reaction of the sunfish undermined Vonnie's success.

—Young Matriarch sways Biting Female! they cried. *—The female is unstable. She chafes at Young Matriarch's experience and wisdom. She challenges her. She challenges us. She yearns to prove her own depths.*

Vonnie and Ash both flushed in embarrassment. Vonnie stammered for the right thing to say.

Ben wisely kept his mouth shut, too, but O'Neal was waving again. O'Neal patted at the air as the sunfish writhed up his thighs onto his abdomen.

"Ash, I didn't mean..." Vonnie began.

"They don't know people, and you're not in command." Ash yanked the climbing tools from Vonnie's arm as the ice trembled. "Feel that? Let's go. You can talk to them somewhere else."

O'Neal won't last much longer, Vonnie thought.

Every suit had emergency spills. He should have been able to dump his waste heat through the vents on his shoulders. The damage was too extensive.

His mangled armor had become a form-fitting sauna. Dehydration, vomiting and increased heart rate would kill him. If she'd been in his place, she didn't think she could have been as methodical. His bravery made her brave.

"He's doing a new pantomime," she said, although he barely had the use of his left hand.

Did he want them to move lower?

"He's showing one group beneath another," Ben said. "Mid Clans and Top Clans..."

"...and we're the Mid Clan?"

"Tell them we want O'Neal," Koebsch said.

"I'm not convinced he's a prisoner. He isn't hurt."

"They crippled his suit."

"Koebsch, most of these sunfish are new to us. O'Neal left camp with eight matriarchs." Vonnie glanced at her display and said, "We've identified Brigit, Krista, Natalie and Michelle. Where are the other four?"

Ben said, "Why doesn't he jump over to us?"

"He wants to stay. He..."

Ash had loaded the bolt gun with molecular wire. She swung out onto the wall and the matriarchs screeched: *—Are you death!? Are you death!? Lead us home!*

More sunfish emerged into the chimney. Some of them carried dead albino eels in their arms. Some carried icy black wads of gravel or dust, which didn't make sense to Vonnie. Others held soft hunks of lava rock like clubs. Many of them held pieces of metal or plastic. A few carried chest kits from O'Neal's suit. The chest kits were intact.

—Eat!? Eat!? Lead us home! they screamed.

—Your behavior is as it should be. You are fierce, but we rule the ice, Vonnie

cried. "Ash, stop!" she said. "They're offering food to us. They want an alliance."

Ash stretched for her next toehold.

—Biting Female leaves us? She spurns us?

—No! You misread her! Willing herself to believe the lie, Vonnie embellished it with the truth. *—She is a scout. Her restlessness is her strength.*

—She will deceive us? Attack us?

—No.

—You deceive us.

Vonnie rose to her full height with her sword. *—I am Young Matriarch! I lead many sunfish and I can provide homes for your breeding pairs! Listen to my body! You know I want peace!*

But the matriarchs were losing control. Ash was level with them now. She'd relinquished her dominant position.

Two males screamed their war cries. Another male gorged abruptly on the eel he'd been holding as a gift for Von. Like gasoline on a fire, his selfishness ignited more individual acts. Among the tribes, independence was anarchy. It bred hysteria.

Six males stuffed everything they were carrying into holes in the ice, stashing their rock clubs, their icy kernels of dust or the kits from O'Neal's suit. Then they wrestled with the selfish male for the eel. They cut him with their beaks. They snapped at his torn skin and the eel.

The other sunfish screamed at Ash. They were united by the danger she represented. The matriarchs drew the raving males into foursomes, then eights.

Vonnie expected them to hurt O'Neal. He looked like he was shouting. He snatched at the sunfish with his good hand but they melted bonelessly around his arm. Even so, he disrupted their groupings long enough for Vonnie to see they were going to swarm Ash. Any assault would end with people and sunfish plummeting through the chimney.

Vonnie extended her sword. She could have poked the blade's tip against Ash's feet, but she slashed into the ice.

She was asserting her territorial claims. She was boasting about human weapons and quickness. *—Don't make us kill you!* she screamed. *—We will defend Biting Female!*

The matriarchs rustled among themselves.

—Attack? Attack? the males shrieked.

Vonnie repressed the urge to grab Ash's leg and drag her down. "Goddammit, you're provoking them."

Ash kept climbing. "Follow me," she said. Her voice was hoarse, but she wasn't speaking to Vonnie. "Ben, make her follow me! We need to get out of here!"

"What about O'Neal?" he asked.

"We'll shoot a wire to him," Ash said, and Ben looked at Vonnie. His gaze was imploring.

"The quakes are getting worse."

"Our mecha will be here in sixty seconds," she said. "They can drop a web into the chimney. They'll extract us and the tribe if—"

"Watch out!" Koebsch yelled.

There was an eruption in the chimney's depths. On the wall, Ash braced herself. *—Beware!* Vonnie cried at the sunfish.

A yellow-tinged cloud heaved upward, thrusting the rain sideways into the chimney's walls. Mostly gas, it also contained flurries of mist. The astronauts recoiled but the sunfish opened themselves to it, slurping at the moisture with their beaks.

—You are death! the matriarchs screeched. *—Death! You bring nutrients and gates!*

They were rejoicing.

"Christ," Vonnie said with her wet arm in front of her face. "Ash, are you okay?"

"Roger that." Ash sounded out of breath. The flurries must have slammed her against the wall.

O'Neal was taking cover among the sunfish. He rose unsteadily as they bucked and screamed, feasting on the yellow moisture.

Vonnie questioned O'Neal with a hand sign and he returned it. Thumbs up. Crouching with Ben inside their pocket in the wall, Vonnie let him see her elation. “That spray was full of bacteria,” she said.

“I’m also reading toxic levels of sulfur and iron. It’d kill us if we weren’t in our suits.”

Vonnie smiled. “You moron. The lack of air pressure would make you bleed out first.”

Ben laughed.

So did Vonnie — a crazy giggle — sharing her terror and her affection.

“Are you flirting with him?” Ash grunted as she climbed. “If you are, I’ll kill you myself,” she said. Her anger was a different method of sublimating her fear.

Koebsch intervened. “Von, what do the sunfish mean by ‘gates’? Could they survive swimming down into the chimney?”

“We could, too. The water isn’t boiling.”

“You’d get lost or stuck or burned,” Ben said. “No way. We need to evacuate.”

“I wish we could talk to O’Neal.”

Unlike the astronauts, the sunfish were in harmony. The males participated in the matriarchs’ celebration. They were exultant. —*We deliver ourselves to you! New food! New gates! We hunt and fight for you!*

Vonnie motioned for Ben to stand beside her. It would have been better if Ash rejoined them, but Ash clawed her way into the largest branches at the top of the chimney.

“Oh,” she said.

Vonnie knew what Ash was seeing because her display was lit with beacons. In the fog-riddled catacombs were five mecha. The machines had tiptoed through the last kilometer, their movements disguised by the ongoing tremors.

“Koebsch, let me run the mecha,” Vonnie said. “Ash, follow my lead.”

“Mm.” Ash wouldn’t say *yes* or *no*.

—*We offer a treaty with you if you leave this chimney!* Vonnie cried. —*Become our clanmates! Help our colony!*

Stay! they screamed. —*Stay!*

Vonnie lowered her voice into a grumble. —*Come with us or we will deny you.*

—*No! Lead us home!*

"We're missing something," Ben said. "They're using a different word for 'home' than you are. The connotations are more about up and down than finding a good place to live."

Vonnie couldn't help believing the matriarchs would have been less likely to defy her if Ash hadn't gone off on her own. She let her irritation show. She tipped her head in a warrior's pose. *—This chimney belongs to us!* she cried. *—You may return if we allow it. Merge with our clan. We have weapons and shelters and…*

—No.

The matriarchs' refusal spread through the tribe like a wave. They undulated apart from each other on the chimney wall, preparing again to swarm from many angles. Less obvious was the current that directed the nearest males to turn on O'Neal. Two of them wrenched their arms around his leg. They did not hurt him but the threat was made.

Vonnie summoned her mecha. She walked all five units to the top of the chimney and said, "Ash, move with them. Be loud."

The machines were ROM-12 GPs. With their arms and sensors folded into their transport position aboard a ship, each one was as big as a car.

Unfolded, they were demonic. They looked like the steel skeletons of gigantic ten-legged spiders — if spiders had skeletons — bristling with mandibles and eyes. Along their spines, they carried fusion reactors and data/comm. The rest of their bulk consisted of hydraulics. GPs were intended to build and dig and transport. They were construction machines.

They had been used in Africa and Asia as combat units. Small arms fire couldn't stop them. Barbed wire and tank traps barely slowed them down.

As each mecha appeared at the chimney's edge, it stabbed with a digging arm. Ash punched her fist. A halo of ice flashed down the chimney walls, sandblasting the sunfish and the three humans in their suits.

O'Neal threw his arm over his helmet. Vonnie and Ben stood motionless. They'd anticipated the small avalanche, and they were impervious to it.

The sunfish screamed. They must have been startled by the appearance of the machines. Nevertheless, they issued war cries. They promised bloodshed and victory.

In response, the mecha amplified Vonnie's cries. —*WE ARE GHOST CLAN THIRTY!* she roared.

Overwhelmed by the sound, the matriarchs wriggled clumsily. The males released O'Neal, hunching their bodies to shield their ears.

—*The mecha obey me!* Vonnie screamed. —*Resist us, you die! Join us, you thrive! We rule the ice!*

—*Treaty? Treaty? Treaty? Treaty?* they shrieked.

What was different about this group compared to the previous tribe? They had fewer females, although half of their females were matriarchs from the ESA camp. They were familiar with suits and mecha. More important, they were healthy. They weren't as desperate, which, ironically, meant they were more inclined to accept help.

—*Our clan is strong!* Vonnie screamed. —*We grow because we want more workers and scouts. We want your breeding pairs. You may return to this place if you earn the right.*

—*We deliver ourselves to you.*

—*Treaty, yes. Peace, yes.*

—*We obey! Our strength is yours and yours is ours!* the matriarchs cried with new energy.

"Can we trust them?" Koebsch asked.

"For now," she said. She didn't doubt there would be unrest. Once they were well-fed, some of the sunfish would run away. They might steal things or sabotage ESA mecha for ceramics and steel.

She dreamed of maintaining an eternal truce, but she was hard-eyed enough to accept this was unlikely. Everything was temporary with the tribes. That didn't mean each new treaty wasn't a milestone and it didn't mean the sunfish weren't sincere in swearing loyalty to her.

For now.

The main thing is to get some distance between us and more eruptions. O'Neal needs repairs.

But the sunfish weren't finished. They ran around the chimney walls, a howling flock. Most of them jumped at Vonnie and Ben. Eight scrambled up toward Ash and the mecha.

"Von!?" Ash shouted.

"You know what they want." Vonnie locked her sword onto her back and met them with open arms. Their culture demanded the exchange of touch and scent.

Above her, the mecha were as gentle as elephants. Bending and swaying, the machines allowed the sunfish to crawl in and out of their steel frames.

Ash cringed beneath two males' rubbing arms.

Ben was more adept. He accepted kernels of ice and bloody gunk from the sunfish, stuffing everything into his kits without examining it. They gave him eels. They gave him gravel and dust in black icy wads.

—*Good! Good! More! More!* he cried. Scouts and matriarchs joined the throng. They brought steel artifacts. "I have O'Neal's kits!" he said, clamping the extra kits onto his suit.

Vonnie danced as the tribe enveloped her. Like Ben, she accepted their offerings. She also led them in a new song. The affirmation ritual was a sharing of voices. They were exploring the many parts involved in their new sum.

—*We are Ghost Clan Thirty!* they cried.

Vonnie felt a convoluted joy at this simple declaration. The sunfish were baffling in so many ways, and, in others, as forthright as dogs.

Reaching through the swarm, she found Ben and squeezed his hand. "We did it," she said.

9.

The next minutes were both tedious and frightening. As the mecha extended wires to the astronauts, the sunfish interfered, not maliciously but because they were curious. They wanted to stay close to their new tribemates.

Vonnie was reminded again of dogs. The sunfish clung to her suit or scurried up and down the wires. The congestion was aggravating.

—*Move! Climb!* she screamed.

O'Neal was lifted to safety. Vonnie and Ben were still in the air when the chimney belched.

The yellow-hued mist sent the tribe into a frenzy. They rioted. Vonnie's line jolted from the impacts of four sunfish. Two males smacked into her head and chest. The undersides of their arms — their rasping, puckering carpets of pedicellaria and tube feet — sponged through the moisture on her suit.

They guzzled from their dripping arms, slurping with their beaks, inhaling through their gill slits. They were eating the water for its bacteria content *and* stripping its oxygen.

The mecha dragged her over the top of the chimney. Vonnie fell on her knees as Ash swatted the convulsing sunfish. She peeled one from Vonnie's helmet.

"They're as psycho as you are," Ash said. "They act like they're starving."

Her first comment might have been the bridge they needed to mend their relationship. Vonnie could have acknowledged the jab. She could have thanked Ash for helping her… but like a pair of sunfish, they were engrossed in a personal challenge.

Vonnie snubbed the younger woman. She looked at Ben.

"I can't explain why they're going nuts," he said. "That spray has more poisons than nutrients, and the bacteria can't give them more than a taste of protein."

"Maybe it's more important where the water came from than what it is," Vonnie said. "Maybe it smells different than their home territory."

"Get out of there," Koebsch said. "I don't care if the sunfish go with you. Leave."

"I have your routes, sir," Ash said. She wanted to show she was reliable and prepared even if they all had the same sims. Koebsch had drawn real-time maps of the catacombs leading north, where the ice looked more solid.

"What about O'Neal?" Vonnie asked. He sprawled on his back underneath four males. Vonnie hurried closer. She screeched and the males shrank from her.

They were protecting him, she thought, crouching down.

She set her forehead against O'Neal's faceplate. Doing so put her eyes above the bridge of his nose, one of the few spots where abrasions didn't obscure his face.

Even in this clear patch, it was difficult to see him. The inside of his helmet was fogged. He was roasting. His cheeks were no longer pink. He was pale. His eyes were red orbs and his lips were purple.

"What happened to your suit?" she asked. "Were you attacked by a different tribe?"

"No. This tribe."

"They crippled your suit, then they brought you to us? Why? What the hell were you doing out there?"

His voice was faint. "Thank... you, Von." He obviously wanted to say more, but he was fading. He coughed out three more words. "Saved my life."

"You better say so to Ash if you know what's good for you. That girl is pissed off. You're too hot, aren't you?" Vonnie unspooled a line from her waist. A hard connection was the only way to get a diagnostic from his suit. She tried to plug it in but couldn't.

She leaned away from him to scrutinize the problem. His panels were crammed with dust and ice. She whacked his suit. She shoved the plug into its socket. Medical reports scrolled over her display, and her heart sank.

Oh God, she thought. Then she recovered her voice. "Koebsch, are you seeing this?"

"Roger that. Can you... Uh, let's get his temperature down. We'll deal with his internals next. Tell him everything looks good. Keep him awake."

O'Neal's body was giving up its extremities. Low blood pressure had caused his veins to contract in his fingers and his legs, forsaking these non-essential parts, but the skin on his torso was blotchy and dry where the blood vessels had dilated in an attempt to increase heat loss.

His temperature was 42 degrees Celsius, 108 Fahrenheit, well above levels causing brain death. In fact, he would have died by now if not for the hyper-efficient medical systems of his scout suit

Vonnie willed herself to act cheerful. *Be amazed.* She set her helmet on his faceplate and said, "You must have found something important."

"Access points. Library. Empire. Breeding program."

The handful of words implied far more than she'd expected, but there wasn't time to quiz him. She said, "Don't forget to say thanks to Ash. I'll fix you in a sec."

She sat up. Disconnecting their helmets left O'Neal in silence, so she scooched around until her knee touched his thigh. She didn't want him to feel alone.

She used a mag key to release three plates of armor from his chest. Beneath the interlocking sections of plastisteel were universal ports, ducts, and LRAs — line replaceable assemblies. Everyone carried spares. They were meant to adapt to a thousand contingencies in situations where help could never arrive. Once she'd seen a crew survive in Earth orbit for thirty-six hours by tapping the oxygen tanks of their dead comrades.

Unfortunately, his armor was wrecked. One plate wouldn't give. Vonnie tugged at it.

The ice heaved again, throwing her from O'Neal. Her display lit with radar alerts. The chimney had cracked. Yellow steam washed over their suits and the cavorting sunfish. Koebsch and Ash shouted.

At least Ben kept his cool. He'd organized the five mecha in a phalanx with the unit on the left wing standing near Vonnie, poised to grab O'Neal.

Ben tried to herd the sunfish toward the machines. They skimmed past him, piping at Vonnie and O'Neal.

Would they betray her real emotions? O'Neal must know he was almost terminal. She pulled on his mangled armor and yelled, "This fucking plate!"

Ash shouted, "Can't you help him on the move!?"

"He's hyperthermic. He has severe arrhythmia and internal bleeding. You won't believe how much shit he's taken to reduce cerebral damage."

Their suits were walking pharmacies. O'Neal had ingested dozens of pills and mainlined ten vials of biological agents, but even nanotech hadn't been able to seal his hemorrhaging organs. The miracle was how long he'd kept going. He'd only stayed on his feet because his suit had propped him up.

"She needs to deal with him now," Koebsch said. "Ben, Ash, you should evacuate."

"Screw you," Ben said.

Koebsch couldn't let the affront pass. "Ben, I can overlook your attitude when..."

"Both of you stop." Vonnie sliced her laser into O'Neal's suit. She knew Koebsch hated to see his people in trouble while he was on the surface. He wanted to be with them. Clashing with Ben allowed Koebsch to be a part of their group, but she didn't need the distraction.

If she cut too deep, she would puncture O'Neal's chest.

"Got it!" She switched off her laser and tore the panel loose. Beneath his armor was a secondary layer, a pliable network of circuitry and conduits. The network was torn. Flecks of ice were embedded throughout the damaged spots.

Her main concern was his inner shell. It seemed intact. He could have saved himself if the sunfish hadn't reduced his spare LRAs to crude weapons and scrap.

She removed a component from the damaged area. It was smaller than her hand. She inserted a new component.

The response from his suit was immediate.

"His airco is back up," she said. "We'll lower his temperature soon. What about the bleeding?"

"Inject him with your nano kits," Koebsch said.

They were grasping at straws. O'Neal had overdosed himself to compensate for the unbearable heat. By now, more fever reducers or blood pressure meds would kill him. His lungs were sluffing apart, his liver, his stomach. Their AIs said his odds of stroking out were three in five.

Short of erecting a pressurized tent and operating on him, O'Neal was down to his last hope. Even with her nanotech, the AIs put his survival at forty percent.

"I can't get my kits into his suit. His jacks were in his collar. The fluids inputs on his back are gone."

Ash shouted, "Let's go! We'll figure it out!"

O'Neal might die while they were on the run, but Vonnie nodded. "Now," Ben ordered the mecha.

The sunfish shrieked when the machines came to life. One of the mecha clutched Ben. Another took Ash. It looked as if the machines were attacking the astronauts. Four males ran away into the ice.

—*Come back! Come back!* Vonnie screamed.

The matriarchs let them go.

The rest of the tribe wedded themselves to the machines, shinnying up their legs, clogging their hydraulics. The nearest mecha paused, adjusting its midsection to keep from squashing a matriarch.

Vonnie bent down to O'Neal. His face was white. His lips were blue. "You're going to be okay," she said.

The mecha took them both. It lofted Vonnie on its right, using her as a counterweight for O'Neal on its left. Somehow it also compensated for eight writhing sunfish.

It raised O'Neal gracefully.

Then it ruined the illusion of tenderness by tucking his suit against its small head like a spider eating a fly. Its wire probes groped at his battered armor. It impaled him, sealing each hole with nano mesh.

The machines were agile and sure-footed as they charged into the catacombs. They dodged through the labyrinth, unaffected by tight spots or low ceilings or debris.

Ash and Ben weren't carried by their mechas' arms. Both of them had been slotted in the "rider" position, their suits clipped onto brackets at the front of their mecha's spines. All of the machines juggled the weight of the sunfish, who leaped and squirmed.

"We need them to calm down," Koebsch said. "Von, call to the matriarchs."

But she was staring at her mecha. More wire probes reached for her chest. *Don't scream, don't scream, don't scream,* she thought, clenching her fists.

The probes dug into her suit, not her body, but there was a blunt pain in her side and she loathed hanging from the mecha's grip like a slab of meat. Stripping her nano kits for O'Neal was a good thing. She would have given blood if needed yet she felt helpless and exhausted.

—Quiet! Stop moving! she cried. *—Your chaos impedes us! Your lack of discipline harms our clan!*

Brigit and Michelle berated the other matriarchs. They scolded the males. Clinging to the mecha in fours and eights, the sunfish continued their song of jubilation, but they reduced their movements to arm strokes.

Vonnie's datastreams flared as the mecha transmitted information to Koebsch. O'Neal's mem files were intact. They would learn everything he'd seen and done.

She hoped it was worth it.

The mecha removed one of the three probes in her ribs and stabbed O'Neal with the same wire, injecting him with her nanotech. His vital signs were bleak.

Patient's heart rate is 153 bpm, the mecha reported. **Blood pressure 60 over 43. Cardiac arrest is imminent.**

Most of the nanotech had been swept up by the typhoon of his pulse, then dispersed among his leaking veins. Their nanotechnology wasn't magic. Its main purpose was to scrub their bodies of the cancerous cells caused by Jupiter's radiation.

The nanotech could minimize trauma by closing wounds or reducing swelling. It could even rebuild nerves and flesh, but there was a cost. It demanded as much energy as it expended. It ate red blood cells for fuel, and it needed raw materials similar to what it constructed.

It had taken microscopic amounts of chest muscle from O'Neal to repair his heart. It used tissue from his neck to maintain the blood vessels that served his brain.

None of this was enough.

Patient is seizing. He's in arrest. Initiating emergency life support. Systems nonresponsive. Suit diagnostic indicates extensive damage. Systems nonresponsive.

"No!" Vonnie yelled as if her grief could overcome the mecha's soulless report.

It bent its head, repeating the illusion of tenderness. It looked like it was praying until it thrust a probe through his torso with a *crunch*

Attempting defibrillation via electrical shock. Attempting emergency transfusions of plasma.

The mecha tightened its arms on Vonnie, immobilizing her as another wire pierced her chest. She yelped. The mecha was dispassionate; it imprisoned her for her own safety; but to Vonnie, its actions were obscene. She had been awash in fight-or-flight adrenaline for hours. Humiliating thoughts of rape and violation tore through her mind as the mecha sucked a clear fluid from her med packs and pumped the juice in O'Neal.

The sunfish attacked the mecha, shrieking.

10.

The males went for the mecha's head. The matriarchs thumped against Vonnie and O'Neal, attempting to free her from the machine.

—*No! No!* Vonnie cried. She shouted at her mecha, "Let me go or they won't stop!"

Her mecha stumbled beneath the onslaught of sunfish, but it did not comply with her demand. Its priority was the transfusions from her suit to O'Neal.

The sunfish yanked at its probes. Suddenly the discomfort in her side became agony.

"Gaaaaaah!"

"Von, what did you do!?" Ash shouted as Ben said, "Look out!" His broadcast ended with a crash.

Koebsch said, "They hit Ben's unit!"

"Where is he?" Vonnie yelled. Her pain was fading but she couldn't see. The matriarchs covered her faceplate. They banged on her chest, where they dislodged the probe but not its nano mesh seal.

They shrieked in confusion when there was no blood. They couldn't smell or taste the plasma being siphoned from her.

At the same time, Ben's plight unfolded on her display. Four males had hurled themselves into a crevice beneath the mecha on the far right. They split the ice. When the mecha swerved, the four males pounced at its head. Their weight exaggerated its reeling movement.

They'd brought it down. Then it had struck the mecha holding Ben. Both units joggled onto their feet again, but he cried out in pain.

"Ben?" Vonnie yelled.

The transfusions to O'Neal were complete. Her mecha released her and she dropped to the ice among the half-crazed males. —*Stop!* she shrieked.

The mecha aimed the speakers in their heads like guns, strafing the sunfish. —*STOP! STOP! WE ARE CLANMATES!*

The matriarchs quit fighting. They scuttled into the crannies in the ice, bringing the males with them. Vonnie saw a foursome duck into another branch of the catacombs. Radar showed them running away from the humans and the mecha.

Ben said, "I'm okay, I twisted my leg."

Ash checked in, too. "Von? How are your ribs?"

"I'll be fine."

Her mecha issued a new report. **Patient is responding. Heart rate 120 bpm. Blood pressure 80 over 55.**

Combined with her relief that Ben and Ash weren't badly hurt, the words made Vonnie light up. She couldn't contain her emotions. Pity and guilt. Frustration. Impatience. —*You've misread us again!* she screamed. —*Our warriors were not attacking me! They were healing Wise Scout! You are stupid animals like fat, slow prey!*

The matriarchs slunk among their males, buzzing to each other. One matriarch was bruised. Another had cuts on her arm.

They shared the taste of blood among themselves as they reflected upon Vonnie's rage. The sonar call she'd used for *misread* was a foreign concept to them because the tribes communicated precisely with each other. They associated *misread* with the deceit necessary to trap their enemies. They thought she'd accused them of treachery.

—*We are Ghost Clan Thirty!* they cried.

They were affirming their loyalty to her, and Vonnie's mood quieted. The sunfish couldn't comprehend mechanized field surgery. Why should they?

—*Danger? Attack? Metal warriors attack their females and scouts?* the males asked.

—*No! Join us!* Vonnie cried.

The matriarchs waited. They couldn't hear radio broadcasts, but they noticed the shift in her mecha's posture as its cocked its head over O'Neal, issuing its next report. **Patient is improving. Heart rate 125 bpm. Blood pressure 85 over 60. Urgently recommend additional transfusions. Urgently recommend additional nanotech.**

"Von, let's trade spots," Ben said, instructing his mecha to set him down.

The matriarchs piped as Ben limped toward Vonnie and O'Neal. She wanted to embrace him. Instead she touched his shoulder as he passed.

"Love you," he said.

"I love you, too," Vonnie blurted. She wasn't positive if she meant it, but she needed a special moment. She needed to love him.

Ben instructed her mecha to lift him in its arms, using him as a new counter-balance for O'Neal.

Meanwhile, Ben's unit clipped Vonnie into the "rider" position, where she hung against its underside. Like a torpedo, she was aimed head first beneath its spine with her hands free for weapons or tools.

As soon as Vonnie and Ben were secure, the machines ran. Reluctantly, the sunfish climbed aboard.

The matriarchs shrieked with new aggression when Ben's mecha perforated his suit, raiding his nanotech and blood plasma. Vonnie couldn't watch. Enduring the procedure herself had been easier than seeing her lover treated like a donor corpse.

The sunfish rearranged themselves into fours and eights. Brigit had been with Vonnie on the first unit. Now she appeared at her side again. She brushed Vonnie's shoulder with the same intimacy as Von had touched Ben, stroking her arm tip on Von's armor. —*We did not misread you*, Brigit cried, but Vonnie was watching her datastreams.

Ben's suit reported ligament tears in his knee and hip.

Seismography predicted more quakes in sixty seconds.

They'd traveled 1.15 kilometers from the chimney while gaining in elevation, but their maps of the local fault lines were hazy. Koebsch thought they were beyond the potential borders of a sinkhole if the area collapsed. Magma and floods were other obstacles, and, if the surface blew out, explosive decompression would kill their sunfish.

"Ash, I want you to drop the ceiling behind you," Koebsch said. "Seal the tunnel."

"What about..." Vonnie stopped herself. *What about the foursome who deserted us or the males who ran the other way when we left the chimney?*

They were gone.

Koebsch said, "Let your mecha fall back. Put a charge in the fissure on your display."

"Yes, sir." Ash stayed behind. Some of the matriarchs piped after her. Brigit and Michelle tugged at Vonnie, who ignored them. She watched her radar as Ash placed an excavation charge, then ran after the rest of them.

They bounded through the catacombs. Brigit and Michelle screamed at Vonnie, pestering her about *Biting Male* and *Wise Scout,* their names for Ben and O'Neal.

—*Wise Scout is alive? Biting Male gives him blood?*

Vonnie answered suddenly when the det code flashed on her display. —*Cover your ears!* she cried.

In the enclosed tunnel, the charge exploded like God clapping his hands. *KWHAM.* The blast wave gushed over them, thick with ice and moisture.

The sunfish snapped at the wind with their beaks. Others seemed to taste it with the undersides of their arms.

"Hang on!" Koebsch said.

Two kilometers away, the chimney blew. The devastation started with a *boom* more profound than their explosives. The sound resonated through Vonnie's suit. Then there was a subliminal rumbling in the ice.

From the surface, ESA rovers reported a huge, expanding blossom of heat. At its center was a main column that unfurled into a hundred petals as it bashed against the ice. On its edges, the offshoots were more irregular.

The blossom spread south easily yet backspilled into itself on the north and east, driving its growth upward. It claimed .26 of a square kilometer, then .59, then 1.17.

They were on the northern edge where the blossom rippled upward rather than outward.

"You may be too close," Koebsch said.

"It'll reach us!" Ben shouted, highlighting three segments of their map. "We need to find solid ground. Ahead of us. This is part of the foundation layer."

For once, the two men cooperated seamlessly. Koebsch said, "Ash, more charges. You'll have to dam yourselves in."

Damn ourselves? Vonnie worried.

On all sides, the ice roared. Inundated by the noise, the sunfish were reduced to touch and smell. They flailed at Vonnie.

Shards of ice rattled against her faceplate as the mecha rocked with the quakes, striving to maintain speed. Her unit lost its footing. Nearly thrown, Brigit cinched four arms on Vonnie's head. Vonnie dropped one of the charges she'd pulled from the mag locks on her arm. The charge bounced on the cracking floor and vanished. The ceiling cracked, too.

Vonnie and Ash reversed course as Vonnie screamed at her passengers. — *Run! Survive!*

The males obeyed her. They scampered after Ben.

Brigit and Michelle stayed with Vonnie as she took manual control of her unit.

Guiding the mecha was surreal. She was no longer a bipedal human. She became a creature with sixteen extensions — the sensors in her helmet, the sensors in the mecha's head, her own limbs and ten mandibles — but it was impossible for her nervous system to coordinate this frankenstein.

Her ROM programs were based on virtual assists. An AI anticipated every step, every turn, each burst of acceleration. Vonnie felt like she was hang gliding inside the mecha's steel frame. She galloped into the din with Ash. After seventy meters, she yelled, "Here! Here! We can't go any farther!" Rearing up, her mecha swung toward the wall and she jammed two charges into the ice. "Put one in the floor there!"

They wanted the ice to fall sideways, creating another buffer between themselves and the oncoming destruction.

Ash heeded her instructions without a word. Like Ben and Koebsch, the two women were beyond any rancor. They placed their explosives. Then they ran.

On the surface, their rovers had differentiated the many parts of the blossom into various densities and temperatures.

The larger petals were scalding gas that whipped through the catacombs. The gas cooled as it spread but its insane rush weakened the ice. A full square kilometer slumped apart.

The offshoots were boiling water. Like a weed extending vines, the geyser rammed through each path of least resistance. The flood yielded some of its vigor as it washed away to the south… but on the north and east, the water shoved upward.

Vonnie's group was 2.1 kilometers from the epicenter. The blossom had expanded 1.45 km in their direction. Very soon, a blowtorch of gas would reach the first spot where Ash had sealed the tunnel.

Their det codes counted down.

Brace yourselves! Vonnie cried to Brigit and Michelle. She wasn't sure if they heard her, so she also communicated the warning with her hand.

She scrunched her fingers on Brigit's topside, shaping her fingers like a sunfish knotting itself down to hide. She felt Brigit poke at Michelle. The matriarchs wormed onto Vonnie's belly and she tucked herself into a ball, cradling them.

The charges went off like cannon fire. Unseen in the blast, Ash screamed. Their mecha staggered, then staggered again when the blowtorch hit the first buffer. Some of that ice must have evaporated. Their radar showed colliding masses as the flood rose, compressing the gas.

The catacombs imploded. The flood bubbled through and hit the second buffer, where it fused the shattered ice. The water swept east. Nevertheless, their safe ground was eroding. Fractures broke the tunnel walls.

Vonnie shouldered through a chattering burst of ice with Ash close behind her. "Ben!" she yelled.

"Von!"

He'd arranged his mecha and the two spare units like a clam shell. One was on its back with its arms reaching up. The other two leaned over it with their arms drilled into the ice. Inside this protected space, two dozen sunfish clung to Ben and O'Neal and the mecha, using their bodies like shock absorbers.

They sang of death and home. They were accepting. They had given themselves to fate.

Vonnie and Ash detached from their mecha. They ducked into the protected space, where Ben and the sunfish made room for them. Their mecha glommed onto the other units. Vonnie and Ash grabbed onto the men. O'Neal was frail, but he closed his hand on Vonnie's, completing the circuit. She was aware of the matriarchs on her shoulders. She drank in her friends' faces, so close yet isolated by their helmets.

Meeting their eyes, Vonnie felt herself suffused by a mindset like the deathly peace of the sunfish.

The feeling was bittersweet. She wasn't quitting. She would always fight, but their circumstances were too vast. Either they would live or they would die. Her best chance was to conserve her strength. Maybe she could influence her fate.

If their last words were *Ben* and *Von,* at least they'd had their time together. She was glad she hadn't been shy with him like she'd been with potential lovers in her past. She was glad they'd had sex and quarreled and laughed and shared a few secrets. She wished they'd done more of those things. She wished she'd been even more candid with him, but she knew the balance of her life was in her favor.

She'd conducted herself with determination and skill. Hard work had made her a success.

We're going to live, she thought.

Shrapnel pelted the mecha from every side. The floor listed like a sinking ship. Vonnie caught Ben's hand, trying to convey all of her dreams and plans in one avid squeeze.

Suddenly everything grew still.

Ash said, "Is it…"

The walls collapsed. The ceiling hammered down. Two of the mecha were smashed. One was torn from their shell. As the machine spun away in a turbulent white cloud, half of the sunfish were taken with it.

Most of them returned in an avalanche streaked with blood. Vonnie was hit by screaming bodies. Then the floor turned over. She heard water.

It sloshed over her suit and dragged her down.

11.

Just as quickly, the water sluiced off her helmet and sleeves. It poured away through their bodies.

The sunfish screeched: a song of luck and conquest.

Numbly, Vonnie stared at the drips solidifying on her faceplate. She wondered why the tribe wasn't louder until she remembered the spew of blood. How many had died?

"You're okay, it's okay," Koebsch said. "The floods are receding from your area."

She found herself on a slope. Their slab of ice must have seesawed or floated, settling with a 25 degree tilt. The tunnel had flattened into a narrow plain. They were caught between their slab and a massive iceberg. Filling the borders around these two pieces, the ice lay in piles.

Ben, Ash and O'Neal were inside the remains of the mecha with Vonnie. They stayed on their bellies with their gloves locked on each other's arms.

Incredibly, Ben ignored her. He scanned his display. Ash's face scrunched in terror or pain. O'Neal seemed to be unconscious. As for the mecha, nothing was left of the missing unit except its dismembered arms. Another machine draped over them like a fallen bridge, its spine ruptured, its sensors bashed in. The other three units maintained their grip on the astronauts.

Vonnie counted fourteen living sunfish and a corpse. She thought her ankle was sprained. Her chin was sticky with blood where she'd struck the base of her faceplate. Her friends' suits reported no significant injuries. In fact, O'Neal's vitals were improving. The matriarchs tended to their wounded. Most of the sunfish had suffered contusions and gashes.

Ash spoke first. "Sir, is there a way out?"

"The mecha need to dig through two slides," Koebsch said. "Let's move. There may be aftershocks."

"Yes, sir."

One unit stayed above the astronauts. The other two extricated themselves and went north, easing down the slope. Four males bounded after them.

The mecha shoveled and carved. The males searched the rubble. They shrieked when they discovered another corpse. Then they screamed again, responding to the distant cries of a survivor.

"We'll be through in a minute," Koebsch said.

Ash let go of Vonnie and Ben. She sat up. Vonnie felt like she was returning to her body, but her arms were too heavy and her brain was slow. She still hadn't said anything.

Koebsch spoke to them like a coach after a bad game. "You chose a great spot to ride it out. Von, Ash, Ben, I'm recommending all three of you for the Union Cross."

"Yes, sir." Ash continued to give her rote response, unmoved by the possibility of receiving the EU's highest civilian medal.

"The stars," O'Neal mumbled. "Stars."

Vonnie glanced up, which was dumb. *If we could see into space, the atmosphere would've blown out.* Suddenly she was babbling. "How close are we to the surface? Did the flood lift us? My links to our rovers are down."

"The rovers are gone," Koebsch said.

"He sacrificed 'em for us." Ben's tone was approving.

Vonnie had never heard him say anything nice about Koebsch. Caught off guard, she fumbled through her display. "Oh my God," she said.

Ben laughed. "Impressive, isn't it?"

In orbit, ESA and FNEE spy sats studied a plume more than three kilometers high. The plume was tall enough to engulf one of their lowest satellites. O'Neal must have seen its alerts when the stars were blotted out.

The plume's structure was unlike geysers on Earth. It jetted into space without falling back on itself and only its base was liquid water.

During its first kilometer, it transformed. Above that point, it dispersed into a magnificent storm. It froze into dust and knives. Some clumps were as large as mecha. The fog glittered, and the sulfur content added colored formations. So did the iron, ammonia, rock dust and bacteria. Many of the gossamer clouds were yellow or black.

The plume also contained ejecta like house-sized chunks of old ice and basaltic lava. Parts of a fin mountain had been driven through the surface.

Some of the larger pieces burst from the sides of the plume. So did pulverized bits of mecha. In order to provide better readings, Koebsch had kept his rovers above the chimney until the end.

Three of his five units had been demolished. Of the remaining two, one had been sucked down by an offshoot of steaming water. The last rover was flung seventeen hundred meters to the southeast, spinning end over end until it slammed into the icy plain.

"We're underneath the plume?" Vonnie asked.

"Almost." Ben was cheerful. "We're about a klick northeast."

"What happens when the plume stops?"

"It might last for days."

"But if it doesn't..." If it diminished, the gargantuan tower would collapse.

"If it stops, it'll squish us like grapes," Ben said, but he grinned. "Koebsch will get us out of here. If he doesn't, he'll have a bad mark on his record."

Europa's surface had buckled over ten square kilometers, opening chasms or thrusting up new ridgelines. Puffs of air leaked through forty-two of the thousands of cracks, killing any lifeforms below. Clear water and red sulfuric acid bled through other places. Around the base of the plume, fresh ice grew into fantastic castles and serpents.

In camp, the bombardment of rock struck their northern perimeter, annihilating three beacons and a listening post. Quakes split the plain on the west.

The FNEE soldiers had deployed two gun platforms, firing missiles, disintegrating a hunk of ice that would have landed within half a klick of their position. Vonnie wanted to ask about Tavares. She wanted to ask about Harmeet and Lam and the sunfish. What if the tunnels in Zone One didn't hold?

Fortunately, the top of the plume bent toward the horizon. Most of the gauzy clouds and ejecta had been drawn away by Europa's orbital velocity. Some of this material would blanket other parts of the moon. Some of it would add to Jupiter's rings.

"The mecha are finished digging," Koebsch said. "One is coming back. One will stay in front and test unstable areas. Both of the other units can carry two of you."

"I'll ride with O'Neal in case he needs help," Ash said. Her suit hadn't been stripped of plasma or nanotech.

"Don't worry that he isn't talking," Koebsch said. "We put him in a medical coma. Harmeet is monitoring his progress. He's going to make it."

Vonnie and her friends were lifted by the mecha. Brigit pawed at her suits. The matriarchs were concerned because the astronauts had been taken in the machines' arms rather than clipped into the "rider" positions.

—Climbing out? Climbing out? they screeched.

—Yes, follow us, Vonnie cried. *—If you are quiet, you can hold onto our mecha.*

The sunfish jumped up. The injured ones tucked themselves among the machines' undercarriages. Bleeding from her topside, Brigit chose Vonnie's unit again and crawled along its arms. Michelle was more agile. Unhurt, she rebounded from the ceiling and landed on Vonnie's back.

Vonnie and Ben's unit went first.

The mecha ducked into the tunnel they'd excavated. The ice creaked. Vonnie bit her lip. The mecha had formed struts in this passageway by melting solid bands into the walls, which wouldn't last. Nothing in this area would last.

—Where are the four males who followed our machines? she cried. *—Did they find your survivor?*

—They have him, Brigit screeched. *—They are singing.*

She looked at her sonar displays, which were affected by the noise of the plume. She placed the males' voices below her to the west. —*Why are they moving toward the geyser? Our course is up and northeast.*

—*Up is where your warriors take you?*

—*Yes. Call your males.*

The undersides of Brigit's arms tangled with Michelle's. Vonnie closely recorded the fine patterns of their pedicellaria, but the translation from her AIs was indefinite. Brigit and Michelle were debating something in the private language of the matriarchs.

Vonnie screamed for the males. —*Join us! Follow us!*

If they answered, she was unable to detect it.

—*Here!* she screamed. —*Here!*

The mecha carried her team away. The ice was always the same because it was never the same, thin holes, wide caverns, smooth lines, broken edges, clear water ice and opaque stains of iron or sulfur.

Ahead of her, the lead mecha propped up a teetering wall as her unit passed, then the unit holding Ash and O'Neal. The machines averaged less than 10 kph. But with each step, the males were left further behind.

—*They will not join us,* Brigit screeched. She stroked Vonnie's shoulder mournfully. —*You showed mistrust.*

—*We welcome your males!* Vonnie cried.

—*You misread us. We did not misread you.*

—*I don't understand.*

—*The sunfish who left us chose to live as refugees rather than ally themselves with your metal warriors. You fear your warriors. You wanted us to attack.*

Vonnie stared at Brigit with creeping doubt. —*No! Our mecha serve us!*

—*They are your savage males.*

—*We rely on them. If not for our mecha, we would have died.*

—*You use your warriors but you do not trust them like we cannot trust our savages. You resent their strength. You command them. You kill them.*

Vonnie turned her head, a human gesture that the sunfish were learning.

—*Talk? Talk?* Brigit cried.

She said, "Ben, where are we?"

"We're almost safe. In another klick..."

Like a monster with a plaything, their mecha yanked Ben down among its legs to avoid whacking his helmet on a jag of ice. Simultaneously, it extended Vonnie on its other side to compensate. The sunfish shrieked in praise at its dexterity, but she also saw agitation in their shapes.

She looked at Brigit and Michelle. —*Our mecha serve us without question*, she cried.

Brigit curled four of her arms to expose her beak. She clacked at Vonnie's eyes, and Vonnie jerked in the mecha's grip. The mecha held her tight. Its priority was speeding through the catacombs. Vonnie would have shouted an override, but intellectually she knew a sunfish couldn't chew through her synthetic diamond faceplate.

Emotionally, she was at the end of her rope. Fury drenched her heart and she thumped her helmet into Brigit's pulsating underside. —*The mecha has its tasks and I have mine!* she screamed. —*I control its functions! You will lose if you challenge me!*

But she was bluffing. Everything she'd said was an equivocation because she'd never felt a whole, honest faith in her AI or her mecha.

Brigit was a veteran of the earliest tribes to form a treaty with the ESA. She remembered the FNEE gun platforms that had murdered dozens of sunfish. She remembered the diggers that had been loaded with pony bombs.

She couldn't possess more than an inkling of how quarter-ton warheads would burn the ice, but she had witnessed the arguments among the ESA crew, who had been divided in their efforts to stop or support the FNEE. To Brigit, the mecha were a conundrum. Even now, Vonnie was resisting her unit.

—*Your anxiety is what we hear,* Brigit screeched. In twelve swift gestures, she portrayed the machine and Vonnie's frantic body when it stabbed her with its probes.

—*You are wrong!* Vonnie cried. —*The mecha aren't alive. Sometimes they seem dangerous because they think faster than humans or sunfish. They are powerful. They have value but they're disposable if necessary.*

—*Yes. Like our savages.*

—*Not like them! Obedient! Reliable!*

—You fear them.

The mecha rose through a chain of tunnels where the ice had fallen in stages, creating steps as little as a table and as wide as an ocean liner.

The mecha played leapfrog. Pushing and pulling at each other, they formed pairs like impromptu ladders, using Europa's low gravity to fling or lift their partners. Their coordination was dizzying. They were no more human than a swarming tribe.

Brigit is right, she thought. *Subconsciously, a lot of us are afraid of mecha, especially after the war.*

The suspicion she felt was common. It stemmed from an innate wariness of any creature as large as a buffalo or an elephant. It was why people went into space when mecha could perform any job at less cost, less risk — and less glory.

Not everyone felt the same qualms. Harmeet was willing to stay in the modules as their mecha acted in her place. Dawson was so spellbound by his own ego that he couldn't fathom feeling threatened by a machine.

As for Vonnie, she wanted to build as much as possible with her own hands, see with her own eyes and walk on her own feet. She had the nomad gene that had led her earliest forefathers out of Africa and across their planet over mountains and deserts and oceans.

Even after today's catastrophes, she knew she would go back into the frozen sky.

12.

Returning to camp was only one of their triumphs. Days later, looking back, Vonnie felt that sense of history again. The thrill permeated everything she did.

In her enthusiasm, she had a hard time sitting even long enough to eat lunch or dinner. She waved her hands and laughed too much when she recorded her mission reports or fielded interviews from Earth.

She couldn't sleep.

Her insomnia was partly because she had nightmares when she closed her eyes. It was difficult to relax with dreams about being drowned or squashed.

The health teams in Berlin wanted to medicate her. She refused, although she agreed to extensive therapy sessions with an AI. So did Ben and Ash.

Some rumor about the FNEE soldiers had reached Earth. The net simmered with unconfirmed reports of discord among Colonel Ribeiro and his squad, which made Berlin uneasy about their own crew.

In private, Ben and Ash confirmed their therapy sessions were much like Von's. The AI asked about their sex lives and rigorously pursued gossip of any kind. No doubt Berlin was mining their transcripts for information on everyone's well-being.

Vonnie didn't withhold much, although she insisted she'd heard nothing about the FNEE's interpersonal headaches. She felt like the ESA crew had a few points of friction but otherwise excelled as a team.

They were participating in extraordinary events. They'd influenced the futures of two worlds. Their accomplishments had been tremendous.

Some of the clean-up was mundane. When her group returned, everyone had watched as the new sunfish integrated themselves into the existing clan; the linguists added sims to their databases; the biologists and genesmiths analyzed their various samples from sunfish, eels and bacteria; the engineers tested the integrity of the ice, then reseated Hab Module 02; and they deployed new beacons and GPs on the perimeter.

Koebsch and Ribeiro chose not to relocate. After six hours, the plume had subsided, its main column diminishing by seventy percent. Now it was a gurgling crater.

Most of its spray and ejecta had missed camp. As an unexpected bonus, the hunk of ice that landed on their northern border might prove useful as soon as their ecology and planetary experts could spare a day to examine it.

Another reason to stay was the homes they'd constructed for their sunfish. Zone One had ridden out the quakes with minimal damage. Zone Two had experienced slides and a cave-in, but the sunfish were accustomed to losing territory. The matriarchs cried in adulation when Vonnie restored an air pipe in Zone Two, and their songs had caused a glow in her heart.

The same couldn't be said for the bland letters of recognition issued mutually from Brasilia and Berlin for heroism in the face of disaster.

Ben mocked the letters. "They're congratulating us for not getting ourselves killed," he said.

Vonnie tended to agree. The FNEE soldiers had shot down one piece of ice that wasn't going to hit them anyway. Her group had been close to oblivion. They'd survived because they were clever — and lucky — but they shouldn't have been in trouble in the first place.

The events leading to the plume had started with O'Neal's curiosity and hubris. They'd learned a great deal, but their mission had had all the grace of broken, bloody drunks crawling out of a single-vehicle crash on the autobahn.

They'd shown resourcefulness and valor. Even so, the whole had been an accident.

The reality was Earth wanted to be impressed, so their governments emphasized the good and neglected to mention the bad. Their letters were written in bureaucrat-speak with phrases like *solidarity and commitment, joint ventures, intellectual prosperity* and *furthering our strategic gains.* Ben called 'em as phony as a hug from your fat uncle, although the signatures of the EU prime minister and the Brazilian president were as good as gold.

Gold ammunition.

Vonnie decided to leverage her new fame to the hilt. She had her supporters and fan clubs. She was also a popular target. From the beginning, prominent figures in the scientific communities had slandered her qualifications. Military men condemned her decision-making even though she wasn't a soldier. In the media, she'd been second-guessed by personalities across the political spectrum, the right, the left and everywhere in between. Her behavior had been declared too liberal, too imperialist, too feminist, too subservient, too anything they wanted to vilify.

Now she'd received a multi-national commendation and Koebsch hinted more was to come. What if despite so much abuse, she was under consideration for the Union Cross?

Top officials in Berlin might be receptive to the idea for selfish motives. A medal ceremony would heighten the public relations campaign that had prompted them to issue their letters, which allowed Berlin and Brasilia to thumb their collective nose at China. They needed to brag because the PSSC crew had diligently labored for months without setting off any geysers, fighting with the sunfish or losing a single astronaut as far as anyone knew.

The Chinese were digging. Seismography confirmed that much. Their territory was riddled with catacombs and lakes like most of the southern pole, but they'd tented their camp to hide it from spy sats and they did not communicate with their neighbors.

One area of progress was overt. The Chinese had doubled their production of deuterium. Their camp was surrounded by an army of mecha, and their automated tankers sent a steady stream of shuttles back and forth to the surface.

The PSSC destroyer parked above Europa was another bald statement of ownership. It had settled into position yesterday like a yellow jacket hovering over a plate of food. It didn't need to sting to scare them. Its presence made them think twice about everything they did.

With two new FNEE ships on final approach, leaders in Brasilia and Berlin must have been chewing their nails. If they needed to hand out some medals, Vonnie wouldn't say no. Maybe she deserved it. She wanted to make the most of her letter of commendation before it was overshadowed by an award, so she attached a copy to every interview she recorded for Earth. She hoped it would convince her detractors to keep their venom to themselves.

She also wrote a seek-and-spam code to post her letter wherever she was represented on the net. There were news feeds and media sites where people — mostly men — half of them lunatics — thrived on refuting each other's politics.

Her program also reported hundreds of high-trending sites that didn't quite meet the criteria she'd assigned. When she investigated, she found porn feeds where people — mostly men — half of them lunatics — used her old Arianespace medical files to generate sims of her performing unspeakable acts.

Ben had a few things to say about that. "At least thirty percent of guys are deranged by their gonads. Every thought in their head is affected by penis penis penis whether they know it or not — and mostly it's 'not.' Lots of people are short on self awareness. They lack empathy. They lack ethics. That's why the news is crime crime crime, cheat cheat cheat, rape, divorce and celebs. Following celebrities is just a different kind of porn. It's hero worship. The most popular shows fill the same need. The characters are beautiful and rich and always breaking up with each other. People need sex and drama vicariously if they can't find it in their own lives."

Ben and Vonnie were in Lander 04, naked on his bunk, which wasn't meant for two people. The room itself was a rectangular box meant to sleep four with the bunks folded down from the walls, two on each side.

She and Ben always used the bottom bunk on the right as a courtesy to their crewmates. Living in close quarters was demanding enough. Some of them were finicky about having a bed exclusively for sleep because everybody knew what Vonnie and Ben were doing. Dawson had commented distastefully on the smell. Tony had twice asked them to tidy up.

Talkative and euphoric, Ben reclined on a pillow. Vonnie had wriggled into her panties when they were done, then snuggled beside him on her stomach with her head by his feet, her hips tipped up with one leg scissored across his chest. Occasionally she bit his toes. He traced his fingers up and down the length of her thigh.

She sulked over a pull-out display. *Grumpy* couldn't describe how she felt. Her program had posted her letter on 1,092 popular news feeds and political sites. It had also located 1,139 porn feeds where it was prepared to add her letter after identifying her likeness.

"A thousand of each, Ben! It's late afternoon on a work day in Germany and early morning in North America and *this* is what people are looking at."

"You should be flattered. Some of the guys on the porn feeds probably can't understand where you are. Jupiter. Wow. At least they think you're important and pretty."

"I think it's obnoxious."

"Von, we've been in space for a hundred and fifty years, but you know what? The two biggest moneymakers on the planet are guns and porn, and not in that order. Food is sixth."

"I'm glad I'm a woman."

"Christ, no." He pinched her rump. "You're hardwired to jockey for social standing and put on sexual displays and babies babies babies. Who do you think fuels the celebrity business or the most lucrative dramas on the net? Chicks are crazy. How much of your hate mail comes from women who don't like how you look or call you a slut or say you're evil because you're helping the government or fighting the government or whatever?"

"Not all of it. Some of them say I shouldn't hurt animals or I upset someone in their church."

"Same thing. This is basic primate behavior — segregate and ostracize. They make themselves feel righteous by telling you everything you're doing wrong. It doesn't matter if they don't have the education or the guts to come here. They have their opinion. They cling to it. They find other people who agree with them and they'll defend their little cliques until hell freezes over."

"Ben, we do that, too."

"What?"

"We do that, too. Cliques. How snarky were the people in your biology department?"

"The snarkiest." He grinned. "I didn't say Einsteins are better than idiots. Look at who's in camp. There are only nine of us plus the FNEE and we maneuver for power blocs even if it's three or four people. Everybody seeks out like-minded individuals. Dawson can't get along with anyone because he's the only upper crust lord in the group. The women tend to make friends with each other like you and Harmeet and Tavares, but Ash sides with Henri and Koebsch because they're authority figures."

"Henri isn't an authority figure."

"He's a spy like her, and she has a father fixation in case you haven't noticed."

"Her father died in the war."

"A lot of people died in the war. Does that make it okay if I pretended I was a biologist, didn't do some of my real work and spent as much time as possible feeding classified data to a bunch of manipulative assholes in London?"

"Ash is better than she used to be. I think she wants to be one of us. They must have gotten to her when she was very young. She feels like she has a duty, not just to MI6 but to her family. Her dead family."

"I don't like her."

"You never told me that." Vonnie changed the subject. "What do you think about Tavares?"

"She calls you more than she needs to. You should talk to her. She must be lonely over there. We need all the connections we can get with the FNEE."

"What about us, Ben? Why are we together?"

"My looks, your brains. Classic example of the beauty and the beast."

"Hmm." She'd wanted more than another joke. She gestured at her display and said, "What am I going to do about this garbage? Can the agency get an injunction and make these pigs take everything down?"

"Von, you could spend the rest of your life and a stack of money sending lawyers after every porn feed on Earth. You should be flattered."

She had been panning through the least hardcore sites as they talked. There she was in lingerie. There she was on her knees. The permutations were endless and most of the animation looked as real as life.

"Whoa!" Ben hollered. "Let me see that one."

"What? No!" she said, but she blushed and laughed. She covered the screen with her fingers instead of turning it off, which would have blanked the image.

"C'mon." Ben nudged her leg off of his chest and crawled around on top of her. He nipped at her ear. "We haven't done anything with blindfolds."

She giggled. "That wasn't me, you idiot."

"It could be."

The sex was another reward. Ben delighted in her body. Vonnie enjoyed the distraction of his hands and his mouth. Her lean figure wrapped nicely around his squat shape. She reveled in feeling vigorous and young. They were protected from the hellish environment outside by his cozy bunk. It was a pleasure to drowse beside him or to catch up on their notes in a warm slinky bundle like a pair of cats.

Their first days after rescuing O'Neal were the happiest she'd ever been. A hero. A lover. A winner.

Ash was still furious about the rescue mission. So was Koebsch. Vonnie was not. Their most significant breakthroughs had been the direct result of O'Neal screwing up.

He remained in a medical coma. Berlin had also placed him under house arrest and flagged his personnel file. Ben summarized the flags as "This guy is an impractical son of a bitch but he's a genius and he's eighty bazillion klicks from Earth so we need him to get back to work."

Vonnie asked Koebsch about O'Neal's punishment, but Koebsch was fretful when he was alone with her. On the showphone, they were fine. In person, he steered clear of her unless their crewmates were present.

She knew why. He was envious of the time she spent with Ben. She and Koebsch needed to figure things out. She thought she saw her chance.

They had watched O'Neal's mem files repeatedly. Grilling him was overdue. Berlin had tasked Koebsch and Vonnie with the interrogation today, and, according to the schedule they'd posted, O'Neal was awake at last. He'd been allowed a few hours to eat and wash and look through their reports.

Very soon, Koebsch would be forced to deal with her.

She wasn't sure which made her more nervous, facing Koebsch or hearing what O'Neal had to say.

On Earth, thousands of scientists continued to evaluate O'Neal's files. More revealing, Vonnie had spoken with the matriarchs. As suspected, the eldest and most prestigious females had concealed vital facts from the astronauts for the same reason they deceived their males or lesser females.

O'Neal had said six words before Vonnie repaired his suit. *Access points. Library. Empire. Breeding program.*

Once she demanded to know more, the matriarchs had been as blunt as ever. They denied nothing. They also volunteered nothing. Until she learned which questions to ask, too many of their answers felt like she was being misled. She could only guess at the unvarnished truth.

The matriarchs had blindsided their human allies.

They'd thought they ruled the ice, but they had been like children making sandcastles while the tide was out. Ultimately, they were small and weak. They'd camped above thousands of tribes — and if they weren't vigilant, they might be devoured by a rising wave of sunfish.

ESA EUROPA BASE
Revised 1 September 2113

Command
Koebsch, Peter Günther

Engineering
Gravino, Antionio Leonardo
Sierzenga, Ashley Nicole
Vonderach, Alexis Rose

Life Sciences
Dawson, William George
Frerotte, Henri Charles
Johal, Harmeet
Metzler, Benjamin Todd
O'Neal, Dublin David

Koebsch	COMMAND - PSY - DATA/COMM
Dawson	GENE SMITH
Johal	GENE SMITH - MED - HAB
Frerotte	BIOLOGY - HAB - ASST. SUIT MAINT - ASST DATA/COMM
Metzler	BIOLOGY - PLANETARY - ASST. ROM
O'Neal	LINGUISTICS - BIOLOGY - ECOLOGY - ASST. ROM
Sierzenga	PILOT - NAV - MED - DATA/COMM - CYBERNETICS
Vonderach	PILOT - NAV - MAINT - MED - ROM
Gravino	ENGINEERING - PILOT - MED - HAB - DATA/COMM

Mission Control:
ESOC – Darmstat

Craft:
Deep Space *Intruder*-class *Clermont*
Deep Space Reconnaissance *Marcuse*

Support:
DSSC Hab Modules (2), ROM-12 Lander Flightcraft (2)
ROM-4 APAQS Modules (1), ROM-12 ATMP Vehicles (3), ROM-12 Rovers (7), ROM-12 GP Mecha (14), ROM-12 Beacons (29), ROM-12 MMPSA (2)
ROM-12 Rovers (1), ROM-12 MMPSA (3), ROM-12 MMPSA (14) // Japan
ROM-12 GP Mecha (9), ROM-6 Beacons (4) // United States of America
ROM-6 GP Mecha (1) // Australia

Constructed On-Site:
DSSC Hab Module 06
Submodule 07 Exploratory
ROM-12 "Doppelganger" Probes (10)
ROM-12 MMPSA (12), ROM-12 Beacons (5)

13.

"I'm going to see Koebsch," Vonnie said. She pumped her hips playfully beneath Ben's weight, but there was another message, too. *Get off me.*

Ben didn't like it. "There's no rush," he said. He let her roll onto her back. Then he pinned her down by nuzzling her collarbone and neck. "You could stay here. Talk to him on the group feed."

"Not dressed like this."

"I'll come with you."

"You need to get back to the lab."

Frowning, he let her up.

She sorted through their undergarments and jumpsuits. He lowered his eyes, which was unusual. Normally he watched her dress or undress.

Was he brooding about his work? As their planetary expert, lead biologist and acting linguist, Ben had more responsibilities than anyone. He'd spread his chores as widely as possible, leaving Henri to analyze the new strain of bacteria. Then he'd invited Lieutenants Carvalho and Santos to join him in C Lab, where they used spectrometers, magnetometers, core drills, jet sieves and chem packs to study the Top Clan's granite tools.

Vonnie had briefly assisted when their sieve lost its feeds to Earth. Bringing her tool kit, she had sidled into the lab among the three men until Ben asked the FNEE lieutenants to take a coffee break. Although they were gracious, they'd left eyeball tracks all over her jumpsuit.

Later, she recalled, she and Ben had been extra energetic in his bunk. She hadn't flirted with the soldiers. She had been virtuous, but she'd also felt desirable. Had Ben felt empowered as the alpha male?

'Basic primate behavior,' she thought. *He's mad about me seeing Koebsch by myself. Why? I'm not promiscuous. I'm the one who chickened out when we could have played a kissing game with Henri and Ash. Who knows where that would have led? When I was in university, I might have swapped with them even if it made me uncomfortable. I let peer pressure make my decisions for me. Then I guess I grew up. After a few bad experiences, I turned shy. I put my energy into my work.*

Maybe Ben and I should have traded partners with them once or twice. I wonder if our crew would be better off. Ben and I might feel closer to them… or maybe we'd have even more trouble between us.

Ben is getting possessive. Doesn't he know how I feel?

Vonnie finished dressing. She bent to kiss him. "I'll see you at dinner."

"Call me if O'Neal says anything about the granite," he said. She walked away. But when she opened the door, he stopped her with a word: "Von."

She smiled, expecting him to blow her another kiss.

His tone was a complaint. "You don't take me seriously," he said.

"*You* don't take you seriously, Ben. There's nothing going on with me and Koebsch. Got it?" Vonnie stepped through the door into data/comm, where Henri and Dawson stood at two stations.

Crud, she thought. They'd heard everything. Dawson's nose was wrinkled. He kept his gaze on his display, where he was comparing DNA sequences, yet he'd paused to listen. The old man might have been scandalized, but he was drawn to his comrades' romances like everyone.

Henri was more blatant. He'd muted his display to hear Vonnie and Ben.

She reddened. Some of it was indignation. Some of it was the self-conscious awareness that she hadn't showered and Henri was tall and handsome. His hands were slender. He had the hooded eyes of a hawk.

"O'Neal is awake," he said.

"Thanks. Are you… Does anyone need a ride? I'm leaving in ten minutes."

"I'd like to transfer to B Lab," Dawson said.

"Yeah." Vonnie hurried out of the room before she blushed again. Two orgasms made her emotionally sensitive and she couldn't deal with Henri — or Koebsch — until she got her head straight.

She walked to the toilet for a quick wash. Inside the closet-sized room, she stripped, turned on the fans and stepped into the shower bag. Hot water was plentiful. When she was done, she grabbed a fresh towel. Her cubby held clean undergarments. The laundry ran daily. Fusion power meant unlimited washing and drying, one of their few luxuries.

She ran a blower on her short hair. She dressed and stepped out like a new woman. Ben had joined the other men in data/comm. "Dawson, are you set?" she asked. "Ben, please tell them I'm driving over."

If Ben made the call himself, he might feel like he'd scored a point on Koebsch. She saw she was correct when he threw a *told you so* smile at Henri.

Had they been talking about her?

She should've asked Ben what he thought of Henri when he said he didn't like Ash. Ben and Henri were friends, which was unfair. As an agent of the French Directorate, Henri worked for a bunch of scheming assholes in Paris, but men judged men by one set of rules and women by another.

Ben even used phrases like *au contraire* as if to please Henri. Didn't he see his hypocrisy?

She led Dawson to the ready room, where she ignored the scrutiny of Dawson's eyes as they donned pressure suits and checked each other's seals.

In the air lock, Dawson said, "You and your young man are making a go of it, are you?"

She was flabbergasted by the personal remark.

"Ben is an intelligent man," he said. "My concern is you're both less than even-tempered."

The lock opened and they walked from the lander to a jeep. Vonnie fed it directions. The jeep trundled through the spotlights and mecha.

Were his contacts on Earth asking for gossip, too? The money their crew represented was an inconceivable sum from the cost of their ships to stock futures in genetics, deuterium and water. *Berlin is afraid someone else will go bonkers, so a microgram of prevention is worth ten tons of cure,* she thought. *That's why they sent our letters — to make us feel good.*

She laughed at the image of puppet strings curling all the way from Earth to Europa. Then, mischievously, she said, "What about you, Billy? Who strikes your fancy?"

"I beg your pardon?"

"Since we're talking about who's in what bed, how's it going? You got a hottie back home?"

"You know perfectly well I'm a widower." His voice was severe.

Hers was merry. "That was ages ago, old chap."

"Vonderach. Control yourself."

"I thought we were good fellows now, William, since you're asking about my shenanigans with Ben."

"I apologize for the conversational gambit."

"Shenanigans with Benjamin." *Share that with him later,* she thought. *And... Dawson apologizing? No one will believe it.*

"I have a serious matter for you," he said. His bony, distinguished features were framed inside his helmet. "We're corrupting the sunfish."

"Oh, Jesus, here we go."

"We're altering their natural balance." He raised one hand to stall her protests. "Our ancestors tried to help many less developed native peoples, and, time and again, the indigenous culture fell into steep decline."

He was speaking of the early naval powers who'd spread across the globe during an age when men believed Earth was the center of the universe. Vonnie said, "Our ancestors pillaged their way through Africa and the Americas. Disease and guns wiped out the natives, not good intentions."

"Our teachings and our missionaries were equally devastating to savages living in huts."

"I'll grant that do-gooders were part of the poison, but you've seen how resilient the sunfish can be. They're not going to lay down and die because we have heap big science."

"You jest, but I know you share my observations."

"I'm excited to hear you admit they're sentient. That's an important step for you."

"They're *not* sentient, not most of them. This is incontestable. It's why you should reexamine your entire approach, which, at its core, resembles Catholic missionaries attempting to beat the devil out of aboriginals who functioned quite handily in their local environments."

The jeep stopped in front of Module 02.

"We're here," she said. Haggling with Dawson was like chewing on her toes, all pain, no gain. "Get out."

14.

He didn't move from his seat. "There are other reasons to cease your welfare program for the sunfish," he said. "Your tools and food are creating a native superpower."

"Dawson, we can't put the genie back in the bottle. Someone will deal with the tribes. I want it to be us."

"Because you can save them."

"What's the alternative? Kill them or capture them as specimens or pets?"

"Nation-building has a sordid history of failure on Earth. The sunfish you equip today will march on their neighbors tomorrow. They may attack us."

"You've been listening to the chowder heads on the net. I get their hate mail. They think the sunfish will fly to Earth, eat our babies, rape the women and make everybody worship an octopus."

"We have the right *not* to intervene in their affairs. You're on a slippery path."

"Speaking of slips, I'll walk you in," she said. He was an old man. She didn't want him to fall on the module's steps. She exited the jeep and walked around to his side.

Dawson stepped out by himself.

Vonnie shrugged when he refused to take her hand. "I just don't see why you hate them," she said.

"I've told you: 'Hate' is a sophomoric word. I find them repellant. More to the point, I'm perplexed that we've allowed ourselves to be drawn ever deeper into their chaos. This moon is a bottomless snake pit."

"Right." Vonnie returned to the jeep and waited until Dawson entered 02.

She drove toward 01, ruminating on his greed. It still disturbed her that he'd accused her of not receiving enough attention as a child.

Was that why she felt attached to the sunfish? Ben would say *yes*. Everyone needed validation in their lives, but one of the ironies of human interaction was that people tended to accuse others of their own shortcomings. They saw the world through the lenses of their personal demons.

When people didn't understand something — when they felt stupid — they called it stupid to disguise their lack of comprehension. Vonnie believed this was the main reason for the abuse she took on the net. Small minds couldn't deal with giant realities. They found things to offend their political or religious beliefs, which allowed them to stop thinking, then wallow in their outrage.

Ben was correct that geniuses did this, too. Weeks ago, during another argument, Dawson had been showing off when he compared his disgust with the sunfish to the revulsion anyone would feel toward a black widow or a *Sloane's viperfish.* Despite her vacations to the South Atlantic and the Caribbean, Vonnie hadn't heard of the viperfish, a nasty-looking abyss predator. She'd had to look it up. He'd cited the viperfish to impress her, which meant he felt intimidated by her, which meant she had the upper hand in their relationship.

What was Dawson afraid of? Maybe his worst fear was losing the acclaim of his peers and business contacts.

Then a more insidious thought struck her. What if Dawson loathed being cared for like she cared for the sunfish? He took exception to needing help himself.

By that logic, Ben is possessive of me because he wants me to possess him. We flirt and joke and I even said 'I love you' when he said it first... but every time he talks about a commitment, I duck it.

She stared at the busy mecha as her jeep rolled through camp. In this safe, tranquil setting, she admired their invincibility. The machines were immune to the cold and to the vacuum. They did their jobs. Nothing else. It was only in the extreme when her deepest feelings were revealed.

My family wasn't close. With five kids and a job, dad never had time for us. My brothers always won when we punched each other or wrestled. It was every kid for himself.

Now look at me. As an engineer and a diplomat, I put things together. I build mechanical systems and I build peace, but I fight with the people involved whether they're on Earth or here on the ice. Are my lousy relationships with my brothers why I keep Ben at arm's length?

The jeep rescued her from worrying. It halted in front of Module 01. She sent it to the charging station.

She didn't want to be a heartless thing. The need to improve herself was part of her fascination with the tribes. Being involved with them allowed her to explore her slightly inhibited emotional state.

Using them as substitutes for her estranged family didn't mean she was frigid or delusional. In fact, she felt better for dissecting her own motives.

She hit the air lock's outer hatch and walked in.

As the lock cycled, she glanced through her display to confirm who was inside. O'Neal. Koebsch. Ash.

The inner hatch opened and she stepped into the ready room, where she unclamped her helmet. Koebsch and Ash were in data/comm. Vonnie wanted to talk to Ash before Koebsch. She stowed her helmet in a locker but didn't hurry with the rest of her suit. She opened the hatch into the corridor. "Ashley! Hey, Ash!" she called.

The young woman's footsteps sounded on the deck as Vonnie removed her gloves. Ash appeared but stayed in the doorway. "I should be at my station," Ash said. "We have messages from Earth."

"I wanted to say I'm sorry."

"For what?"

"I've barely seen you since we got back. I'm sorry for everything that happened. This place does things to people. It makes me feel upside down."

"I know what you mean," Ash said. Her eyes were cautious, but she manufactured a smile. "I've lost track of how many times we saved each other's lives."

"We make a good team."

"No, we don't," Ash said. Stung, Vonnie opened her mouth to cite examples of how well they'd anticipated each other in the ice, but Ash said, "We can be friends. People like you. I do, too, but it's hard for me when… I want you to admit you're undisciplined. That's why you like the sunfish. They do whatever they want."

"That's not true. They have as many rules as people. Maybe more."

"They can't stick to a plan. They're disorganized."

"The environment is disorganized."

"Don't make excuses for them. You make me angry when you make excuses." Ash banged her palm on one side of the door. She looked at Vonnie, maybe intending to say more. Then she left.

This must be my day to fight with everyone, Vonnie thought. Ash didn't make it easy. Ash was by the regs, which was why Berlin idolized her. She was a girl-shaped mecha. At least that was what she wanted to be.

Vonnie went back to taking off her suit.

What is Ash compensating for? Is she so uptight because she's afraid how she'll act if she doesn't follow orders?

An orphan in post-war London, Ash might have been a rebellious child without a home where she felt accepted. The ESA and MI6 offered new kinds of structure. They were surrogate families. Ash would submit to the most exclusive group first — MI6 — while heeding the second — the ESA — to the best of her abilities. It made her schizophrenic.

In her soul where she wouldn't question the fundamental axioms of her reality, Ash must believe that no personal relationships were forever; people died; yet her surrogate families would live on. Her assignments gave her meaning.

As an explanation, it seemed too pat, but Ben's armchair psychology had been on target with everyone else, which meant Ash had been incredibly candid with Vonnie.

If we're in the ice, I can count on her to watch my back. On the surface, she'll defend us against the PSSC or rogue tribes. That's the extent of our friendship.

For her to say so was a backhanded compliment. She must have been instructed not to burn any bridges. A spy needs to ingratiate herself with everyone. Drawing a line with me made her vulnerable, which is what she hates more than anything.

So do I. We should be friends.

Feeling inexpressibly sad, Vonnie stowed her suit in a locker. She would take what Ash had to give, but she needed to talk to someone about Ben. Could she arrange a time to sit down with Tavares?

I don't trust mecha. I don't trust men. It's amazing I fit the ESA psych profile for this mission, although I guess all of us have quirks. We're geeks and workaholics. Who else except crazy people would fly to Jupiter?

She set her hand on the door exactly where Ash had banged her palm, wanting to share Ash's frustration.

We'll talk again, she thought.

Then she strode into the corridor, mentally preparing herself for another difficult conversation. She walked into data/comm. "Koebsch, I'm ready," she said.

15.

He was sitting at his console. He glanced at her, but he didn't stand. He turned to Ash. "You'll tell me as soon as we have a response from Berlin?"

"Yes, sir," Ash said.

"I also want to hear Ribeiro's decision."

"Yes, sir." Ash kept her gaze on her display, shunning Vonnie. Her behavior was clear. She was saying she'd had enough for now.

Vonnie put a pleasant smile on her face. Of course a sunfish would have perceived her internal discord. Ash and Koebsch probably felt it, too. Koebsch stood up, but he laid his hand on his chair as if tethering himself. He didn't want to walk down the corridor alone with Vonnie any more than she wanted to stay and deal with Ash's silence.

Vonnie tried to coax him from the room with an easy question. "What is Ribeiro deciding?"

"Mecha detachments."

"Will he stay in command when the new ships arrive?"

"Yes and no." Koebsch seemed to realize how terse he'd been. He let go of his chair. "The FNEE sent two colonels who'll act as a tribunal with Ribeiro. He may have seniority. They may have orders to assume command. I think he's trying to put everything in place before they arrive. He wants precedents for how his men work in shifts, for his patrols, and for dealing with us."

Koebsch was setting his own precedent. He must have hoped that by swamping her with business, they wouldn't have time for personal subjects.

Vonnie had hoped to reconcile with him. If she and Ash were forging a new trust — even if it was a limited, piecemeal trust with restrictions and taboos — couldn't she and Koebsch get past their mutual attraction?

The two of them walked into the corridor. She said, "I saw Berlin issued a letter of commendation to you, too. Why didn't you tell us?"

"It was a political statement."

"You deserved it."

He shook his head. "Berlin wants to boost my standing before I meet with the FNEE tribunal. The good news is we're seeing fantastic coverage in the media. We're also gaining ground in the legislature. That won't last. In a few days, the opposition will introduce a new motion to cancel our efforts with the sunfish, but I'll stay on top of it for you. At the moment, we'd win any vote in EU or NATO proceedings."

"I don't care about Earth."

"You should. They're in charge. They control the money. We can't do whatever we want."

What would you say to me if you were a free man, Koebsch? And why do I keep calling you by your last name like you're Dawson or a FNEE soldier? To maintain our distance?

"Peter," she said, "thank you for handling the politicians. I couldn't finesse my way out of a plastic bag."

"You do fine when you aren't hotheaded."

"Engineers aren't hotheaded. We're heartless, remember?"

"Heartless is the last thing you are."

He wants to talk about it. I gave him an out, but he steered us right into the topic we've been avoiding. Suddenly she had butterflies. She gestured at the door to the infirmary and said, "O'Neal is waiting."

"He's not going anywhere."

"Peter, I shouldn't..."

"Have dinner with me tonight. Here. The two of us."

She feigned laughter. "In the corridor?"

"Of course not. I mean at a table. With chairs. Napkins. Wine."

They had been jockeying with each other for weeks. Even most of their words held innuendos. *I'm ready. On top of you.* Vonnie wanted to kick herself.

Prior to Ben, she'd had seven lovers. All but one of them had been at university or during her tour in Earth orbit after the war. She had been eighteen, nineteen and twenty at the time, inexperienced, eager, and some men had taken advantage of her. Those early trysts might explain why she had such trouble allowing herself to be wooed now.

"I'll talk with Ben," Koebsch said. "We're all adults. We're a long way from home."

He wanted to make their predicament as simple as possible for her, but she seized on his last comment. *How many times have we made that excuse? We are a long way from home. The cameras are always watching, the mikes record everything, and the constant surveillance makes us want to rebel, even Koebsch, even Henri and Ash. All of us want intimacy. All of us want more control over our lives. Is that why Koebsch won't let me go? He follows so many orders. Courting me, stealing me, is his way of demonstrating he's more than a puppet.*

By now, the slowness of her response was embarrassing. He was watching her face, reading her thoughts. She tried to ambush him with grin. "You've got it all figured out, huh?"

"Yes. We're on for dinner?"

"We are not on for dinner," she said, but even her denial sounded like teasing.

What she disliked most about Koebsch was how he *managed* everyone. At the same time, she appreciated his planning because she *was* hotheaded at times.

Her critics said she was strident. Koebsch was steadfast. As their armchair psychologist, Ben might point out that her difficulty with authority figures was the very basis of the temptation she felt.

Koebsch was completely unlike Ben. He was a little older and physically fit with good shoulders and a square face, but it was his self-restraint that foiled her. He was so damned stalwart. When she contemplated his precision, she knew he would treat her body with the same thoroughness.

Rehearsing what to say, she thought, *For the sake of the mission, let's put our attraction to bed, no, Christ, put it to* <u>*rest*</u>*, not bed, put it to rest and improve our working relationship.*

"Peter..." she said.

He didn't budge. "You don't need to decide right now. Let me talk with Ben."

"No."

"We can both do it."

Was that another double entendre? He was wearing her down with the same stamina that intrigued her, so she grabbed his arm roughly. "You don't say anything. You don't do anything. We don't hurt Ben. Got it?"

"Yes."

"This can't be about who's better than who. We're crewmates. No divisions. No fighting. I don't think you and I are a good idea." But she was drawing deeper breaths, standing too near. She let go of his arm and stepped back.

"I value our friendship," he said. "I'd like to be more, but I won't push, okay?"

"Okay."

"Let's talk to O'Neal. I think that's what Berlin expects me to be doing," he said, cracking a rare joke at his own expense.

Vonnie liked the effort he'd made to de-escalate the many undercurrents between them. "Thank you."

"My pleasure."

Another loaded phrase. First he'd been a gentleman. Then he'd emphasized their physical chemistry. Vonnie averted her face. She hit the infirmary door, and, as it opened, she deliberated with herself like a woman considering whether or not to move in a new direction. She thought, *Did the two of us finish something or are we just getting started?*

16

Reclining on a bunk with a pull-out display, O'Neal looked pale and dirty. His jumpsuit was wrinkled. His curly hair was unwashed. There were bags under his eyes, yet his eyes gleamed. "Von!" he said. "I was dreaming..."

"About what?"

"We were in the chimney, but it wasn't bad. The sunfish weren't violent. The ice was fascinating."

"I must have missed that part," Vonnie said. She was definitely teasing now. O'Neal was a bumbling *wunderkind,* all intellect, no social grace.

"It'll be peaceful next time," he said. "They'll lead us to a chimney willingly."

In the small room, Vonnie perched on the bunk by O'Neal's knees. Koebsch stood near the door, frowning at the IV lines. She rested her hand on O'Neal's shin.

More and more, she found herself wanting to connect with her friends. Physical contact made them feel larger and more secure. Touching O'Neal's leg calmed her, and it seemed to quiet the fanaticism in his voice.

"How soon can we go back?" he asked.

Koebsch said, "You're not going anywhere. You're under house arrest."

O'Neal blinked at Koebsch. Then he turned to Vonnie. "You know why I went into the ice."

Vonnie was keenly aware of being recorded. When their superiors watched this interview, she needed them to regard her favorably. "I think I do," she said, "but we need to be careful. Nobody goes off their own. Nobody goes against orders."

O'Neal lifted his turbulent gaze to the camera block on the ceiling. "I see. I made some poor choices. I'm in trouble. That doesn't change what we've learned."

"Why did you leave Zone One?" Koebsch asked.

O'Neal's leg tensed beneath Vonnie's hand, and she knew why Berlin had asked her to attend. O'Neal saw her as an ally. Koebsch was mindful of her feelings. A female presence counteracted the testosterone in the room.

"You have my sims," O'Neal said sullenly.

Her tone was mild. "Some of your files are degraded and there's no telemetry at all after they smashed your sensors. We need you to walk us through it. I'm sure the psych teams will evaluate every word. Try not to use scatological humor or talk about your parents. They think anybody who says 'shit' and 'mommy' in the same sentence is neurotic."

O'Neal laughed. Koebsch frowned.

"Don't say 'fuck' or 'daddy,' either," she added. "I made a joke in one of my therapy sessions and they said it pointed to my deep-seated girlhood issues."

"You're in therapy?" O'Neal asked.

"Me and Ben and Ash. Welcome to the club."

"What's wrong with you?"

She smiled like the devil. "Well, my parents were less strict with my brothers than they were raising a daughter because they couldn't deal with my sexuality. They're Catholic. Fortunately, I was a late bloomer. They treated me like another son until I was fourteen. Unfortunately, nothing was going to stop me from having breasts or hips. Then things got weird, which explains why I pursued engineering and ROM. Those are male-dominated fields. I wanted to make them happy but I wasn't happy even though I loved what I was doing and it all blew up in their face when I was eighteen and I overcompensated by sleeping with three boys at university. Conversely, Ash never had a stable family, which is why she's hungry for patriarchal relationships even if London doesn't deserve her. She's too good for them."

"Von, enough," Koebsch said. "If personal information has been divulged to you, we shouldn't hear it."

"We're gonna hear O'Neal's private stuff. Aren't we about to massage his head on camera?"

"The psych teams will conduct their own assessments. You don't have the training and nothing is ever that simple. Let's stay on task."

"A lot of the time, I think our motivations are pretty simple, Koebsch."

"I don't want to argue."

"Fuck," O'Neal said with a sly, troublemaker's grin. "Mommy. Diapers."

Koebsch said, "Tell us why you snuck out of Zone One."

"I was collaborating with the matriarchs. I'm their equivalent of a scout. As a male, I asked them questions I shouldn't have known to ask."

"What questions?"

"Let's back up." O'Neal indicated his display. "We should talk about the plume."

"The plume doesn't have anything to do with—"

"It has everything to do with what's happening. Me. You. The tribes. Earth."

"Let's hear him out," Vonnie said. Koebsch was annoyed at the other man, but he was willing to accommodate her. He nodded. She said, "What was unusual about the plume?"

"Nothing!" O'Neal said with zest.

Koebsch started to say something harsh. Vonnie stopped him with a look. O'Neal had opened dozens of sims. Most included DMsP radar or chemical analysis. She also saw grainy surface photos taken by twenty-first century hardware.

"It was a normal eruption," O'Neal said. "There are thousands of places where the ice is breached. As far back as 2012, the Americans detected vapor plumes as tall as two hundred kilometers. Typically the strongest eruptions are on the equator or at this pole because the Great Ocean is shallower here and there's more volcanic activity. Northeast from our position, we found a whorl in the ice where the subduction of three colliding masses causes the ocean to seep through, but it doesn't meet our criteria because those eruptions are generated by lateral grinding, not vertical displacements of gas or heat."

"And what's our criteria?" she asked.

O'Neal blinked owlishly. He said, "We want access to the Great Ocean, of course."

A thrill shot up Vonnie's spine. *The ocean!* she thought. "If we can find a stable channel—" she said, but now Koebsch stopped her.

"Nobody is going into the ice."

"Ah," O'Neal said. "Berlin needs to send us back in if we want to compete with the PSSC. That's why they're digging. They intend to beat us."

"Why?"

"Why? We've barely scratched Europa's surface. If there's a native civilization, it will exist in the Great Ocean. It may center around the fin mountains or drift with the tides, but the ice is the thinnest shell around a volume of water greater than all of Earth's oceans combined. I guarantee you. After we discovered complex lifeforms in the ice, we knew equally complex lifeforms must swim in the water."

"This is an Earth-like world, so we assume many of the same mechanisms," Vonnie said, quoting Ben.

Koebsch glanced up sharply, but he didn't say anything to her. He peered at O'Neal. "You're talking about lifeforms other than sunfish."

"Once life evolves beyond single-cell organisms, any ecosystem will diversify. Europa is younger than Earth but it hasn't suffered as many extinction events. As a water planet, it experiences less turmoil after meteor strikes. It lacks exposed land or what we regard as a conventional atmosphere, so there haven't been long-term calamities like our greenhouse periods and our Ice Ages."

Koebsch said, "The Great Ocean was sterilized hundreds of thousands of years ago. We have samples from plumes and seeps. There are lethal concentrations of acid, sulfur, iron, salt. Nothing can live down there."

"Nothing that hasn't adapted." O'Neal grinned again like a boy. "Look at the sunfish. They exude or store accumulations of toxins that would kill a human being. The sulfur and iron provide the coloration in their defensive spikes and the hardest cartilage strands that encase their organs. Haven't you wondered why their spikes are pigmented when their skin is albino?"

"The ocean is too acidic."

"It's also boiling hot in places. That doesn't mean it's lifeless. There will be dead zones and populated zones just like we've seen in the ice."

Vonnie said, "We won't know until we get mecha into the water."

Koebsch paused.

Come on, she thought. *Come on, Peter. I know you're with us. I can see your excitement, but you're afraid of how your bosses will react.*

"Getting through the ice won't work," Koebsch said. "We've lost fifty probes trying to drill."

"That's why the PSSC spread their camp over a series of chimneys," O'Neal said. "They're searching for one that goes all the way down. Look. China has always been ahead of us in genesmithing. Their hybrid soldiers are more advanced. So are their hybrid astronauts. They want to maintain their lead."

"Those programs are rumors."

"Koebsch, I saw PSSC super soldiers myself when I was with Arianespace," Vonnie said.

"Think of the meds you could design from lifeforms who are immune to intense poisons. Beijing still hasn't solved the problem of fertilizer runoffs into their drinking supplies. They need to grow too much food. They have algae blooms and cholera in fifteen districts, including their capital. That's a humiliation to the People's Supreme Society. They don't like being reminded of their peasant heritage even if most of their population resides in villages or slums."

Koebsch startled Vonnie by laughing. "O'Neal, sometimes I can't tell if you're showing off or if what you're saying is actually relevant."

O'Neal didn't blink or smile now. He gazed at Koebsch without expression. Vonnie realized he'd taken offense. "I'm not here to generate sound bites for the media," he said. "In most circumstances, background is more than relevant. It's vital to our comprehension."

Koebsch accepted his scolding with a nod. "Go on."

"The PSSC want to find the real power on Europa. The sunfish are useful, but if there's a central power, it will be inside the ocean."

"They want to find a king," Vonnie said.

"Yes."

Her eyes widened. Then she shook her head, berating herself, and, by extension, the entire ESA. "We're not even thinking on that scale, much less pursuing a major operation."

"Sometimes totalitarian societies accomplish more than democracies. I don't condone it. They treat their people like slaves. But the trains run on time."

"If they reach the ocean before us..."

"I've seen the data from our flybys and sats," Koebsch said. "We would have hard evidence if the ocean was full of civilizations."

"The sunfish evacuate before the most powerful eruptions. They use their scouts like early warning systems, and it's logical to believe ocean life avoids the chimneys altogether. The regions below the chimneys have the worst currents, volcanic eruptions and acute fluctuations of heat and cold."

"The water would show traces of life."

"It does. We missed the signs."

Beginning in 2032, Earth probes had swept through Europa's plumes, sampling the vapor. By 2094, spy sats were in orbit and mecha explored the surface. Because this moon held so many organic compounds, there had been several instances of false positives or inconclusive readings.

Only a handful of mecha had traveled deep into the ice. Missions to the Great Ocean had been limited to a few crawlers or batches of nanotags injected into hot springs.

Most had transmitted emergency signals as they were crushed or burned. The rest disappeared. Deep missions looked like an expense with zero return. NASA and the ESA had suspended these operations. The FNEE hadn't even attempted to send mecha. Everybody was focused on the tribes.

We need to sway Berlin, Vonnie thought, *and no one puts a puzzle together like O'Neal.*

She gave him a leading question. She said, "You've talked about vestigial features in the sunfish like the tailbone or the appendix in people. They have gills. They can withstand incredible pressure. Why would they leave the ocean?"

"Competition. On Earth, life originated in our oceans during the Precambrian. Sedimentary rocks as old as four billion years hold fossils of our very first microbes. I'm talking about simple individual cells. For an extraordinarily long time — for the next three billion years — nothing else existed until one strain mastered the process of oxygenic photosynthesis. Earth developed an atmosphere, which led to aerobic cellular respiration."

Koebsch said, "What does this have to do with the sunfish?"

"Their timeline is like ours, except they faced much stronger competition for the few areas where an oxygen-rich, non-reducing atmosphere emerged. Let's stick with Earth for a minute. A billion years ago, we saw the advent of multicellular organisms. The next jump was the Cambrian explosion. There was an expansion of more complex body plans, although everything continued to live in the water. The land was dead rock. Gradually, plants and fungi spread over the continents… and by the end of the Paleozoic, the oceans were crammed with fish and sharks and brachiopods. Favorable mutations allowed a few creatures to thrive in the shallows. They climbed out to escape the feeding frenzy in the water."

"You think that's what happened here."

"Yes. In people, smell is processed differently than our other senses because the earliest mammals were rat-sized things who coexisted with the dinosaurs. We were nocturnal. We only came out when the giant lizards were asleep, so smell was more useful than sight. We grew a bump of brain matter called the neopallium to sort through the ambiguous cues provided by scent. Eventually the neopallium evolved into our cerebral cortex without losing its preference for scent. That's why fragrances are so evocative. Scent goes directly to our limbic system."

Vonnie thought of Ben's pleasant salt smell, the aroma of her favorite chocolate or the morbid stink of a sweaty scout suit. In each case, the feelings in her mind sprang from their association with those scents.

She could remember her mother's perfume and the unwashed odor of her brothers bustling into the house after *fussball.* She had tried to keep herself clean like *mutti* while competing with her brothers in sports, a fine line she'd rarely walked with success. Just the memory of pungent grass on her clothing was associated with her father's righteous gaze.

Every time she stepped inside the rank confines of her armor, her subconscious flickered with images of him. Was that why she disliked suiting up?

"One of their vestigial features are the photoreceptors among their tube feet and pedicellaria," O'Neal said. "Europa is a lightless environment, but their optic nerves run directly to their dual cortexes. Sight does an end-run around their other senses. It occupies an amount of brain power that could be used elsewhere. Their aptitude for hearing and spatial relations should be even stronger, but sight affects them like smell affects us. Once upon a time, it was among their primary senses."

"They live in volcanic environments," Koebsch suggested. "Couldn't that explain it?"

"They didn't need eyes to avoid magma. All life inside Europa is heat sensitive. Their photoreceptors are specifically geared to detect shortwave bioluminescence."

"I don't know what that means."

"It means there are predators in the ocean," O'Neal said.

17.

Vonnie sat up straight. "You don't think the tribes are at the top of their food chain?"

"Here in the ice, yes. That wasn't the case in their past. It may not be the case now. If the sunfish hunted creatures who used bioluminescence, they wouldn't need to see. Their other senses are ideal for locating prey. In the ice, light only shines as far as the next bend in the catacombs. Among the mountains submerged in the ocean, the same limitations apply. Noise and scent travel farther than light. But when their ancestors crawled out of the water, the sunfish were in this world's most precarious environment — the middle zone."

Vonnie shivered. She enjoyed his brilliance. She cherished Europa's distinctive beauty and its exotic past.

Far below, the Great Ocean's tides thumped against the slush that made up the underside of the frozen sky. Along the mountain peaks, there would be drowned shores, and, inside the rock, water-logged grottos and lava tubes.

That's why the sunfish adapted so well. During their transition from the ocean into the frozen sky, they moved from one set of catacombs to another. They traded rock for ice, but both environments were labyrinths.

Leading him again, she said, "Why would they develop photoreceptors in the middle zone?"

"They lived there for millions of years. Originally, the sunfish were aquatic, and they weren't a dominant lifeform. Like the earliest mammals on Earth, the sunfish were a niche species. Something down there ate them.

Staying alive demanded sharp instincts. Roaming from one mountain to the next demanded memory."

"And there were predators in the middle zone who could see."

"They never had eyes like ours, but yes. The spaces between the water and the ice must be noisy — congested — and covered in the rotting scum of sea-life. Sonar and scent wouldn't suffice. The carnivores began to generate their own light. They needed it to find enough calories. For the sunfish, natural selection favored the ability to evade them. Running from predators also made the sunfish smarter."

Vonnie crossed her arms over her chest as she pictured a glowing monster as it lunged out of the water. "Christ."

"The predators may not have died out. Both breeds of sunfish have photoreceptors. Their optic nerves haven't atrophied despite who knows how many eons since they climbed into the ice."

"Some of the tribes might live near the ocean or go in and out of it!" she said. "If they still see those predators..."

"In the Mid Clans, the optic nerves are particularly robust. They may be close cousins of a third breed. They may visit the Great Ocean themselves."

Koebsch intervened, dulling the energy between Vonnie and O'Neal. "None of the sunfish have made any claims about the ocean or a third breed or predators. Let's get back to what they really told you."

"We don't know what's down there," O'Neal said. "What we do know is the tribes kept us from discovering the portals for as long as they could."

"Portals," Vonnie said, savoring the noun.

"The chimney we found is well-guarded by the matriarchs. It's sacred to the Top and Mid Clans. It opens and closes, but it's been an access point for longer than they remember."

O'Neal tapped his display. His first sim was a basic cross-section. Europa's surface was always in motion, bulging, gyrating. The pole was an eye at the center of the storm. The tides and the volcanoes eroded vertical shafts in the ice. The chimney had stabilized to some extent.

Next he brought up his projections of the local sunfish population. The tribes were concentrated at the chimney. They formed a stack of rings around it with stray groups spread throughout the catacombs.

The known locations of bacterial mats, bugs, eels, and ruins from the sunfish empire were clustered in the same manner. The chimney was a spoke. It was a lightning rod. All life radiated from it. All life was drawn to it.

O'Neal said, "Since our very first landings, mecha and people have stayed away from hot spots. We mined the plains. We drove back and forth and decided we'd seen everything. Even when Vonnie, Bauman and Lam fell into the ice, they never got closer than eight klicks to the nearest chimney."

"That's why the Americans have found so little," Vonnie realized. "They're exploring beneath their original mining site. Those tunnels are old and dead."

"The PSSC are willing to risk an eruption because the heat's done most of their work for them. Less digging. More exploration. They've moved fast."

"Is it possible they met the sunfish before us?"

"We would know, wouldn't we?"

"Maybe not. Their security is ironclad. Their few public announcements are scripted. What if they've been dealing with the sunfish for years?"

"We can't worry about intangibles," Koebsch said. "Speaking practically, what difference would it make?"

"What difference would it make?" Her tone was thick with derision. "Four people are dead because we didn't know how to talk to the sunfish. We've killed entire tribes."

"I think it's far-fetched to assume the PSSC encountered the sunfish years ago, then hushed it up and sent Choh Lam with your mission as an elaborate ploy to hide the truth."

"Have you talked to their commanders?"

"Briefly."

"We should meet. We can use our recovery as an excuse. Say we need medical supplies. We'll trade some of our genesmithing, whatever they want."

"That's not how it works."

"Koebsch, we need to know what they know. If the PSSC established their own treaties with neighboring tribes or if they've fought, it could have influenced everything we've done. It may influence what we do next."

"Von, I'll be honest," Koebsch said. "I think you need someone to blame."

"What? I don't—"

"We can't just visit them and start asking questions. You will also take care not to say *anything* like this during your interviews or in broadcasts of any kind including our short-range transmissions in camp." Koebsch was not her suitor now. His expression was stern and his words were clipped. "Are we clear?"

"Yes."

"I recognize your concerns, but pursuing this subject is beyond your pay grade. We do think PSSC mecha have encountered sunfish. It was after you lost Bauman and Lam, not before."

That was an interesting choice of words, she thought. *He didn't say 'After you were rescued.' He said 'After you lost Bauman and Lam.' Does that mean the PSSC ran into sunfish while I was in the ice?*

She didn't want to believe Koebsch was withholding information, although he did try to manipulate her. Maybe the two of them would always be in opposition despite what they'd shared. Koebsch's best trait was his dedication. Foremost, he would protect his crew from physical harm. Would he also keep them in the dark to circumvent a public relations debacle?

How many secrets are you keeping, Peter Günther Koebsch? Would you be honest with me in bed?

I can't love someone who treats us like we're assets — like we're mecha or spy sats. It's better if we stay friends. I can never get involved with you.

18.

Feeling a pang of regret, Vonnie turned to O'Neal and said, "Tell us about the library you found."

"Von." Koebsch touched her shoulder.

He wanted to apologize. She brushed off his hand. "We're done talking about the PSSC. You made your point. I want to talk about the library."

O'Neal didn't look at them. He was uncomfortable with the friction between them. Vonnie thought he was also grappling with friction inside himself. She knew a thing or two about the burden of remorse, and O'Neal had played a part in eradicating what he loved most. Knowledge.

There had been rock islands near the chimney. Big islands. Every centimeter had been inscribed with hieroglyphics, and he'd recorded less than a twentieth of the islands' surfaces before everything went wrong.

Very likely, the matriarchs themselves hadn't inspected many of those surfaces for generations. Wherever the rocks grated together, wherever they pressed into hard, old ice, the carvings were hidden from the sunfish.

Who could say how much the matriarchs had forgotten?

No one could say how much had been lost in the plume and the collapse. There had been hundreds of genetic samples tucked into the ice alongside the hieroglyphics.

"This library was their Alexandria," O'Neal said, referring to an irreplaceable collection of scrolls, scholars and lecture halls in ancient Egypt. Many historians believed the Library Of Alexandria had been the greatest center of academia in the world. "Two thousand years ago, Alexandria was looted and put to the torch by Roman armies. Now, because of me, the tribes destroyed their own heritage."

"It was inadvertent," she said.

He hadn't told them to cause the flood that led to the chimney opening up. On the other hand, if he hadn't persuaded the matriarchs to bring him to the chimney, Koebsch wouldn't have sent Vonnie, Ben and Ash.

"I should have waited," he said, "but you know how they are — quick decisions, quickly acted upon. When they agreed to take me, I couldn't let them change their minds, so I went."

"The sinkhole didn't destroy everything. Someday we might dig far enough to recover the islands."

"We're fortunate Ben saved as much as he did. The genetics are exceptional. Some of the samples are new to us. But the hieroglyphics were better."

"I read the translations. Nobody can make sense of it. The AIs don't agree with each other. Neither do our people on Earth. There are conflicts in the age of the hieroglyphics, there are conflicts in what's written, and the matriarchs dodged too many of my questions. If they were human, I'd say they were lying, but I think they might not have the answers themselves."

"They don't. The messages recorded in the hieroglyphics — and the ages of the messages — vary because so many were altered over time. Some were erased by the matriarchs. Others were modified."

Reading from his display, she said, "It's like the signals at a railroad crossing. Stop. Go. Stop."

"Very good, Von." He nodded. "They changed the most fundamental part of their history when the chimney opened or closed. It set the course for everything they did. They gave accounts of their wars against the Mid Clans or they provided advice on establishing treaties with other Top Clans. They kept lists and maps of the other creatures in the ice or they counted their savage males."

"Are you saying it was one or the other? They either fought with the Mid Clans or they turned their attention to the other Top Clans?"

"It's not that simple. They're always scouting for ways down — but in a nutshell, yes. When the chimney is open, they have more room, more resources, and more wars. The Mid Clans aren't the only species down there. There's no question that our sunfish met something else."

Libraries were more than fables from the empire or commands to the next generation. They were life rafts. They held the sperm of healthy males and the eggs and pheromone-laden scat of healthy females. The ESA had also found painstakingly insulated blots of fresh water, salt water, bacterial mats, fungi, the blood of eels and mashed remains of various bugs. Ben thought these samples were meant to provide clues for starving tribes much like search and rescue dogs on Earth were given personal items from missing people. A tribe that hadn't encountered eels for generations might improve their chances of locating a new food source if they memorized the scent or the compositions of different waters from specific environments.

The new library — the biggest library, their Alexandria — had contained a special vault. The matriarchs hadn't objected when O'Neal dug samples out of its main area. Nor had they barred him from entering the vault, where he discovered eight pellets of gore. Each had been buried beneath distinctive symbols molded in the ice.

Drilling from the side, leaving the symbols undisturbed, O'Neal extracted the pellets inside cores of ice.

He'd put six of them in his kits when he fumbled the seventh. He had been rushing like a boy in a candy shop. The ice core struck his boot. It chipped. The sunfish caught its scent. The males went berserk. Even the matriarchs seemed to lose their intelligence. They'd dropped part of a rock island on him, battering his suit, ravaging their hieroglyphics. They'd kept at it until they heard Vonnie's trio ascending the chimney.

She said, "Those blood samples must have come from the predators. What else could trigger that kind of response?"

"You're probably right. I wish they could tell us. Whatever the blood came from, ninety four percent of its DNA is identical to DNA of the Top and Mid Clans, but we share more than ninety percent of our DNA with every primate on Earth. The sunfish may be closely related to the predators. Maybe the samples belonged to a third breed, our hypothetical Low Clans.

The symbols in the ice weren't much help. Every symbol was a variation on the sunfish shape for welcoming and warning. My guess is the Top Clans have had mixed success with this species."

"They represented an opportunity with a cost," she said, glancing at Koebsch. *I know the feeling.*

"Those samples were put in the library five hundred years ago," O'Neal said. "Then something happened. The chimney closed. Other samples go back a few decades, but most are recent. So are many of the hieroglyphics. The matriarchs are perpetually revising their history."

Vonnie didn't like where this was going.

"'Revising,'" she said. "That sounds like a fancy word for 'fraud' or 'propaganda.'"

"Yes."

O'Neal wanted to treat this as an intellectual exercise, but Vonnie hated corruption in any power structure, especially when it was systematically applied for the benefit of a few at the expense of the many.

"It's been thousands of years since the empire fell," he said. "For every chimney that closes, others form, and the Top Clans and the Mid Clans had a covenant once. They built the empire together. Why haven't they rebuilt?

"They're hindering their own recovery, aren't they?" Koebsch asked. "It's intentional. We've seen them arrange fights among the tribes."

Her skin prickled in horror. So much pain. So much ignorance and cold and starvation. "I know there's not enough food, but what good would come from endless war? Are the matriarchs doing it so they can stay in charge?"

O'Neal shook his head. "I believe they've come close to recreating their empire over and over again. Several factors prevented it."

Despairing for the sunfish, she closed her eyes.

"Their life spans work against them. Males average twenty years, females barely twenty-five. That's if they aren't killed. Their leadership has so little continuity. Most of what they learn is hearsay. Their records are impermanent."

"Or they erase their own carvings," she said bitterly.

"There's a good reason why."

"A good reason to exist as barbaric tribes?"

"The same events unfolding here occur in every populated zone. When a chimney closes, it's often due to volcanic activity. That means more flooding, more quakes, more blowouts. The pocket ecologies burn or freeze. So do the bacterial mats that provide most of the free oxygen. The tribes' food supplies temporarily improve as they dig through the rubble. Then the cold sets in. The atmosphere is gone and they've lost their catacombs."

"Why not work together and expand their territories? Build more reservoirs and farms?"

"That's how they built the empire. At some point, the matriarchs chose another solution. They changed their history and wrote new commands. That was at least fifty generations ago."

O'Neal's voice was ominous. Each word reached back through difficult centuries on the threshold of extinction.

"Their wars are meticulously planned," he said. "They don't lead their tribes into random conflicts. It's a breeding venture like a poor man's genetic program."

"We've seen them butcher their savage males."

"It's far more than that. The matriarchs are selective in who's allowed to procreate. There are incentives. The tribes who improve the health of their males are permitted to expand into better regions. Those who stagnate or regress are banished."

"Or they're killed."

"Yes. Or they're killed and used to feed the stronger tribes." O'Neal blinked. "I don't see why you're upset. They're doing the best they can."

"They murder their own. They set them up to fail. It's cruel. It's immoral."

"You can't apply our morals to their society."

"I can if I love them," she said. She caught herself and explained: "I want to love them. I want to root for them. Some of the matriarchs and their scouts are my friends. We've worked too hard to learn they're the bad guys."

"They're not. Listen to me. This goes beyond weeding out disease or savagery. They share with each other. The healthiest males are moved among the tribes like stud bulls. The matriarchs cooperate. There's a prevailing strategy."

Vonnie lifted her head with haunted eyes. It had been a long day. Weariness and trepidation lingered in her soul. It made her feel alone. She yearned for Ben. "How many have they sent to die in the cold?" she asked.

"You can't apply our morals to their world."

"How many? You said it's been fifty generations since they *revised* the commands from the empire."

"And they breed like rabbits. Even when they're starving, they breed. That's part of the problem. There hasn't been enough food or habitable territory since the upheavals that decimated their civilization."

"We're talking about millions of lives, aren't we?"

"During the same period, billions of human beings have died of sickness and poverty, not to mention our wars. Who's to say we're better?"

"We are. You and I. Our crew."

"Because we're trying to shape events beyond our control? That's what the matriarchs have done. You should root for them. You're right to admire them."

I hope that's true, she thought, and, reacting to her distress, Koebsch took her hand. She flexed her fingers inside his grip, needing his hand yet feeling guilty for it.

O'Neal said, "Some of the empire's instructions were never changed. One command was emphasized. We've seen other, younger rock walls where the sunfish repeated this message. You found these symbols when you were lost in the ice."

"The command to share."

"Yes. We thought it was a forgotten decree, but it serves as the primary tenet of the matriarchs' plan. Their scouts and hunting parties seed the ice."

"What do you mean?"

"They don't eat everything they find. If they did, the ice would be lifeless by now. They stock the seas with eels' eggs, they stock the catacombs with bugs, and they carry bacteria everywhere."

Vonnie wanted to feel optimistic. She took her hand from Koebsch and said, "Do all of the Top and Mid Clans contribute? This is a joint venture by both breeds?"

O'Neal said, "There are renegades who raid and steal, but for the most part, the tribes cooperate. The matriarchs decide which areas are restricted. They seed the ice, then leave it. After a few generations, they return. Sometimes an area has flourished. Sometimes it's dead."

Vonnie thought of the pocket world she'd discovered after Bauman and Lam were killed... a lively space with two species of bugs and growths of bacterial mats... but part of his explanation didn't make sense to her.

"The tribes fight every day," she said. "Their battles are only staged to kill off savage males?"

"Sometimes a well-established tribe will bully a newer group into yielding territory, and tribes who belong to the pact will eliminate renegades. There are marauders who've degenerated beyond any capacity to read or think."

"We ran into some of them before we saved you."

"No. The sunfish you encountered with Ben and Ash were outcasts. They were ill, but they were serving the pact. That's why they tried to drive you away. They were protecting the chimney."

As he spoke, Vonnie's subconscious made a new connection. Some memories would always taint her thoughts. Blood and darkness. Her own savagery.

O'Neal saw it in her body language. "The first sunfish you ever met were animals," he said. "Their speech patterns were rudimentary — and when you ran into the larger breed, their minds were made up. They assumed you were another animal."

"I killed them."

"You didn't know," Koebsch said.

"I tried to talk to them."

"You were using the animals' sonar calls," O'Neal said. "You sounded like a beast."

Vonnie put her hands on her face, overwhelmed by the blackest emotions. *Put it behind you. Put it behind you.* She could still feel the rubbery spasm of a sunfish popping between her gloves.

"Let's stop for now," Koebsch said.

"I'm all right."

"You need to remember the sunfish are doing their best in a horrendous situation," O'Neal said. "Things might have been different if our rovers hadn't found the tunnels for another century. We came during a bad cycle. Their lives are worse when the chimneys are closed."

"But if they've been cultivating the ice, why are there so few lifeforms? What happened to creatures like that ferret?"

"Maybe the fur-bearing species couldn't be tamed. Maybe the sunfish decided they were too competitive. For all we know, the ferrets were wiped out during the extinction event that destroyed the empire. Von, we're talking about enormous periods of time. It's remarkable that the tribes exist at all, much less that they shepherded other lifeforms through the upheaval like a fleet of Noah's Arks."

"There's an inspiring image," Koebsch said. "Mention it in your interviews. We could use the support of the church."

"I don't want to debate the religious implications of an alien race. Leave that to Harmeet. My point is the sunfish have gone to incredible lengths to survive. Our lab work proves it. They've harvested the bacterial mats, nurturing certain strains for productivity and heartiness. They not only seed these strains throughout the ice, they share their best samples with other tribes."

"That's why they were so riled in the chimney," Vonnie said. "There were churned-up flecks of bacterial mats inside the spray."

"Yes."

"Hold on," Koebsch said. "If the chimney was closed for years, but it opened after the flood caused by the outcasts… Why haven't they kept it open all this time?"

"It's not open anymore," O'Neal said. "The outcasts weren't acting in concert with the matriarchs. They gambled on a better outcome, hoping to earn the matriarchs' favor, but centuries will pass before that sinkhole reforms into vertical shafts. The survivors need to begin all over again."

"We should send mecha to find them," Vonnie said. "Our shelters are big enough."

"Our resources are limited," Koebsch said. "We could pump heat into the ice forever, but we can't provide food for hundreds of sunfish unless we're resupplied."

"Our mission here goes beyond the sunfish."

"That's not your prerogative."

"We can show Berlin there's a living environment between the water and the ice. There might be Low Clans and ferrets."

"We don't have the people or the equipment to mount that kind of expedition."

"What if parts of the empire still exist?"

"We'll get to them."

"If they form a treaty with the PSSC, it could set us back. Restricting our operations due to short-term costs might ruin everything in the long run."

"I'll share that idea with Berlin. You have your own contacts and, uh, your therapy sessions. Bring it up. I'll support you, but you said it yourself. We need to be careful. Nobody goes off on their own. Nobody goes against orders."

He was quoting her like she'd quoted Ben, using her words as a harness. Vonnie growled, "Fine. I'll talk to Earth."

"Not to the media. Talk to our people in Berlin. You're a hero. That means you have a responsibility to watch yourself. Everything you say affects public opinion. Be patient, Von. You have enough enemies at home."

"We could modify our probes to push through the chimney. The cost is minimal."

"You're not listening to me."

"Our fusion reactors mean we can pump heat into the ice forever," she said, steering him with his own words exactly as he'd steered her. "We don't need to give more of our supplies to the sunfish. We can help them feed themselves."

O'Neal smiled, matching her enthusiasm. "If we drop cables into the sinkhole..."

"We'll melt through the chimney! Our mecha can help the sunfish dig out everything that died in the collapse. We might establish contact with the

Mid Clans. Then we'll find a way into the Great Ocean."

"You're talking about a significant redistribution of mecha and crew," Koebsch said. "First things first. We need to complete our repairs. The new sunfish have barely settled in."

"I'll talk to the matriarchs."

"Don't promise them anything."

She stood up, needing to get away from him. She saw the hurt in his eyes, but she thought, *I can't talk to you when you're like this.*

"We need to hurry," she said. She walked to the door, where she paused and surveyed the two men. "Thank you, Koebsch."

"It's my job." He amended his words. "I'm glad to help."

But you won't tell us what you know about the PSSC or how far they've gone into the catacombs. That bothers me. Earth is pulling strings and you let them.

Feeling like she was closing a door on their relationship, Vonnie left the room.

I know who can tell me about the PSSC, she thought.

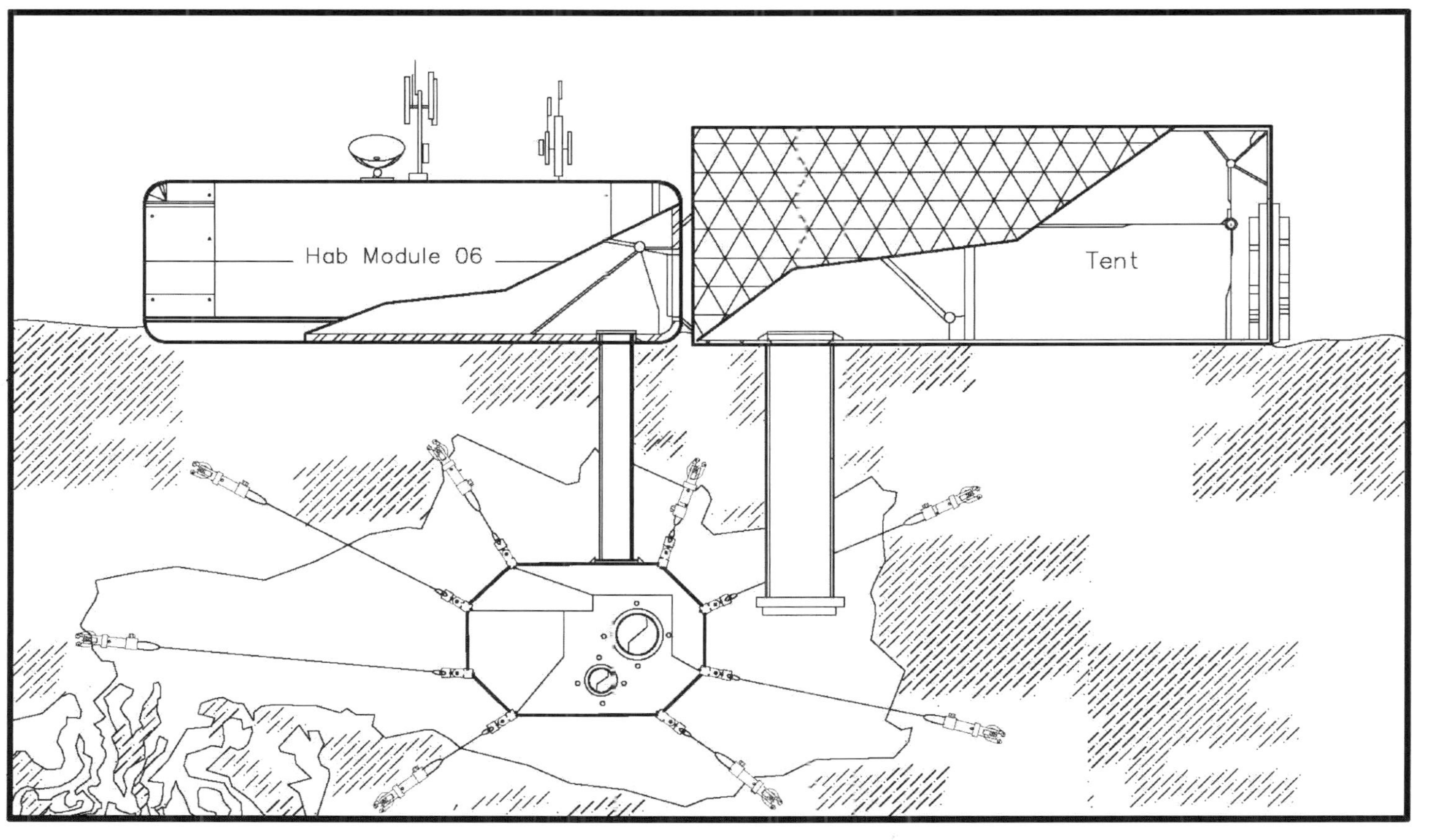

Submodule 07

19.

The next morning, Vonnie returned to the ice. She'd told Koebsch she would talk to the matriarchs. In reality, she wanted to find her answer.

She wore a new scout suit and packed a full load of weaponry. Sword. MP7. Explosives. Flares. She'd also surrounded herself with two burrowers and five of the doppelgänger units. Including herself, they made a group of eight, a powerful number for the sunfish.

"Team theta standing by," she reported from the cargo tube beneath Module 06.

"Hold for my command," Koebsch said on the radio. He'd left his station in Module 01 to monitor her progress from 06. "We're checking our arrays."

"You've already checked them twice."

"We're comparing data."

"I'm on schedule. It's safe."

Rather than answering, he patched her display into his datastreams. Directly alongside the cargo tube, Submodule 07 was outfitted with passive sonar, active sonar, radar and cams. Their MMPSAs provided surveillance of the nearest caverns and other sections of the colony.

Weeks ago, O'Neal had assigned an AI to every sunfish in the clan. These watchdogs maintained individual profiles and evaluated the clan as a whole.

"I don't like their mood," Koebsch said.

"They're jumpy because you're making me wait." High-pitched shrieks rubbed up and down the cargo tube like fingernails on a wine glass. "They're screaming my name."

"We've added so many newcomers to the tribe. What if they're out of cycle?"

"Koebsch, let me go!"

Even before Ghost Clan Thirty was formed, Harmeet and Ben had guessed at the peculiar composition of sunfish intelligence. Then their watchdogs proved it. Berlin had ordered them to conduct their missions according to new rules of engagement. Ben called this edict '*Let sleeping fish sleep.*' It was based on four provocative facts.

First: the tribes had rest-wake-rest-and-wake patterns that matched the physical properties of Europa much as lifeforms on Earth had biorhythms attuned to day and night. The sunfish consistently slept for 5.33 hours, which was a sixteenth of Europa's orbital period around Jupiter.

Second: the implication was that long before they met human beings, the tribes possessed hints of *when* if not *why* the ice moved. They felt the tides caused by Jupiter and the tug of other moons, although some of this activity was randomized. Europa endured close encounters with asteroids and larger masses. Saturn added its gravitational pull each time it passed. So did Uranus and Neptune. Their world was subjected to inscrutable forces… but like everything else, the sunfish used their pattern of sleeping and waking to their advantage.

Third: neighboring tribes tended to alternate. One rested while another was awake. It had taken several cycles for the many sunfish of Ghost Clan Thirty to adjust. Nobody knew if the tribes' alternating rhythms were a collaborative effort — a way to reduce strife between hunting parties — or a predatory adaptation to allow raids into each other's territories.

O'Neal believed their swift 5.33 hour rotations were a more complex evolutionary trick. It meant some tribes were always alert. If there was a catastrophe, the active groups had a greater chance of survival.

Fourth: the most intelligent sunfish were bipolar, not in the casual definition of the word, which people might use as slang to describe a moody friend. Throughout the day, the sentient male scouts and the matriarchs literally shifted their consciousness from one hemisphere of their brain to the other. They did so with drastic consequences.

The majority of a sunfish's central nervous system was devoted to its musculature and involuntary functions like heartbeat and digestion. For the savage males, those demands were everything. They generated an inkling of self-awareness, no more.

Even the sentient male scouts and the matriarchs were hard-pressed to spare any portion of their minds. Like autistic humans, they were overpowered by their own responses to stimuli. They heard too exquisitely, scented too sharply.

They maintained their sanity with intervals of rest. They relinquished themselves two periods out of every four. For them, the dormant-active-dormant-active cycle actually meant sleep, intelligence, reduced intelligence, intelligence. They always seesawed to an inhibited state.

During this phase, a tribe surrendered its memories and its strongest leaders. They tended to rut like animals. They rampaged through their territory. If confronted with astronauts or mecha, sometimes the matriarchs reestablished themselves. Sometimes not. They experienced confusion and personality changes.

Clenching her hands on her sword, Vonnie thought, *How many sunfish have died who might've been intelligent if we'd met them an hour later?*

O'Neal posted schedules that listed when the colony should be receptive. The sunfish were able to skip an occasional rest period or delay it. At times, they changed their pattern as if realigning themselves with neighboring tribes, but when they refused sleep, they experienced longer stretches of reduced intelligence.

Less challenging was matching their cycle to Earth's twenty-four hour clock. Vonnie rose early or stayed up late to approach the sunfish on their own terms.

This morning, she was ten minutes into their intelligent phase. "Koebsch, unlock the hatch," she said.

"Something's off today. Their behavior is… strange."

"Let me go."

Silence. Her pulse was loud in her ears. Finally he said, "Beacons up. Now."

One of her doppelgängers opened the hatch. It dropped through. Another followed it, then Vonnie. She landed in a crouch with her blade protecting her face, sweeping the cavern with a spotlight and infrared. Beside her, the doppelgängers struck equally assertive poses.

She was surrounded by fifty-two sunfish. The cavern was jammed with matriarchs and savage males. Lashing, snapping, they recoiled from her spotlight, a mob of albino bodies and dark beaks.

—*Metal scouts!* they screamed. —*Young Matriarch brings her killing scouts!*

—*We are Ghost Clan Thirty!* she cried.

Her burrowers and the rest of her doppelgängers scrambled from the tube. The burrowers cast more lights. Above her, the hatch shut automatically with a *bang.* The doppelgängers stepped toward the sunfish and bared their steel beaks.

Like a pool of water stirred by an unseen hand, every lifeform and machine in the congested space moved in a clockwise pattern. As the mecha advanced, the wave of sunfish retreated up the cavern walls or surged over the cables and struts of Submodule 07.

—*Attack? Attack?* the males shrieked. They squirmed in knots of four and eight, inciting each other.

Vonnie had confronted this dilemma many times. There was always a bad moment when the hatch opened. Standard protocol was to announce the arrival of astronauts or mecha with unique sonar cries, one for each crewmember, one for GPs, one for doppelgängers and so forth.

The sunfish heard people or machines before they arrived, but the specialists in Berlin hoped to teach them concepts such as schedules, set ranks and a fixed chain of command. The announcements also gave the matriarchs time to prepare the males.

As the doppelgängers and the sunfish moved in their busy dance, Vonnie muttered to her radio, "You were right. Something's different."

"There are more of them," Koebsch said.

O'Neal was monitoring her datastreams. "Actually, the male-to-female ratio is in our favor," he said. "I see more matriarchs than we regularly attract. We can expect this group to exhibit self-control."

"They're about to jump my mecha."

"They're posturing. They're afraid of something else."

His words eased Vonnie's tension. Suddenly she ignored their screaming. Beneath the noise, her thoughts steadied and she glanced through her radar displays.

"Look how the sunfish are distributed," O'Neal said. "I mean all of them inside the colony and beyond."

"I see it."

O'Neal opened ten sims from their mecha. He turned off the seismography. He turned off DMsP, thermal and atmospheric. He focused on the sunfish. His first sim was dated twenty-four hours ago. The tenth was current.

"During their most recent cycles, the sunfish bunched near the surface except for two groups on our southeast perimeter," he said. "There's a third anomaly in the center, a cluster of breeding pairs and matriarchs. Otherwise their distribution would have been more obvious."

He did it again, she thought. O'Neal had put his finger on one pattern hidden among a thousand details.

Koebsch said, "Are they preparing an invasion?"

"I don't think so. Most of the sunfish on the perimeter are males. If they wanted to cause a blowout underneath us, the males would be here."

"Then what are they doing?"

"I don't know."

"I'll ask them," Vonnie said. "Lights out, mecha to me." Her suit went dark. So did the burrowers. Several steps in front of her, the doppelgängers scuttled backward and took submissive postures at her feet.

The matriarchs slithered onto the cavern floor, where they assumed positions as equals with Vonnie and her mecha.

The males stayed on the cavern walls or Submodule 07, but now their song was one of acceptance. —*Thirty! We are Thirty!* they screamed.

The sunfish and the doppelgängers embraced. Two of the matriarchs included Vonnie in their ritual, wriggling against her suit. What could they smell? Stray molecules of plastisteel? What mattered was their physical exchange — the act of rejoining the tribe.

Vonnie stroked their muscular bodies with her left hand as they investigated the pommel of her sword. The oldest matriarch wrapped an arm around the blade and grazed herself. The wound spurted blood. The males frolicked.

—Metal and flesh! Young Matriarch leads! She provides! they screamed.

Vonnie knew better than to offer sympathy to the bleeding female. *—I am here for my friends!* she cried. *—I seek the ones we call Brigit and Michelle.*

Her names for the two matriarchs depicted the individual scars on their topsides and a missing hunk of pedicellaria beneath one of Michelle's arms. She included gestures to imply age and size.

—Brigit, yes! Michelle, yes! the sunfish shrieked. *—They are deep in the ice.*

—Guide me to them.

—No. Stay. They will come to you. Harmony and food! The clan pivots on Young Matriarch.

—Do as I say. Guide me to them.

The savage males howled at Vonnie's orders. Somehow the matriarchs communicated by touch among themselves, sustaining a conversation despite the males' interference, but they couldn't hide it from the ESA. Using radar, the mecha caught snatches of the matriarchs' discussion, and their AIs combined previous samples with a million extrapolations.

The translation was instantaneous. Koebsch ranked its accuracy at 85%. "The matriarchs want to stop you from going into the ice," he said. "If they can, they'll delay you with more songs."

Vonnie barged forward in her suit. *—Are we clanmates? Will you ambush me!? Guide me to Brigit and Michelle! Scouts, listen! I will reward those who bring me to the females I seek!*

Sixteen males jumped away from Vonnie. They hurried from the cavern until they were restrained by the matriarchs.

Four of the males bit at their captors. The others rustled and screeched, but the matriarchs were larger. They worked with a higher degree of cooperation. They gripped the males in their arms and used the mass of bodies as a dam, sealing off the main entrances into the tunnels.

—*Stay! Stay!* the matriarchs screamed. —*We hear. We sing. All of us will come to you.*

Vonnie leveled her sword with as much conviction as she could fake. She wouldn't hurt them. The females must have known it. —*Move!* she roared. —*Males, obey me!*

—*Obey us!* the matriarchs sang. —*We lead the clan, not Young Matriarch!*

Why were they opposing her? Dawson had warned that the ESA was creating a native superpower. Unparalleled wealth had surely affected how the sunfish viewed the future, but would they reject their human allies?

—*I have earned my role among our councils!* Vonnie roared. —*The peace in which we thrive began with my strength, my food, my tools!*

The males renewed their clash with the matriarchs. They added to the insufferable noise.

—*Obey me!* she cried at the matriarchs.

—*Obey us!* they screeched at the males. —*She is a rogue! She brings food but she can never breed with you! Her strength is here! She is weak in the ice!*

They wanted to set the males against her. After everything she'd done, they were willing to fight to keep her from leaving this cavern. Why? She'd come to ask about the chimneys and the Great Ocean. She intended to propose a far more substantial union between their species.

She clamped her sword against the magnets on her back and advanced with her gloves balled into fists. They would read her irritation as thoroughly as they perceived her unwillingness to maim or kill. She could throw them out of the way.

"Mecha, sync with me," she said, bringing the doppelgängers with her on either side.

The sunfish screamed. Some of the males instinctively aligned themselves with the matriarchs. Others continued to fight on Vonnie's behalf.

—*Defend us! She is a rogue!* the matriarchs screeched.

—*My strength goes beyond tools or food,* she cried. —*I <u>can</u> breed with you. Our machines are capable of producing the healthiest sperm and eggs. We can cure your diseases. <u>That</u> is what we want! If our goal was utter domination of this world, we wouldn't need you!*

The matriarchs seemed to unwind. They were intrigued by her claims, but, more critical, they expected her to stop asking the males to support her. They wanted consensus, not loners.

—*If you are true to us, stay here,* they sang. —*The deep ice has dangers you haven't met.*

—*We know more than any sunfish!* she cried. —*We see farther than you hear. This is why I seek Brigit. Let me pass. I must speak with your eldest females.*

—*The ice holds many dangers!* the matriarchs screamed.

But even now, they were unpredictable. As they screamed their message of caution, they released the males they'd imprisoned.

Four of the matriarchs rushed into the catacombs. —*Follow us! Follow us!* the foursome cried.

Twelve males went after them in a swarm.

Vonnie gaped in surprise. The foursome's voices were deferential. They were compliant. They were going to take her to Brigit.

Among the sunfish that remained, the males and females screeched back and forth. The matriarchs sang of the Old Ones. They began to coach the males through a ritualized oral history of their ancestors' rise and fall.

Vonnie had heard it before. When she originally discovered the written legends of the empire, the tale had enchanted her. Now she wondered how much of it was accurate.

Lies within lies, she thought. *Can I trust them any more than Dawson or Ribeiro?*

20.

Vonnie led her mecha after the band scampering into the darkness. Small and agile, they weaved through the ice. Vonnie ducked a low spot. She jumped over a crevice.

The sunfish accelerated when they reached an open pocket. Then they swerved into a zigzagging maze of holes, where the males doubled back on her. Vonnie didn't waver. She barreled on, making them avoid her. The males sprang off the walls and ceiling, howling at the doppelgängers.

The tunnels in Zone One were well-traveled, but the males insisted on scouring for spoor. They were like demented puppies. They screamed at every scent. They dug at every crack. Hoping to draw them off, Vonnie sent two of her doppelgängers behind her. She needed to think. The frenetic males were too much to handle.

Her doppelgängers led them away. When she glanced back, they were snuffling at a dirty patch of ice where a GP's hydraulics had leaked. Then they were out of sight.

Vonnie pursued the four matriarchs, emerging from the maze of holes into a wider space.

—*Close! We are close!* they cried.

Her sonar detected other sunfish screaming far below. She saw a steel bulkhead reinforcing the ice. It was labeled **ZONE ONE Section 19.** Suddenly she passed a bundle of cables leading through a smooth, man-made shaft. She was almost in Zone Two.

Her helmet crackled. "Radio check," Koebsch said. "All signals clear."

"Yes, sir."

"I'm reading a localized malfunction in your left glove. There's a dead spot from the wrist down. The sunfish must have damaged the circuitry."

"Yes, sir." Every segment of her scout suit reported to their grid.

"Vonnie, does your glove work?"

"Yes." Her mind felt as honed as her sword. *They called me a rogue,* she thought. *I thought they were urging the males to stay loyal to them by pointing out my shortcomings. Did they hear my reservations when I spoke with O'Neal and Koebsch? I'm a liar, too, and for what? Small lies for the greater good. That's what I tell myself. It doesn't feel right.*

The tribe is planning something... but if they aren't preparing an assault, what are they doing? There's nothing east or south. The Americans and the PSSC are eighty klicks away. Could they know we're at odds with the PSSC? They've intuited so much about us. What if they send males to the PSSC camp to raid for metal and food?

She rapped her knuckles on her helmet, chastising herself. *Don't give them any ideas! If they aren't going to attack, you can't suggest it. They're so quick to make connections. Quit thinking about the PSSC.*

Ahead of her, the matriarchs hurtled off a cliff into a black, cluttered maw. The chasm dropped forty meters.

They exulted in their freefall. Shrieking, they sounded out the chasm's sides and the piles of debris at the bottom. Vonnie jumped after them. The matriarchs landed first. They rolled lightly on the debris. Her doppelgängers thumped down, then Vonnie. Her burrowers came last.

The matriarchs went into a low tunnel camouflaged by the piles of ice. The tunnel was short. Its ceiling and floor were marred by gaps and stumps where material had been removed or stacked. It was an air lock, a native lock, not a man-made seal.

—*Join us! Join us!* they cried.

They encouraged Vonnie and her mecha to squeeze into a bunch. They dropped more ice behind her, gluing new blocks in place with saliva and urine. Waiting in the jammed space was torture. She felt like she was suffocating. She hummed a bit of Beethoven.

They opened the lock.

Thinner, colder air cascaded over her as she knocked her mecha aside. The sunfish chirped at her casual violence. They treated their males in the same fashion. What piqued their curiosity was the panic in her body language. A fear of tight spaces was aberrant to them.

In front of Vonnie was another cavern. She said, "I've exited Zone Two. This isn't an air lock we've used before."

"Roger that. I'm watching your radar and your cams. The doppelgängers are patrolling above you, and we have other mecha nearby."

"Thank you, Koebsch."

"You're... welcome." He was taken aback. She'd tried to put as much tenderness as possible into her voice.

Will you forgive me? she thought. She felt awful for deceiving him. She'd told Koebsch she wanted to chat with the eldest matriarchs, but she was looking for someone else, a friend she'd known longer than any sunfish.

The matriarchs had probably sensed her ulterior motive. If they tried to delay her again, she would bribe them, which was why she'd stashed meat and juice in her chest kits.

As they led her into another tunnel, Vonnie laughed to distract herself from her claustrophobia. Sunfish loved orange juice like she loved chocolate. Last month on Earth, an American juice company had hyped this revelation with an ad featuring a virtual sunfish cavorting with human children after they'd shared a refreshing snack on a sunny playground.

Retail sales in grocery stores had tanked while bulk sales to restaurants, bars and sports venues went through the roof. The drink traditionally known as a corkscrew became a worldwide fad when it was renamed a "sunfish" or a "fish me" after a Swedish pop star was recorded drunkenly hollering *fish me* with her blouse open at the bar of a New York City club. Among twenty- to thirty-year-olds, orange juice and vodka was the "in" thing for two weeks after the juice company pulled its ads. Comedians and market experts ridiculed them on the net, fueling the drink's popularity, and Vonnie wondered again if the tribes could accurately comprehend *homo sapiens.*

So much of what people did was frivolous, trendy, sarcastic or cruel. The sunfish were merciless but they never mocked each other or wasted resources or splurged. Of course they had no sense of humor. Vonnie wished they could laugh. Sunfish displays of affection were also sorely lacking in comparison to the intimacies of human beings.

Ben will support what I'm doing, she thought. *Peter won't. He can't.*

The tunnel ended in a rift. Beyond it, the ice had fallen in blocks with only the thinnest dust-filled cracks available to enter or climb.

—*Here? Here?* the matriarchs cried. They bared their undersides and screeched.

Vonnie shuddered at the idea of threading herself into the stacked blocks. *I'll get stuck.* Then she realized they didn't want to go farther. Other sonar calls wafted from the ice. A new band of sunfish was approaching.

Her AIs identified the voices. The oncoming group was also a foursome, although it included two of their intelligent males, Tom, the seven-armed scout, and Hans, an older, less active companion to the matriarchs who was likely in his final months.

O'Neal will want tissue samples, she thought as Hans jostled into view with Angelica, Brigit and Tom. She wished she could offer her condolences, although she was careful to mask her sorrow with upright body language. They didn't understand pity. They regarded it as an insult just as they thought pleading was taunting.

A natural death hit a sunfish like a time bomb. When they experienced renal failure, even if they quit eating since their food chain was contaminated — even if they drank only fresh water — they were paralyzed by the iron and salt concentrated inside their bodies. They lapsed into toxic shock and unconsciousness.

Such deaths were rare. The ESA had recorded only two natural fatalities during all these months of surveillance. More commonly, older sunfish experienced cognitive lapses like senile human beings. They became more aggressive, but they did so with impeded faculties and reflexes. They picked fights. They went hunting alone. They were killed by savage males or were lost in the ice until their starved, frozen corpses were retrieved and added to the tribe's larder.

Vonnie noted that Hans had red blotches on two arms. What did he think about his own mortality? Did he feel rage or regret?

Probably not. His sickness was a badge of honor. He'd served his tribe long and well. Vonnie guessed he was used as a breeding male, so she bowed, taking the dominant position yet inviting Hans and Tom to approach. She lowered herself into a ball and greeted them with an inward motion.

—*We are Ghost Clan Thirty!* she cried.

—*Thirty! We are Thirty!* they screeched.

—*I have come for Brigit and the eldest matriarchs. There are questions I must ask.*

—*Food? Food?* Tom shrieked.

—*Yes. Meat and juice.*

Tom and Hans crawled on her back as Brigit sang. —*Feed the males. Strengthen them,* Brigit cried.

—*Hans is sick?* Vonnie dared to ask.

—*He is wise! We mate with him!*

Vonnie nodded. There was poignant dignity in serving as a breeder. Hans had left his mark on the future of his kind. What more could anybody want?

She'd meant to dole out her treats in small amounts, one bite for one answer. Instead she gave them a feast, opening two packets of chicken and three tubes of juice. The matriarchs allowed Hans and Tom to eat before they swarmed in, tearing at the chicken, slopping juice on each other.

Vonnie's glove found Brigit's topside. Then she activated a program that drew her hand against Brigit in meticulously arranged patterns.

Last night inside Lander 04, under the guise of updating their CEW codes, Vonnie had written these patterns with a temporary AI. She'd deleted the AI after saving its work to a data tab. This morning she'd stored the tab in her hip pack. When the sunfish led her into the catacombs, she'd cut the circuitry in her suit's left arm, removing it from their grid. Next she'd installed the tab in an auxiliary slot for welding or construction routines.

Her glove's movements were based on the matriarchs' fifth language, their private language, and the intricate patterns of her fingers boiled down to one awkward request. —*Tell me to turn off the mecha and my gear block*, she said.

Brigit wrapped two arms around Vonnie's wrist. Her pedicellaria brushed against the plastisteel with a repeating stroke. It meant the same as the ESA's *Say again?*

—Tell me to turn off the mecha and my gear block.

Brigit wrenched herself upward. She snapped at Vonnie's helmet. Without her faceplate, Brigit's beak would have flayed her nose and lips. —*Off! Off!* Brigit shrieked.

Vonnie flinched. Tom and Hans were a sudden enemy. Their arms beat on her suit.

"What's happening!?" Koebsch shouted.

"I'm okay! She's trying to tell me something!"

—*Off! Off!* Brigit shrieked as the females chorused with her. —*Your head makes noise! There are dangers in the ice! New dangers you attract!*

The doppelgängers yanked at them. The combined weight of mecha and sunfish knocked Vonnie down.

"Tell them to let you go!"

"They're not hurting me," she said. "There's something out there. That's why they put their skirmish lines on our border. Koebsch, they want me to shut off our sensors."

"I'm bringing reinforcements."

"Don't. Please. Something's different. Let them tell me what it is. This is their home. Their rules. I'm going to power down the mecha."

"Absolutely not. That's a direct order."

Vonnie sent commands to her doppelgängers and her burrowers. The mecha shut off. Tom whined, pawing at her suit as the matriarchs screeched.

—Your noise? Your noise? they cried.

She prepared to switch off her gear block. "Give me five minutes," she said to Koebsch.

"Vonnie!"

"I'll leave on my transponder so I can signal you in an emergency."

"If they hurt you…"

"That's not what this is about. They want to show us something, but we need to be quiet. No radar. No mecha. I won't know what it is until I see it."

"I have every mecha in Zone Two on alert including a FNEE gun platform. We can reach you in seconds."

"Yes, sir." Vonnie's heart was in her throat. She hoped her deception would be worth what she learned. Could she convince Koebsch to give her more time?

She shut off her primary sensors and data/comm. No one was watching now. She kept her short-range sonar and the program that converted sound waves into a holo display. The sonar also allowed her to speak to the sunfish.

She swept her arms toward her body in a gesture like bringing them to her. —*We are alone,* she cried. —*The mecha cannot see or hear.*

—*Your mate will attack us?* they screeched.

—*He is not my… None of our people or machines will threaten you,* she cried. How had they known she was talking with Koebsch? —*He cares for me. He is troubled.*

—*You asked us for your silence. You arranged this ambush so you could hide from him. Why? Why? Why? Why?*

—*I want to speak with the metal scout we call Lam. My mate cannot know. The two of them would fight.*

—*You deceive your mate? You hurt him?*

She began to deny it, but their interpretation was accurate. The matriarchs schemed against their males every day. Would it increase their affinity for her if she said she'd crossed her 'mate'?

—*Yes!* she cried. —*I'll blame you for my silence and he'll be angry, but we may learn new ways to defend our clan.*

If the matriarchs were capable of smiling, she thought they might have grinned. Their arms darted among themselves as if snatching prey from each other, grabbing at nothing, then raising their empty arms.

—*Defend us!* they screamed. —*We will deal with your males. They know little. We know more.*

—*He'll be angry,* she warned them, but the matriarchs responded with self-assurance and something else she couldn't quite distinguish. Was it conceit?

—*We know more!* they cried.

—*Let's go. Can you find Lam?*

—*No. Yes. Yes. No.*

Their reluctance baffled her. Hadn't they agreed to cooperate? She couldn't afford to waste more time.

—*Take me to him!* she roared.

21.

Among the worst of Vonnie's sins were her roles in the karma of Choh Lam. The AI had been her friend before he died. Long before Ben, long before Koebsch, Lam had been her first nascent romance on Europa. They'd had potential.

Like Ben, Lam was a genius with a rebellious streak, which he covered by publicly supporting the Communist Party of the PSSC. Like Koebsch, Lam was polite.

Unlike Ben or Koebsch, he was unimposing. Vonnie had underestimated him during their weeks aboard the *Marcuse* as they traveled to Jupiter. Lam scrupulously allowed Bauman and Von their privacy. In the past, she'd had crewmates who'd ogled or groped her. Lam was kind. Foolishly, she'd dismissed him as all-brains-no-guts until they landed on the ice.

Then he'd blossomed, dazzling her with his drive and his integrity. Every glimpse inside Lam's genius inspired Vonnie to grow herself. For the sake of Beijing, the man pretended to be a cloudy day, but when he abandoned his masters, he'd shone like a nuclear explosion.

His words had electrified her.

Physically, the two of them shared no more than a hug and several glances. Emotionally, they became soulmates. Vonnie had been with Lam when he was crushed by a rock swell. Then his ghost saved her life. He'd been her only friend in the dark.

After she was rescued, Koebsch chose to erase Lam's fragmented personality. To save him, she'd sent him back into the ice. Now he inhabited one of their doppelgängers.

Lam had helped them develop their treaties with the sunfish, but he was erratic. He was feral. The doppelgänger he'd taken as his body lacked the processing power for human intelligence or human memory. In his last encounter with Von, he'd seemed more like an alien than a man.

He should have been repaired. The lockers inside Module 01 contained enough hardware to augment dozens of mecha like him. They could have performed those upgrades at a negligible cost.

Unfortunately, his existence was classified. Choh Lam had been a Chinese national. If anyone learned that the ESA possessed a Level II intelligence based on his mem files, the PSSC could accuse them of espionage as well as human rights violations.

The highest circles in Berlin considered him a liability. So did most of the ESA crew. Too many lives were at stake to allow an unstable AI to run free.

Months ago, without realizing Lam was more than a sabotage and control program, the FNEF soldiers tried to destroy him with missile fire. More recently, the ESA had swept the ice with slavecasts, hoping to drive him to the surface.

He'd disappeared. She didn't blame him. She would have run, too, and his suffering was her cross to bear.

Vonnie would not have received her letter of commendation if more people were aware of Lam. In this case, she'd benefited from the blind spots in top-down bureaucracy and one hand rarely knowing what the other was doing.

Vonnie, Ash and Tony were the ROM and cybernetics team responsible for killing Lam, but her heart wasn't in it and Tony and Ash had their plates full with other tasks.

They'd deployed new beacons and spies. They'd adjusted their grid from time to time.

The chase had been fruitless.

Tony thought Lam had fled the southern pole. By traveling less than fifty kilometers, Lam could have left behind everything from Earth except a few long-range surface rovers and their spy sats. Lam had no limitations. He didn't eat. He didn't sleep. It was anyone's guess what attachments he felt since his memory banks were shattered and he had none of the physical attractions of a man or a sunfish. By now, he might be anywhere, a wretched phantom who'd forgotten why he existed or what he was looking for.

Vonnie didn't believe it. She thought Lam was in the area, although he might have gone far, far below to escape them. They knew he'd traveled among the Mid Clans.

O'Neal had caught several references to *Metal Scout* in their clan's songs. The sunfish were non-linear in most of their thinking, but O'Neal said they mentioned Lam in the present tense. Vonnie had asked about him repeatedly. The matriarchs always claimed he wasn't near.

—*I see it in your bodies!* she cried. —*You know where to find him! Show me!*

The matriarchs crawled onto each other's topsides, literally obscuring their thoughts. Half of them eclipsed the rest. The others called for the males to shield them.

—*Metal Scout is far away!* they screeched. —*We do not always recognize him. Like you. Sometimes you behave as a matriarch. Sometimes you behave as a male. You deny our consensus.*

—*You are ignorant!* she snarled. —*I am devoted to your safety, and you cannot imagine the dangers beyond your world! Dangers that approach you! Take me or I'll go myself! Do you prefer that I create noise and heat stomping through the ice?*

Their test of wills was at its breaking point.

Beneath the clustered sunfish, Brigit and Angelica rasped at each other. They reached out. Their arms encircled Vonnie's ankles, and, at this key juncture of her body where she bore her weight, they read her seething mood.

—*Come with us,* Brigit sang. —*Come quietly. No mecha. No noise. Our voices must be soft.*

—*Yes!* Vonnie cried. She signaled Koebsch with her transponder as Brigit, Angelica, Hans and Tom separated themselves from the other sunfish. Using a shorthand form of Morse, she sent: **I'm fine. Need 20 min.**

His response was shorter: **No.**

20 min.

Brigit's foursome sprang into the air, sailing toward the gigantic blocks of ice. Vonnie wouldn't fit through the cracks… but the sunfish landed above her.

An opening lay behind a crag of ice. At low power, her sonar had missed it.

Vonnie looked over her shoulder at the other foursome. They had gone toward the air lock. Vonnie walked after Brigit. She climbed.

Koebsch continued to signal through her transponder. **Return to surface. O'Neal says savages on the move.**

Toward me? she asked.

Some, yes. Most leaving colony.

She reached the crag and hauled herself up. Tom and Hans latched onto her arm. They pulled. Vonnie scrabbled up.

—*Softly. Many listen. None must hear,* Brigit cried.

Vonnie set one palm on Bright, one on Tom. The gesture meant acquiescence. It demonstrated the effort she'd made to become their clanmate, and Brigit piped once like Vonnie was a stupid male who'd improved.

Vonnie smiled. Their praise was harsh and it didn't come cheap. It meant more to her than a letter from Berlin.

They led her through the opening. She was forced to kneel, then worm after them on her belly. Her sonar was a whisper. The words on her display felt too loud.

ESA/FNEE on full alert, Koebsch signaled. **Return to the surface or we'll send mecha after you.**

Don't. I have the matriarchs' protection.

This wasn't what we agreed.

Please. 20 min.

The passage branched. It widened. Vonnie rose to her feet. She dashed after the sunfish through several turns and two drops, plummeting in elevation. They were moving deeper.

They were heading east.

The catacombs stretched through long funnels and caverns. The sunfish glided through the open gulfs. Somehow she kept up. Her feet were louder than the whisking touches of their arms, but she gave off no scent and she kept her sonar to a minimum. For the most part, her suit was able to use their chirps and the vibrations from her boots and gloves to create her holo display. All she needed were outlines of the ice. Her suit made adjustments for every step.

We're going farther than I thought.

There was no indication that Koebsch had sent mecha in pursuit. They were definitely outside Zone Two. Despite what she'd said, that made her nervous. The ESA hadn't explored the eastern catacombs. The FNEE had sent diggers in this direction, but that had been months ago and their search had been brief. This was a cold zone, a dead zone.

Her display said she'd hiked 2.4 klicks when she heard sonar. Brigit halted their group. The voices were unfamiliar. Her AIs couldn't identify any known individuals.

Overhead, the ice creaked with the sounds of scurrying bodies. *It's a trap,* she thought.

She reached for her sword, but Brigit wrapped an arm around her ankle and rubbed her armor. In the cold, each little scratch sounded like teeth chiseling bone. Vonnie had to guess what Brigit meant. From their alert postures, her sunfish were wary but they didn't expect an ambush.

She left her sword attached to its magnets. On her left, the ice carried another breath of movement. *Krik.* The sound was a creeping premonition.

Vonnie jumped when new words scrolled across her display. **What's happening?** Koebsch asked.

I'm with the sunfish.

What do you see?

Stay off the transponder. Let me concentrate. She began to raise her Lance 515.

Brigit glommed onto Vonnie's wrist. Hans joined them and took Vonnie's other side, hugging her leg. He was guarding her back. Angelica and Tom tasted the air with their arms.

Was it Lam?

Angelica called into the dark, a cry like a lighthouse sweeping through heavy fog. —*Here!* Angelica piped.

Vonnie's sensors tracked the sound as it bounced through the catacombs. Ahead and to her left, the ice formed lopsided pockets. Overhead the ceiling was a drooping mass.

Nothing moved. The mysterious voices weren't repeated.

Maybe the other sunfish are farther than I thought. Those noises might have been the ice settling...

An avalanche of eight-armed bodies crashed over Vonnie. Savage males slammed into her. Twelve. Sixteen. Twenty-eight. Angelica and Tom did nothing to impede the swarm. Hans and Brigit dragged Vonnie to the floor, immobilizing her.

The males scraped their beaks against her helmet. They clawed at her chest.

The horde buried her alive.

22.

Screaming, Vonnie heaved herself upright, thrashing through the savage males. Brigit held onto her wrist. Hans was torn loose by the horde.

Vonnie swung her arm like a bat, slamming Brigit against two males. She cleared the space in front of her.

In that split second as Hans scurried to rejoin them, Vonnie realized the savage males weren't inflicting damage. They just wanted to get past her. They were running from something. Except for the stampede of their bodies, they were silent. Vonnie had been the only one who was screaming.

—*No! Quiet!* Angelica piped.

Vonnie ducked to the floor again. Two stragglers careened overhead. The horde vanished. Their body language had imparted descriptions of pain and death… and predators?

A fleck of ice dropped from the ceiling.

Tracing her fingers on Brigit's topside, Vonnie sketched a wordless apology. *Did I hurt you? What's chasing them?*

Brigit extended her arms to Angelica and Hans, sharing Vonnie's questions. Tom nestled himself into their conversation. All four brushed at Vonnie's armor.

—*Do not provoke him*, Angelica whispered.

Who? Vonnie signaled. *Where?*

Angelica twisted herself away from Vonnie. She pointed east with two arms. The other sunfish wanted to leap and fight. Instead, they held themselves in check, shivering, as if tied by invisible ropes. Their postures were contentious and hostile and saturated with respect.

"Oh," Vonnie said when she saw what had prowled out of the fractures overhead.

A sunfish with a mutilated arm clung to the ice. The base of his limb was encrusted with scabs, and sprouting from the puffy, mangled skin was an arm fashioned out of alumalloy. The metal arm resembled an artificial skeleton, although sunfish did not have bones. They had no solid parts like this metal arm, which marked Lam as an imposter. He was a doppelgänger revealed.

He was bathed in gore and moisture. Behind him, he dragged two half-dead males. One of them mewled. The other was unconscious.

—Lam? she cried. *—It's me.*

He lifted two arms like a sunfish scenting the air. Then he cinched himself around the unconscious male. The cartilage encasing the male's brain popped. In the pregnant quiet, every crackle was a thunderclap. He'd killed the male.

Tom and Hans quivered, wanting to strike. Brigit and Angelica stroked their topsides. The matriarchs urged composure. They stroked Vonnie's legs, too.

She swallowed hard. She could only think of one reason why Lam would hunt rogues and savages. He didn't eat. He had no territorial needs except to hide from slavecasts or mecha… but the last time they met, he'd assisted the matriarchs in butchering the tribe's weakest members.

How far had he drifted into madness?

—It's me, she tried again.

Lam speared his arm tips into the corpse. He sorted through its flesh, but he didn't bring the gore to his beak. He flicked it away.

Drawn by the smell, Tom and Hans bucked with hunger. So did the wounded male behind Lam. Vonnie thought even Angelica was seduced by the scent of blood. The four sunfish at her feet rippled among themselves, tugging on each other, signaling against her legs.

All of them wanted to feed. Brigit demanded that they suppress their cravings.

Vonnie's impulse was to retreat. Her hands ached for her laser or her blade.

Unlike a real sunfish, Lam was powerful enough to bash through her faceplate.

He yanked an arm from inside the corpse. The same arm clenched into a knot. It unfolded and he squashed its messy underside against his body, washboarding it against his spikes, adding to his icy sheath of gore.

—*What are you doing?* she cried.

When he answered, at last, his voice was lucid. —*I couldn't save him. His lungs were scorched. I thought we could find liquid water. His gills were okay, but he asphyxiated before we could reach the nearest streams.*

—*You killed him.*

—*He asked me to.*

—*Why? Why? Why? Why?* Brigit and Angelica screeched.

—*He was suffering and his blood left the spoor behind us. Better to end it here. Let him die. Feed you. I'll lay a false trail if I can.*

—*What are you running from?* Vonnie cried.

The matriarchs responded for him. —*Predators! The ice has dangers you haven't met. We told you! We told you!*

—*Lam?* she asked.

He threw down the corpse. Tom, Hans, Brigit and Angelica pounced. So did the wounded male. Brigit and Angelica gorged on the corpse's arms, making room for Tom, Hans and the other male to feast on its innards.

—*We need your help,* Vonnie sang, but Lam countered her plea with an accusation.

—*You're here to capture me.*

—*No. I swear it.*

—*You've deployed slavecasts and HKs.*

—*Berlin will never trust you. I do. That's why I came. Ask the matriarchs.*

—*I can read you myself.*

—*Then you know I'm your friend.*

—*You stink of fear.*

He couldn't possibly smell her. She was sealed inside her suit, yet he spoke like a sunfish, using their verbs and imagery.

—*You frightened me,* she admitted. —*You ripped him apart. Of course I'm scared.*

—*Your sensors are off.*

—*Yes.*

—*Mine too. No radar. No data/comm. Short-range sonar. That's what I told them. Stay quiet.* Six of his arms fanned the air as if gauging how long the sunfish needed to finish eating… or was he listening to the ice?

—*There are more females near the surface than usual,* Vonnie cried. —*The rest have gathered to defend their hatcheries. They put skirmish lines of males on our colony's east side, this side. Those males are close. They're above and behind us.*

—*I know where they are,* Lam sang. —*I sent my refugees through the lowest catacombs to elude them.*

—*Why?*

—*Look at the wounded male with Tom and Hans.*

Vonnie ran her glove over the bloody male. —*He has bruising and lacerations. The cuts aren't consistent with beaks or rock weapons. There's also a superficial wound where something was dug out of his skin.*

—*Nanotags,* Lam sang. —*I extracted the same tech from the dead male and most of the refugees before they ran too far ahead.*

That was why he'd clenched his arm before smearing the bloody mess against his topside. He'd pulverized the nanotags, which only functioned as transmitters in groups. Destroy the group, destroy its function.

Vonnie sagged in relief. Lam was protecting the sunfish! But her joy was short-lived. Nanotags meant they'd battled the Americans or the PSSC.

NASA's camp was nearest to the ESA/FNEE and even their operations were forty kilometers away. Forty klicks was a long distance for American GPs to pursue an elusive band of males. American GPs were barely on par with the ESA's best, whereas Chinese mecha were top-of-the-line war machines. If anyone could patrol such an immense region of the ice, it was the PSSC… and according to O'Neal, the Americans were unlikely to have encountered sunfish in their zone.

Vonnie didn't believe the Americans would send their mecha without warning. Only the Chinese had the brawn and the audacity to go where they pleased.

—*Why are you fighting the PSSC?* she cried.

—*Not fighting, fleeing,* Lam sang. —*They've had enough of our looting and ambushes. They've learned they can't chase us off. We come back. Now they're exterminating all native life.*

She noticed he'd said '*us*' and '*we*.' Did he actually think of himself as a sunfish?

—*They sent three platoons to kill us,* he sang.

Three platoons was thirty mecha. —*How close are they behind you?* she cried.

—*Fifteen kilometers. We damaged four units and trapped a fifth. Then we brought down the ice and left eight males to fight.*

—*Your refugees are inside our lines. They'll be safe.*

—*That isn't true. Most of them belonged to a rogue pack before the PSSC offensive. The rest are all that's left of four Top Clans. That's why I herded them into the lowest sections of the catacombs. We needed to elude your males. They wouldn't have survived another fight.*

—*Then where are they going?*

—*Anywhere they can.*

Her anger and her doubt intensified into a new, brighter wrath. —*You used us as a shield? What if the PSSC invade our colony next!?*

—*And start a war? They won't risk it.*

—*If they think we're harboring combatants…*

The matriarchs turned their attention from the last of the meat. Brigit piped at Vonnie and she caught herself, trying to bring her emotions under control. —*You've sent refugees in our direction before, haven't you?* she cried at Lam. —*That's why our colony has been on edge.*

—*Yes.*

—*The last time I saw you, you advocated the slaughter of dozens of males. Why save them now?*

—*Those executions were necessary for the formation of your clan. An empire-class population cannot include so many savage males. This is a different scenario. There are no longer any tribes beneath the PSSC site.*

The tough, adaptable nature of the sunfish made it hard for her to accept their total defeat. The catacombs were so vast. There were too many places to regroup.

—*That's impossible!* she cried.

—*It's already happened. I've met hundreds of refugees who witnessed the elimination of their kin. Von, I fought the PSSC mecha myself.*

—*They don't have the firepower to kill everything in a warm zone. No one does. Why would they even try?*

—*The PSSC have traveled 5.8 kilometers down through a series of catacombs and hot springs. The tribes sabotaged their efforts until the PSSC decided to clear the area. It was touch-and-go at first, but their mecha wore down the tribes. They destroyed bacterial mats, reservoirs, air locks. In places, they used bombs. Some of the quakes your crew registered were caused by those detonations.*

"Oh God," she said.

The sunfish were connected almost telepathically to their world like the neurons of a single brain. Scouts carried impressions through the dead zones, and they felt every shudder in the ice.

Had the violence of PSSC emboldened the tribes beneath the ESA/FNEE to seek their union with humankind? She knew they yearned for power. So did people.

She'd thought their treaties were founded on symbiosis, not a sour thing like fear.

—*I don't want to believe you,* she confessed. She knelt and set her hand among the closely knit sunfish. —*Brigit? What have you heard?*

—*Trembling and quakes! Stray packs in the ice!*

—*Attack? Attack?* Tom and Hans screeched.

—*Predators with human eyes follow the strays,* Brigit sang. —*They taste our heat. They pace and hunt.*

—*You're safe inside our territory. Their machines won't challenge ours,* Vonnie cried, but the sunfish lashed in disbelief. They described the known coordinates of PSSC mecha. They writhed with bloodlust.

—*Hundreds are dead,* Lam sang. —*Thousands more fled downward where they'll meet other refugees or the Mid Clans. The females will find new homes. Only a few dozen males ran in your direction because they'll die if they're intercepted by your warriors. Ghost Clan Thirty is too strong.*

—They're safe with us. Tell them! We've had our own losses. Our clan needs hunters and scouts.

—These males are hurt. Your males would kill them.

—They are stinking and weak! Brigit cried.

—In time, they'll heal, Lam sang. *—They'll be more acceptable once they regain their strength. I can find them. Then you can introduce them to your tribe.*

Vonnie nodded, but Brigit and Angelica bristled at Lam's suggestion. They wanted to punish him.

Playing on her role as *Young Matriarch*, Vonnie gestured for Lam to approach them. He was more than savvy enough to act like a male. He obeyed Vonnie, leaping past her.

He submitted to Angelica and Brigit. They were rough with him yet welcomed the gore caked on his topside. His artificial form blended among the real sunfish as they cleaned him of blood and moisture.

They ate, and Vonnie sang.

—Lam serves us. He is better than any scout. We need his strength and his eyes, she called to the matriarchs.

Brigit squeezed his body. Her grip would have been painful for a living male. Lam bore it without feigning discomfort. *—He is not a sunfish!* Angelica hissed. *—He resists us! He resists you!*

They coveted his might, but in their judgment he was a traitor and Vonnie hadn't resolve her own suspicions. Even as she defended him, the matriarchs perceived her lack of faith.

—He is like Biting Female, she cried. *—His independence is his worthiest trait.*

Angelica screeched to Hans and Tom. They wrapped themselves around Lam, adding their arms to hers. Hans was a vice. Tom was a sanding belt. They taxed Lam's durability. His skin peeled. Synthetic blood welled up.

Vonnie couldn't stop herself. She knocked Tom aside. *—What are you doing?* she screamed.

—He will never die, Angelica hissed.

—You're damaging him!

—He cannot breed. He does not sleep. He follows voices we cannot hear.

—He is a new species, a living connection between us. He is human and sunfish. My friend. Your scout. He is unique but he has always served our clan.

—His mind is stranger than his insides, Brigit sang, prying at Lam's metal arm.

ESA biologists and military advisors had refused to equip the doppelgängers with nanotech like the med systems in Vonnie's suit. The biologists wanted to avoid contaminating native lifeforms while the military cited a more strategic concern… that the doppelgängers might transfer the capacity to heal major wounds to the sunfish… so Lam's trauma systems had been restricted to med beetles, which could seal his injuries but not reconstruct tissue and nerves.

Would the matriarchs have been more likely to assimilate him if his metal frame was concealed? Or was it his behavior that doomed him? They treated the other doppelgängers as exceptional workers, but the other doppelgängers were subservient. Lam was an individual, a *rogue* by definition.

Maybe his prospects would improve if he stripped off his false skin. The matriarchs expected the ESA/FNEE mecha to contradict them. It was because Lam resembled a male that they wanted him to act like one, but he dictated terms to the matriarchs, speaking as more than their equal.

He spoke as their superior. He ranged in and out of their territory at will. He dealt with enemy mecha and enemy tribes, defeating some, saving others.

He was too much for the matriarchs to integrate.

That they'd always lived for the short term could not obscure their most hidebound tradition: Females rule.

Vonnie was done bickering with them. Was he less trustworthy than Ash or the FNEE soldiers? *—You're no better than savages! You are selfish and deaf!* she cried.

—He undermines the clan!

—Lam did not cause this upheaval. It will find us even if we hide. He will help us if you permit it.

—He cannot lead.

—I lead! He collaborates with me!

—*His voice is solitary. We banished him many sleeps ago,* Brigit cried, lunging. Her beak clacked on Lam's metal arm. Vonnie shoved Brigit away and Tom snapped at Vonnie's glove, twisting her fingers.

They despise him, she realized. Of course the sunfish sensed her thoughts.

—*We would kill him if we could!* Brigit screamed.

23.

—*Stop!* Vonnie roared. —*He belongs to me!*

—*Attack!* Hans screamed.

—*Consider him one of my mates. He holds a special place among my kind. His life is more valuable than yours,* Vonnie cried, accepting that they would parse some of the falsehoods in her words. She wanted to confuse the matriarchs. She needed them to back down.

Brigit's arms heaved as she bustled in complex patterns among Angelica, Tom and Hans. But they did not attack.

They yielded to Vonnie.

—*I will send our mecha into the ice,* Vonnie cried. —*You will reinforce your home. When I bring refugees, you will adopt and feed them. We need more warriors.*

—*Yes.*

—*You will accept Lam. He is not a savage male. He is like me when I wear my suit.*

—*No. No. No. No.*

Vonnie pursed her lips in a thin smile. The matriarchs had grown but they would never be pushovers. —*If there is war, it will exceed anything your race has known. We will survive only by our unity, not your intolerance.*

—*No.*

—*Yes! Tell every matriarch. Go. Lam will scout the dead zone. I'll organize our defenses.*

—*Yes.* Brigit's assent was grudging.

The others rubbed against Vonnie's legs or piped at Lam. Hans and Tom prodded him briefly. Their physical contact meant *hello*, not *farewell.* For now, at least, they had obeyed Vonnie's command to regard him as an ally.

Then the sunfish hurried west. As her mother would have said, they were on pins and needles. They worried that the refugees had penetrated their air lock into Zone Two, although there had been no din of combat. Lam had wisely steered the horde away from entering clan territory.

Vonnie spoke in English with her speakers at a murmur. "I'm sorry," she told him.

—*I'm not.*

"You shouldn't be down here on your own. Eventually I planned to bring you back to camp. Then everything went wrong. I never meant to torture you."

—*This isn't torture. It's exhilarating.*

The real Lam had been willing to forsake family and country in order to walk on Europa. Now he'd become a part of this world, and she recalled how she'd summarized his metamorphosis to Brigit. '*He is a new species, human and sunfish. My friend. Your scout. He has always served our clan.*' How perfect if it was true.

"Are you sure?" she asked.

He formed body shapes that warned there were instabilities in the ice, then shapes that meant the ice was solid. —*Should I be unsure?* he cried. —*I've streamlined millions of errors in my core. Some of my memory is gone. All of my processors are back online. I know you. We were friends.*

"Lam, we were almost lovers."

—*I don't remember.*

"I meant everything I said to Brigit."

—*So did I. I'm certain I've taken the best actions for the sunfish. Some choices were easy. Some were difficult. There's been so much death.*

Standing with him on the blemished ice, Vonnie winced. Their past would always be tainted by blood.

Guilt and shame were lodged inside her fondness for him. That wasn't a healthy relationship. On a lesser scale, the same emotions had corroded her ties to her oldest brother, Andreas, who'd dominated her with his size and weight. In their teens, Andreas had conducted what she saw in retrospect as a low-level terror campaign by marching his friends through the house in callous groups. They'd harassed her with dirty jokes and leers and not-so-gentle wrestling.

Boys will be boys, her father had said.

Her father tacitly approved of their manly behavior and thereby spurred his only daughter to dress modestly, keep quiet, stay in her room, and turn to computers instead of boys for companionship.

Twenty years later, look at her: an elite engineer who felt as committed to an alien species as to her own kind. Some people called her a traitor. They said she was misguided, an idealist, a fool, a slut, any belittling name they could use to demean her or impede the mission.

It pissed her off. If anything, they'd propelled her farther from acquiescing to their demands. She felt more driven, not less… but in this case, she was the monster. She'd created Lam. She couldn't bear to act like her brother, blame the victim and refuse all culpability.

"I am sorry," she said. "I thought I was doing the right thing for you."

—My prompt codes confirm.

"What?"

—Some of my memory is gone, but I reduced the key personal data to prompt codes. My colleagues. My origins. What happened to Bauman and myself.

"But if…" She nearly didn't say it. "If you know you're Chinese, why are you helping the sunfish?"

—I am not Choh Lam. I am Metal Scout.

He'd erased parts of his mind to bring peace to himself. His transformation broke her heart, and she disguised her misery by cheering for him. "We need you. It may be years before the tribes accept how small they are in comparison to the outside world. You can coach them."

—I want to be your friend again.

"Me, too."

—Stop hunting me. I can be useful like you said.

"Koebsch is under orders."

—I can demonstrate that I'm on your side. I have intel. Let me show you.

Caution sprang through her like a dagger of ice. "Intel is good. You've been near the PSSC site?"

—Let me show you.

I can't do that, she thought. She wanted his sims, but she couldn't let him upload directly to her suit. The last time he'd had full access, he'd compromised her systems.

There was an alternative. She unspooled a cord from her waist kit and jacked it into her side. She could secure his files in a mem bank, then bring it unopened to camp. "Here's a hard line," she said.

—Roger that.

He didn't question her mistrust. He plugged the cord into a jack obscured by his gills, binding them together.

She gazed at him as they waited in the dark. *His life has been harder than mine,* she thought. *He's stronger than I am. Would anyone else feel content, much less happiness if they were turned into an AI inside a doppelgänger? Would I?*

Berlin couldn't afford to provoke the PSSC, but she wondered if Lam wanted his family to learn what he'd become. How could she tell them that his essence had survived?

—Transfer complete. Disconnecting.

He pulled his jack and Vonnie tucked the cord into her kit. "Thank you," she said.

—Tell Koebsch. Stop hunting me.

"I will. Stay away from our skirmish lines. Listen for PSSC mecha. I'll radio you as soon as I can."

—What about Koebsch?

"If your sims are as valuable as I think, he'll ask for new orders from Earth. We'll bring you in."

—No tricks.

"I swear it."

He rapped twice on Vonnie's boot. Then he sprang away from her, catapulting off the wall. He vanished into the ice.

Vonnie had gained more than she'd anticipated, although it seemed like she went one step back for every two steps forward. When she was in her twenties, her career path had been a straight line. Now everything was crooked angles and misfires. The floor kept falling out beneath her.

She needed to mend her rapport with the matriarchs. She needed to apologize to Koebsch.

She signaled with her transponder: **Returning to camp.**

You've been stationary for 13 minutes, Koebsch replied. **In two more, our mecha were going to advance.**

Keep them where they are. I'm coming back. This is a sensitive zone and I've made an incredible discovery. Don't rile the sunfish.

Like her, his head must have been whirling. **What discovery?** he asked.

Meet me in Zone Two.

Are you hurt?

I'm fine. Let me hike.

Vonnie peered into the catacombs, but she couldn't see Lam without her radar. She rapped on the brittle floor as he had done to her boot. *Tok tok.*

Closer than expected, the sound was mimicked by an unseen presence. *Tok tok.*

She smiled. There was a childish pleasure in trading knocks like goodbye. "I'll see you soon," she said, uncertain if her speakers' low volume would carry her voice to him.

His raps were an oath of loyalty. He'd positioned himself between Ghost Clan Thirty and the PSSC, although one doppelgänger couldn't stand against three platoons of war mecha. Neither could the sunfish.

If they attack our colony, the most we'll do is slow them down. Her smile vanished, but the good feelings of friendship and defiance remained.

Vonnie and Lam were a team again.

24.

Koebsch and Ben met Von in the cargo tent above Submodule 07. Wearing pressure suits, they caught her shoulders as she lurched out of the tube.

Koebsch didn't speak. He shut the hatch and held onto her side, looking her up and down.

"Are you all right?" Ben asked.

"I am, but I have new information and most of it is bad news. Let's get inside."

From his expression, Vonnie could see Ben was upset with her even though he adored her independence. Koebsch was petrified. She'd rarely seen him at a loss for words. Koebsch knew how to manage any situation... but when he motioned for her to walk ahead, his glove was unsteady.

"We thought we'd lost you," Ben said.

"I'm sorry." Yesterday had been her day for arguing. Today was a day for apologies. That didn't change how urgently they needed to deal with the PSSC.

They walked through the tent's decon units, then into Module 06's air lock.

As soon as the lock equalized, Vonnie opened the inner hatch. She hurried into the ready room, where she approached the assists that would remove her scout suit. Koebsch and Ben stripped off their pressure suits. Both men wore jumpsuits underneath. Vonnie wore nothing except a bra after the assists detached her chest piece.

"See me in data/comm before you do anything else," Koebsch said.

"Don't shower. Don't eat. See me."

"I—"

He left before the assists removed her pelvic component, then the sections on her thighs. Like always, the ready room was chilly after the confines of her suit. Vonnie hugged herself as the assists pried at her shins and boots.

Ben spoke quietly. "He's under a lot of pressure."

"Who? Koebsch?"

"We had another directive from Earth."

"Since when are you two friends?"

"We're not."

"You're making excuses for him."

"He's running the show. We want him to make good decisions and he's out of wiggle room. You keep putting him in bad situations."

She opened the locker where she'd stored her clothes. "You don't know what I saw in the ice," she said. She felt his gaze on her naked figure until she shucked her jumpsuit up over her ribs. She wiggled her arms into the sleeves and zipped the chest. "Let's go." She walked past him.

"Wait." He kissed her.

She turned her mouth away. Then she reconsidered. She kissed him back. She laughed and said, "I thought we were fighting about something dumb like which one of us is friends with Koebsch."

"You're his friend. Not me. I hate how he looks at you."

"He doesn't..."

"I hate how you look at him. We're a couple, aren't we?"

"Yes."

"Next time let me come with you. We can't count on the sunfish."

"You sound just like him."

"Von, I'm not your boss and I'm not your husband. I'm also not an idiot. Something could have happened to you like O'Neal."

"I didn't want to get anyone else in trouble."

"I like trouble. Trouble is my middle name. I'm in love with you, aren't I?"

She met his eyes. "Yes. And I love you. I do. We can talk about it later. Right now I need to see Ash and Koebsch. Let's get everyone on the group feed."

He kissed her again — possessively — and she put a little fire into it, biting his lip.

They held hands as they strode into the corridor.

She pulled free before they reached data/comm.

Inside, Koebsch stood alone, although he'd filled his display with datastreams and two faces. One was Ash. The other was Colonel Ribeiro. Koebsch said, "If we redistribute our sats, we'll be worse off. We need the Americans to expand our grid."

"You must tell them to join us," Ribeiro said.

"I've already made official and unofficial requests to their commander."

"You must tell them again."

Vonnie felt little except contempt for Ribeiro. He was an arrogant ramrod and she thought he deliberately conducted himself like a cliché because this was the easiest stance for him to take. He repeated himself like a pigheaded bulldozer until Koebsch acquiesced just to move onto the next subject.

Koebsch didn't always do what Ribeiro wanted. He'd learned to sidestep the bulldozer by agreeing to one thing, then announcing a change of plans after the fact.

White lies weren't good for ESA and FNEE relations or for ESA morale. No one wanted to see their boss getting bossed around. Vonnie wished Koebsch would give Ribeiro more flak, although she was cognizant that she'd used the same ploy of saying one thing before doing another.

So had O'Neal. So had the matriarchs. Stubbornness was a trait linked to vision and productivity.

If so, Ribeiro should have been a great leader. He was an ass. His deficiency in protecting Tavares from his men was enough to condemn him. That he'd willingly killed sunfish should reserve him a place in hell.

Vonnie couldn't let him know about Lam. "Sir, I have priority sims from our mecha," she told Koebsch.

Ribeiro looked at her and said, "Ah, Vonderach. My government would very much appreciate for the gorgeous Berliner to denounce the aggression of the PSSC."

The slime ball thinks he's charming. He and Dawson love their fancy talk, she thought. But as she walked to Koebsch's side, she matched Ribeiro's well-mannered grace. "I beg your pardon, Colonel, I've been installing supports in Zone One. I'm not sure what you're talking about."

"The PSSC destroyer left its position above Europa's southern pole," Koebsch said. "It's moving to intercept the inbound FNEE ships."

"They can split up or alter course," she said.

"You are a pilot," Ribeiro said. "You must be aware that Jupiter's rings and moons do not present many safe routes, and China has no cause to blockade our ships. Brazil and China have been close friends to each other."

"The destroyer says otherwise," Koebsch said.

Jesus, we don't have time for this. Maybe that's why the PSSC are doing it. If they shake us up, we're less likely to respond well to their mecha beneath the ice. "What does NASA think?" she asked.

Ben said, "They're with us, but they're not soldiers, either."

"Everyone's scrambling for the correct response," Koebsch added, and Vonnie frowned. Ben had denied that they were becoming friends. Yet more and more, Ben and Koebsch seemed to be on the same page.

"We must have access to the American grid," Ribeiro said. "Contact me as soon as they grant permission."

"Roger that," Koebsch said.

Ribeiro signed off of the group feed.

"Every time I listen to that guy, I want to stab him," Vonnie said. Ash smirked, but, uncharacteristically, Ben didn't participate in the fun.

"Don't laugh," he said. "We're going to need Ribeiro if this turns hot."

"I can't believe the PSSC want a fight."

"It won't be much of a fight if they blockade the new FNEE ships," Ash said. "Their destroyer can handle everything we've got, and the *Jyväskylä* won't arrive for another week. Even at close range, I don't think the *Jyväskylä* can protect us."

Koebsch said, "You know which destroyer they sent, don't you? It's the *Dongfangzhixing*, 'the Eastern Star.'" His voice was rocky.

Infamous for pounding the U.S. and Japan, the crew of the

Dongfangzhixing were purported to have been in space without leave since the One Day War. They were more than veterans, more than war criminals. They were fanatics.

Without thinking, Vonnie laid her hand on Koebsch's shoulder. Then she realized what she'd done and extended her other hand to Ben, drawing him close.

Ben hesitated but he didn't protest. Awkwardly, they gazed at Koebsch's display.

Five of his datastreams were tactical sims. Tracking billions of objects in real time, each sim was a chaotic three-dimensional field. Most of the dots were gray for natural debris like dust and asteroids. White for moons. Green for ESA, FNEE and NASA. Red for PSSC. They also used yellow for unidentified or suspected devices like sleepers and HKs.

Yellow dots hovered around Europa in a malevolent cloud, outnumbering the green by 1.7-to-one. Adding the red, that ratio increased to 2.3-to-one.

The *Jyväskylä* was the EUSD missile platform sweeping into orbit behind Jupiter. The new FNEE ships were six days ahead of it, although their arrival was questionable now as they veered away from the *Dongfangzhixing*.

Vonnie cleared her throat. "What are our directives from Berlin?" she asked Koebsch.

"They told us to hunker down. We want the eyes of the world on us and we want to show we can inflict a fair amount of pain ourselves. We've suspended deuterium production. Our tankers are on standby. They're programmed with collision courses and I instructed the *Clermont* to open its launchers."

"Jesus Christ."

"I don't expect our ships to last. The tankers won't reach their targets and the *Clermont* may not get off more than one salvo before it's hit, but we'll go down fighting. Best case scenario, the PSSC won't call our bluff."

"I bet they don't," Ben said. "They can afford a stand-off. Their deuterium production won't stop. Neither will their exploration teams."

"We won't stop, either," Vonnie said.

"Someday we'll run out of food unless we start eating bugs. A blockade could last for years."

Ships had a finite number of openings through Jupiter's rings. The *Dongfangzhixing* couldn't cover every angle of insertion, but it was deploying drones.

They're setting the chess board, she thought. *It's like they're building fences around Europa.*

As she watched, five more red dots appeared on the display, although the new dots were set on top of the *Dongfangzhixing* due to the limitations of scale. Even high-gee drones needed several minutes to meaningfully distance themselves.

From personal experience, Vonnie knew warfare in space wasn't much to look at. Combat amounted to drawn-out stretches of tedium punctuated by sudden death. Naval battles spread over too much distance and time. Missiles could take hours — even days — to reach their targets. Defensive tools like decoys, chaff and mines might drift tens of thousands of kilometers from their sources while ships and HKs jockeyed for position.

"It gets worse," she said. "The PSSC are in the ice."

"You saw them?" Koebsch asked.

"No. Lam has sims of their mecha."

Koebsch opened his mouth but seemed at a loss. "You met with Lam?"

"Yes."

"I can't allow more unilateral actions," he said. "I need my crew in sync, no matter what. Our best defense may be a preemptive strike. If I order an assault on the PSSC camp, will you comply? Otherwise we're better off without you."

"Peter, I'd do anything to save lives. That doesn't include leading a sneak attack."

"Henri and I can lead an offensive," Ash said. "If we need more people, ask Ribeiro. Most of his guys have seen action in Colombia or the Korean peninsula."

Koebsch said, "That doesn't solve the issue. I can't keep looking over my shoulder to see if Von is with us or against us. Nobody gets to choose which orders to follow."

"Let's talk about what I found."

"I am so frustrated with you."

"Don't be." She tapped an empty window on his display, keying the data from her suit. "Our AIs have q-and-e'd my files." Quarantined and evaluated. "Lam saved a number of tribes from PSSC mecha. They wiped out the sunfish in their territory. I don't think it's a coincidence that chasing the sunfish means they have thirty war machines on our borders."

Koebsch forgot his voice again as he studied Lam's sims. "They've got us in a pincher, above and below," he said haltingly. Then he looked at Ash, making his admission to her rather than Vonnie or Ben. "I don't know what to do."

"We're outgunned, sir," Ash agreed.

"We'll move ten of our GPs and Ribeiro's gun platforms to the outskirts of Zone Two." He was regaining his voice, and, with it, his decisiveness. "Ash, put excavation charges on each unit. I'll talk to Ribeiro about his pony bombs."

"You can't!" Vonnie said.

"Where is your diagnostic of Lam? Is he reliable? Our last encounter was… None of us liked it."

Vonnie wondered how Koebsch had been about to describe that massacre. *Frightening?* "There is no diagnostic," she said. "I couldn't risk any broadcasts. I hard lined his files into a secure bank."

"You don't trust him."

"Mostly I do. He doesn't want to die, and he doesn't want to be alone. He knows we've been hunting him. So have the sunfish. Lam is nominally male, but he's no good as a breeder and he's too powerful for a rogue. The matriarchs would prefer to kill him. He needs us to mediate."

"Sir," Ash said, "maybe we can trade him to the PSSC."

Vonnie glared at her. *You bitch,* she thought, but Koebsch said, "If it'll save lives, that's a possibility. We'd have to scrub his memory."

"Lam is helping us!"

"We need a bargaining chip. Find him."

25.

Everybody in the ESA crew transferred to Module 01 or Landers 04 and 05. Module 01 housed their primary data/comm and their armory, and Koebsch wanted them ready to move, which is why he put most of his people in their flight craft.

Huddling with Koebsch inside 01, Tony and Ash marched ten ESA mecha down through the ice. From inside the FNEE hab module, Lieutenant Pereira directed two of his gun platforms.

Ben and Tavares had splashed each unit with lab-grown pheromones. They hoped the smell would ensure safe passage through the savage males, and they transmitted recognition codes to advise Lam of their approach. If he responded, they would ensnare him.

Lam was silent.

"Where is he?" Ash said, but Vonnie shrugged. They had her maps. She'd told them everything she'd seen, but she wasn't exactly champing at the bit and Koebsch hadn't included her in his search team. He'd assigned her other responsibilities.

From inside Lander 04, Vonnie used a doppelgänger to communicate with the matriarchs. She warned them to keep their males in check even if they heard rogue sunfish or mecha. They couldn't afford to engage the PSSC by accident. The catacombs offered very short distances for projectile weapons. Any combat would be close combat. The PSSC would overrun them unless their defensive positions were flawless.

Vonnie skipped lunch. Riveted by her display, she didn't notice Harmeet until the older woman touched her arm. "Don't sneak up on me like that!"

"You should eat." Harmeet held a packet of chicken soup.

"I didn't mean to snap."

"It's okay. Eat."

Vonnie barely tasted the soup. Fretting over her sims, she tried to arrange her sentries where they could guard a three-dimensional section of the catacombs more than five klicks wide, five clicks high and a klick deep.

She only had ten mecha. Koebsch, Henri and their AIs worked with her. They gamed a thousand possibilities. Few were viable. In most of their simulations, the PSSC outflanked their mecha and trampled the sunfish. Then the PSSC broke through the caverns beneath the ESA/FNEE camp.

"I see two options," she said. "Either we back up almost all the way to Zone One or we send more mecha into the ice, but then we won't have any units on the surface."

"We can load the ice with explosives," Henri said. "We'll turn it into a minefield."

"They'll jam our command-and-control. If we lose our feeds, we can't detonate unless somebody sits out there with her hand on the trigger."

"We'll set magnetics. The mines won't go off unless their mecha get close."

"What about Lam?"

"If he answers, we'll tell him to stay clear. If he doesn't, well, maybe the PSSC got him."

"That's incredibly selfish."

"Von, even you don't think he's sane."

"Not all of the PSSC units are ferrous metal. They use ceramics like we do. I don't like it. There are too many ways to outsmart a mine."

"It's our best shot," Koebsch said. "Do it."

Despite her reservations, Vonnie obeyed. The soup gurgled in her stomach as she and Henri sent their mecha to place dozens of excavation charges with crude magnetic sensors — intentionally crude — because simple devices were unlikely to be hacked by SCPs.

Fortunately, the charges stank of the lab-grown pheromones they'd splashed on their mecha.

Lam would smell it, wouldn't he?

That night, despite feeling frazzled, Vonnie was required to attend a virtual ceremony with Koebsch, Ben and Ash. They gathered in Module 01 wearing fresh jumpsuits. The men had shaved. The women applied lipstick.

Materializing as rigorously scripted proxies in immaculate suits or uniforms, a rotation of bigwigs and officials lauded them for rescuing O'Neal. Vonnie was awarded the Union Cross for valor. So were Ben and Ash.

Next the media personalities had their turn. Few wanted details about saving O'Neal, which was old news. Most asked about the ESA's capacity for war.

Oddly, Brazil had yet to publicly complain about the interdiction of their ships. Berlin and Washington were trumpeting in outrage. Governments around the world called for an emergency session of the Allied Nations, although Brazil must have been communicating directly with Beijing.

Vonnie presented herself as a voice of reason. "We're supposed to be the good guys," she said. "We should conduct ourselves as examples to the PSSC."

"What if they fire on the *Jyväskylä* or march into your camp?" asked a proxy.

"They can shoot us, we can shoot them. I suggest we leave each other alone. Europa is a big place. Blasting each other is self-destructive."

Afterward, Vonnie and Ben returned to Lander 04, where Harmeet ate dinner with Henri at the lander's controls. Henri had been ordered to stay in 04 as an assistant pilot. Harmeet was free to move between 04 and 05 depending on available space. Ben asked if she could sleep in 05, which would allow him some privacy with Von. Harmeet said, "Of course." Henri said, "I'll take first shift in the pilot's seat."

Vonnie was grateful. She felt like she could sleep for a week. She and Ben ate a light meal as she reviewed their evacuation plans.

Then she and Ben went to bed. Spooning in their bunk, she watched some of the media sims from Earth. He kissed her neck and traced his fingers down her thigh until she said, "Not tonight." She was too wrung out for sex.

Stress had put her in a discouraged mood, which bordered on masochistic.

She'd tried to sound sensible, but the stance she'd taken wasn't winning many hearts and minds. The most popular twits on the net either excused what they saw as pacifism or they cited her as proof of everything rotten in Western civilization.

Energy prices were spiking in the financial markets. Worse, the A.N. had drafted a swift resolution — more like a plea — to protect their deuterium production and shipping lanes. The wording of the resolution implied that Washington and Berlin were willing to remove their human crews from Europa to prevent hostilities.

What would happen to the tribes?

"I can see why she doesn't want to fight. The ESA is no substitute for a military presence," said an apologist in Romania while a sneering hawk from Ireland explained, "Vonderach exemplifies the moral appeasement of our welfare culture. Too many of us feel entitled to subsidized medicine, subsidized education and subsidized housing. Austerity is the answer, not politicians who'll say anything to stay in power. We've raised millions of coddled fools who vote the same liars into office because the socialist bureaucracy promises free money with deflation and taxes. It's unsustainable. The time will come to pay our due. When it does, I don't want Vonderach next to me."

Ben said, "Remind me why you're watching this dreck?"

She keyed her display for biographical data. "This prick is one of the top commentators in the U.K. with a six figure income. He failed at two businesses before getting into the media. Now he sits around riling people up and they worship him for it. His show has three million followers."

"Most of 'em are underemployed. Check the demographics. Getting riled up keeps them busy."

"I earned my scholarships in school. I had the fifth best grades in my class and I beat out hundreds of applicants for the engineering program. I don't like high taxes. I didn't even vote for our prime minister. I wanted the other guy."

"Von, it's not personal. His angle is fire and brimstone. You say you don't want to fight, so he says you're a wimp, but his life isn't on the line. He just gets the advertising money for his show. Our system is in awful shape. No one denies that. The problem is nobody knows how to fix something that's so big. Overpopulation soared on cheap energy, cheap medicine, mechanized agriculture and mechanized industry. That's how we got into space. We could finally afford the infrastructure, but there are a lot of people without jobs."

"Energy prices are up."

"Historically, they're at all-time lows. Fusion ruined oil and coal. Cheap power means cheap production. The average joe owns more stuff than ever but unemployment has skyrocketed. The post-war construction boom is over."

"You make it sound bad."

"It's always bad. Bad is a normal state of affairs for humankind. We have the technology to make paradise on Earth. Instead we point fingers, we lie, we steal, we kill for land or God or other ideologies. The independence movements are growing in the U.K., Italy and Belgium. They want out of the Union."

"They'd lose their assets in space."

"They'll sue for a couple orbital stations and two or three ships from the fleet. Careers will be made. The lawyers will lawyer, the politicians will wave their flags, and the locals will feel bigger when Italy and Belgium reinstitute the draft for their national armies and rehire in their factories."

"What about you and me, Ben? Are we that selfish, too?"

He rubbed his palm judiciously on her hip. "You're tired," he said. "I'm not going to answer that one."

"Meaning yes. You're helping me and the sunfish because you weren't happy growing up. You were too fat and too smart. Now you can show everyone you're so great..."

"Ouch."

"...and I'm still trying to prove myself to my father by outperforming every man in the world. That's why I don't listen to Koebsch."

"They really messed with your head by giving you a medal, didn't they?

You don't like being part of the establishment. It goes against your self-image."

"No, it doesn't."

"You appeared on the global feeds with our prime minister. We should be celebrating, but you want to pout. You'd rather be an outcast. A workaholic."

For a moment, she wavered. Part of her was irked. Part of her accepted that he was right. She laughed and rolled over so her breasts grazed his chest. Opening her thighs, she lifted one knee and set it on his hip. "You think you're so smart," she teased him.

He hardened against her thigh, but his expression was serious, almost quizzical. "Is that why you're watching these dipshits on the net? So you don't feel too mainstream?"

"I need to know what people were saying."

"There'll always be someone who wants to dish out abuse. People are scared. You're a convenient punching bag."

"I should be doing more. Maybe I can field more interviews or explain what we found in the chimney. We should call the PSSC admiral on the destroyer."

"If you contact him, they'll say it's treason."

"They'll wish I had when the shooting starts."

"It won't come to that. Like you said, there's plenty of room to stay away from each other. What everyone wants most is deuterium for their fleets, then fresh water for their stations and farms. Genesmithing is a distant third. Dealing with the sunfish comes last."

"Then why are the Chinese mobilizing?"

"They'll strong-arm us. We'll make concessions. They'll let us stay here if America downgrades its missile bases in Vietnam and we stop sending weapons and advisors to India, which is what most of the Union wants anyway. The Kashmir will fall again to Pakistan and the PSSC."

"You're really that cynical," she said.

"I thought we both were." His hand slid to the small of her back and he pressed her belly against his erection. "It's late. Let me help you sleep."

"Sex doesn't solve everything, Ben."

"It'll help you relax."

"Don't be mad if I say no. Just hold me. Please."

Vonnie's dreams were serpentine. She wandered through small dark spaces and white avalanches. Somewhere she heard wailing, but it wasn't a sunfish. The forlorn screams sounded like a woman. Was it herself? Her mother?

She woke after an hour and listened to her heartbeat. She felt anxious and lost.

She roused Ben by stroking him. His penis stiffened. She bent to lick him. The seduction made her wet. She sat up and wrapped her hand around his erection and mounted him before he said a word.

In the dim light of the life systems read-outs, Vonnie lifted and rocked, riding him until she came. Then he rolled her over and thrust into her as she crossed her ankles on his butt, increasing the tempo of each stroke. She held onto him with her double embrace, arms and legs, savoring him. She almost came again. He orgasmed first. He withdrew and used his fingers on her and she moaned louder than she wanted before she reached her second climax.

Is anyone else in the lander? She couldn't remember until she thought of Henri at the controls. He shouldn't have heard her through the door.

She and Ben mopped up with his shirt, which he dropped to the floor. She slid on her undies. They nuzzled. She slept again. Her nightmares returned but seemed to leave her after a while. She rested.

When she woke, the display read 06:27AM.

Henri was supposed to have woken her at 04:00 to take the pilot's seat. Her personal alert was winking. The ID said the message was from Koebsch. She extracted herself from Ben. If she and Koebsch needed to talk, she'd call after she washed up and brushed her hair.

She opened the door. "Henri?"

He sat at the pilot's station with two coffee packets, not looking any worse for wear. He was a handsome man. "Good morning," he said. His mouth curled. "Harmeet said I should let you sleep if I knew what was good for me."

"I snapped at her yesterday."

"You're under more pressure than most of us. Too much attention from Earth. Ben. Peter. The sunfish. I envy how you've been accepted by them."

"Thank you." She considered kissing his cheek, but she was aware of how she must smell and her tousled hair.

He said, "I can stay on station if you need breakfast."

"Koebsch wants me to call."

"I talked to him. It's not urgent. Berlin has a new construction project for you."

"Okay." She didn't leave. She shuffled her feet, wondering if she should address her grievances with him.

Henri had been her supporter at times. Like Ash, he acted aloof, but Vonnie believed his demeanor was a charade. All of them shared a brisk, pragmatic attitude or they wouldn't fit the ESA psych profile. Too often, it was only in private moments that their individuality shone.

Henri was a hard worker and a neat freak and a man who'd exhibited a certain latitude in his thinking when it suited him. Vonnie had watched him become friends with Ben despite Ben's messy habits and loud mouth. Henri had his tidy romance with Ash and he honestly seemed to enjoy the overblown zeppelin of Dawson's genius, playing to the old man's narcissism. Henri often remarked that his bio research was enhanced by Dawson's genesmithing. He was a smooth guy.

It shouldn't have taken this long for us to develop our own connection, she thought, so she bent and planted a kiss on his cheek. "I'd like to be friends."

His mouth curled again. "I'm on your side, Von."

"You work for the Directorate."

"They paid my way through school and… other debts. I send them reports. They ask me to keep my eyes open. There's nothing sinister about it."

"Is that why you're sleeping with Ash? They must have told you to watch each other's back. Paris and London will remain allies even if Britain leaves the Union."

Henri didn't take the bait. He offered nothing political. He said, "Actually, sleeping with her is against the rules."

"She's younger than you."

"She's a grown woman."

"She's twenty-four. You're forty-four."

"It was her idea. I don't see the problem."

"My problem is you're a biologist who armed FNEE nukes to exterminate native lifeforms."

"We expected an attack *en masse* by the Mid Clans."

"Before that, you were involved in creating our alliance with the FNEE. You must be some kind of super spy to have the clearance to initiate back-channel deals *and* the skills to handle foreign model neutron weapons."

"My orders are to protect the crew. In the same circumstances, I'd arm those warheads again. Don't forget I've bent the rules to help you with the sunfish. I am a biologist, Von. That's my first love."

"I'm worried that we'll let a fight develop on Europa to solidify our gains with Brazil on Earth. The threat of war would also keep Italy and the U.K. in the Union."

His mouth curled. "Now you're looking at the big picture. You should work for us."

"Don't the sunfish factor into your thinking?"

"We've had this conversation before. The sunfish are fantastic. Having said that, we need to put our species before a diseased alien race."

'Diseased,' she thought. *One word gives you away, but our world isn't much cleaner and our waste is self-generated. Chemicals. Heavy metals. Megatons of carbon dioxide and sewage. We have cancers and respiratory illnesses created by our own pollution.*

He said, "Cooperation is everything. We survived the last war with China because of our pacts with America and Japan. If Brazil aligns itself with us, the geopolitical map tips in our favor. China will back down."

"And the only loose ends are beneath the ice. It's nice and neat how you like it."

That was a rude description of his motives, but Henri nodded. "We'll do what we can for the sunfish."

Vonnie was afraid to test him further. Maybe she'd made progress. "I appreciate you letting me rest. Give me five minutes."

"Shake Ben, too."

She walked away. She poked her head into the living quarters, where Ben stirred like a bear. "Let's go, lover. We can eat at our stations."

Ben wasn't a morning person. He rubbed his eyes blearily.

Vonnie rushed through brushing her teeth, a sponge bath, clean clothes. She ran a drier through her dirty hair. That would have to do.

When she returned, Koebsch was on Henri's group feed. "Von," he said. His expression was neutral, but he glanced up and down her body as if taking stock. He probably wasn't aware of it but his look was covetous.

She was losing him as a friend.

"Put on a scout suit," he said. "Tony and Ash will rendezvous with you outside."

"What's happening?"

"We have a new directive from Berlin."

26.

Vonnie met Ash and Tony beside Module 01. She didn't know Tony well. He wasn't a loner like Dawson but he often kept to himself, volunteering for extra shifts or maintenance. He was olive-skinned with dark hair, dark eyes, and a by-the-book attitude that Berlin treasured and the media hated.

His single quirk was his full name, Antonio Leonardo Gravino, which had led Ben and the others to dub him "Triple-O," but Tony downplayed this nickname until even Ben gave up on it.

The interviewers and pundits who bothered with Tony portrayed him as conservative at their most charitable or bland at their worst. Vonnie admired his work ethic but the two of them were opposites. For once, she was in tune with the media. Tony *was* boring.

With him were a rover and four general purpose mecha. The rover dragged ten slabs of plastisteel like a sled. Two of the GPs held welding equipment. The others carried tanks of con foam. All of them blazed with lights and radar.

Beneath the fathomless sky, Vonnie greeted Ash with a hug before she said to Tony, "I don't see how this accomplishes anything."

"It's a feel-good effort," Ash agreed.

"Berlin must know we have higher priorities."

"Right now it's a waiting game," Tony said. "Personally, I want all the armor I can get."

"Here we go," Ash radioed Koebsch, who was inside 01. The mecha lifted the module like jacks. Vonnie and Ash scanned the ice, which they'd reinforced months ago with alumalloy plates, glue and nanotech.

They were looking for pressure points where Module 01 had settled. Berlin wanted them to add vibration-absorbing insulation to prevent the sunfish from eavesdropping on their conversations. That was the public explanation. Incidentally, the new foundation might protect them from attacks from below.

Vonnie regarded this as wishful thinking. Tony was a company man like Koebsch and he talked a good game, but short of building an impregnable castle on the ice, their modules could not withstand the guns of PSSC mecha. Even if they wanted to spend the next month erecting a fortress, they lacked the materials. Ten slabs of plastisteel and five tanks of foam were everything they had to spare unless they dismantled the *Marcuse.*

More bullshit from Earth, she thought. *Playing a shell game with our few resources is stupid.*

"How does it look?" Koebsch asked.

Vonnie shook her head and frowned. "We can finish the job in thirty minutes," she said.

"What about reinforcing the landers?"

"Bad idea. We want all the speed we can get. If we had more steel, we could graft it onto the landers' walls, but weighing them down isn't worth the trade-off. PSSC mecha use VRAP loads." Variable rapid-fire armor-piercing rounds. "They'll go through steel like butter."

She let Tony and Ash direct their mecha. The GPs arranged a broad, low tent in preparation for spraying foam. On Tony's command, they pumped heat into the tent.

Vonnie fidgeted as Tony laid foam in a ten-centimeter-thick block as long and wide as Module 01. Next he added two slabs of plastisteel. Watching their meager resources committed to a flimsy barrier was disheartening.

"Koebsch," she said, "let's move food and gear into the ice. We're not safe on the surface."

Tony made a disapproving sound. *Eh.* "You're so ready to give up."

"The hell I am. Standing toe-to-toe with the PSSC isn't a battle we can win. We need to find other ways to get what we want."

"We can put up a fight if the Americans join us. We'll have a strong umbrella." He meant an orbital shield of spy sats and HKs.

"You're dreaming. Ash, tell him. Unless the Chinese let us bring in more ships, they've already beaten us."

"She's right. Maybe we can hide in the ice."

While the machines fought each other, the flesh-and-blood astronauts could ride it out with the sunfish. They would need to run deep. Their explosives would set off blowouts and quakes, but, left behind in the collapse, their MMPSAs could generate a blizzard of electronic noise. The blizzard should conceal them from the PSSC. Then they might counterattack.

"Let's put our supplies on the west side of the colony, away from their mecha," Vonnie said. "Everyone should have a scout suit prepped at all times."

"I'd rather be in a lander," Tony said.

"Landers are high-value targets. Individual suits are harder to track. We can program the landers to take off and draw their fire."

"That can't be our first option," Tony objected.

"No, but it's a fallback position," Koebsch said. Then he added, "We may lose communications with Earth."

Vonnie said, "We need to prepare the matriarchs. If they're in the wrong cycle and we rush into the catacombs with Ribeiro and the Americans..."

"They're sleeping now, but they'll be awake in forty minutes," Koebsch said. "Finish the job, then gather supplies. Moving food and gear into the ice is a good plan, but listen to me, Von. You are not allowed to search for Lam on your own. Tony will accompany you with a pair of mecha. If you go against my orders, we'll take you into custody. If Lam tries anything, we'll burn him."

"Yes, sir."

An hour passed — much longer than Vonnie would have taken. Tony's attention to detail while he laid their armor beneath Module 01 might have been genuine, but she thought he also wanted to delay going into the ice.

The job was visually impressive. They'd improved the module's footprint. Certainly it was well-shielded from the ears of the sunfish. So what?

"Tony, let's go. Ash, I'll see you later."

Ash stopped her with another embrace. "Be careful. For me. You take too many chances," Ash said. Her last words sounded tough, like she was admonishing Vonnie, but the first things she'd said had been uncommonly warm.

It was their friendship that stayed with Vonnie as she ran toward Module 06. Almost in spite of themselves, she and Ash had grown close. She was glad.

She was scared.

Tony pursued her with two mecha. She heard his breathing in her radio. Jupiter's pale colors traced over her faceplate. And in her heart, there was darkness.

She reached 06 and the cargo tent. "Stay close," she said. Tony didn't like the sunfish and they knew it.

Their name for him was *Hiding Male.* He'd only visited the catacombs three times. When he wasn't helping with a construction project, he tended to hang back with his hands on his hips or his arms folded over his chest.

Vonnie led him through the tent's decon bubbles. Their mecha would follow, although she didn't think decontamination mattered. The sunfish were unlikely to contract microbes from suits or machines that had been exposed to surface temperatures, but protocol was protocol. She needed to adhere to every rule for Koebsch's sake.

As the UV lights hummed, she studied their datastreams. Below her were two doppelgangers and twenty-six sunfish, mostly breeding pairs and older matriarchs like Angelica and Michelle.

They sang. They had listened to Vonnie's approach and they'd unraveled the emotions conveyed by every step. There was anger. She was always angry now. It had worn a rut in her thinking, and inlaid with this habit was dread.

She tormented herself with apprehension, remorse, dismay, and the longing to right so many wrongs — but the sunfish didn't care about injustice. They cared that evident in her was a sharp, rising edge of aggression. They took her complex feelings and isolated the one trait they revered more than any other: her willingness to fight.

—*Young Matriarch brings new killing and raids! Blood and fire!* they screamed.

The doppelgängers grabbed some of the males, trying to soothe them. —*You misinterpret her plans. Young Matriarch will deliver food into the ice,* the doppelgängers cried.

—*She leads us to feeding and death! Show us! Show us!* they screamed. They wanted war. To them, the reservations she felt were a hoax. Once upon a time, the sunfish had marveled at the energy she expended on guilt. Now they assumed the busiest parts of her mind were a facade, a masquerade of pointless questions and moralizing.

They knew she was a killer.

Her mood was influenced by their perception of her. As she walked from the decon bubbles, the cold wind in her soul heightened the aggressiveness in her stride.

—*New enemies! New territories!* they screamed.

"Wait," Koebsch said abruptly on the radio. "I need you in data/comm."

"What's going on?" Tony asked, but Vonnie said, "You can't tell me to stop. I won't. The matriarchs are with us. They'll do what I say, and we need them, Koebsch."

"I heard from the *Jyväskylä.*"

Her heart jolted with adrenaline. "Oh my God. Are they under fire?"

"They're fine, but some of their probes have been hit. One was a collision with an asteroid. PSSC drones may be responsible for the rest."

Tired and short-tempered, Vonnie snapped at him like she'd snapped at Harmeet. "We knew they'd lose a few probes! I can't help them."

"They found sunfish on Io."

She stammered over her next words. "On… they…"

"I'm looking at the sims." Koebsch was thrilled. He sounded like a man who'd dropped a burden. If only for the moment, he'd again become the administrator of a deep space exploration team rather than a bureaucrat caught between a hard place and the might of the People's Supreme Society of China.

She loved his spark. She shared his astonishment. His announcement felt like meeting an entirely new alien race because the implications were breathtaking.

Europa was the second of Jupiter's four largest moons. Io was the first, which made Europa and Io neighbors, but they were never closer to each other than 250,000 kilometers of vacuum. Typically, much greater spans lay between them. How could there be sunfish on both moons?

The discovery was more than amazing. It left Vonnie electrified and dumbfounded. Enunciating every syllable, she said, "Sunfish on Io. Are you sure?"

"Yes."

They'd been blindsided again.

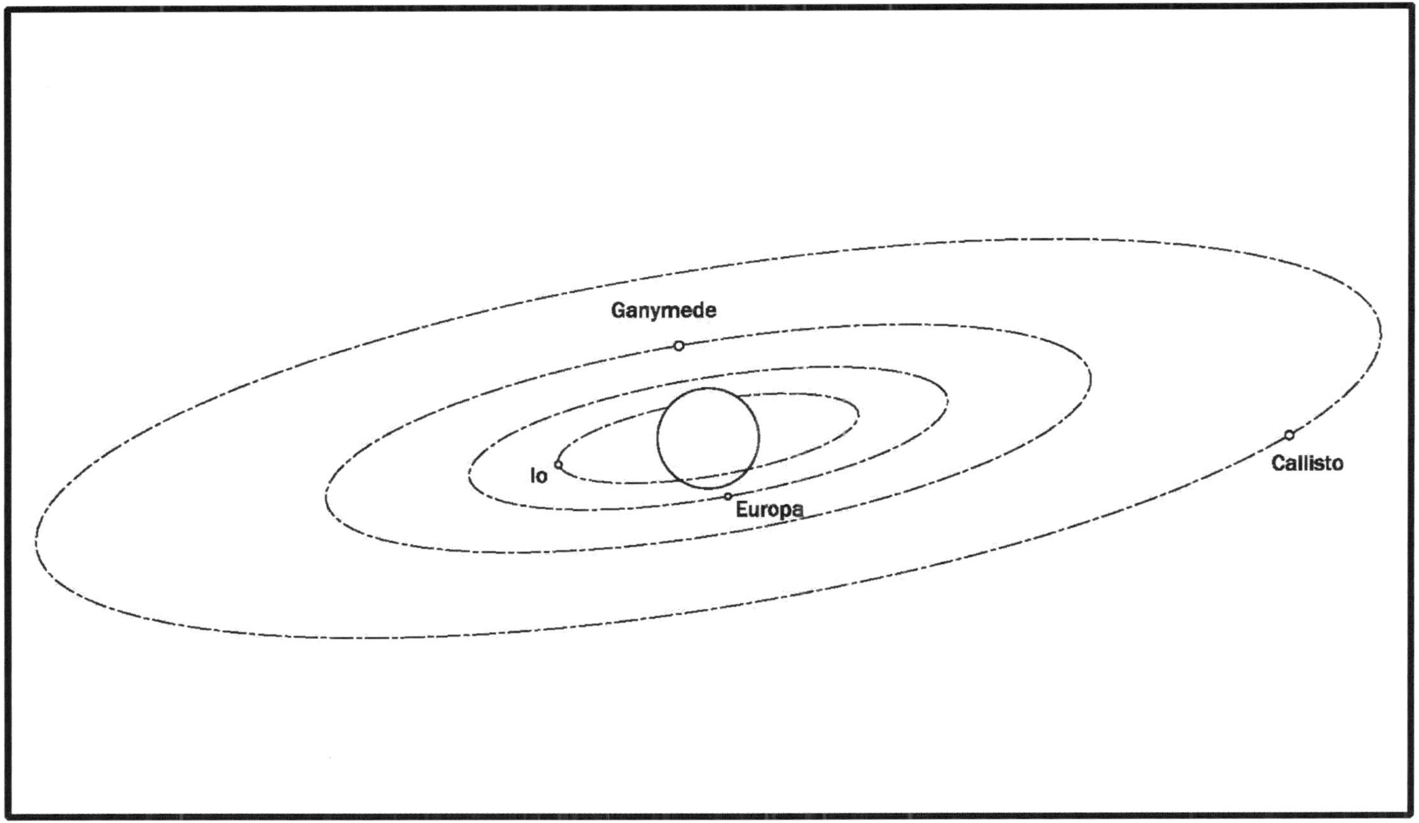

Callisto

Europa

Ganymede

Io

Jupiter's Largest Moons

27.

Through the doppelgängers, Vonnie offered a quick explanation to the matriarchs. —*We must go. We have urgent strategies for the clan.*

—*Mature Male calls you? He needs you?*

—*I will return.*

As she watched her display, the sunfish thrashed and screeched. They heard her excitement. Not incorrectly, they believed she'd gained new information.

They knew they faced a dominant force in the PSSC. From the changes in her voice and in her bearing, they thought she'd found an advantage over their enemy — and it continued to spook her that they could tell who spoke in her ear by her physical response. Did she act that differently with Ben or Koebsch?

She walked through the tent's air lock in a daze.

He thinks finding sunfish on Io gives us leverage, but I don't see it. Yes, the chess board just got larger. That doesn't affect their destroyer.

Outside, lights covered the surface. She saw listening posts and hab modules, which looked like gray blocks scattered on the ice. One handful of missiles could pound them into atoms.

Tony stepped through the lock beside her — but as he jogged across camp, she stayed, pacing above the matriarchs. Her head felt cluttered.

Will the PSSC reconsider moving against us? With the FNEE ships, the Jyväskylä *could blockade Io. We'll redraw the lines of ownership. We can deny them access to the new sunfish unless they back down on Europa. Gamesmanship.*

That's what Koebsch brings to the table.

Ordinarily, she didn't appreciate his administrative skills, but on a chess board populated by real weapons, they needed him as king. She couldn't ignore her attraction to him. Koebsch was their alpha male.

He's not a genius like Ben or a fighter like me, but the way he grinds at every setback is a different kind of talent. I was wrong to shut him out.

I can't hurt Ben, but I should talk with Koebsch again. I need to tell him how I feel.

She took one step toward Module 01. Beneath her, the sunfish screamed at her doppelgängers. —*Show us! Show us what you learned!* they cried.

—*First I need to hear more.*

—*Attack? Attack? Attack? Attack?*

She held herself motionless, trying to convey a diligence that was worthy of Koebsch. —*We will not attack. Stay quiet. Let our machines protect you.*

—*We hear rogues! We hear enemies!*

—*You also heard our machines spread into the catacombs. If we are threatened, our mines will explode! Stay inside the colony!*

—*The rogues are close. Metal Scout is close.*

—*Bring him to me.*

—*No. No.*

—*He is a friend.*

The tribe boiled with animosity, but they were seasoned by their respect for elders like Brigit, and the elders respected Vonnie. —*Young Matriarch goads us! Young Matriarch hears farther than the clan!* they cried.

—*I will return. Find Lam.*

Tony was at Module 01. He entered the air lock. Vonnie sprinted after him.

She'd run thirty meters when an alarm lit her faceplate. A malfunction in the lock's pressure gauges? As she neared the module, her display advised her that Tony had moved into the ready room. The air lock was clear.

She opened the lock's outer door and stepped in. The door wouldn't close behind her. New alarms riddled her display. The lock had failed. Back-up systems were coming online.

Outside, portions of their grid faltered. Their mecha and listening posts were shutting down.

"Koebsch?" she asked.

"Go to SRHEL." He used the slang pronunciation of the acronym as one word — *shrell* — and her nerves tightened like violin strings.

Short-range high-energy lasers operated on line of sight, one module or suit blinking at another to evade SCPs. Koebsch wouldn't ask her to communicate via blips of light unless they were under attack. Sabotage and control programs were the front wave of a PSSC blitzkrieg.

Module 01 had been infected.

"How bad is it?" she asked as her suit translated her words into flashes.

On the ceiling was a sensor bubble with cams, X-ray, infrared and laser scan. The lasers winked. Her suit rendered the light into meaning: **Stand back. The door will close. Shut down all systems and prepare to jettison your suit.**

Vonnie began to tremble. She'd lived this nightmare before. Her suit was an expensive miracle, but its sophistication was its Achilles heel. If hacked, it might be crippled. If coopted, it might serve the PSSC. It could smash through Module 01 with her trapped inside, screaming or dead.

I can't breathe, I can't breathe, she thought.

The outer door lurched. Stopped. Lurched again. She grabbed the front edge and yanked before she could stop herself. If she pulled the door out of alignment or stripped its gears, she would need to run to Landers 04 or 05 before she could get out of her suit. By then, the PSSC might shut off core systems like life support. No data/comm. No oxygen. No lights.

I can't breathe.

The door shut with a *boom.* Vonnie backpedaled from it like an animal in a cage, touching the wall behind her. She listened for the heaters and airco, but the lock was a dead steel box.

Her helmet flashed as she yelled, "Koebsch, are you there!? Talk to me!"

The bubble winked: **Stand by.**

"Okay, okay, okay," she chanted.

The heaters kicked in and she watched the fine grates in the floor, deluding herself that she felt the warmth shimmering through her boots. Her stomach flip-flopped. The pressure rose as the airco went on.

I need to kill my suit, she thought, but she couldn't bring herself to blind her helmet even if her data/comm components were the most likely to host an SCP.

She turned off her radar, her sonar, her links to their grid. She kept her lights and external mikes. If she couldn't see, she would go crazy, so she found other chores to attend, turning off her mem files and her translation AIs. She hesitated over her weapons systems.

The bubble flashed: **Tony is coming.**

The inner hatch opened. Tony had taken off his scout suit. Now he wore a pressure suit and he'd darkened his faceplate, which left him expressionless. He held an M7.

His empty scout suit stood behind him. Its left arm jerked. An SCP was consuming and reanimating its systems. How long before it attacked them?

More frightening was his weapon. He aimed the M7 at Vonnie's feet.

"Tony?" she said.

The speaker in his collar squawked, "Open your helmet and your chest piece. Kneel and pull yourself out."

"Did the SCP come from Lam? Was I seeded with it?"

"It's Chinese."

"Lam said he fought them. Maybe they infected him with trojans or frags."

"Take off your helmet, Von."

"I'm trying!" Her gloves shook on her collar assembly.

"What do you see? Am I alone?" Tony lifted his M7. He thought she was immersed in false images and voices generated by PSSC bogey packets. Datastreams laced with lifelike shams had caused EUSD soldiers to fire on each other during the war.

If I scare him, he'll shoot, she realized.

Somehow her terror fell into an icy calm. "I see you. Yes, you're alone. Communications are off except for audio and SRHEL. I can remove my suit if you let me."

"Go."

She released the seals on her collar. She lifted her helmet. The air lock stank of an electrical fire. She saw no smoke, but somewhere components had fried inside the module. "I'm going to set my helmet down."

Tony nodded. He aimed the compact, lethal shape of his M7 away from her but not too far.

She lowered herself onto her knees. She opened her armor, then pushed one shoulder out like a baby bird emerging from an egg. She reached back inside to disconnect the plumbing and heaved her torso and legs up through the chest piece. Goose bumps studded her skin. "Now what?"

"My suit is coming in. We're going out." Tony gestured for her to walk into the ready room. She did.

His empty scout suit lumbered past them. Its arm twitched.

"Clear," Tony said to his radio.

Their suits collapsed, thudding on the floor. Koebsch had sent kill codes. Tony shut the lock, leaving the suits inside like dead giants.

In the ready room, a new feeling swept through Vonnie, stark and bleak. She opened a locker with Ash's name, taking socks and underwear and a blue jumpsuit. None of her belongings were in 01. Ash's clothing was clean if too small. "Is someone fixing the outer door for us?"

Tony said, "Santos and Tavares should be here soon. Their suits are okay. Our guess is China and Brazil are negotiating on Earth. Ribeiro might be told to get his people out of here. He might be told to commandeer our camp."

"They're on China's side again?"

"The SCPs started in a FNEE satellite. That's how we lost our grid."

"Then why are they fixing our lock?"

"Santos and Tavares were on their way before we traced the SCPs to the source. Either they're really going to help us or it's a set-up."

"They wouldn't do that. Claudia wouldn't."

"We'll see," Tony said.

She finished dressing. Looking past him, she saw that the hatch into the corridor was shut. Sealing every door was standard operating procedure. The

AP/CEW pod he'd clipped to the hatch was not.

He'd prepared for the FNEE to breach Module 01 as a hostile force. Santos and Tavares were engineering and ROM specialists. If coming to help was only a cover story, they made the story plausible… but Ribeiro must be aware that Vonnie and Tavares were chummy. Wouldn't he send someone else?

Maybe not. Claudia Tavares was a soldier. She had approached Vonnie with her most intimate concerns, but she wouldn't oppose Ribeiro. She'd given too much of herself to her squad. To her nation. Her integrity and her self-worth depended upon her patriotism.

Maybe I can talk to her, Vonnie thought as Tony undogged the hatch from the ready room into the corridor. They strode through. Tony shut the hatch and set a companion AP/CEW pod on their side.

He walked to the armory. She went to data/comm and closed its door as well. Every room was a cell. Every door was a line of defense.

Koebsch and Ash stood in front of group feeds, Koebsch with unfamiliar men and women wearing black uniforms. He and Ash were both wrapped in datastreams. Some were from distant probes. Others were from much closer spy sats and mecha. Many were distorted by static.

"—through Ceres or the USAF if possible," Koebsch said as Ash said, "Here's our entry key."

Koebsch was communicating with the *Jyväskylä* through heavy jamming. Encryption codes swept through his display, reporting thousands of updates at AI speeds. The codes flashed green and orange and red, mostly orange.

Ash was speaking with Santos and Tavares. Wearing clunky, over-muscled FNEE scout suits, the two soldiers stood outside an ESA storage shed.

Its lock opened. Santos entered, then Tavares. The shed was packed with containers. It was also inhabited by five mecha — slender, long-armed machines designed to pull and stack. Ash had transmitted a parts list. The mecha sorted out replacement sensors, wiring and motors to fix Module 01.

Vonnie stepped into Ash's display and said, "Lieutenant? We need more AP/CEW pods." *More* was a threat. If their repair mission was an excuse to breach Module 01, she wanted them to know it was well-defended.

Santos said, "Uh, *sí.* Where are those located?"

Ash muted her feed and snarled, "Most of our weapons are in the armory! Why did you say that?"

"If they don't think they can take our module, they won't. They'll call Earth for new orders. Every second they wait is in our favor."

Ash shoved Vonnie aside. She reopened communications and said, calmly, "Thank you, Lieutenant."

"Affirmative," Santos replied.

His face was neutral as Ash instructed the mecha to retrieve a case of AP/CEW pods, adding it to their stock of replacement parts. Tavares looked antsy.

Santos lifted two containers and the new case. Slowly, Tavares took the other three containers. First she touched her sidearm like a gambler revealing the strength of her cards with a nervous tic. "Von, is there anything else before we go?" Tavares asked. Now that she'd heard Vonnie, the situation was more personal for her, which had been Vonnie's intent.

Hurting each other, capturing or killing each other, should be personal. They weren't machines.

Studying the young sergeant, Vonnie read her as easily as a datastream. Claudia Tavares was determined but unhappy. She wasn't looking forward to rescuing a friend. She was distraught.

She and Santos had been ordered to take Module 01.

Vonnie bowed her head, a heavy, brooding posture from her childhood when Sunday mornings were spent in church. She remembered the hard slat benches. She remembered the grown-ups' rote voices and feeling like she was trapped.

She prayed for everyone caught on the sprawling chess board from Jupiter to Berlin. *I can't fight Claudia, too,* she thought. *Somehow we need to convince the FNEE to stay with us.*

** * * Intercept * * * Eyes Only * * * Intercept * * * Eyes Only * * * Intercept * * **

Força Nacional de Exploração do Espaço
Missão 298 30 De junho de 2113

Personnel
Colonel Ribeiro
Major Correa
Captain Alvaréz
Captain Araújo
Lieutenant Santos
Lieutenant Carvalho
Lieutenant Pereira
Sergeant Tavares

Ribeiro	COMMAND - NAV - ROM - ASST. ENGINEERING
Correa	COMMAND - MED - PSY - HAB - ASST. ENGINEERING
Alvaréz	PILOT - WEAPONS - MED - HAB
Araújo	PILOT - WEAPONS - ASST. ROM - ASST. MED
Santos	ROM - ENGINEERING - BIOLOGY
Carvalho	ROM - NAV - TECH/COMM - BIOLOGY
Pereira	ROM - WEAPONS - ASST. NAV - ASST. PILOT
Taraves	TECH/COMM - NAV - MED - HAB - ASST. ROM

Mission Control:
Alcântara

Craft:
FNEE *Leopard*-class *M4*

Support:
ROM-4 Hab Modules (2), ROM-6 Orbital Shuttle (1)
ROM-2 APAQS Modules (3), ROM-4 Rovers (5),ROM-4 AP Mecha (15),
ROM-6 SD Mecha (10), ROM-4 Sentries (10), ROM-2 Beacons (15)

28.

Santos and Tavares walked out of the shed. He spoke on an encrypted frequency and Ash's datastreams flittered with intercepts translated from Portuguese.

SANTOS TO TAVARES: Remember your training.

Tavares nodded.

SANTOS TO BASE: Colonel, we have their replacement parts.

Ribeiro's answer was a single burst of squelch. Typically one meant *Yes*, two meant *No.*

"That was a 'go' sign," Vonnie said.

Ash glanced over her shoulder, where Koebsch hollered, "Captain, I need those satellites!"

Ash met Vonnie's gaze and said, "He's coordinating with the *Jyväskylä.* I'm in charge of security. It's a disaster, but I got a few bugs into the PSSC grid."

"Why is Tony in the armory?"

"He's rigging a new scout suit." Ash pointed at Santos and Tavares. "Can you stop them? This time, don't hint around. Try anything you can. Tell her you're scared. Tell her she's your buddy."

"Claudia won't go against her squad. Anything I say will just get her in trouble."

"Better her than us."

"If I embarrass her, she'll do something to prove herself like taking out our cameras with her pistol. Then they're committed."

"Vonnie, *I* need to commit. If they come inside, I can't let them in without a fight."

"Let them pretend to fix the lock. We'll gain a few minutes."

"Koebsch won't hear from Earth that soon. Neither will Ribeiro."

Santos and Tavares were a hundred meters from Module 01. Hurrying from the shed brought them past several ESA rovers and listening posts, none operational. Vonnie said, "Do we have any mecha at all?"

"Not on the surface. Most of the units beneath the ice are fine, but if they climb out they'll walk into the SCPs."

"What about our landers? Can they come for us?"

"Nav was the first thing to go. Ben thinks he can fly by hand but he doesn't have the training." Ash lowered her voice and said, "Koebsch should have left a pilot in 04."

Henri was in 05 now with Harmeet and O'Neal. Ben and Dawson were in 04.

"Koebsch needed you here," Vonnie said, although she agreed with Ash. Koebsch might not have grasped the severity of the attack when he ordered Vonnie to join him, but gathering all of his pilots in Module 01 had been an error.

She was his weakness. A king needed to play every piece on the board. He couldn't safeguard his favorites.

Santos and Tavares were at the lock. They set down their containers as Santos radioed Ash. "Verify your inner doors are sealed," he said. "We will inspect the outer door."

"Wait, please. We're having trouble with the inner hatch to our ready room," Ash said. Then she muted her feed again. "I hate this polite fucking dance. I'd rather haggle with the sunfish. They're psychotic, but at least you know they'll eat you if they can."

"The sunfish..." Vonnie touched Ash's display, enlarging five views.

The largest groups in the colony had dissolved. Many of the scouts and matriarchs were leaving. They descended into the catacombs while the savage males roiled beneath the surface in packs of eight or twelve. They could no longer hear inside Module 01, but they had calculated Vonnie's emotional state before she went into its air lock. They'd listened attentively to Santos and Tavares.

They were screaming for *Young Matriarch.*

"The sunfish can immobilize Santos," Vonnie said. "Opening the ice will kill them, but they can pull him down. With luck, we'll only lose a few males."

"God." Ash's tone was grim, yet her eyes gleamed with approval. "You've changed."

I haven't, she thought. *If we take Io and hold our position here, Brazil will forget any deal with China. Everything stops. We'll go back to our stalemate.*

Ash thought she'd put the well-being of their crew before the lives of the sunfish.

Vonnie thought she was behaving like matriarch.

This is survival. It serves the tribe.

She contacted her doppelgängers even though each transmission was a danger. SCPs blanketed their camp like an unseen tide, attaching code to anything that listened, so she reduced her message to its barest elements. The sunfish had never needed more. She screeched the equivalent of six words — her name — their description of Santos — and a cry for blood.

Young Matriarch. Rival Male. Kill him!

He was nearly invincible in his suit, but they could prevent him from raiding Module 01. If necessary, Vonnie would squander more lives to stop Tavares.

A wave of savage males spilled through the catacombs. Their screams rose into a howl. The sound was raucous and rapturous and cruel. Santos and Tavares recoiled from the ice at their feet, stepping like people who'd walked onto coals.

The males divided into four shrieking packs.

They fractured the sides of four tunnels. The tunnels collapsed, falling laterally.

One digging pack of males was in front of Santos. One was beside him. Two were beyond the oblong shape of Module 01. Santos backpedaled. He pulled at Tavares.

Beneath the surface, the males labored at their cave-ins, packing each heap of ice to block the tunnels, cementing their work with urine and saliva. They sealed a bowl-like area near Module 01. Most of the males were outside of the walls they'd fashioned.

Six males were inside. They started to dig *upward.* They pried at the cracks in the ceiling… but they targeted a patch of ice several meters from Tavares and Santos.

Santos drew his sidearm.

Tavares called on her radio, "Von?"

The surface split with masterful precision. The widening cracks chased Santos. Heroically, he pushed Tavares, wanting to save her. The ice bulged under his feet. It exploded. Shards clanged against Module 01.

The six males were expelled into the vacuum. Their cartilage skins left one opening for the terrible pressure change. They were turned inside out. Their foaming stomachs and lungs protruded from their beaks. Air and blood crystallized into grotesque confetti.

With their last breaths, two of them latched onto Tavares. Gagging, they chomped through their own guts, scratching their beaks against her faceplate.

The other four grabbed Santos. One knotted itself over his thigh and the pistol in his hand. It used its spasming body like manacles, pinning his weapon even as it choked, went limp and died. The rest of them glommed onto his head.

They formed an unwieldy lump. Bent like a hunchback, Santos stumbled and ran. He almost got away. The cracks outraced him. The ice buckled under his feet and Santos fell.

Tavares began to fall, too, but she fired a magnetic clamp from her left forearm. The clamp glommed onto Module 01, holding her in place. Simultaneously, Ash's datastreams spiked with intercepts.

TAVARES TO SANTOS: Sir!

SANTO OPEN FREQUENCY: They're all over me! They're—

TAVARES TO BASE: The aliens took Santos! I can't—

He landed badly, striking his neck. His pistol barked. Once. Twice. Then it chattered on full auto. The weapon was silent in the vacuum, but the impacts of its bullets vibrated through the ice.

Less than two meters from him, the surviving males screeched. They were still packing their walls. Was he shooting blindly or trying to kill them?

RIBEIRO TO SANTOS: Cease fire!

SANTOS: They're on my suit and—

RIBEIRO: Cease fire! Cease fire! The aliens are dead and a stray round may hit the ESA.

SANTOS: My arm—

RIBEIRO: Sergeant, can you reach him?

TAVARES: Yes, sir! I see him! I need to retract my clamp! Lieutenant, are you all right?

SANTOS: They dislocated my shoulder.

TAVARES: You drew your weapon anyway? Sir, you stopped them from hurting me.

"Gah." Ash stuck a finger in her mouth. "If she pours it on any thicker, I'll vomit."

"She has an injured teammate."

"She's talking like his girlfriend. She sounds like a little buttercup."

Vonnie should have expected the catty remarks. Ash was strict in judging everyone's conduct except her own. Especially during a crisis, Ash wanted one-size-fits-all behavior, emotionless and genderless, based solely on rank, even if Ash treated Koebsch like a father. She rebelled against him, aiding Vonnie when she shouldn't, then scrambled to make up for her transgressions with renewed zeal.

Ash made no allowance for the circumstances Tavares had endured since leaving Earth. Everything was black and white to Ash. She couldn't even see the gray in herself.

These thoughts flew through Vonnie's mind as Tavares grabbed her sidearm. Had she guessed that Vonnie personally directed the tribe to attack?

There were thirty-six males in screaming packs all around Tavares. The ice quivered with their shrieks.

Santos rolled onto his hands and knees. Above him, Tavares peered into the pit where he'd fallen, and Ash's datastreams translated their broadcasts from Portuguese.

TAVARES: Sir, I can extract the lieutenant, but the aliens are everywhere. I need assistance to carry him to sick bay.

SANTOS: I don't need a medic.

RIBEIRO: How bad is it?

SANTOS: I can complete the mission.

TAVARES: I have his telemetry, sir. His rotator cuff is bruised, maybe torn.

RIBEIRO: Lieutenant, you're no good to us with one arm. Sergeant, I'll contact the ESA commander. Abort your mission. Return to base.

TAVARES: Yes, sir.

Ribeiro switched frequencies and said, "ESA 01, have you been monitoring our people?"

Leaving her cameras off, Ash said, "Yes, sir! Are they okay? Our mecha are offline. We are experiencing cyber-attacks and cannot assist." She managed to sound afraid but her eyes were delighted. She muted her feeds and whispered, "Did you see Santos smack his head? That was beautiful."

Vonnie gazed at the dead males.

Ribeiro said, "My lieutenant requires medical attention."

Ash couldn't resist needling him. "What about our air lock, Colonel? Our crew will be stuck if you can't do the job."

"Vonderach knows the aliens better than anyone. Have her tell them to stand down. My people will not return to your module until you verify our safety."

"Colonel, I can't explain what happened except we're obviously in trouble. The sunfish can't hear cyber warfare. They might not have understood why your soldiers approached us. Von is a matriarch. You've seen what they'll do to protect her. She's trying to talk to them but our grid is down."

Outside, Tavares dropped a cable to Santos. He climbed out, swearing, "Christ. The dead ones keep moving."

They stood back to back near Module 01, weapons out, surveying the gauntlet of sunfish with radar and infrared. "Colonel?" Tavares asked.

To Ash, Ribeiro said, "Vonderach can use two of our mecha. Tell the sunfish. They must allow my people to safety."

"Stand by." Ash muted her display and smiled gleefully. "What a mook. I'll infect the hell out of his mecha as soon as I have access."

Vonnie said, "Our doppelgangers in the ice are fine. We don't need FNEE mecha."

"Don't be dense. Ribeiro doesn't know if we're in control of our units or not. Let him give me access."

"He'll hear us talking to the sunfish. Ash, *I told them to commit suicide for me.* If they ask why we let Santos go after I killed six males, Ribeiro will know."

"We have bigger problems. The PSSC are infiltrating even our basic systems like lighting and meal counts. I can redirect some of their SCPs with our signals to Ribeiro's mecha, and I'll include our own spyware."

"What about our air lock? If you take out Ribeiro's grid, he won't help us."

"We'll fix it ourselves with Tony's suit. The important thing is to beat the PSSC jamming. If we don't, we can't go outside anyway. But if we fox Ribeiro and the *Jyväskylä* does its job, Brazil could decide to stay on our side." Ash had spoken faster and faster as she activated her CEW packets and checkbacks.

Her plan mirrored Vonnie's thinking.

"Okay. Do it." Vonnie opened a third station and touched their group feed.

Henri was offline. So were Dawson and O'Neal. Sweating, Ben had immersed himself in pilot lessons. Harmeet was collating demographics on the sunfish, which struck Vonnie as bizarre. Did she want to finish a genesmithing program before their grid failed?

Vonnie said nothing to Ben or Harmeet. She needed to concentrate on the FNEE mecha because reasoning with the savage males was like juggling swords. They would cut through her.

Right now we can all pretend the FNEE weren't planning to take over and I didn't hurt Santos.

If the males give me away…

29.

But when they were confronted by a FNEE mecha claiming to speak for *Young Matriarch*, the savage males didn't challenge the machine. They were accustomed to scouts bringing messages from one leader to another. They recognized her voice, and their utmost gifts were for deception and improvisation.

Minutes ago, she'd told them to kill Santos. Now she ordered them to let him go.

They didn't dispute the contradiction. They screamed in tribute to her. They also howled for the matriarchs far below, describing their fatalities and Vonnie's praise. In reply, the matriarchs screamed their own praise. The songs of the clan permeated the ice.

Soon, two matriarchs and two scouts scurried up through the catacombs. They joined the savage males.

FNEE translation programs lacked the sophistication of the ESA. To Ribeiro, the clan's screeching sounded like more calls for violence — and as Vonnie's mecha walked among the sunfish, Ash thieved her way deeper into the FNEE grid, filching codes, faking handshakes. Then she backed off. There were PSSC watchdogs throughout Ribeiro's systems.

Vonnie was more intrigued by the ESA translations of the matriarchs' body language. Their arms whisked in their private language. The FNEE missed it, but the ESA deciphered something new. The matriarchs had caught onto Vonnie's game. They gossiped like magpies. They were amused.

They like our traps and lies, she thought. *I invited Santos into my home.*

Then we hurt him. Then we saved him. For the sunfish, it was a joke. The prank cost us six males and it wasn't fun for Santos or Tavares, but the sunfish are learning humor from us.

She brushed the matriarchs with her mecha's legs, wanting to share their mirth. They snapped their beaks without biting. A playful act?

A calm settled upon the ice and Vonnie marveled at how they'd grown.

On her radio, she said, "Santos, run."

He and Tavares sprinted away from Module 01. Beneath them, the savage males shrieked and Tavares yelled, "Don't let them get us!"

The matriarchs increased the pace of their writhing arms. The FNEE unit lacked the tactile sensors of a doppelgänger, but the ESA had saturated Zone One with MMPSAs. Vonnie linked with the nearest segment of their array, potentially exposing it to PSSC jamming. She needed to know what the matriarchs were saying. All too soon, the ESA and the FNEE might need sanctuary. Preparing the sunfish to accept both crews was critical now that the males had had a taste of battle.

She expected bloodthirst. Instead, she heard swift, unfolding wisdom. Lam had said, *They may be smarter than the average human being.* The females who used both hemispheres of their brains probably exceeded the IQs of human geniuses. Combined, they were the equivalent of an AI.

They knew she wanted to bring twenty people among them. They had meticulously sorted the astronauts into factions whose memberships overlapped. Foremost to them were Vonnie and her friends. They included Koebsch in her faction, although they also counted him among the standouts who held various kinds of power over the other astronauts.

The standouts were Koebsch, Henri, Dawson and Harmeet — the commander, the spy, the two genesmiths — all of whom were indebted to Earth for different reasons.

Correctly, the matriarchs thought each of these four people represented larger groups who had yet to appear on Europa. They regarded Dawson's group as predators and Harmeet's group as allies with some reservation.

What had they felt in Harmeet that Vonnie couldn't see?

The matriarchs regarded the FNEE as a rogue pack even if Ribeiro had aligned his squad with the ESA. The sunfish hadn't forgotten their battles with FNEE mecha, but they knew the FNEE soldiers could be manipulated.

Tony and Ash were rogues. Both of them supported Koebsch, yet Tony couldn't hide his fear of the catacombs and Ash was inconsistent. She would follow Koebsch for long periods, then break off like a contrary scout.

—More and more, she is my friend, Vonnie cried. *—She wants to be a part of us.*

—No. No. No. Yes. The matriarchs were less optimistic than Vonnie. They emphasized that they were committed to Ghost Clan Thirty. They wanted Earth's wealth, but they were aware of the fissures between Vonnie and many of her crewmates.

They're trying to talk me into kicking people out of the clan! she realized. *They'd prefer it if we got rid of Dawson and Henri and Ash.*

The matriarchs clacked with their raw new humor. They jabbed at her mecha, biting its cameras and radar. Frightened, Vonnie bumped them — hard — like she was swatting her brother Andreas.

Their message changed. They bowed to her. They would accept any man or woman on her recommendation, but they were explicit about the amount of trust they'd extend to each human. Too many of the ESA and FNEE personnel were suspect. Worse, they resented her for coercing them to accept Lam.

I took the sunfish for granted, she thought. *I assumed they'd do what I wanted, but males know who the matriarchs don't like. They know who I don't like. Hiding in the ice won't be simple. What if they assault Henri or Ash because he's Directorate and she's MI6? The sunfish don't rationalize people's shortcomings. They don't forgive.*

We'll only have a few minutes to escape. I can't let them hurt anyone, not even Dawson.

Across camp, Santos and Tavares reached the FNEE hab module. Beneath the ice, a pack of males screeched, taunting them as Santos and Tavares hurried into their air lock.

—You will not harm my people! Vonnie cried. *—Your males will die for us. This is how the empire begins. It starts with new enemies and killing.*

—*New killing!* they screamed.

—*New territories. New food.* Vonnie walked her mecha like an arrogant dragon, stamping on the ice.

Despite their intelligence, the matriarchs exulted in the grandstanding of her movements. They would pay any price to rebuild their empire. They shrieked at their males, who issued another war cry.

Ash said, "Are you almost done? I'm as far as I can get into the FNEE grid without Ribeiro catching on."

"Can you fox the PSSC jamming?"

"Maybe."

—*I must attend other threats,* Vonnie screamed at the matriarchs. —*Guard our borders. Find Lam. He is essential to our clan.*

They reluctantly agreed. —*We listen. We listen.*

—*I will return,* she cried. Then she shut off her links with the FNEE mecha.

"Von," Koebsch said. He waved for her and she stepped out of her display, leaving her clash of wills with the sunfish.

She knew at a glance that another test waited for her on Koebsch's display. His group feed held the clean, blunt face of a man in his fifties with buzzed gray-blond hair. The man wore a black EUSD uniform. Stitched onto his chest were four combat ribbons and the gold-ray-on-blue patch of the *Jyväskylä.* His chin jutted to one side. He was grinding his teeth.

Koebsch said, "This is Captain Leber. Captain, this is Alexis Vonderach, our engineer."

"*Gutentag,*" she said to the German officer.

Leber had her sympathy. She felt like a speck in a hurricane, but the *Jyväskylä* was a bug surrounded by giant fly swatters. At least he could move. Her people were stationary targets. The question was if they'd kept his discovery of sunfish on Io from the PSSC. That seemed unlikely. What about her discussions with Lam or the matriarchs?

Vonnie examined one of the datastreams most affected by enemy jamming, a ground-to-orbit altercast between Module 01 and their spy sats. "How long ago did they initiate their SCPs?"

"This feed is secure," Leber said.

"That's not what I asked. The PSSC took us down in seconds. That shouldn't have happened, which makes me think they've been infiltrating our grid for weeks. They could know everything we've done since we allied with Ribeiro. They could be stealing everything you know about Io."

Leber's jaw clenched. This was a man accustomed to giving orders, not allowing debate. "Our command-and-control is secure," he said. "We're openly broadcasting everything else to Earth. None of our sims from Io are encrypted."

"Why would you do that?"

"An HK penetrated my screens, two of my people were killed and we have SCPs inside our life support."

Her stomach rolled. "I apologize. I didn't—"

"They don't want the world to hear about Io. Our findings may open new sessions in the A.N., and they don't want me to set terms. If they can, they'll burn my ship. You're ROM. I wanted to speak to you myself."

He wanted to evaluate me and I screwed up.

"We may need a diversion," Leber said. He grated his teeth, considering her. Then he reached into his display. "Lieutenant Wade will coordinate with you. Do what he says."

Leber signed off. His image was replaced by a man twenty years younger but carved from the same mold, short hair, black uniform, his face wrought with stress. "I have overrides and flash codes," Wade said. "Verify your altercasts."

"Cycle seven, cycle one."

"Stand by for transmission."

"Please tell Captain Leber I'm sorry."

Wade seemed to notice her for the first time. "I will. Prepare your assault. Hold for our mark. Codes include dead-mans. Copy that?"

"Yes, sir."

Wade sent his packets in a squeal. Then another. Then he signed off, too.

Vonnie hadn't anticipated such short bursts. He'd transmitted simple ROM-4 codes. Their plan wasn't to confront the PSSC sabotage and control programs with elaborate countermeasures. Their plan was for the ESA *to cripple their own machines*, torching the very processors that hosted the SCPs.

When she was done, their mecha would be incapable of high-level interaction with each other or the astronauts. Their mecha would exist as brute metal skeletons with functioning hydraulics and extremely constricted data/comm… but the stupid machines could march on the PSSC camp.

She should have known the EUSD would arrive at Jupiter with detailed manifests of every piece of hardware in the ESA mission. Each mecha had a specific kill code as a failsafe. Koebsch had the same overrides, but too many of his systems were down. Now the *Jyväskylä* had replaced what he'd lost.

The obstacle would be sending the overrides to their mecha. Module 01's exterior was studded with dozens of transceivers from radio dishes to neutrino pulse components. Most had been corrupted.

"Koebsch, I need laser comms." She opened a map of their units on the surface.

"Delete that map," he said. "Q-and-e your work. Don't do anything until they give the order." He didn't want enemy SCPs to catch her preparing.

It was good to stand beside him. If they were going to die, she wanted to acknowledge how she felt. She wouldn't poison what she had with Ben, but she hoped she could forge a deeper if platonic relationship with Koebsch. They'd been through too much. He wasn't her colleague. He was a dear friend. Somehow the three of them needed to work together.

She felt gutsy and brave. They could die at any instant or stand in their module for hours as the space war played out. Waiting was the hardest part.

"About dinner," she said.

He froze.

Behind them, Ash turned with a scowl, so Vonnie lowered her voice and said, "I'd like that if your offer stands."

"It does."

Her pulse was like a drum. "We'll talk. Later. When this over. What about Io?"

"I wanted Leber to tell you. He has sims and analysis. It's mixed news."

It's bad news, she thought. *That's why he wanted Leber to tell me.*

Koebsch said, "Long-range instruments confirmed the presence of four sunfish on Io's surface and nineteen more in caverns below ground."

"That's incredible!"

"There are no indications of life. No movement. No sonar. The sunfish we found are dead."

She laughed. The sound had the reckless air of a woman facing her own execution. The PSSC could kill her, but they couldn't take away what the ESA and EUSD had learned. "We've barely explored Europa, and Io is bigger," she said. "It could take years to find a living colony."

"Leber doesn't think so. There's no water. No oxygen."

"How did they get there?"

"We don't know. They've been dead for thousands of years. The bodies are mummified."

"Is he looking at Ganymede or Callisto?"

"We're going through old data, and Leber cast defensive screens across the system. He's gathering what he can. His first priority is his ship."

"The *sunfish* must have had ships!"

"It could be a case of parallel evolution."

"Not if they're actually sunfish. Their physiology is the same?"

"As near as we can tell."

"Smaller breed or larger breed?"

"Larger." Koebsch put five sims on his display.

Vonnie gaped at the detailed X-rays and neutrino pulse scans. She said, "How can you suggest parallel evolution would produce a species with identical size, identical cartilage structures, eight arms, beaks, lungs, gills, and no eyes? A species native to Io would have their own morphology. They wouldn't look like the sunfish."

"I admit his sims are convincing."

"Ha! Koebsch, at some point there was a technological civilization in the Great Ocean. They got through the ice and into space."

"It's possible." He wrapped his arm around her experimentally, then let her go. "Back to work," he said. "I'll tell you if there's anything new."

"Yes, sir."

"Call me Peter."

"No, sir." She continued to work on her display as she spoke. "We need to make sure Berlin hears everything. If there are sunfish on Io, they must have colonies on Ganymede and Callisto, too." She was obsessed. "What if they landed on Mars or Earth's moon while we were still living in caves?"

Koebsch brought up a new datastream. It showed comparisons of Jupiter's largest moons. "Here's something else to consider," he said. "Ganymede has an ocean like Europa. It also has more landforms."

Ganymede was two times larger than Europa and far denser. Callisto was closer to Europa's mass. Both had been candidates for deuterium mining. Callisto wouldn't have been as hazardous to human crews because she was outside Jupiter's main radiation belt, but mecha didn't care about radiation and what Earth wanted most was bountiful water ice.

Ganymede's surface was a frozen crust like Europa's, although it was infused with clay, sulfur dioxide, cyanogen and hydrogen sulfate — a mess of dirt and toxins left by meteor impacts and primordial swellings from her iron core.

Callisto was dirtier. At her center was a weak silicate core. She had no mountains, no volcanoes, no tectonic pressures. She was the coldest of the four moons. The compressed rock and ice of her shell had never been smoothed. Many of her innumerable craters dated to four billion years ago. Callisto was a museum of timeless filth. She had an ocean, too — layers of slush and water more than ninety kilometers below her surface — but it was Ganymede's profile that drew Vonnie's eye.

These moons had been excluded from mining because of their foul crusts. Nevertheless, Ganymede's ocean was greater than Europa's, equally warm and less volatile. The swellings in her mantle had occurred early in her creation.

Ganymede was steadier than Europa, and she had dry pockets and shores among the landforms suspended in her ice. Water-rock contact was considered vital to the development of life. Some of Ganymede's caverns might have filled with oxygen atmospheres. Also, Ganymede had a higher iron content than Europa. Iron meant steel.

Koebsch said, "If the sunfish came from somewhere else, that would explain the gaps in Europa's evolutionary history. They were more likely to discover fire and metallurgy inside Ganymede's landforms than underwater. We know they had eyes in their past. They looked up. They saw the stars, and the low gravity made it easier for them to achieve escape velocity than it ever was for humankind."

Vonnie nodded slowly. She had mourned the loss of the sunfish empire inside Europa. Now she could barely grasp how far their civilization had fallen.

"You think Ganymede is their home world," she said.

"Maybe not. They could have come from Io or Callisto." Koebsch pointed at the *Jyväskylä*'s imagery.

Four sunfish lay entombed in a black-and-umber snowfield, their corpses withered. Alongside them were the eroded granite pieces of what had been a hieroglyphic.

"What if we've been in the wrong place this whole time?" he said.

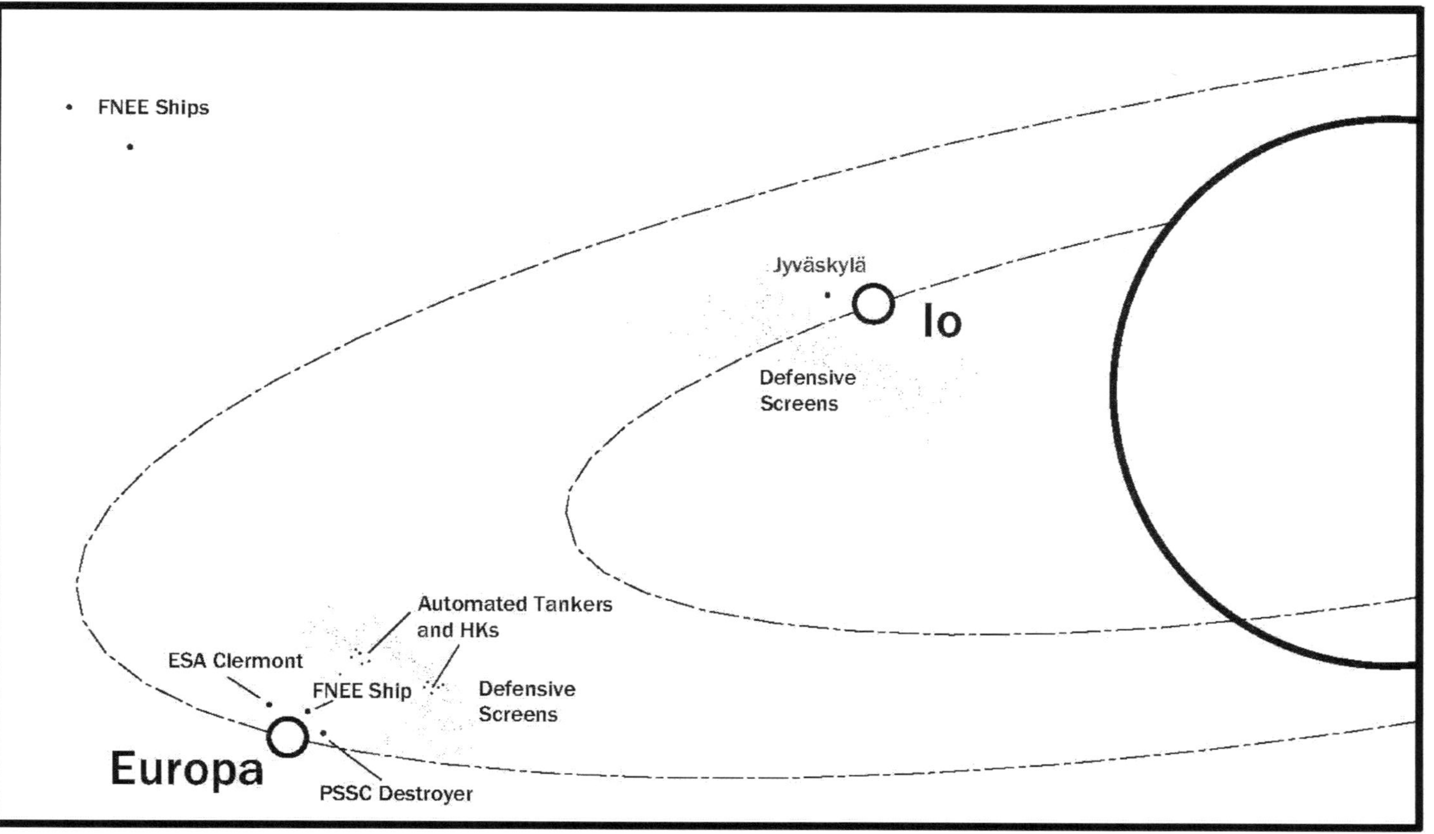

Ships and HKs

30.

Before leaving Earth, Vonnie had done her homework. Everyone studied outside their specialties. She knew their star system was not unique in possessing a yellow sun and planets. If these were the only requirements for life, their spiral arm of the galaxy might have teemed with advanced civilizations.

The spiral arm was barren. No one, no *thing*, had ever been detected by the SETI radioscopes.

Their star system was an unlikely oasis.

They were far from the galactic core, so they'd been spared the radiation of giant suns and chain-reaction supernovae. If a jealous God had placed Earth at the center of existence, their oceans would have boiled away long, long before the advent of single-celled organisms.

Their star was also remarkably stable. It spluttered and flared, but it hadn't reduced its companions to husks, which was the fate of many planets in other systems beyond the galactic core. Such worlds might have lived. Instead, many were abused by their own suns. Thus humankind and the sunfish won another roll of the dice.

Next, Jupiter was both an anchor and a broom. Its presence had allowed the formation of smaller terrestrial worlds closer to the sun. It also swept up most of the debris throughout the system, reducing the meteor and comet impacts on Earth as primitive vegetation crept across the continents, building a future for air breathers.

More than once, the cosmos had punched Earth with fiery blows — but not often enough to annihilate the young, growing things in her oceans or on her lands.

There was another stroke of providence. Jupiter was not only well-positioned, it was ideally sized. If the old god had massed ten percent more, it could have ignited as a second sun between Mars and Saturn.

More than half of all systems had double or triple stars. The result was catastrophic on terrestrial worlds like Earth and Europa. If the additional gravity hadn't sent the inner planets careening like billiard balls, the additional heat would have roasted Earth, making it a greenhouse like Venus. Io, Europa, Ganymede and Callisto would have been incinerated if they'd formed at all.

Even as a gas giant, Jupiter bathed its moons in radiation.

A more sinister peril was the inexorable drag of its gravity. Over time, Jupiter had swallowed everything in its grip, creating and recreating its children as if each moon was a phoenix.

One night in her bunk, basking after sex, Ben obstinately bragged about his research and his lack of media coverage on Earth. "If you look at the numbers, we can prove our theories, but people hate thinking about how tiny we are, so it's business as usual. They don't want to hear that we were created out of dust with the sunfish."

"I do," she said, massaging his chest.

Ben said in its earliest days, Jupiter had gathered a circumplanetary disk of gases and solids. This stuff coalesced into moons — but the disk remained so thick, it restricted their orbital momentum.

The moons spiraled in. They were torn apart. Some of this material replenished the disk.

Meanwhile, new bodies were born.

Each group was short-lived. The moons currently surrounding Jupiter were its fifth, most enduring family. They were nearly as old as Earth and the other planets, having spun into existence with unimaginable speed and force.

From the waning volume of Jupiter's disk, Io, Europa and Ganymede had been birthed in the exceptionally brief period of 10,000 years while Callisto, accreting at the edge of the disk, took 100,000 years.

The speed with which they'd formed wasn't the miracle. It was that as each family of moons came and went, the available materials changed. Less water, more water, more rock, new chemicals and more heat arduously led to a pre-biotic soup.

"Earth swept up a lot of comets, too," Ben said. "We got our share of water and organics, but compared to Earth, the number of combinations that took place in the Jupiter system was higher — much higher — and the tempo was faster. I won't be surprised if we prove life on Europa is older than on Earth."

Foolishly, Vonnie admitted these parallels made her ponder the existence of a higher being. "Two intelligent species around one star makes me believe in God," she said.

Ben laughed at her. "You're being anthropocentric. Everybody thinks they're the hero of the story. We weren't *chosen* by Allah or Jehovah or Odin or Pan. We're a fluke blend of elements and there are quadrillions of empty systems where things didn't line up, so there's no story to be told, right? We happen to be in the ideal star system to look around and decide we're special."

"We are special, Ben."

"But people want to believe it's eternal, world without end, the earth is immutable and so are human beings. That's wrong. Our planet has been host to some wildly different environments. Deserts used to be jungles. There are ancient cities beneath the oceans. Several branches of primates died out before *Homo sapiens* came along. The same thing is happening here with who knows how many breeds of sunfish. Once upon a time, Europa itself didn't exist, but I can't get anyone except the science channels to bother mentioning that even our planets are temporary."

"How temporary?"

"Uh, we're not talking about next Monday," he conceded, tickling her until she giggled and fought back and he pinned her wrists to the bed, kissing her neck.

By the twenty-second century of the Western calendar, Jupiter's disk had dwindled to rings… yet even its faded rings were abrasive. For its innermost daughters, the battering would not cease until they were worn into powder.

Metis and Adrastea orbited extraordinarily close to Jupiter at a dizzying pace of thirty-one kilometers per second. Vonnie loved that number — *31 klicks per second* — which was more than one hundred thousand kilometers an hour or 70,000 miles an hour. Year after year, Metis and Adrastea whacked through trillions of particles and asteroids drawn by Jupiter's gravity.

Metis's leading face had disintegrated into a concave, absorbing blows, spitting debris.

Io was also shotgunned by the maelstrom, but she was large enough to withstand her beatings. Her pain came from her center. Like Europa, Io possessed a molten iron core. She was stretched and squeezed as she reeled around Jupiter.

Ice spotted Io's surface, although she'd cooked off most of her water. The frozen substances were yellow snowfields of sulfur dioxide, yet she vomited magma at temperatures exceeding 1,650 degrees Celsius — 3,000 Fahrenheit. The snow mixed with floodplains of incandescent lava.

Io was sick. She pulsed like an aneurysm. Pumping gases and ionized plasma into space, she added to Jupiter's rings.

The magnetized, radioactive fields of the inner system played hell with radar. Ships relied on defensive screens consisting of thousands of probes, using AIs to knit each jot of information into a gestalt.

Vonnie's ship, the *Marcuse*, had accessed the preexisting grids of their satellites and tankers to reach Europa. She'd come straight in. The *Jyväskylä* was handicapped by false signals and blackouts — and in addition to weaving through the natural ship-killers, the *Jyväskylä* dueled with the PSSC destroyer, HKs and nano weapons. Also in play were the new FNEE ships, who might join either side.

Vonnie wouldn't blame Captain Leber if he abandoned Io. Dead sunfish didn't matter to a man with a gun against his head, although he could protect himself by staying in Io's shadow. Defense as the best offense.

The PSSC held most of the cards. If they disabled or killed Leber, they could invade the ESA camp. The safety of her crew — and her clan — hung on Leber.

Alternatively, PSSC mecha could strike the ESA camp to gain concessions from the *Jyväskylä*.

Would he surrender or would he fight?

Vonnie's nerves were frayed and her stomach felt like Io's mottled surface. Part of her wanted to get it over with. Part of her whispered to be patient.

Beside her, Koebsch ended a call with NASA. Vonnie had been fidgeting with her overrides. "I'm done," she said. "Do you want me to help Tony in the armory?"

"Stay. Ash and I need to q-and-e our grid or the Americans won't share their spy sats. You keep us alive."

"Got it." Vonnie opened their diagnostics of Module 01. Food, water and sewage were unimportant. Power and air took priority. Same with heating. Same with the lights. Regaining control of their doors was also preferable.

Christ, she thought. SCPs had shut off their airco, which was why the copper-and-plastic stink of their electrical systems hadn't dissipated.

They could wear pressure suits if the air stayed off. But if the doors never opened?

That didn't bear thinking about.

She said, "If I was the PSSC, I'd land probes on Io. I wouldn't waste time with us. Do you think they've already been there?"

He said, "Ezekiel's wheel."

"What?"

"Ezekiel's wheel. The Bible has accounts of visitations by what sound like alien spacecraft. So do Indian writings from 4,000 B.C., Egyptian writings from 1,500 B.C., and other cultures all over the world. Those could have been ships from the sunfish empire."

He's done his homework, too, she thought, but she shook her head. "Sunfish couldn't withstand Earth's gravity."

"If they had spaceflight, they must have learned how to deal with acceleration. Maybe they had crash couches in their ships. Maybe they landed in our oceans or rivers like the Bay of Bengal or the Nile."

He meant because the water's buoyancy would reduce the strain of Earth's gravity. Vonnie wasn't convinced. Her shuttle from Darmstat into Earth orbit had maxed three Gs. On the other hand, the earliest rockets of the twentieth century had maxed over six and seven.

Positing space travel by the sunfish was a stretch. She couldn't imagine they'd refined their craft from rocket engines to fusion jets. That they'd visited human civilizations seemed preposterous — and yet at most, sunfish leaving Ganymede or Europa might have experienced .75G for a few seconds.

She said, "They could tolerate escape velocity from one moon to another, but those liftoffs wouldn't feel anything like touching down on Earth."

He smiled. "It's just a crazy theory, Von. How else do you explain Io?"

He was a welcome distraction from her fear. So was brooding about Ben. She shouldn't let herself feel tempted by Koebsch, but the shame gnawing on her conscience was another bright emotion to sidetrack her from her anxiety.

How much help can NASA provide?

Will the FNEE ships attack the Jyväskylä?

Vonnie pressed her hands against her temples. "I can fix the airco," she said. "Our heating units are fried. We'll have to yank them."

"What do you need?"

"An hour. Less with Tony's help."

"He's still rigging his suit."

"If we freeze to death—"

"Let's make sure we can evacuate. We need that suit to repair the lock."

She nodded. Then, suddenly, she took his hand. "Thank you. I don't always see the bigger picture."

He closed his fingers on hers. "That's not true. You're the heart and soul of our crew."

"You're in charge. You've done better than I ever could." *I sound like I'm saying goodbye,* she thought, and it was a miserable feeling.

He almost kissed her. She saw his desire in his expression. She tilted her chin up to encourage him. They both knew what was coming. She wanted it. Then his gaze darted toward Ash and he let go of her hand.

"Peter," she said.

The module shook. Beneath the ice, she saw PSSC mecha advancing through her sims, detonating mines, causing sinkholes and avalanches.

Fractures zigzagged across the surface. A chasm ruptured the eastern border of the ESA/FNEE camp and devoured two listening posts. Far overhead, their spy sats tracked the seismic upheaval. So did their arrays in the catacombs.

"We have enemy mecha inside our lines!" Ash cried as Vonnie yelled, "Goddamn it, they were five klicks away! How did they get so close?"

"I'm alerting Colonel Ribeiro," Ash said.

"You were watching us instead of doing your job!" Vonnie yelled, but Koebsch said, "It's not her fault. Our subsurface grid was compromised."

One of their doppelgängers had been paralyzed by an enemy slavecast. SCPs had created other gaps in their arrays. Radar, gone. Seismography, gone.

Shutting off the infected MMPSAs, Vonnie switched to neutrino pulse where she'd lost everything else.

Their mines had exploded in three clusters, one low, two high. Her display showed the skeletal parts of five PSSC mecha sliding apart with the ice. The mines had destroyed them.

More spearheads of PSSC mecha were hurrying north and south. Soon they would curl in toward the colony.

At the same time, four packs of screaming males raced outward through the devastation. She saw more than a hundred males, but one pack was thwarted by a cave-in. Another was pulled into the vacuum of a blowout.

The catacombs shuddered. Cave-ins filled the opening and reduced the bawling winds to a sigh.

Other males hurtled toward the invaders.

Vonnie patched into an array of MMPSAs with functioning sonar. —*Stop!* she cried. —*Their metal warriors will kill you!*

—*New enemies!* they shrieked. —*New food! New death!*

She should have known better than to try to deter savage males. As they scrambled through a rock field, an alumalloy shape leaped from a cranny. It moved to the head of the pack.

"That's Lam," Koebsch said. "Tell him to get out of there. He's too close to our mines."

—Lam, stop them! Go back!

He rapped at the ice, conveying his own message to the savage males. One group altered direction. They swarmed down through a fork in the catacombs, turning from the enemy mecha. "Is he…?" Vonnie wondered, but Lam's group rushed on.

"Maybe they can damage a few units," Koebsch said. He was willing to see them die.

—Lam, it's me! she cried. *—Lam!*

She directed her GPs and doppelgängers to meet the enemy at five choke points. Several FNEE mecha and a gun platform mingled among her units, but the FNEE mecha did not acknowledge her signals. They stood motionless while her units scurried forward.

Shit. If they don't back us up, we won't have any guns. And if they fire on us…

"Sir, no response from Colonel Ribeiro," Ash said.

"I have no response from their mecha," Vonnie said with that sick, hot sensation in her stomach.

At the center of the colony, the matriarchs were gathering tools and food. The breeding pairs collected their eggs. Where would they go?

To the west, the chimney where she'd rescued O'Neal had become a swamp encased in hard new ice. Northwest, the tunnels were shattered and wet. If they went southwest, they might evade the PSSC mecha. Or they could go down. There were fin mountains and Mid Clans beneath their colony.

—Lam, don't attack! Vonnie cried. *—Block the tunnels, then come back to us!*

He kept running. He added his sonar to the males' shrieks, whipping them into a frenzy of sheer, unthinking bloodlust.

—We are Thirty! they screamed.

Further east, among the cavities where the mines had detonated, a GP was being drawn into the largest sinkhole. So were two unexploded mines.

Vonnie's sims anticipated the currents in the ice. She instructed her GP to wade sideways through the avalanche. If the mines went off, the blast would drag down their northern border as well as the PSSC mecha. That might have been an acceptable trade-off if the males weren't so close.

Koebsch signaled Landers 04 and 05. "Ben, Henri, get out of here. Watch out for the FNEE. Von, what can you do about their gun platforms on the surface?"

"My overrides are ready. Our mecha can attack theirs," she said as calmly as she could.

"Ash, try Ribeiro again."

"Sir, they're offline. I'm hailing them with everything we've got."

"I'll airlift your module," Ben said from Lander 04.

"Don't," Koebsch said. "We'll just weigh you down."

"Vonnie?" Ben asked. With one word, he'd stated his willingness to defy Koebsch.

Her heart swelled with affection. She was proud of him, but she said, "Go. Please. We can't protect you from close-range fire if Ribeiro—"

Far below, outside Zone Two's eastern border, more cave-ins dropped the catacombs. A new slide brought an unexploded mine toward Vonnie's GP. She sent it scrambling away, but loose ice impeded its progress.

The mine's sensors winked to life. In another meter, it would detonate.

On her display, a different alarm winked. The ESA's ravaged grid finally determined where Lam sent his stray pack of males. The pack had split in two. Both groups were digging. Soon they'd open the compacted slush along the belly of a lake and the thawing side of a gas vent.

They were nowhere near the fight. They'd gone 2.7 klicks beneath the mecha — 5.9 beneath the surface — but Vonnie was all too familiar with blowouts in Europa's gravity.

Another explosion would increase the downward pressure. If the mine went off, more avalanches would compress the flooding and the gas.

"Ben, get out of here!" she yelled.

"This is Frerotte in Lander 05," Henri said. "I have a visual on the FNEE squad. They are outside their hab module. I repeat, they are outside their module."

O'Neal was with Henri in 05. "They're heavily armed. I see assault weapons and SAMs. They—"

The mine exploded.

31.

To Vonnie, it felt like a thousand events happened at once. Beneath the ice, the concussion tore through her GP. Fire and shrapnel set off the next mine.

More ice dropped in heaps, spilling and pouring and crashing down. The chain reaction sprang toward the savage males and PSSC mecha. Like crunching jaws, the ice became a monster in its own right. It crushed two packs of males into jelly.

The rumbling took longer to converge on the other males and the PSSC mecha. Before it reached them, they collided with each other.

Lam was with these males. He'd directed them into four arrows, two in front, two from above.

There were five mecha. Forty-forty males enveloped them. The mecha opened fire. Their chain guns were loaded with VRAP rounds.

Lam shielded himself with three males, bouncing from the ceiling into the wall into the floor. Their next move would have been to bounce underneath the nearest mecha.

They were cut down. The armor piercing rounds were like needles with small entrance wounds, small exit wounds and little gore — but the hollow-point rounds and the explosive squash heads literally tore them apart. Their insides splattered like Rorschach inkblots.

Lam was struck by two armor piercing rounds. One splashed through the lab-grown skin and blubber on his metal chassis. The other severed the tip of an arm. He rolled into a gap blown through the tunnel wall, smearing the blood of real sunfish on the ice as he scurried away.

He jumped and soared and climbed.

Behind him, eleven injured males clawed at other rifts in the ceiling. Bleeding, gasping, they dropped four tons of ice. Two mecha were hit. The others were obstructed. There was nowhere for the mecha to retreat. One unit pried at the hole where Lam had gone, its chain guns stuttering as it attempted to widen the gap and pursue him.

The battlefield imploded. Living and dead, the sunfish popped like fruit. The machines were pulverized. Some of their ordnance exploded, creating new vibrations.

Lam zigzagged up through a fissure with unearthly dexterity, better than a man, better than a sunfish. Below him, the ice jounced. The fissure widened. He leaped through the open space.

Abruptly, the fissure shut. He clawed at the grinding morass. Then the ice fell in. It took him.

A kilometer overhead, two beacons traded signals with Lam when he broadcast on multiple wavelengths. —*This is ESA Probe 114!* he radioed. He knew the PSSC would target him if they learned that he held the personality of Choh Lam.

Vonnie couldn't watch him die again. She averted her eyes as he disappeared from their grid. There was nothing she could do to find Lam. The ESA mecha on the surface were useless until she transmitted her overrides. The rest of her assets were inside the colony or committed to its southern border. If the buckling ice didn't engulf them, she needed every last GP and doppelgänger for combat.

Far below, the males opened their lake. The water fell into the blistering gas vents. They were broiled alive. Steam jetted upward and sideways, rupturing other gas pockets. Some held thin atmospheres of carbon dioxide. Some were superheated balloons of sulfur and hydrogen.

Shockwaves pummeled the frozen sky. Then the flood belched up through the sinking ice.

Above the surface, the ESA landers bent away from each other. Ben angled toward Module 01. Henri flew over the FNEE soldiers. Vonnie's display flickered with PSSC jamming, static, and glimpses from Henri's cams.

On the east end of camp, Ribeiro's squad fled in scout suits. Their mecha had not accompanied them. They ran on foot with insulated machine pistols and surface-to-air missile launchers. One man held a short-range mortar. He fell when the ice heaved. Another man grabbed him.

A third man aimed some sort of device at Henri.

"They're too close! I can't fox 'em!" Ash shouted, but Henri said, "He's pointing a surveyor's dish, not a weapon. They're radioing me."

"*Henri, clear out!*" Vonnie screamed.

"I have Ribeiro online," Henri said as Ribeiro himself signed onto their group feed.

His eyes were seared with urgency. PSSC sabotage and control programs had debilitated his grid, which was why his squad had run outside. It was why his mecha had gone dark. The PSSC had ruthlessly disposed of Ribeiro's soldiers as pawns in their offensive against the ESA.

Ribeiro said, "Koebsch, I need—"

Vonnie was still screaming: "*Clear out! Henri! The surface will—*"

Geysers blew through the ice in six places. The largest spouts were on the east side of camp. Another splattered up beneath Module 02.

The ice lifted in shards as heavy as Berlin's skyscrapers. Pieces like houses and cars and fifty thousand knives ripped upward, a billowing white cauldron. Flash frozen water erupted as towering snakes that twisted and cracked.

Ribeiro's people were flung from the surface. Their hab module puffed with orange fire when a cache of missiles or mines exploded.

One man slammed into the bottom of Henri's lander. So did gas and ice. The man — it was Alvaréz — died as the geyser evaporated against the lander's fusion jets. Seething crosswinds dismembered his corpse.

Pereira's suit was compromised by the same burns that killed Alvaréz. Within hours, he might have died from radiation sickness, but he didn't have that long. His plastisteel armor weakened. It repelled most of the ice clattering against his suit until a dagger shot through his arm. Another perforated his thigh. Explosive decompression finished him.

The ice bashed Carvalho's hands into his helmet. He was carrying a

FiveSAM, a five-round surface-to-air missile launcher. The titanium barrel cracked his helmet. His faceplate blew out.

Three blocks of ice folded Santos like a doll, rupturing his spine. He went into cardiac arrest. His suit tried to revive him. It restarted his heart, but dislocated ribs went through his lungs. The suit couldn't compensate.

Ribeiro and Tavares were knocked clear. He sprained his elbow. She struck her temple on the inside of her helmet, drawing blood. Nevertheless, they lived.

Araújo was the only member of the FNEE who wasn't injured. As their point man, he'd led them from their hab module, so he was ahead of the squad. He was thrown on his belly and dropped his weapon in the thundering white sleet. When a huge plate of ice tilted up, he slid away.

By luck, he missed two cracks. Then he fell into a chasm, grabbing at its sides.

If there was any benefit to this massacre, FNEE emergency signals overpowered the PSSC jamming. Beneath the ice and on the surface, the FNEE mecha were gone. Their spy sats had repulsed PSSC incursions. The same could be said for their ship above Europa's southern pole and their two ships in deeper space.

Without interference from camp, the FNEE spy sats and their spacecraft realigned their net. They boosted their signal strength. In orbit, Major Correa took control of the scout suits worn by Ribeiro, Tavares and Araújo.

He did the same for Santos and Carvalho. They were dead but their sensors added radar and data/comm as they sailed upward, tumbling inside the geyser.

Tavares was shaken by the blow to her head. She said nothing as her suit sprinted toward Araújo. He clung to the chasm until his suit located a thin shelf below him. It pulled his hands from the wall and jumped *down*, ignoring his shouts. It landed in a crouch. It lifted its arms and fired two cables at Tavares. Her suit missed one cable but caught the other. Then her suit dragged him up.

In another setting, Vonnie would have been impressed by their teamwork — but Ribeiro's suit ran from the epicenter. First and foremost, Correa was saving his commander.

You bastards.

Lander 04's jets blazed as slick white dust surged over its port side. Ben was on the outskirts of this geyser. He surfed away as it buffeted him with condensation and gas. With him was Dawson, who squeaked inarticulately. Otherwise the old man conducted himself well, operating Lander 04's cameras for Ben, who lacked nav or radar.

Ben circled around, taking hits, rolling into a nosedive when a glob of ice thumped his front side. He regained control, shouting, "Henri! Henri! Harmeet!"

Alvaréz had clanged against Lander 05 with several tons of ice. An AI might have steered itself to safety. Henri could not. He must have intended to ride the geyser into space. He was on his side when he accelerated.

Lander 05 shot from one geyser into the next, flipped and shot clear again. It whacked into the splintering plain on the northern end of camp. Good clean air gusted from its hull, then a clotting necklace of red beads. Then it was obscured by the pillows of mist around a bubbling spring.

In the opposite direction, two kilometers south, the *Marcuse* issued an alarm as it pitched against its mooring cables. They'd mothballed the *Marcuse* where its fusion jets wouldn't melt the ice above the colony. One of its cables snapped. It tilted.

Much closer, a paroxysm of water and gas took Module 02. The empty module sent alerts as it was squashed.

Lander 05 issued many of the same alerts, although its signals were distorted by SCPs. Hull breach. System failures. Critical injuries to personnel. Nobody inside answered the radio as Ben yelled, "Henri!"

Module 01 shook, but it held to its new foundation. Ash staggered into Vonnie. Clutching at her station, she cracked her knee.

Their displays fluttered and went black. The datastreams that returned did not include most of the ESA mecha. Outside the colony, their doppelgängers and GPs had been crushed. On the surface, many of their infected units were also gone.

Inside Zone One, their machines survived with the breeding pairs. Floods swept through Zone Two. Most of the air locks separating One and Two were demolished, but the work Vonnie had done to reinforce the colony paid off now in minimizing the loss of atmosphere, maximizing the retention of habitable space, and shielding them from the deluge.

In three places, water encroached into Zone One, then froze, creating new bulkheads and splinting the fractured ice. Throughout the tunnels, Vonnie's arrays reported four matriarchs wounded and a breeding pair killed.

Then they lost ten times as many.

Twenty-four breeding pairs had taken shelter near Submodule 07. This was the cavern where Vonnie appeared in person. It was where mecha entered with food. The sunfish had imbued this cavern with the aromas of pheromones and urine. They'd scratched carvings into the ice. Few places in their world were as sacrosanct.

As the PSSC mecha loomed near the colony, the older matriarchs had sent their healthiest males and young females to Vonnie. One of them was Michelle. Natalie was there, too. The breeding pairs were meant to escort Vonnie and her crew if they ran into the ice — and to perpetuate the tribe if necessary.

They died when the surface she'd fortified wasn't substantial enough. Submodule 07 and Module 06 jackknifed with the quakes. 07's struts pushed up. The cargo tube screwed down. The ice blew out.

The breeding pairs were sucked into a vortex of machinery, supply cases and decontamination bubbles.

The tent retained a wisp of air. Fourteen sunfish lived longer than the rest in cloying sheets of plastic. It muffled their shrieks. Then they died, too, frothing blood. Vonnie screamed for them. "Nooooo!"

Module 06 overturned. Submodule 07's roof dented in. Then the quakes closed the labyrinth. The blowout was contained. If the breeding pairs hadn't been waiting for her, they wouldn't have died, but Vonnie was beyond grief. She was beyond guilt.

She wanted to save her friends.

Then she wanted to hurt the PSSC.

32.

Hatred made her stronger. She felt larger than herself as she returned to her station. Too many of her windows were black with PSSC jamming or the ghastly silence from Lander 05.

Frerotte: NO LIFE SIGNS

Johal: NO LIFE SIGNS

O'Neal: NO LIFE SIGNS

She paged through FNEE satellite imagery downward onto Europa's surface and outward into space. Orbital radar couldn't show the blood rubies that had spurted from Lander 05, but she saw that red necklace again and again in her mind.

The Jupiter system churned with death. The explosions beneath the ice had been a starting gun, awakening man-made rings from Metis out past Callisto.

Thousands of drifting objects had fired their jets in groups and waves, accelerating toward each other or the ships. Many cloaked themselves in CEW. The HKs packed warheads or nanotech. Defensive screens used chaff, flares, EMPs and clouds of nanotech. Missiles and interceptors played hide-and-seek, detonating by the hundreds.

Like the battle on Europa, the space war occurred on many levels — tangible, microscopic, electronic. Even the mental states of their personnel influenced the fight.

"I have authenticated flash codes from Captain Leber!" Ash shouted. "The *Jyväskylä* has attacked the *Dongfangzhixing,* not the FNEE ships. I repeat, the *Jyväskylä* has attacked the Chinese destroyer, not the Brazilian ships. He's ordered us to engage the PSSC."

"Hold for my command," Koebsch said.

"Sir, we can't—"

"Hold for my command."

Vonnie had memorized the distances on the surface. Her mecha would need an hour to reach the PSSC camp, but they had other weapons at their disposal.

"Let me send our tankers," she said.

Koebsch was yelling at the FNEE and Ben. "Ribeiro, can you hear me? Lander 04 is due west of your position! Activate beacons or lights! Lander 04 will find you!"

Ben said, "I need to get Henri and—"

"They're dead!" Koebsch yelled. "Damn it, Metzler! Go for Ribeiro's squad!"

It had been weeks since Koebsch addressed Ben by his surname. Doing so was significant in the same way that Vonnie had begun to call him *Peter.* She'd drawn him closer. Koebsch was divorcing himself from his nascent friendship with Ben and reasserting his authority.

"I won't do it!" Ben shouted.

"Dawson, can you fly that lander?" Koebsch asked.

The old man said, "The AIs are down. No. I can't. What would you have me do with Ben, arrest him?"

"Try it! Go ahead and try it!" Ben shouted. "I'm going to lift 05 out of here, then I'm coming back for you. Ribeiro has to make it on his own."

"I can reach 05," Vonnie said. "Ben, get out of the air. We can't stop their missiles."

"I'm not leaving you."

"I can reach 05. If anyone's alive, we'll take them with us. We're evacuating the module. Get out of the air. You have to trust me."

"I do," he said.

Those words were special to them. She smiled.

Listening, Koebsch softened his tone. "Ben, Major Correa is online," he said.

The FNEE radio bands crackled. "This is Correa. We have three survivors on the ice. They're running northwest but there are chasms ahead of them. They'll be cut off."

Ben said, "Shit." Then, "I hear their transponders."

"They've added lights. Do you see them?"

"Von, I love you. Major, patch me into your team." With that, Ben quit talking to Vonnie and Koebsch. He yelled, "Colonel, stop your men where they are! Back up! Back up! That area is sliding! Dawson, find me a place to land!" Ejecta rattled against the lander and Ben yelled, "Hold on!"

Koebsch turned to Vonnie. "How can you reach 05?"

Behind them, Ash worked ceaselessly at her display. "Sir, my links with NASA are down. I'm totally offline."

"I have executive channels."

"I've lost my feeds from our spy sats. I cannot raise the *Jyväskylä*. Our last authenticated report showed them brushing back ten HKs before an EMP cut us off, but they had more bogies inbound."

"Take my station." Koebsch stepped out of his display.

Ash hurried over.

The room was colder, and their breathing was shallow and fast. Low oxygen. If they wanted to counterattack, it needed to be soon. Vonnie glanced at her few datastreams.

She saw Ben land near the FNEE soldiers. They charged into his air lock. He lifted off, pitching to starboard.

"Send our tankers at their destroyer!" she said. "Launch our missiles aboard the *Clermont*. Do it before they shut us down."

Koebsch shook his head. "I haven't fired on the PSSC because they've restricted themselves to electronic warfare."

"Peter, they're killing us."

"The geysers were caused by our mines and the sunfish. The PSSC took out our grid, but they haven't hurt anyone and that's not a line I want to cross."

She grabbed his arms. "Leber lost two men! Their mecha invaded our camp!"

"Their mecha approached our border. That's it. Leber's casualties were in space. I don't think they'll fire on Ben, not if we hold our fire. We're no use to them dead."

"You're going to surrender?"

"If it comes to that, they'll repatriate us through the Red Cross on Earth. We'll be interrogated but we'll be alive."

"Peter, Jesus Christ." She let go of him like she'd been scorched — like she'd been branded by despair or cowardice. She preferred her rage.

Like most people on Earth, the PSSC considered themselves more advanced than the sunfish.

What kind of species butchered its own for a water source as big as a moon? She recognized the strategic advantage of controlling the deuterium supply, the deuterium markets, and the genetic bounty represented by the tribes. There should have been enough for everyone, but only angels shared.

To the ape, nothing was enough. The ape invented higher motives like national security or national wealth, but these ideals were steeped in lust and greed.

The fighting would never end. It might pause, but it wouldn't end, not in her lifetime or centuries to come until humankind evolved into something that was no longer quite human. Her whole life she'd known this like she knew the sky was blue and grass was green. Now she felt conscious of a solemn truth. It was horrific. It was freeing.

She felt homicidal.

Her transformation might have been as preordained as entropy. Evil was a communicable disease. Bad people made good people bad until there was no good left except in babies and young people and saints.

Vonnie was no saint. She said, "We can't let them take sole possession of Europa, and I'd rather die than rot in a Chinese prison."

Koebsch nodded. "Let's make sure it doesn't come to that. How are you getting to 05?"

They had several mecha near Module 01, but her overrides would erase the machines' intelligence with the SCPs. That meant the machines were unlikely to extract wounded people from a crash site in a vacuum environment.

"Tony and I will clip ourselves to GPs and run them manually," she said.

"He has the only scout suit."

"I'll wear a pressure suit. Tony and I go for 05. You and Ash run into the catacombs."

"The flooding—"

"The matriarchs can protect you. You're legends to them, *Mature Male* and *Biting Female.* Tell them to help. Tony and I will catch up."

He kissed her. He cupped her jaw in his big square hands and brought their mouths together.

If she refused his kiss, it was out of shock. He should have prepared her with a word or a look. She would have returned his desire. Instead he stole one kiss. Then his eyes became self-conscious. He gave her another peck on her cheek. He must have meant it like a correction, like a non-romantic gesture, but the second kiss could not expunge the first.

"Peter," she said, grazing her fingers on her lips.

He wasn't looking at her anymore. He assessed the frozen inferno outside. "Don't waste time at the lander. If our people are dead, leave them."

She nodded.

Aftershocks were propelling short white sprays from the east side of camp, where the ice toppled. The charred hull of the FNEE module fell in.

"Ash, I want five MAID/comms," he said, pronouncing the acronym as two words — *maid comms* — for Mobile Artificial Intelligence data/communication units. "One goes with Von. You and I keep the rest. We leave in three minutes."

"Yes, sir," Ash said. She hadn't noticed their kiss. She was consumed with her display.

Vonnie returned to business, too, wondering if she would see Ben or Peter again. It was a horrendous feeling. "Initiating overrides," she said.

Many of their rovers and GPs were gone. The rest had slid into troughs and pits, but she'd tracked each unit with a low-level AI designed to capture scenery for the media. Now she lit up Module 01's laser comms.

The machines convulsed as their core processors melted. Then they slumped into cockeyed positions. Four were permanently incapacitated. The others responded dully to her homing signal. They limped toward Module 01.

"Our first MAID/comm is ready," Ash said.

A light glowed on Vonnie's station. She yanked a briefcase-sized component out of the wall as Koebsch called the armory. "Tony, how's your scout suit?"

"Good to go."

Koebsch met Vonnie's gaze. "We need pressure suits."

"Yes, sir." She wanted to explain why she hadn't expected his kiss, but she moved to the door.

It didn't open. The motors inside the wall groaned. It gave her thirty centimeters and she squeaked through. Smoke rolled over her. Another electrical fire had filled the corridor with fumes. She coughed as she ran into the haze.

Before she reached the armory, Tony emerged in a scout suit. He banged his shoulder on the door. His arms were loaded with gear. So were the mag locks on his back. She saw med kits, rations, a sword, an axe and four M7s, but she didn't believe their weapons and equipment had affected his balance.

"Your suit," she said.

"It'll work."

It's compromised, she thought. *Their SCPs jumped into his systems but he's wearing it anyway.*

She had never really liked Tony. He was a company man, a straight arrow. Now she whacked her fist on his chest plate and shouted, "Great job!"

Inside the armory, she rummaged through the cabinets. She took a few items.

She ran back into the corridor, where Tony deactivated the AP/CEW pods. Ash appeared with three MAID/comms.

"Where is Peter!?" Vonnie yelled.

"He's still making calls."

They entered the ready room. Vonnie slapped her palm on four lockers. Three held pressure suits. One was stacked with trauma and repair kits.

She and Ash dressed as Tony dealt with the AP/CEW pod into the air lock. It flashed green but he didn't open the hatch. He stuffed his gear into the kits on his waist and chest. He clipped the M7s to his belt. He took several trauma and repair kits and attached them alongside his sword.

"I'd like a weapon," Ash said.

Tony handed an M7 to them both. Vonnie gave Ash five excavation charges. They holstered their weapons.

Koebsch arrived with another MAID/comm, breathing hard in the smoke. As he dressed beside Vonnie and Ash, he said, "I got through to Leber. He took two missiles but one was a kinetic strike and his screens defused the other warhead. They're okay. Three wounded. The FNEE ships have fired at the *Dongfangzhixing*. They're on our side."

Vonnie said, "What about our tankers and the *Clermont?*"

"He wants us to launch."

"Do it! We can't make Leber fight alone."

"The FNEE ships are supporting him and it looks like NASA took out a few enemy spy sats."

"Peter, we're going outside with *nothing*. You're playing by one set of rules while Leber's crew puts themselves between us and the PSSC."

"You have your mission," he said. His voice was curt. He sealed his helmet.

Vonnie's cheeks flushed and she glared at Koebsch. He obviously regretted their kiss. She didn't, but she was mad at him for being mad at her.

"Tony, get us out of here," he said.

Everyone had suited up. Vonnie closed the lockers. Ash shut the hatch into the corridor. They didn't want loose materials striking them when the air rushed out.

Tony opened the hatch into the air lock. He stepped over the hollow scout suits they'd discarded. At the outer hatch, his laser sizzled against the wall. "Get down!" he said, and the three of them knelt.

Koebsch's MAID/comm blared. He stared at its small display with Vonnie and Ash.

"Those are American signals," Vonnie said. "Why?"

The anguish in his face was terrifying. "We… You were…" He couldn't find the words.

He lifted his MAID/comm for both women to see.

Its display showed new magnitudes of destruction. Multiple targets had vaporized in orbit. American radar pulses flitted through the wreckage, quantifying each loss. Most of the remains were miniaturized sensors, fusion reactors, jets or missile housings. The PSSC had annihilated the ESA and FNEE satellites in a coordinated strike.

The larger trails of debris included the most precious of elements. Blood. Water. Oxygen.

Iranian HKs had pierced the *Clermont* amidships. Smoke from short-lived fires formed gray ribbons around its mangled shape. Crystallized water added a white wreath.

The FNEE ship above Europa's southern pole had been similarly gutted. It pinwheeled toward the moon's surface in gray and white ribbons. It also threw off drizzles of red. The telltale streamers were Major Correa's blood. Radar identified his torso — a hand — a leg.

Much farther away, the other FNEE ships deployed new screens to protect themselves.

Loosely coordinating with the Brazilians, the *Jyväskylä* glimmered like a Christmas tree. Drones rushed ahead or trailed behind in wide formations, independently launching weapons or broadcasting corrections to each other.

The FNEE ships lacked the *Jyväskylä*'s defenses. Their vessels relied on heavy firepower, heavy armor, and strength in number. One of them blocked a PSSC kinetic strike with its crude screens — but its screens were too close to its hull.

Shrapnel peppered the ship. Its fusion engines burst. Throbbing radiation baked its crew. Ten men and women. In the thickly shielded cockpit, only their colonel lived long enough to commit an act of retribution.

He emptied his silos. A hundred warheads raced away from the dying ship before its screen deteriorated. PSSC kinetics tore it apart in gales of air and fire.

Closer to home, a single kinetic strike lanced down onto Europa's surface. Leaning pathetically on its cables, the *Marcuse* exploded. Its destruction was an arrogant, almost jeering feat. One strike. One kill.

Vonnie took it personally — *that was* my *ship* — but like flirting with Peter, fixating on the *Marcuse* was a way to steady herself against overwhelming losses.

Frantically, she looked for Landers 04 and 05. They hadn't been hit. Peter might have saved Ben by refusing to shoot at the PSSC, but now the option to return fire was gone. The *Clermont* had been eliminated. Without their spy sats as relays, their MAID/comms couldn't reach their tankers.

They were helpless.

Vonnie's hands clenched on Peter's helmet. She dragged his stunned expression against her faceplate and screamed, "You son of a bitch!"

33.

She stopped herself before she cursed at Peter again. "I'm sorry," she said. She pushed him away with shaking hands.

"He made the right choice," Ash said. "Our tankers might have been a nuisance to them, nothing else. Now let's make the best of it."

"*I'm* sorry," Peter said. "I didn't think they'd escalate. I didn't. If—"

"Tony, how long do you need?" Ash called into the air lock.

"Twenty seconds."

"Two PSSC flightcraft just took off from their camp." Ash showed Peter and Vonnie her MAID/comm. Enemy troops would arrive in thirteen minutes, taking them prisoner unless they fled into the catacombs. Ben, Dawson, Ribeiro, Araújo and Tavares needed to get out of Lander 04.

"Are you in contact with Ben?" Vonnie asked.

"Yes. He knows they're coming."

"Remember what I said about 05," Peter said. "Stay away from the crash site if it's not safe. Leave them if they're dead."

"She should be okay." Ash switched to another MAID/comm. "There's outgassing here and here, water seeping through crevices here." She touched points on their north, east and south. The catastrophe had been widespread but short-lived.

"Let's assume the worst," Peter said. "Von, as soon as we're outside, have our mecha strip this module and the sheds. I want every bit of food and gear."

"Where are the sunfish?"

"Most of them have taken off," Ash said. "They're going southward and downward. A few groups stayed behind, mostly males. Brigit is with them. I see Angelica, too. They're closing holes where the catacombs are leaking air. The tunnels below Submodule 07 are intact. That's where we should dig into the ice."

"We're leaking here, too," Tony said. "Brace yourselves."

Ash tucked herself against the bulkhead. Peter grabbed onto her and Vonnie. Like a prayer circle, they lowered their heads to protect their helmets.

Holding them was bittersweet. It was lovely. It was a fleeting moment.

If she reunited with Ben and Peter, they could straighten out their triangle. Why was it so important who was exclusive and who shared?

The noise of Tony's laser was joined by a scream when the outer hatch lost its seal. The smoke in the air twisted into braids. He kept cutting. The air gushed out. He put his shoulder into the hatch. He bent it open and walked through.

Vonnie was first on his heels. She would have liked to say something else to Peter and Ash. She wanted them to know how much she adored them, but her claustrophobia was yowling in her head. She ran through the hatch.

She stepped into a familiar apocalypse.

The plains formed ridges where there had once been clear lines of sight. The sky was painted with clouds. A light beamed up from a chasm where a listening post had fallen.

Their nine mecha were caked with frost and gas-infused lumps of new ice. So was the exterior of Module 01. Tony began to inspect the mecha and Vonnie joined him, singling out two GPs for Peter and Ash. "Here," she said.

Her commander and her sister did as she indicated. They turned their backs as the GPs reared up, securing them in the rider position.

Ash's unit failed to clasp her left wrist. Vonnie manually connected the bracket.

"You have eleven minutes," Ash said.

"Do *not* stay at the lander," Peter said. "Look it over, then get into the ice. We'll see you soon."

"Soon."

He touched Vonnie's glove. She wished she'd kissed him back. Then he and Ash started toward Submodule 07. His unit had a dead leg. Hers had internal delays that made it wobble.

Tony instructed the next best GP to approach Vonnie. "Take this one," he said. "I have my suit."

She nodded, tracing out primitive dots on her MAID/comm. Her goal was to connect the remaining mecha with Module 01 and the storage shed, mark supplies, and provide directions for them to follow Peter and Ash. The mecha were in lousy condition. They might not complete the job without supervision but she couldn't stay in contact.

SCPs were already causing glitches in her signals. Her MAID/comm dropped her maps and she swore. She had to draw her stupid little dots again.

The ice swayed beneath her. Overhead, the stars held the teeming arsenal of the PSSC. She felt naked among the white-and-black swirls of fog and vacuum. Enemy spy sats must have predicted their evacuation as soon as the hatch blew. Every step she took would be tracked.

"Done," she said, letting her MAID/comm bang against her thigh as she clamped herself onto her mecha. Tony attached his scout suit onto his GP.

The other mecha limped to fulfill her commands. Two GPs and a rover approached Module 01. Another GP hobbled toward the shed. The last unit, also a rover, rolled with her in the direction of Lander 05.

In thirty meters, Vonnie and Tony outpaced the rover. It kept drifting off-target and pausing to correct.

Her GP had six functioning legs, five on its left, one on its right. She scooted diagonally like a crab. Hop. Stab. Hop. Stab. Pain stretched and clawed through the muscles in her shoulder and her hip.

Tony's GP was slower, but his course was straight. Staying on her strong side, he said, "Why did you bring the rover with us? Peter told you—"

"We need it to transport wounded or carry supplies. We'll never get back to camp before the PSSC landers."

"Right," Tony said, accepting her leadership.

"Find someplace we can dig into the catacombs."

He nodded. His radar was out, so he swept the ice with X-rays and neutrino pulse.

Behind them, three mecha thumped on Module 01. The module's loading ports were stacked with interior components as large as a sofa or as small as a lunchbox. The mecha released fifty locking bolts. Then they pulled cases of food, meds, tools and spare parts from the hull.

A lone GP hammered on the storage shed, unable to release its locking bolts. Vonnie watched their mecha with her cameras but she did not intercede. She had to save her MAID/comm for the most vital transmissions.

She and Tony had covered half the distance to Lander 05 when they reached a fissure. It ran more than a kilometer across the surface. The bottom was thirty to sixty meters down. Its sides were twenty meters apart. Their mecha could jump that far but lacked the agility to land well.

"You first," she said. "Get out a repair kit. I'll try to roll, but if my suit rips..."

"You'll be fine."

She appreciated those three words. The positive remark was as personable as Tony had ever been.

Choosing his spot to jump, he swept the bottom of the fissure again. There were large, solid blocks, but mostly it was loose ice. It might offer a route down into the catacombs after they finished with Lander 05.

Tony located a seam where they could dig through. Beneath one of the larger blocks, the ice formed a diagonal channel of narrow holes and pockets. He concentrated his X-rays on the seam. Then he stiffened. "Look out," he said as new alarms lit Vonnie's faceplate.

Her MAID/comm was receiving ESA signals.

Two hundred meters away, Lam squirmed out of the base of the fissure. Sonar was useless in vacuum. He didn't shriek like a sunfish. Nor did he announce himself like a mecha. Most of his sensors were quiet. An encrypted radio burst was his sole transmission. —*This is Probe 114!* he cried.

"How did he get so far west?" Tony asked as Vonnie waved desperately, not at Lam but at Tony.

"Be careful how you answer. Something's wrong with it," she said, referring to Lam as a machine, not a him. She had been careless earlier when she called Lam by name. She also had legitimate concerns about the doppelgänger.

Her leery feeling increased when Lam slipped in the ice. She didn't like how he wandered and groped, struggling to extend four of his arms. The floods hadn't damaged him. Nor had the grinding ice, although his synthetic flesh had been pulped against his topside. He was a patchwork of bloody wounds and steel, but those injuries were cosmetic.

He'd been targeted by PSSC spy sats as soon as he breached the surface. There were SCPs in his core.

"Probe 114, report," she said.

He sputtered with recognition codes and transponder blips, pointlessly verifying his location.

He must have known what was waiting for him. Why had he climbed up? Yes, the cave-ins and the deluge had solidified an enormous swath of ice. *Up* might have been the only direction available to him, but he could have stayed in hiding until the battle was over. Why would he sacrifice himself?

Was he coming to attack them?

"Tony, move," she said.

Tony leaped. He sailed in the low gravity. On the far side, he touched one of his GP's legs on the ice like a gymnast sticking his landing, but his trajectory was too shallow. His mecha couldn't run with the momentum. It toppled, rolled, stopped.

As his GP clomped onto its feet, Tony produced a repair kit from his gear. "Go," he said.

Below them, Lam scrabbled ineffectually. His eyeless body strained upward like a creature accustomed to sight. He radioed again as Vonnie took several running hops. She propelled herself over the fissure.

—*This is Probe 114!* Lam cried.

In the air, Vonnie bent her GP's legs into a shield for herself. She'd pivoted as she sprang off the ice, intending to somersault when she landed.

Her GP hit hard. Its legs rammed into the side of her chest. When it stopped, she was on her stomach. She tottered up. Her side hurt, but more worrisome was her neck. A needle-like pain stabbed between the back of her skull and the cusp of her spine.

Tony approached with his GP. He had suit patches in either hand, which she didn't need. "Four minutes," he said.

"Don't wait for me," she said even as she thought, *I can't spend another second on Lam.* She turned away from what was left her friend while he broadcast the same pitiful words.

—*This is Probe 114!*

Were there messages encoded in his transmission? What if he'd passlocked data inside his mem files?

Tony ran. Vonnie pursued him up a long, slanting block streaked with rivulets of ice. Her GP struggled on the slope. Hop. Stab. Hop. Hop. Hop. Stab.

Her neck and lower back both hurt. Exerting herself against the GP's weight was tearing ligaments.

Peter said, "Von, I want overrides for 114."

"No!" she gasped. The pain was very bad. "We can't wipe its core. It found something. It knows something."

Her radio popped with static. Peter hadn't heard her. He yelled, "Von! Von! Do you copy? Take control of 114 and bring it with you!"

She glanced at her MAID/comm. The rover she'd instructed to accompany her had reached the fissure. Of course it was equipped for Europa's surface. It extended pogos from its underside and hurled itself across.

Their other mecha caught up to Peter and Ash at Module 06. Dead sunfish and the cargo tent littered the ice. Normally, GPs or rovers would have done anything to safeguard organic materials. Even a speck of alien DNA was priceless, but the machines marched through the bodies with their supplies. They reached the pit where Submodule 07 sat in a snarl of cables and struts. They descended.

From the background noise in his transmissions, Peter and Ash were digging. Vonnie heard him grunt as he chopped at the ice. He yelled, "Probe 114 could make the difference between your being captured or getting away!"

I can't, she thought, but she could.

The crew of the *Jyväskylä* believed Lam was merely another doppelgänger. She had an override for him like she had overrides for every unit — but if she transmitted Lam's code, she would eradicate his memories and his personality.

"We'll kill him," she said. She had forgotten to call him '*it*.'

"I should've made you come with us!" Peter yelled. "Ben and Ribeiro found a hole down into the ice. They're safe. Ash and I will make it, too."

Near the top of the slope, Vonnie looked east at the incandescent blue pinpoints of fusion jets. She had to assume the PSSC wanted her alive. Otherwise they would have fired missiles into the ESA/FNEE camp.

Behind her, the rover doddered on the ice. Lam was out of sight in the fissure.

Why did he come to the surface?

"114, report," Vonnie said as the crunching noises on the radio stopped. Ash said, "Get in. I'll drop that section behind us." She and Peter were about to run into the ice with their mecha. Peter yelled, "Von!"

If he tried to say anything else, it was unintelligible. As the enemy closed in, she might lose communications with anyone more than a few meters away.

Ahead of her, Tony crested the slope. Vonnie heard a discouraged mutter. "Damn it."

She climbed after him to the peak.

The ice was dotted with metal and clothing and a grisly rainbow of hydraulics, coolants, and liquids like juice and coffee and blood. Everything sparkled with the frozen mist that had wafted over the crash site as the geysers subsided. The trail of debris ran two hundred meters north. Lander 05 was a smashed gray box caught against a corrugated row of ice.

Tony ran toward it. Thermal imaging showed warm bodies inside the lander. One was moving.

"I have a survivor!" Tony said. Somebody was crawling through the lander's ready room. Henri, Harmeet and O'Neal must have suited up before they took off because Lander 05 was no longer pressurized. The survivor was trapped and likely hurt… and Vonnie released herself from her GP.

She handed it three excavation charges. She gave two more to the rover. Both mecha secured their explosives. She sent them after Tony while she remained on the peak. She needed as little ice as possible between herself and Lam.

She designed a slavecast in nine seconds. Ash had stocked their MAID/comms with standard CEW packages. The overrides from the *Jyväskylä* contained Lam's individual serial codes. By combining the two, she could control him.

Alone on the peak, Vonnie flared like a nova. She beamed her slavecast at Lam. His transponder squealed and her MAID/comm redoubled its efforts, shifting through hundreds of frequencies and signal strengths.

She hoped she'd draw the PSSC away from Tony. She hoped somehow Lam could save them. If her slavecast wasn't successful, she would burn him with an override.

As an artificial intelligence, Lam should have been immortal. Deleting his mind was unconscionable, but she would defend her living friends before him. That didn't mean she wasn't sick with herself. Her throat tightened as she rasped, "*Bajonette. Bajonette.* Probe 114, report."

—*Von, listen. Don't close me down.*

Goose bumps rippled up the back of her neck. His plea was his most basic routine.

Tony was at Lander 05. Jamming had shut off her links with Peter and Ash. In two minutes, the PSSC would arrive, but Vonnie stayed with Lam.

Directing his movements, she coerced him up from the fissure and said, "Why did you send those males to the hot springs? We could have stopped the PSSC mecha without a geyser. You hurt us more than you helped."

His arms knuckled in sunfish shapes. —*<Metal Scout heeds Young Matriarch> I saved our clan.*

"My crewmates are dead!"

—*We'll repopulate.*

She stared at him with revulsion. Had he just compared her friends to savage males? She loved the sunfish, but she would never equate a human life with that of an idiot male. In this regard, she and Dawson saw eye-to-eye.

"At least six astronauts died on Europa and thirteen were killed in space," she said.

Lam seemed not to hear. —*The clan will reach the chimneys. So can Young Matriarch. Go down and west. Our enemies are down and north. Far down. We've felt their weight.*

"You've tracked more PSSC mecha?"

He warbled and twitched, an amalgamation of data/comm and sunfish shapes. She denied his broadcasts. His signals must have harbored SCPs, but she was able to translate the physical language of his body and his arms.

—*Larger enemies,* he signed. —*Louder. Deeper. They're in the water.*

She caught her breath.

—*The dark ocean. New threats. Hungry and loud. They'll pounce on you, but we can ambush them if you lead us.*

Lam sketched coordinates among the rippling carpets of his pedicellaria. Her AIs said he'd indicated a region almost twenty klicks to the north. There was nothing there, no crevices, no gas vents, no evidence of catacombs.

If he'd been corrupted by SCPs, he might have been spouting nonsense. Later, if there was a later, she could reevaluate the obscure poetry of his warnings.

She consoled herself with one thought. *Ash probably has copies of his mem files. I'm not killing him, I'm erasing this version of him.*

We'll make you sane next time, she promised.

She burned his core processors.

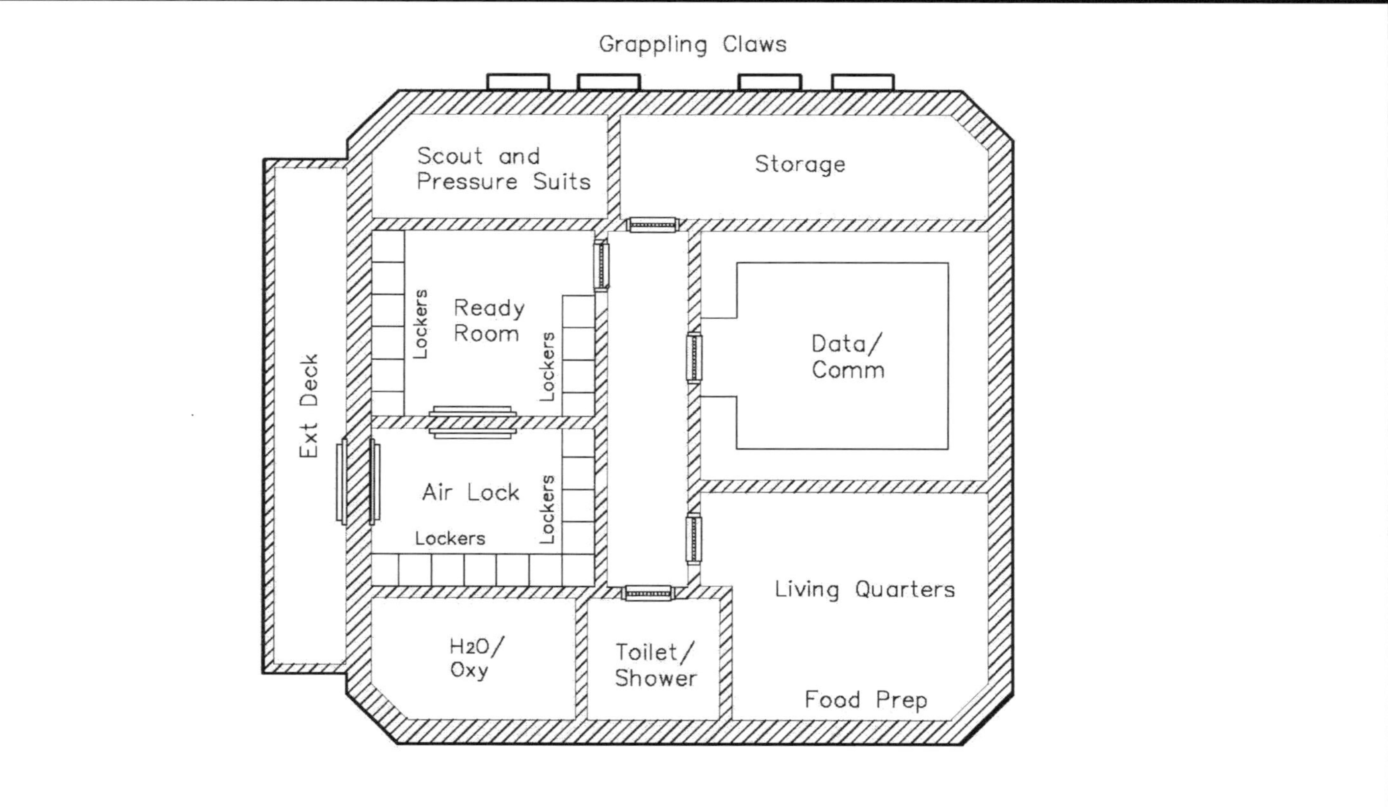
Grappling Claws
Scout and
Pressure Suits
Storage
Lockers
Ready
Room
Lockers
Data/
Comm
Ext Deck
Air Lock
Lockers
Lockers
Living Quarters
H2O/
Oxy
Toilet/
Shower
Food Prep

Lander 05

34.

Lam jerked. He screeched on the radio. And when his metal body rose and hobbled toward her, it no longer contained any trace of free will. It was Probe 114.

Weeping, Vonnie handed it two excavation charges. It clutched the explosives in one arm.

Side by side, they strode over the peak. They descended toward Lander 05. Her radio buzzed with Peter's voice, a snippet of a word, maybe *how*. The jamming was total. Overhead, the jets of the PSSC flightcraft were blue-white torches. Her wet eyes refracted the light.

She had forty seconds before the PSSC swung past or dropped to the surface. "Guard our southern flank," she ordered Probe 114. "Hide by that piece of wreckage. I need you to hit an airborne target."

—Affirmative.

She didn't trust its reduced capacity. She drew dots on her MAID/comm like a teacher instructing a child. "Got it?"

—Affirmative.

Probe 114 scurried off. Vonnie ran to Lander 05. Tony had detached his scout suit from his GP. He was cutting into the hull. Vonnie instructed all three of their mecha to spread out.

She sent two east and one south, setting kamikazes in the most likely approach paths.

Maybe she could hit the PSSC flightcraft before they landed. If soldiers or mecha jumped down, she'd deal with them herself. "Who's inside!?" she yelled as she unsheathed her M7.

"I don't know," Tony said. "His radio's out. Whoever it is, he's tapping Morse. He has a broken leg. We—"

Her vision blurred. The PSSC craft tilted their jets away from Lander 05, but the backsplash of visible light and invisible particles felt brighter than the sun. White-hot vapor spewed from the ice.

Vonnie screamed. "*Aaaaaaaaah!*"

The PSSC didn't care about the condition of their prisoners. Treatment could resurrect almost anyone, and donor organs were abundant in nations where human cloning was lawful, but she didn't want to lose so much of herself that she was like Lam — a hybrid, an amnesiac — enslaved to whomever reconstructed her brain.

Her pressure suit protected her slightly. Tony was better armored in his scout suit.

Her scream tapered into shrieks as a freakish desert cold parched her bones. The cold was counterintuitive. It was supernatural.

She tried to cover her head with her left hand. With her right, she fired into the God-like fusion jets. The recoil of her M7 almost knocked the weapon from her smoldering hand. Her sleeves and chest piece crinkled. Her skin cooked inside her darkened faceplate. Blisters swelled from her temple and her nose. Her open mouth dried like sand. Clumps of hair were desiccated into ash, choking her.

She was driven to her knees.

She kept her arms raised even though she'd emptied her clip. She tried to call her rover and Probe 114. The radiation was too much. Her signals were drowned. Her lungs couldn't draw air.

She fell on the smoking ice. Tony lurched closer with his arms extended to cover her helmet.

At her feet, Lander 05 baked under the fusion jets. Frozen rations boiled with a frantic thumping as hundreds of sealed packets burst. Maybe the sound was their survivor. Was he dying, too?

Probe 114 initiated a futile solo assault. It had puzzled together her instructions and the flightcraft overhead. It sprang at the two craft. Then it detonated its charges before it was within fifty meters — before their AMAS systems negated its attack. It used itself for shrapnel, holding the explosives against its body. The blast drove its chassis and it sensors into the PSSC craft. The impacts were minor. Vonnie's bullets had accomplished less.

Inexplicably, the PSSC craft veered off.

Later, Vonnie learned they'd flown south over the remains of the ESA camp, where their jets slashed through Modules 01 and 06. They caused more damage, then they sped away.

The jamming ceased. So did the SCPs, although the ESA and FNEE mecha would not recover.

Vonnie slithered like a worm. The refreezing ice imprisoned her elbows, hands and feet. She saw a black kaleidoscope but only from her right side. Her left eye wouldn't open. The severed canals in her ear were a caterwaul of noise and pain. It felt someone had reamed her head with sandpaper.

She couldn't pull herself from the surface. Her lips and tongue were dry nubs. She would have wept if there was moisture to spare. "Tuh," she said. *Tony.*

"Don't move!" he said, but his words were noiseless; she perceived each syllable via the contours of his shouting mouth; his helmet was set against her faceplate like a man leaning into the crib of an ailing baby.

Father? she thought. *Where are you? My brothers. They don't know that I forgive them.*

Forgive me.

Pain washed through her like a flood crammed with ice. It numbed her. Froze her. She woke in a smothering panic. Her bones ached. The stars wheeled above her. Blackness.

She woke again. A dead woman knelt beside her in a pressure suit with a hairline crack across its faceplate, helmet dented, shoulders scuffed with filth.

"Hurh," Vonnie said. *Harmeet.*

"Stay with me," Harmeet said, but Vonnie's left eye was a spike driven into her skull. Her abdomen was a nightmare. She would have torn herself open to relieve the rancid, bloating pressure in her guts except her arms were feeble tubes and she gagged and strangled and far away her mother was singing and she wanted to go to her. She needed to peel out her intestines like a sunfish disemboweling its prey.

Where am I? she thought. She couldn't see beyond the interior of her helmet. She was lying on her side. Her faceplate was brown with old blood and vomit, a hideous paste.

"Hurh?" she asked, flailing with her hand.

She struck someone, a woman who said, "Hang on. You're hooked into subdermal packets and IVs."

Nanotech and optimized blood plasma, she thought. That explained why she'd come around, but the woman beside her wasn't her mother. "Hurh?" she asked.

"I can't clean your helmet, sweetheart," the woman said. "We have power but no air. You need to stay in your suit. Hold my hand."

"Hurh… meet…"

"Yes, it's me."

"Guh." *Good.*

Vonnie waded through the math. Tony had scanned Lander 05. Two dead. One alive. Harmeet. Right now, that joy kept Vonnie from wanting to die.

She'd barely known Pärnits and Collinsworth, but they had been crewmates, which was a unique relationship.

Christmas Bauman had been a friend, funny and bold.

Sweet, smart Lam in his many incarnations… attractive… dangerous… loyal… each of his deaths had felt like a beating.

She couldn't bear two more deaths. Henri had been devious and intelligent, and Ash's lover, which made him like a casual brother-in-law to Vonnie. She hadn't agreed with his politics but she'd respected him.

O'Neal had been an innocent. He would approve of dying on Europa but his passing should have been as an old man after another sixty years of exploration as his legacy. This was too soon. He was gone. Too soon.

What about Ben and Peter and Ash and Claudia? What about the Jyväskylä *and Io?*

Her head tangled, Vonnie slept.

Her heart thudding, she woke again, surging with nausea and pain. Somewhere there had been an explosion. Inside her body? Outside on the ice?

She croaked two words. “Help me.”

Nobody answered.

“Harmeet?”

Nobody answered.

35.

Vonnie screamed, "Harmeet!"

There was light beyond her helmet but her faceplate was still papered with dried blood and vomit. The smell must have been atrocious but her nostrils were insensitive holes.

Her teeth were wrong. She probed with her tongue, which was a rag. She sobbed when she found rifts in the top left of her mouth. That was the side where her temple and scalp hurt the most. Feathery ash clung to her face.

I'm missing teeth and gums and hair and my eye. Oh Jesus. We were cremated.

She stretched out her hand and patted the confines of what she decided was the toilet/shower in Lander 05. She felt laundry and towels.

"Tony!?" she yelled.

She thought she could wiggle through the hatch, but what was waiting for her? Bodies? Enemy soldiers? What if Tony and Harmeet had stashed her in the shower because it was the safest place inside the lander?

She concentrated on breathing. She couldn't accept how many friends were gone. She'd killed Lam herself, although he hadn't been Lam anymore. Terminating him had been a mercy.

Terminate me. Forgive me.

Father?

She heard voices and boots. One person was heavier than the other — someone in a scout suit. She knocked on the shower wall, which was the floor, which added to her disorientation.

The hatch opened sideways, creating a square of light outside her helmet.

"Von, I need to lift you," Tony said. "The med droid is working and we restored pressure in the ready room. We'll get you out of that suit as soon as we're inside."

He scooped his hands under her body. Her innards were tender. Her skeleton was frail.

She groaned, "Ben and Peter?"

"They're alive. Dawson. Ash. Ribeiro. Araújo. Tavares. Everyone else bought it." Tony reversed out of the shower with her draped against his chest. Then he crab walked through Lander 05. Something in the wreckage scraped her arm. Something else whacked her knee.

"Why... fighting stop..." she managed to say.

"The *Jyväskylä* negotiated a cease-fire. I'll tell you more after you're stabilized."

"Stupid."

"I am stupid. I should've made sure we were ready. We could've dispersed our weapons from the *Clermont*."

"Me. Stupid."

Tony paused to reposition her in his arms. She felt more than heard the squeal of metal as he bent something aside. "None of this was your fault," he said.

"My fault. Lam. Sunfish."

"The PSSC wanted a fight. Whatever Lam did, that was an excuse." Tony ducked, then jacked his shoulder up against another piece of wreckage.

He heaved his back against the obstruction and jabbed with his elbow. Then they were crab walking again.

He said, "Our tankers are gone, our miners, everything in camp. We lost our deuterium production. We lost our water shipments, so did Brazil, and eighty percent of the American miners and tankers were wiped out, even the *Grissom*."

The *Solar*-class *Grissom* was the American ship.

"China says it was collateral damage. In the last minute, we gave them a little pounding. They said they couldn't distinguish hostiles from neutrals, so they hit everything that didn't have a PSSC transponder. Some governments are calling for punitive strikes. Berlin says no. We don't have enough ships."

Vonnie drifted in and out of his words. She was more attuned to each step. The lander was twenty by twenty meters square. She knew it was on its side and crushed, but why was Tony taking so long?

He said, "They didn't just kill our friends. They're going to beat us to the Great Ocean."

"O'Neal..."

"O'Neal is dead. So is Henri. Alvaréz. Carvalho. Correa. Pereira. Santos."

He listed the FNEE casualties alphabetically. That was a strange thing to observe in her agony. Why had she said O'Neal's name? *The dark ocean,* she thought, recalling Lam's words. *Our enemies are down and north. We've felt their weight. Louder. Deeper. They're in the water.* But the PSSC wouldn't kill people to reach the ocean first, not if it was lifeless, empty water. She had to assume they'd found something valuable.

Tony said, "We're at the ready room. I made an air lock out of plastic but it's crap. My suit's too big. Can you curl up? I'll bend your legs for you."

He eased her into a ball, which was torture. She fought him. She whimpered.

He spoke on a different radio channel and Harmeet opened the hatch from the inside. Tony moved. A taut plastic sheet whapped against Vonnie's faceplate. The hatch slammed shut. The sheet yielded some of its rigidity. Bright lights colored the brown-red paste inside her helmet. Tony set her down.

Harmeet took off Vonnie's helmet. Smoke touched her face — a familiar, friendly smell to an engineer — and she gulped at it. Tony had welded the room in places, resealing its walls. If she was going to die, she welcomed the smoky scent.

Tony brought the med droid to her side. Harmeet removed her own helmet. Her dark eyes were huge with sympathy. "Sweetheart, we're going to put you under."

"Under... the ice..." Vonnie was incoherent.

Harmeet unzipped Vonnie's chest piece. Flesh stuck to her pressure suit. Blood oozed from her roasted skin.

The droid had been affected by SCPs. It couldn't find Vonnie when she was right in front of it. Harmeet guided its tools to her chest, wrists, stomach. Wire probes slipped into her body. Surgery would follow.

How will it know where it's operating on me?

"Don't worry, I'm here, don't worry," Harmeet whispered in a little sing-song.

Vonnie went black.

Thrashing, she woke in agony. Scalpels were carving into her skull. "*Stop,*" she gurgled.

"Don't worry, I'm here," Harmeet sang.

"*Stop.*"

"I cleared the med lines!" Tony said.

She drifted. She woke. There was digging and pain. She heard the pitiless hum of lasers in meat and the *tk tk tk tk tk* of injection stitching. She lost track of where was hell and who was dead and what it meant to see heaven. Suffering and peace. Passion. Malice. Achievement.

When she opened her eye — her right eye — they'd taken her from Lander 05. She was in the armory in Module 01, which they'd converted into living space.

Gel mattresses and blankets were laid on the floor. Along the walls, the armory was stacked with cases of rations and weaponry. Vonnie focused on the mattresses. Ash slept nearby. She'd buried her face in her blankets to obscure the light, but Vonnie saw her hair and one naked leg stuck out. Ash's jumpsuit was rolled at her feet.

Fuzzily, Vonnie associated Ash in bed with Henri and she searched for him. Her neck creaked.

Across the armory, Araújo sat by himself. In his lap was a pull-out display. He was cinnamon-skinned and dark-eyed. He would have made a superb recruitment proxy for the FNEE except for his beard stubble.

"Are you well?" he asked.

She was too busy appraising herself to reply. Araújo returned to his work, but he looked up again when Vonnie said, "Henri is dead, isn't he?"

"My condolences," Araújo said in his lightly accented English. His voice was hushed. He tipped his head at Ash. "Your crewmate knows more, although we should let her sleep. This is her first downshift in quite a while."

The left side of Vonnie's upper jaw felt tender. She had new teeth. Her lips were healing from grafts.

She smelled sweat and food. The armory was being used by more people than it could accommodate. She was glad she could smell its odors. She remembered smoke. Sometimes bad smells were good smells. They meant she was alive.

A stickem gauze patch covered the left side of her face from her mouth to her forehead. Had they transplanted a new eye into her socket? She touched her cheek.

Her hands were pink. So was her left forearm.

Why don't I have two eyes? she wondered, but she said, "Captain Araújo? How long was I out?"

"Six days have passed since the attack. You were placed in a coma. I helped bring you to this module."

"Thank you."

"My apologies. I did not mean you have an obligation to me. I was honored to help. You struck the single blow against the PSSC on Europa. My people wounded them in space, as did yours, but the conflict on the ice was one-sided until your counteroffensive."

"Counteroffensive. Are you talking about the mecha that self-destructed against their flightcraft?"

"I speak of this mecha and the hero of the ESA. Your stand, and your fall, were recorded by a NASA spy sat. The sim continues to play on the net. Is there anything I can provide? Drink? Sponge? We have hot water."

Drained by their short conversation, Vonnie said the only thing she could think of. "Thank you." The so-called *Hero Of The ESA* was repeating herself.

Worse, she suspected all of the combined survivors had been living in the armory, so she'd lain unconscious — and incontinent — among them as they ate and slept. She detested soiling herself like a baby. They would have allowed Harmeet and Ash some privacy to clean her, but her weakness was an insult. A tiny insult.

"Tell me what happened," she said. "I can't believe La— I can't believe one mecha and I chased off the PSSC."

"Administrator Koebsch has been prepared to advise you of our reports. There is a MAID/comm on his desk. Let me retrieve it." Araújo stood up.

Ash shifted in her bed.

"Shh," Vonnie whispered at Araújo. She didn't want to deprive Ash of her own healing.

For spies, everything was supposed to be business — every relationship, every deal — but Ash must have been thunderstruck by Henri's death.

I'll be here if you need me.

Araújo tiptoed to Vonnie with the MAID/comm. Before handing it to her, he cued five menus and said, "I have learned your devices. These are EUSD sims. I will bring you juice. I will call your medic. They're outside."

Vonnie nodded absently, transfixed by the datastreams.

Her last stand had been preceded, above Europa, by the confluence of salvos from the *Jyväskylä* and the FNEE ships. Also sprinting across space were Japanese hunter-killers.

The allies had pinned the *Dongfangzhixing* in a crossfire. A true counteroffensive, their weapons arrived in spectacular waves from multiple angles at multiple speeds. That their formation resembled a swarming tribe was ironic and a compliment to the sunfish. That two of the three FNEE ships had been obliterated before their missiles reached the *Dongfangzhixing* was a testament to man and his machines.

Many of the warheads divided into smaller payloads. Some were decoys. Some were pin-sized "shotgun" kinetics, lasers or EMPs. One was a twenty-kiloton nuclear bomb.

The nuke belonged to the FNEE. When it detonated, it vaporized hundreds of inbound munitions from the *Jyväskylä*. It also opened a gigantic funnel through the *Dongfangzhixing*'s defensive screens.

One of the Japanese HKs stabbed the *Dongfangzhixing*. Accelerating at 17Gs, the hunter-killer couldn't steer itself into vital sections like the

Dongfangzhixing's command center or its engines. The HK perforated the enlisted quarters on the *Dongfangzhixing*'s belly, tearing out cascades of air.

The PSSC crew was at battle stations. Casualties were zero, but the Japanese HK beamed SCPs at the *Dongfangzhixing* as it hit; the damage was significant; and the *Dongfangzhixing* was exposed. Unfortunately, the allies no longer possessed any assets within range to capitalize on their success. More payloads were inbound but too distant to strike.

Three things occurred in that moment.

First, the *Dongfangzhixing* transmitted crisis codes to all PSSC spy sats, mecha and crew.

Second, the *Jyväskylä* beamed a message to the last FNEE ship, the ESA crew, the NASA camp and the *Dongfangzhixing.* This message was public and unencrypted. Captain Leber called for a truce. He said he would allow the PSSC unrestricted access to Io. In exchange, they would suspend hostilities.

The third, most conspicuous event was that Leber's offer resonated in utter silence. Among the many factions, the barrage of signals stopped. It was as if each weapon, AI, soldier and astronaut experienced synchronicity. In their unlikely union, they took a breath.

Everyone was listening to a new sound. It filled the silence, an unidentified, unconventional ELF broadcast — extremely low frequency — at 8 hertz.

The rogue transmission lasted 1.4 seconds. It sounded like an empty burst of static.

Then it was gone.

The pandemonium ended. The *Dongfangzhixing* issued their acceptance of Leber's terms, and the ELF broadcast appeared to be forgotten. A barrage of normal signals inundated the Jupiter system as men and machines aborted their attacks. Thousands of drones turned away from their targets. The *Jyväskylä*, the *Dongfangzhixing* and the FNEE ship dimmed their electronic shields. They recalled their weapons.

But the way they'd uniformly dismissed the ELF broadcast was a charade. Everyone hunted its source as their AIs engaged in rendering and analysis.

"What the hell did we hear?" Vonnie asked, opening one sim after another.

The ESA hadn't recognized the broadcast. Nor had the EUSD, the FNEE or NASA. Extremely low frequency radio transmissions were not a part of any Earth fleet's standard data/comm. Could the broadcast have been Iranian? Russian?

Vonnie had six days' worth of material to review. She'd barely gotten into the most recent updates from Berlin when her MAID/comm beeped, a contact labeled *Koebsch, P.*

She accepted the call. Peter was outside. He wore a scout suit and he was sweating from hard labor. "Von, thank God you're awake."

She smiled unselfconsciously. "How are you, Peter?"

"We're coming in."

"It can wait."

"Everybody wants to see you."

She couldn't deny her friends. *Today I'll even hug Dawson,* she thought. "Is Ben okay? Claudia? Do we have any sunfish in the colony? What about functioning mecha?"

"Yes. Yes. No. Yes." He smiled at her staccato questions and his replies.

She smiled with him

"See you in a minute," he said. When he signed off, she returned to her sims until Ash stirred and poked her head out of her blankets.

Vonnie crawled to the young woman. Wordlessly, they embraced. Ash squeezed too hard.

"Careful," Vonnie said.

"Oh!" Ash released her. "Your surgeries..."

Vonnie smiled again. She needed to smile to keep from crying. "You weren't hurt? What about Harmeet's leg? How much of me is still me, Ash?"

Unlike Peter, Ash couldn't keep up with the rapid-fire questions. Ash shook her head. Her breath hitched, and then Ash and Vonnie were both sniffling.

"We still need to give you an eye," Ash said. "A lot of our stock was burned. Nanotech is fixing what it can. Your lungs and your spine took priority."

Vonnie nodded, feeling spooked. She must have been very, very close to the brink.

Ash said, "Harmeet says you and Tony saved her life."

"She saved mine."

"I take back all the things I said. The mean things. You almost killed yourself getting to Harmeet... and Henri. I won't forget."

"Ash, I've made plenty of mistakes. You have to tell me when I do. It's okay for us to fight."

Ash's voice was inaudible.

"What?"

"'Happy,' I said. That makes me happy."

They held each other. Vonnie was aware of Araújo watching them from the corner of his eye, but he knew how to conduct himself in close quarters. He occupied himself with his display, unwilling to intrude.

Outside their room, the floor banged with the steps of two scout suits. Vonnie heard a *clank* and the roar of pumps. The noise was too irregular for an air lock.

She said, "Is this module intact?"

"Not even close." Ash rummaged in her bed. She grabbed her jumpsuit and pulled it on, glancing at the corner where they'd hung a blanket from a few bolts in the ceiling.

Vonnie assumed the blanket was a curtain for their latrine.

Ash had to pee, but she combed her fingers through her hair and straightened her bed, wanting to present a clean, strong image before their crewmates entered. "The PSSC burned Module 06 and most of this one," she said. "There's nothing left of the FNEE camp. We're down to Lander 04 and this room. We've been repairing suits. We rigged an air lock here so people can eat and sleep. The lander is gathering anything we can find. There are rations and gear and... and corpses thrown over five kilometers. We had to dig for some stuff. Tony, Ben, Claudia and Ribeiro have been in charge of recovery."

Vonnie listened quietly. Ash had tried to conceal their real deadline by listing so many other hurdles. Vonnie said, "How long do we have?"

Contrary to the end, Ash laughed. *Biting Female* was a superb name for her. She was pleased that Vonnie had seen through her little ruse. "Air and water are good. We have power. We have meds."

"How long, Ash?"

"We'll run out of food in ten days. The *Jyväskylä* will send help before then. We've been stretching it with half rations for everyone except you and Harmeet."

"Her leg."

"Three tib/fib fractures and soft tissue damage. The droid replaced her calf muscle and her ACL. She'll be all right."

She couldn't walk but she took care of me, Vonnie thought, remembering Harmeet's song. She shut her single eye to contain more tears. Their losses echoed in her mind, but she celebrated their tenacity in standing against the PSSC.

You motherfuckers, we aren't beaten yet. You'll never kick us off this moon. You might win but we'll always get back on our feet. We'll reconstruct our base. Won't we?

"Tell me the truth," she said. "Is the *Jyväskylä* coming to take us home?"

"No."

The hatch opened. Peter and Harmeet walked through, allowing Vonnie a glimpse of the tent they'd arranged in the central corridor. Beyond the tent, the corridor was a truncated husk. The rest of Module 01 was torn and melted. They'd hung their scout suits on improvised assists. Bare hooks were cluttered with pressure suits, kits and weaponry.

Then she was in Peter's arms. Harmeet wrapped her arms around them. So did Ash. "It's good to see you, it's good, it's good," Harmeet cooed.

Vonnie kissed Peter's cheek. He searched her face. She dodged his gaze and kissed Harmeet, too, hugging them equally close, using the group to avoid the crux of her emotions.

She hoped Ben was coming, too. She said, "Sit with me. I need to hear what's going on."

Peter helped her to return to her bed. The four of them sat together and Harmeet gestured for Araújo to join them. He did. Peter looked at Ash and said, "Did you tell her about the *Jyväskylä* and NASA?"

To Vonnie, Ash said, "The Americans are packing up. They'll consolidate with us. Part of the deal was a mutual 'reduction of forces' around the PSSC camp."

Peter said, "Our spy sats are gone, the *Clermont*, the *Grissom*, the *Marcuse* and two FNEE ships. The *Jyväskylä* will provide rations as 'humanitarian aid,' but the PSSC will monitor any landings to verify that none of Leber's people join us. They don't want fresh boots on the ground."

"We're staying," Vonnie said. "Swear it."

"Yes." Peter took her hand. "Yes. But we might relocate further north or west."

"Not all of us," Harmeet said.

"I won't leave Europa."

"That's not what she means," Peter said. "There's been some... We're sending a new mission into the ice."

"Good. Where are the sunfish?"

"They're waiting for you. A few scouts approached our mecha. They invited us to follow. They said the matriarchs are establishing a new colony."

"I don't blame them. Give me another day, then I can lead the mission."

"Von, it's bigger than that."

She'd expected Peter to say she wouldn't be fit for duty for another week. Instead he'd opened the possibility of needing her soon. She saw anticipation in Araújo's face, distress in Harmeet and that stubborn pride in Ash.

Ash's mood was contagious. Vonnie welcomed it. She lifted her chin and said, "Tell me."

"The blitzkrieg ended when we hit the *Dongfangzhixing*. It wasn't a terminal blow, but it must have scared them. They transmitted crisis codes across the system."

"That's when Leber called for the cease-fire."

"Yes. But there was something else, an ELF broadcast."

"I watched the sims. Was it Iranian or Russian? I know they use old tech in their probes because it's harder for SCPs to fox twentieth century gear."

"It was not Iranian," Araújo said, turning his display to show her. He was a ROM specialist.

Look at what he's consulting on! she thought.

Earlier, he'd opened EUSD sims for her. He was also in possession of classified NATO briefings about the unidentified radio transmission. Araújo had become a liaison with military analysts in Berlin, Washington, Tokyo and Jerusalem. That was how profoundly their situation had changed — a FNEE captain with full access to NATO intelligence.

Extremely low frequency broadcasts were used on Earth for communicating with submarines and mining operations because ELF waves penetrated salt water, earth and rock, which distorted or blocked most radio transmissions.

Salt water, she thought.

Araújo handed his display to her and said, "Here. These are the best calculations from Earth."

In tandem with Japanese and Israeli HKs, the *Jyväskylä* had triangulated the broadcast. It had emanated from a spot eighteen kilometers north of the ESA camp.

North. That's where Lam said he heard new enemies.

No mecha belonging to allied forces were closer than ten kilometers to this location.

The PSSC camp was south and east.

More startling, by measuring the attenuation of the ELF waves, their AIs had proved that the broadcast not only originated beneath the ice. The source had been forty klicks deep in the water.

They'd been blindsided again.

Vonnie stared at Araújo's data. She said, "Something *inside* the Great Ocean is transmitting?"

!!!!!! NOT THE END !!!!!!!

LOOK FOR THE STUNNING CONCLUSION
OF THE EUROPA SERIES IN
FROZEN SKY 4: BATTLEFRONT

AUTHOR'S NOTE

Right now the sound I'm hoping for is: "*Aaauauaagggh! You maniac! Damn you, Carlson! Damn you all to heck!*"

With luck, I'll hear screams all over the planet: "*What? THAT's the ending?*"

I swear on my mother's eyeballs: There are very good reasons for this cliffhanger. It's what Vonnie told me to do.

First let's back up a bit. Writers write to be read. *The Frozen Sky* has been a professional success in sales and fan response. To date, it's been translated into Dutch, German and Japanese. Creating this series has also been gratifying on a personal level.

I grew up steeped in science fiction, so it's the Big Questions that interest me. Why are we here? Where did we come from? Where are we going?

Each installment in the Europa Series addresses these questions with great heaping spoonfuls of biology, astrophysics, politics, cybernetics, even a little religious history plus good old-fashioned sex and violence. I've never had more fun in my life.

The problem (and it's a good problem to have) is the characters took over. The deeper I moved into *Frozen Sky 3*, the more independence they demonstrated. Also, we're not dealing with a small set of circumstances. The storyline is at least as big as a moon. I've tried to narrow the focus so that Earth remains in the background, but what a background! World War 3! Colonies in space! Jupiter! The origins and direction of humankind from our distant past through a harsh yet exciting future!

You can guess what happened. Gradually, while I wrote *FS3*, I realized I had a 750 page manuscript on my hands and I hadn't finished. I still had to wrap up a number of important threads. The book was getting *long*, man.

I'd pulled a Patrick Rothfuss… except I'm not as talented, ha ha.

There's not a publisher on Earth who's going to touch a 190,000 word sci fi adventure. Normally, novels range between 90,000 - 105,000 words. In traditional Big 5 publishing, a book's length plays into printing, shipping, stocking, and, ideally, premium space in stores. You don't want a couple copies spine-out on a shelf somewhere in the back. You want your book on the front-of-store displays, end caps, or the New In Paperback towers.

Plague Year was a perfectly sized novel. Undoubtedly, its length was one factor in the star treatment it received from Ace/Penguin in 2007.

Don't get me wrong. The sheer, dark genius of my high-concept apocalyptic thriller is why Penguin got behind *Plague Year* (he said modestly), but size does matter. Barnes & Noble could put four copies in each slot of their premium displays. Same for the book racks in the regional chains, indies, airports and drug stores.

Publishing has changed dramatically since 2007. As I write this, it's only 2016, but I feel like an astronaut in a crazy future. Ebooks are king. Ebooks have no shipping or shelving concerns, and yet readers still look for "normal" length stories. Ebook distributors assign costs to file size. Printers have expenses. So do audiobook producers. So do publishers overseas.

I put a lot of brain sweat into boiling the rough draft of *Frozen Sky 3* down from 750 manuscript pages to 670 manuscript pages. That's maybe 600 pages in hardcover or umpteen gazillion electrons on your e-reader.

I jettisoned an especially cool subplot. I tightened down the action sequences. I squeezed the scenes between Vonnie and Lam… and I still hadn't written 'The End.'

Considering the many facets of the book, I knew I would add at least another 50 pages before I tied everything together and I wanted to add 70. This is writer math. You have your rough draft. You trim it. You flesh out the most intriguing moments and character arcs. The book gets longer, it gets shorter, it gets longer, and it tightens up again with polishing.

Vonnie said, *740 pages is still pretty big, Carlson.* So I broke the book in half.

There was another factor in this decision. *Frozen Sky 3* was waaaaaaaay overdue. Many, many readers had taken the time to ask when *FS3* would be available.

Fan mail is the coolest thing ever. My job description is I sit alone in a room listening to the voices in my head. Hearing from real live people who want more is beyond encouraging. It's an honor. I told them what I'm going to telling you.

Skip ahead if you want. Here comes a long digression into my personal life because my life contains the seeds that grew into *The Frozen Sky*. Also, I genuinely believe setbacks and pain can be good for people. (Setbacks and pain aren't *enjoyable* but they can be useful.) Here's a saying I admire because I think it applies to any kind of challenge. "Sports don't build character. Sports reveal character."

There have been times when I felt down. Alone. Poor. Unnoticed. Stupid. Those feelings, those failures, motivated me to work harder.

Every day on Earth is full of contradictions. Boldness is rewarded. Recklessness leads to disaster. Brains are an advantage... but if you're too bookish or introverted, you'll miss all the fun. Finding a balance is key. Grow. Push yourself. Never, never get complacent. As the Nowhere Man said, life is what happens to you while you're busy making other plans.

Early in 2015, I got hurt bad. Unfortunately, that's not a new experience for me. Once I broke my hand hitting a guy. Once I broke my kneecap in a 1v1 challenge in soccer. Skiing has been even more death-defying. Over the years, in separate incidents while rolling down various slopes, I've broken my leg (in three places), broken my arm (two places) and fractured two ribs. Believe me, many strains and pulls have been salted in among these larger injuries.

To put my foolhardiness in perspective, my brother, in separate incidents, broke three ribs, tore his MCL, and sent himself to the clinic with back spasms after hucking off a four-story cliff in massive powder. We also know guys who've broken a collarbone, broken an arm, severed an ACL or dislocated a shoulder.

Why would anybody repeat an experience with this track record?

Adrenaline affects your judgment. It's addictive. For me, skiing is peaceful as hell. I mean it scours your brain with raw, fierce excitement. I love the freedom and beauty of slashing through trees in white-out blizzards at 10,000 feet. It's just you and the mountain. That's why I keep going back for more.

2015's injury was less cinematic. I did horrific damage to my back while muscling a 400 pound rock across our yard, which is an idiotic and boring way to get hurt. In my defense, the rock is embedded with the fossilized remains of twelve-million-year-old mollusks. It's an extraordinarily cool rock, but, truth to be told, I was trying to cowboy that monster. Look at me! I'm so strong! I'll roll it by myself! *Crack.*

Doctors, X-rays and physical therapy sessions were expensive and painful. Worse, rehabilitation was time consuming. I tried everything from herbal medications to light therapy, doing stretches, doing exercises, and, everyone's favorite, lying flat on our floor and complaining.

Ugh.

My wife Diana and I are busy enough with her job in the corporate world (she's a marketing analyst for a multinational), an old house to repair, two sons, school projects, field trips, soccer, skiing… you know the drill if you're a parent.

Having kids is the greatest adventure but it's not exactly a cake walk that involves a lot of relaxation, not if you're doing it right. To quote McCartney now, the love you take is equal to the love you make. You get what you put in.

Want to drink or do drugs, watch TV and eat frozen food because that seems like the easy road? In the long run, the easy road is the hard road. Human beings aren't wired for slacking off. Happiness doesn't come out of a bottle or a baggie. It comes from hard work and accomplishments. The real problem is that lazy, selfish assholes tend to raise other flavors of assholes, and God knows we need more dysfunction on the good ship Planet Earth.

Ready to work until you drop? You might raise brave, capable kids who turn into brave, capable adults. That's what I think. But sometimes adventure comes at a price.

Adding to 2015's mayhem, our son Ben got hurt, too.

(Our Ben is no relation to Metzler, by the way, although they're both smart-alecks. Ben Metzler was named after a friend and super fan.)

At least his injury was outrageously dramatic. Both of our boys play competitive soccer, also known as club soccer. This is a different game than you see in rec leagues or AYSO. It's more technical. It's faster. It's rougher.

One fine Saturday afternoon about a week before I destroyed my back, Ben's team was getting walloped by a stronger opponent. These kids were a machine. The final score was 0 - 7, although they didn't go through Ben. He was a lion. He refused to quit even after the game was a blowout, and here's our philosophy:

Winning is more fun than losing, but the Carlsons are playing a deeper game. You score a goal, you save a goal, that's exciting... and it's the intangibles that mean more. We tell our sons that the soccer field is a training ground.

Team sports are life in a microcosm, fighting as a unit in the face of adversity. At its best, soccer is a whole lot more than kicking a ball around on the grass. The sport demands a broad range of abilities that include quick-thinking, discipline, creativity, teamwork, and the capacity to track fluid, situational, interlocking formations.

The structure of your team dictates to and is dictated by the enemy's structure. The puzzle moves. You attack, you recover, you counter again. A friend once told me that — to him — soccer just looks like ants running around. I could only reply, sir, you are willfully ignorant of its strategies and dynamics. This is an opportunistic game in which each position must balance specific responsibilities with vision and initiative. The demands on its players are among the reasons why soccer is Earth's most popular sport.

It's why they call it The Beautiful Game.

By comparison, baseball is static. Baseball has the strict lines of the diamond. It's a very regimented, very cadenced pageant with the spotlight on individuals, not the unit. Except for the batter, one entire team sits on a bench, and, aside from the pitcher and catcher, everybody on the other team stands still. That's a lot of sitting and standing. Yes, baseball has explosive action. Infielders and outfielders must be mindful to adjust to situations like man-on-first… and I'm sure I'll hear from baseball crowd… but have you ever been to a youth baseball game? It's three, sometimes four hours of *yaaaaaaaawwwwwwwn.*

Football is far more cerebral. Every play is a violent, high-speed chess game.

Hockey is soccer on ice.

I don't know much about basketball. We tend not to watch TV and there are only so many hours in the year for sports, but basketball looks like soccer on wood to me.

My point is Diana and I love to see grace under pressure, awareness, communication and tenacity in our sons. Soccer is an arena in which to hone those skills. Not coincidentally, the value of such traits are a recurring theme in my books.

Earth isn't a nice place. People are small and short-sighted and weak, often through no fault of their own. Many were neglected or abused. Some were born with neurochemical imbalances. But whether it's their fault or not, whether they can be reached or not, you have to deal with them even when you're a kid.

What matters is how you conduct yourself.

It can be during a loss that players truly shine. When the other team gets ahead by a couple scores, some kids fold. Others keep fighting until they can no longer stand.

Over the years, our eldest, John, is the boy who's been named captain by different coaches on different teams. Sometimes they had winning seasons. Sometimes they had losing seasons. John is always in the middle of the fight. He has a unique style that can only be described as *heads-up-speed-and-guts.* One of his coaches called him *Captain Crunch* because of his leadership and toughness.

John isn't a big kid, but he's scrappy and quick. On defense, he'll upend much larger opponents — legally — while stealing the ball. On offense, he knifes through 'em. Meanwhile he's yelling commands, warnings or encouragement. He plays his position and helps other kids understand their responsibilities. He's a spark. He increases team energy and team cohesion, forging order out of chaos.

You can tell we've found meaningful joy in our sons' achievements, yeah?

I should add that we're not hyper-aggressive jocks. John and Ben are honor students and they were both invited to join chess teams before we decided they needed a little less thinking and a little more combat. Balance is the key.

As the younger brother, Ben isn't as verbal as John, but he has his own strengths, some physical like burst speed and stamina (plus this kid *really* isn't shy about physical contact), some mental like a gift for spatial relations and anticipating how the enemy is building an attack before it materializes. His best coach called him *Thunderball.*

Before I get too carried away with the sin of pride, here's the deal.

Playing center back against a superior enemy, Ben delivered an impressive sequence of events in which he single-handedly stopped three men. First he challenged the opposing striker and forced a pass to an opposing mid. Next he challenged the mid, stripped him and chased after the loose ball. The opposing wing was closer. The wing secured the ball and sprinted downfield. Ben's outside back was out of position. The wing went on a breakaway! Everyone thought he'd have an easy shot on the stunned goalkeeper.

No, sir. Ben sprinted after him. Ben took him out. All of this happened in a few seconds: challenge, pass, challenge, strip, loose ball, breakaway... intercept and destroy.

Unfortunately, Ben was going full-tilt. He absolutely leveled the wing, saving the goal but wrenching his hip. The ref called the obvious foul. The opposing team took a direct kick. Ben's keeper wrapped it up. Limping, Ben subbed out and our saga began.

We would have preferred if he just let the kid score. He missed half the season visiting his own set of doctors and physical therapists. Ridiculously, he thought going to PT was fun. They have treadmills! They have sleds and weights!

Diana has a real job, so Ben needed me to drive, so now we had two Carlsons in rehab. Getting whole again became our lives for most of 2015. I've calculated that I lost seven months of working time. I edited in waiting rooms. I edited while I was hooked to electrostim. I edited while I was laying on hot pads. I edited while I was lying on cold packs. I kept promising everybody I was almost done with *Frozen Sky 3* and meanwhile the book just wouldn't *stop*. It kept getting longer.

Vonnie told me to be resourceful. She pointed out the story arcs and high points, so what we have is a novel as long as *Plague Year*. Again, I realize *FS3* ends on a cliffhanger of such magnitude, it's unbearable. For that, I apologize. But aren't you enjoying the ride? Email me at **jeff@jverse.com**. Vonnie returns soon in *FS4: Battlefront*.

Before I go, I need to add that the usual suspects kept me honest while we delved into the bizarre and fascinating truths of our DNA, our environments, our histories, and a possible future in the Jupiter system. Please let me tip my hat to Ben Bowen, Ph.D., computational biologist with Lawrence Berkeley National Laboratory; Charles H. Hanson, M.D.; my father, Gus Carlson, Ph.D., mechanical engineer and former division leader with Lawrence Livermore National Laboratory; Matthew J. Harrington, author of many stories in the *Man-Kzin War* collections and co-author of *The Goliath Stone*; and the ever-dedicated, ever-helpful, sharp-eyed Lee Ashford.

The Sierzenga family went wildly above and beyond the call of duty. East Coast Jeff, as he is known, since I am West Coast Jeff, dedicated many weekends to my cause, often with his daughter Ashley and son Jacob at his side. Guys, your maps and engineering schematics are *über* cool. Thank you.

I also want to tell Jeff's wife Michelle what I tell Diana: I appreciate your patience and support! Babe, that lawn doesn't need to be mowed. That cabinet door doesn't need to be fixed. These aren't the droids you're looking for. Your husband *should* be sitting at his computer, yes, again, working on make-believe worlds in 2113 A.D.

Without these contributions by so many brilliant people, I could not have written the Europa Series. Some of them were taken out to dinner or lunch. Some were turned into characters in my novels. All of them earned my gratitude.

You guys are awesome.

Jeff
jeff@jverse.com

If you liked *Blindsided*...

LOOK FOR THE BEST-SELLING NOVELS BY JEFF CARLSON

"Rock-hard realistic."
—James Rollins, *New York Times Bestselling* author of *The 6th Extinction*

"Terrifying."
—Scott Sigler, *New York Times* bestselling author of *Infected* and *Alive*

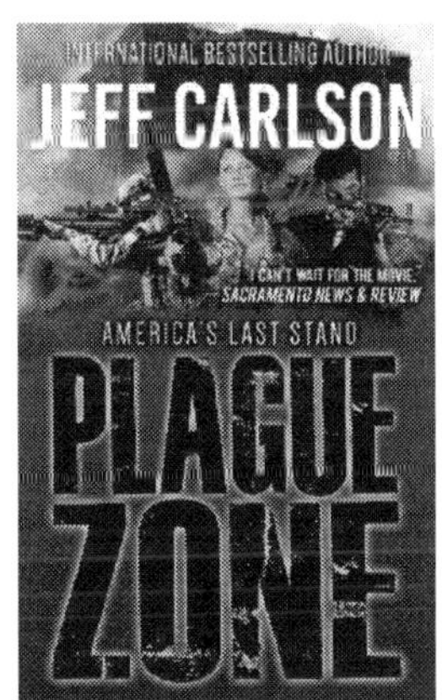

The Next Breath You Take Will Kill You

"An epic of apocalyptic fiction: Harrowing, heartfelt, and rock-hard realistic."

—**James rollins, *New York Times* bestselling author of *Bloodline***

"*Plague Year* is exactly the kind of no-holds-barred escapist thriller you would hope any book with that title would be. Jeff Carlson's gripping debut is kind of like *Blood Music* meets *The Hot Zone*. It might also remind some readers of Stephen King's *The Stand*. He keeps the action in fifth gear throughout."

—***SF Reviews.net***

"One of the best post-apocalyptic novels I've read. Part Michael Crichton, a little Stephen King, and a lot of good writing… Plausible and thrilling. This is a master at work and I can't wait to read the sequel."

—***Quiet Earth* (www.quietearth.us)**

Finalist For The Philip K. Dick Award

"Compelling. His novels take readers to the precipice of disaster."

—*San Francisco Chronicle*

"A mix of sci fi, military adventure, and political intrigue. Strong, dynamic characters bring the story to a conclusion you won't see coming."

—*RT Book Reviews*

"A breakneck ride through one of the deadliest and thrilling futures imagined in years. Jeff Carlson has the juice!"

—Sean Williams, *New York Times* bestselling author of *Star Wars: The Force Unleashed*

"Intense. Carlson has reinforced what I admired about him in *Plague Year*, conveying his story and themes with as much authenticity and emotional truth as possible. Just consider your- self warned. This one is a literary level-four hot zone."

—*SF Reviews.net*

The Next Arms Race Has Begun

"Gripping. Jeff Carlson concludes his trilogy with an epic struggle among desperate nations equipped with nano weapons. This book is an object lesson in why we'd better learn to get along before the next arms race."

—Jack McDevitt, Nebula award-winning author of *Firebird*

"A high-octane thriller at the core—slick, sharp, and utterly compelling. Oh yeah, and it's *frightening*. SF doesn't get much better than this."

—Steven Savile, international bestselling author of *Silver*

"I can't wait for the movie."

—Sacramento News & Review

"This installment opens with a jolt. *Plague Zone* is one of those rare books that you can sit down with and finish in a day due to its unrelenting intensity... If you love dark SF, you can't go wrong with Carlson's *Plague Year* trilogy."

—Apex Magazine

Award-Winning Short Stories

"Striking."

—*Locus Online*

"Exciting."

—*SR Revu*

"Chilling and dangerous."

—*HorrorAddicts.net*

"An amazing collection."

—*Sci-Guys.com*

"Captivating. *Long Eyes* packs a lot of adventure and entertainment."

—*BookBanter.net*

Their Time Has Come Again...

"Edgy and exciting. Carlson writes like a knife at your throat."

—Bob Mayer, *New York Times* bestselling author of the *Green Berets* and *Area 51* series

"Riveting, high concept, and so real I felt the fires and blood. Thumbs up."

—Scott Sigler, *New York Times* bestselling author of *Pandemic*

"A killer thriller."

—John Lescroart, *New York Times* bestselling author of *The Hunter*

"The ideas fly as fast as jets."

—Kim Stanley robinson, Hugo award-winning author of *2312*

"A phenomenal read."

—Steven Savile, international bestselling author of *Silver*

About The Author

Jeff Carlson lives with his wife and sons in California. He is the international bestselling author of *Interrupt, Plague Year* and *The Frozen Sky*. To date, his work has been translated into sixteen languages worldwide. He is currently at work on a new thriller novel.

Readers can find free fiction, videos, contests and more on his website at www.jverse.com including a special Europa-themed photo gallery featuring images from the *Voyager 1*, *Galileo* and *Cassini* probes.

Jeff welcomes email at jeff@jverse.com.

He can also be found on Facebook and Twitter at www.Facebook.com/PlagueYear and @authorjcarlson.

Reader reviews on Amazon, Goodreads, and elsewhere are always appreciated.

Made in the USA
San Bernardino, CA
31 May 2017